Weddings in White

A 3-in-1 keepsake collection that showcases
the enchanting characters and searing passion
that has made Diana Palmer
a legendary talent in the romance industry.

**Ward Jessup. Kingman Marshall.
Callaghan Hart.**

As a rule, these hard-edged, heart-stoppingly
handsome bachelors avoided sweet, virginal
young ladies who dreamed of marriage.
But like moths to a flame, they were drawn
to Marianne Raymond, Tiffany Blair and
Tess Brady. At first, these men of steel resisted,
but when they realized they may lose these
innocent beauties—forever—they found
themselves doing the unthinkable: proposing!

Praise for Diana Palmer:

"Nobody tops Diana Palmer when it comes to
delivering pure, undiluted romance.
Her books have helped define
the romance genre. I love her stories."
—*New York Times* Bestselling Author
Jayne Ann Krentz

"Diana Palmer makes a reader
want to find a Texan of her own!"
—*Affaire de Coeur*

Dear Reader,

I love white weddings, probably because I never had one. My husband and I were married by a justice of the peace twenty-eight years ago this October. I wore a plain street-length white dress without a veil or even a bouquet, and my wedding ring was a plain gold band that cost us $13.00 at a nearby jeweler's. We had dated for just five days. As the saying goes, even the bad times were good. I could not have asked for a better husband or for a better father for our son. When I count my daily blessings, it takes hours.

It is a joy for me to write books about virgin brides. I was always a renegade, even as a child. I never did things just because other people were doing them, or to fit in. I think purity and chastity are noble virtues, and I have enormous respect for young women, and young men, who abstain until they marry. (I did.)

I have to confess that my favorite of these three novels featured in the *Weddings in White* collection is *Callaghan's Bride*. I loved Cag Hart from the time he popped up in *Christmas Cowboy*, and I'm still working on books for his brothers, Rey and Leo. *The Princess Bride* was a book I'd started some years back and never finished, so I enjoyed having a second chance for it to be read. *Unlikely Lover* sprang out of my Silhouette Desire novel *Rawhide and Lace*, in which Ward Jessup was a minor character. I was studying martial arts at the time I wrote it, and the idea of the heroine overpowering the pickpocket and sitting on him until the police came had me in stitches. (No, I never did that—don't I wish!)

I hope you enjoy these stories. I am a hopeless romantic, moving around in a gentle old-fashioned world of hand-holding and poetry while my colleagues (and my friends) write more successfully about corporate advancement and finding quality time and meaningful relationships. I don't really belong in this new world, but those of you who are kind enough to read my books give me a little literary niche in which to shelter, and I thank you most sincerely. When I count those blessings I mentioned, my readers are right at the top of the list.

Your friend,

Diana Palmer

DIANA PALMER

Weddings in White

Silhouette® Books

Published by Silhouette Books

America's Publisher of Contemporary Romance

SILHOUETTE BOOKS

WEDDINGS IN WHITE

Copyright © 2000 by Harlequin Books S.A.

ISBN 0-373-48414-3

The publisher acknowledges the copyright holder of the individual works as follows:

UNLIKELY LOVER
Copyright © 1986 by Diana Palmer

THE PRINCESS BRIDE
Copyright © 1998 by Diana Palmer

CALLAGHAN'S BRIDE
Copyright © 1999 by Diana Palmer

This edition published by arrangement with Harlequin Books S.A.

® and TM are trademarks of Harlequin Books S.A., used under license. Trademarks indicated with ® are registered in the United States Patent and Trademark Office, the Canadian Trade Marks Office and in other countries.

Visit Silhouette at www.eHarlequin.com

Printed in U.S.A.

CONTENTS

UNLIKELY LOVER   9

THE PRINCESS BRIDE   151

CALLAGHAN'S BRIDE   271

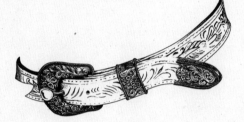

UNLIKELY LOVER

Chapter 1

Ward Jessup went to the supper table rubbing his big hands together, his green eyes like dark emeralds in a face like a Roman's, perfectly sculpted under hair as thick and black as crow feathers. He was enormously tall, big and rangy looking, with an inborn elegance and grace that came from his British ancestors. But Ward himself was all-American. All Oklahoman, with a trace of Cherokee and a sprinkling of Irish that gave him his taciturn stubbornness and his cutting temper, respectively.

"You look mighty proud of yourself," Lillian huffed, bringing in platters of beef and potatoes and yeast rolls.

"Why shouldn't I?" he asked. "Things are going pretty well. Grandmother's leaving, did she tell you? She's going to stay with my sister. Lucky, lucky Belinda!"

Lillian lifted her eyes to the ceiling. "I must have pleased you, Lord, for all my prayers to be so suddenly answered," she said.

Ward chuckled as he reached for the platter of sliced roast beef. "I thought you two were great buddies."

"And we stay that way as long as I run fast, keep my mouth shut and pretend that I like cooking five meals at a time."

"She may come back."

"I'll quit," was the gruff reply. "She's only been here four months, and I'm ready to apply for that cookhouse job over at Wade's."

"You'd wind up in the house with Conchita, helping to look after the twins," he returned.

She grinned, just for an instant. Could have been a muscle spasm, he thought.

"I like kids." Lillian glared at him, brushing back wiry strands of gray hair that seemed to match her hatchet nose, long chin and beady little black eyes. "Why don't you get married and have some?" she added.

His thick eyebrows raised a little. They were perfect like his nose, even his mouth. He was handsome. He could have had a dozen women by crooking his finger, but he dated only occasionally, and he never brought women home. He never got serious, either. He hadn't since that Caroline person had almost led him to the altar, only to turn around at the last minute and marry his cousin Bud, thinking that, because Bud's last name was Jessup, he'd do as well as Ward. Besides, Bud was much easier to manage. The marriage had only lasted a few weeks, however, just until Bud had discovered that Caroline's main interest was in how much of his small inheritance she could spend on herself. He had divorced her, and she had come rushing back to Ward, all in tears. But somewhere along the way Ward had opened his eyes. He'd shown her the door, tears and all, and that was the last time he'd shown any warmth toward anything in skirts.

"What would I do with kids?" he asked. "Look what it's done to Tyson Wade, for God's sake. There he was, a contented bachelor making money hand over fist. He married that model and lost everything—"

"He got everything back, with interest," Lillian interrupted, "and you say one more word about Miss Erin and I'll scald you, so help me!"

He shrugged. "Well, she is pretty. Nice twins, too. They look a little like Ty."

"Poor old thing," Lillian said gently. "He was homely as sin and all alone and meaner than a tickled rattlesnake. And now here he's made his peace with you and even let you have those oil leases you've been after for ten years. Yes sir, love sure is a miracle," she added with a purely calculating look.

He shivered. "Talking about it gives me hives. Talk about something else." He was filling his plate and nibbling between comments.

Lillian folded her hands in front of her, hesitating, but only for an instant. "I've got a problem."

"I know. Grandmother."

"A bigger one."

He stopped eating and looked up. She did seem to be worried. He laid down his fork. "Well? What's the problem?"

She shifted from one foot to the other. "My brother's eldest girl, Marianne," she said. "Ben died last year, you remember."

"Yes. You went to his funeral. His wife died years earlier, didn't she?"

Lillian nodded. "Well, Marianne and her best friend, Beth, went shopping at one of those all-night department store sales. On their way out, as they crossed the parking lot, a man tried to attack them. It was terrible," she continued huskily. "Terrible! The girls were just sickened by the whole experience!" She lowered her voice just enough to sound dramatic. "It left deep scars. Deep emotional scars," she added meaningfully, watching to see how he was reacting. *So far, so good.*

He sat up straighter, listening. "Your niece will be all right, won't she?" he asked hesitantly.

"Yes. She's all right physically." She twisted her skirt. "But it's her state of mind that I'm worried about."

"Marianne…" He nodded, remembering a photograph he'd seen of Lillian's favorite niece. A vivid impression of long dark hair and soft blue eyes and an oval, vulnerable young face brought a momentary smile to his lips.

"She's no raving beauty, and frankly, she hasn't dated very much. Her father was one of those domineering types whose reputation kept the boys away from her when she lived at home. But now…" She sighed even more dramatically. "Poor little Mari." She glanced up. "She's been keeping the books for a big garage. Mostly men. She said it's gotten to the point that if a man comes close enough to open a door for her, she breaks out in a cold sweat. She needs to get away for a little while, out of the city, and get her life back together."

"Poor kid," he said, sincere yet cautious.

"She's almost twenty-two," Lillian said. "What's going to become of her?" she asked loudly, peeking out the corner of her eye at him.

He whistled softly. "Therapy would be her best bet."

"She won't talk to anyone," she said quickly, cocking her head to one side. "Now, I know how you feel about women. I don't even blame you. But I can't turn my back on my own niece." She straightened, playing her trump card. "Now, I'm fully prepared to give up my job and go to her—"

"Oh, for God's sake, you know me better than that after fifteen years," he returned curtly. "Send her an airline ticket."

"She's in Georgia—"

"So what?"

Lillian toyed with a pan of rolls. "Well, thanks. I'll make it up to you somehow," she said with a secretive grin.

"If you're feeling that generous, how about an apple pie?"

The older woman chuckled. "Thirty minutes," she said and dashed off to the kitchen like a woman half her age. She could have danced with glee. He'd fallen for it! Stage one was about to take off! *Forgive me, Mari,* she thought silently and began planning again.

Ward stared after her with confused emotions. He hoped that he'd made the right decision. Maybe he was just going soft in his old age. Maybe...

"My bed was more uncomfortable than a sheet filled with cacti," came a harsh, angry old voice from the doorway. He turned as his grandmother ambled in using her cane, broad as a beam and as formidable as a raiding party, all cold green eyes and sagging jowls and champagne-tinted hair that waved around her wide face.

"Why don't you sleep in the stable?" he asked her pleasantly. "Hay's comfortable."

She glared at him and waved her cane. "Shame on you, talking like that to a pitiful old woman!"

"I pity anyone who stands within striking distance of that cane," he assured her. "When do you leave for Galveston?"

"Can't wait to get rid of me, can you?" she demanded as she slid warily into a chair beside him.

"Oh, no," he assured her. "I'll miss you like the plague."

"You cowhand," she grumbled, glaring at him. "Just like your father. He was hell to live with, too."

"You sweet-tempered little woman," he taunted.

"I guess you get that wit from your father. And he got it from me," she confessed. She poured herself a cup of coffee. "I hope Belinda is easier to get along with than you and your saber-toothed housekeeper."

"I am not saber-toothed," Lillian assured her as she brought in more rolls.

"You are so," Mrs. Jessup replied curtly. "In my day we'd have lynched you on a mesquite tree for insubordination!"

"In your day you'd have been hanging beside me," Lillian snorted and walked out.

"Are you going to let her talk to me like that?" Mrs. Jessup demanded of her grandson.

"You surely don't want me to walk into that kitchen alone?" he asked her. "She keeps knives in there." He lowered his voice and leaned toward her. "And a sausage grinder. I've seen it with my own eyes."

Mrs. Jessup tried not to laugh, but she couldn't help herself. She hit at him affectionately. "Reprobate. Why do I put up with you?"

"You can't help yourself," he said with a chuckle. "Eat. You can't travel halfway across Texas on an empty stomach."

She put down her coffee cup. "Are you sure this night flight is a good idea?"

"It's less crowded. Besides, Belinda and her newest boyfriend are going to meet you at the airport," he said. "You'll be safe."

"I guess so." She stared at the platter of beef that was slowly being emptied. "Give me some of that before you gorge yourself!"

"It's my cow," he muttered, green eyes glittering.

"It descended from one of mine. Give it here!"

Ward sighed, defeated. Handing the platter to her with a resigned expression, he watched her beam with the tiny triumph. He had to humor her just a little occasionally. It kept her from getting too crotchety.

Later he drove her to the airport and put her on a plane. As he went back toward his ranch, he wondered about Marianne Raymond and how it was going to be with a young woman around the place getting in his hair. Of course, she was just twenty-two, much too young for him. He was thirty-five now, too old for that kind of child-woman. He shook his head. He only hoped that he'd done the right thing. If he hadn't, things were sure going to be complicated from now on. At one time Lillian's incessant matchmaking had driven him nuts before he'd managed to stop her, though she still harped on his unnatural attitude toward marriage. If only she'd let him alone and stop mothering him! That was the trouble with people who'd worked for you almost half your life, he muttered to himself. They felt obliged to take care of you in spite of your own wishes.

He stared across the pastures at the oil rigs as he eased his elegant white Chrysler onto the highway near Ravine, Texas. His rigs. He'd come a long damned way from the old days spent working on those rigs. His father had dreamed of finding that one big well, but it was Ward who'd done it. He'd borrowed as much as he could and put everything on one big gamble with a friend. And his well had come in. He and the friend had equal shares in it, and they'd long since split up and gone in different directions. When it came to business, Ward Jessup could be ruthless and calculating. He had a shrewd mind and a hard heart, and some of his enemies had been heard to say that he'd foreclose on a starving widow if she owed him money.

That wasn't quite true, but it was close. He'd grown up poor, dirt poor, as his grandmother had good reason to remember. The family had been looked down on for a long time because of Ward's mother. She'd tired of her boring life on the ranch with her two children and had run off with a neighbor's husband, leaving the children for her stunned husband and mother-in-law to raise. Later she'd divorced Ward's father and remarried, but the children had never heard from her again. In a small community like Ravine the scandal had been hard to live down. Worse, just a little later, Ward's father had gone out into the south forty one autumn day with a rifle in his hand and hadn't come home again.

He hadn't left a note or even seemed depressed. They'd found him slumped beside his pickup truck, clutching a piece of ribbon that had belonged to his wife. Ward had never forgotten his father's death, had never forgiven his mother for causing it.

Later, when he'd fallen into Caroline's sweet trap, Ward Jessup had learned the final lesson. These days he had a reputation for breaking hearts, and it wasn't far from the mark. He had come to hate women. Every time he felt tempted to let his emotions show, he remembered his mother and Caroline. And day by day he became even more embittered.

He liked to remember Caroline's face when he'd told her he didn't want her anymore, that he could go on happily all by himself. She'd curled against him with her big black eyes so loving in that face like rice paper and her blond hair cascading like yellow silk down her back. But he'd seen past the beauty to the ugliness, and he never wanted to get that close to a woman again. He'd seen graphically how big a fool the most sensible man could become when a shrewd woman got hold of him. Nope, he told himself. Never again. He'd learned from his mistake. He wouldn't be that stupid a second time.

He pulled into the long driveway of Three Forks and smiled at the live oaks that lined it, thinking of all the history there was in this big, lusty spread of land. He might live and die without an heir, but he'd sure enjoy himself until that time came.

He wondered if Tyson Wade was regretting his decision to lease the pastureland so that Ward could look for the oil that he sensed was there. He and Ty had been enemies for so many years—almost since boyhood—although the reason for all the animosity had long been forgotten in the heat of the continuing battle over property lines, oil rigs and just about everything else.

Ty Wade had changed since his marriage. He'd mellowed, becoming a far cry from the renegade who'd just as soon have started a brawl as talk business. Amazing that a beautiful woman like Erin had agreed to marry the man in the first place. Ty was no pretty boy. In fact, to Ward Jessup, the man looked downright homely. But maybe he had hidden qualities.

Ward grinned at that thought. He wouldn't begrudge his old enemy a little happiness, not since he'd picked up those oil leases that he'd wanted so desperately. It was like a new beginning: making a peace treaty with Tyson Wade and getting his crotchety grandmother out of his hair and off the ranch without bloodshed. He chuckled aloud as he drove back to the house, and it wasn't until he heard the sound that he realized how rarely he laughed these days.

Chapter 2

Marianne Raymond didn't know what to expect when she landed at the San Antonio airport. She knew that Ravine was quite a distance away, and her Aunt Lillian had said that someone would meet her. But what if no one did? Her blue eyes curiously searched the interior of the airport. Aunt Lillian's plea for her to visit had been so unusual, so…odd. Poor old Mr. Jessup, she thought, shaking her head. Poor brave man. Dying of that incurable disease, and Aunt Lillian so determined to make his last days happy. Mari had been delighted to come, to help out. Her vacation was overdue, and the manager of the big garage where she kept the books and wrote the occasional letter had promised that they could do without her for a week or so. Mr. Jessup wanted young people around, he'd told Lillian. Some cheerful company and someone to help him write his memoirs. That would be right up Mari's alley. She'd actually done some feature articles for a local newspaper, and she had literary ambitions, too.

Someday Mari was going to be a novelist. She'd promised herself that. She wrote a portion of her book every night. The story involved a poor city girl who was assaulted by a vicious gang leader and had nightmares about her horrible assailant. She'd told Aunt Lillian the plot over the phone just recently, and the older woman had been delighted with it. Mari wondered about her aunt's sudden enthusiasm because Lillian had never been particularly interested in anything except getting her married off to any likely candidate who came along. After her father's death, especially. The only reason she'd agreed to come down to Ravine was because of poor old Mr. Jessup. At least she could be sure that Aunt Lillian wasn't trying to marry her off to him!

Mari pushed back her hair. It was short now, a twenties-style pageboy with bangs, and it emphasized the rosy oval of her face. She was wearing a simple dropped-waist dress in blue-and-white stripes and carrying only a roly-poly piece of luggage, which contained barely enough clothes to get her through one week.

A tall man attracted her interest, and despite the shyness she felt with most men, she studied him blatantly. He was as big as the side of a barn, tall with rippling muscles and bristling with backcountry masculinity. Wearing a gray suit, an open-necked white shirt and a pearly gray Stetson and boots, he looked big and mean and sexy. The angle of that hat over his black hair was as arrogant as the look on his deeply tanned face, as intimidating as that confident stride that made people get out of his way. He would have made the perfect hero for Mari's book. The strong, tender man who would lead her damaged heroine back to happiness again...

He didn't look at anyone except Mari, and after a few seconds she realized that he was coming toward her. She clutched the little carryall tightly as he stopped just in front of her, and in spite of her height she had to look up to see his eyes. They were green and cold. Ice-cold.

"Marianne Raymond," he said as if she'd damned well better be. He set her temper smoldering with that confident drawl.

She lifted her chin. "That's right," she replied just as quietly. "Are you from Three Forks Ranch?"

"I *am* Three Forks Ranch," he informed her, reaching for the carryall. "Let's go."

"Not one step," she said, refusing to release it and glaring at him. "Not one single step until you tell me who you are and where we're going."

His eyebrows lifted. They were straight and thick like the lashes over his green eyes. "I'm Ward Jessup," he said. "I'm taking you to your Aunt Lillian." He controlled his temper with a visible effort as he registered her shocked expression and reached for his wallet,

flashing it open to reveal his driver's license. "Satisfied?" he drawled
and then felt ashamed of himself when he knew why she had reason
to be so cautious and nervous of him.

"Yes, thank you," she said. *That* was Ward Jessup? *That* was a
dying man? Dazed, she let him take the carryall and followed him
out of the airport.

He had a car—a big Chrysler with burgundy leather seats and
controls that seemed to do everything, right up to speaking firmly to
the passengers about fastening their seat belts.

"I've never seen such an animal," she commented absently as she
fastened her seat belt, trying to be a little less hostile. He'd asked for
it, but she had to remember the terrible condition that the poor man
was in. She felt guilty about her bad manners.

"It's a honey," he remarked, starting the engine. "Have you
eaten?"

"Yes, on the plane, thank you," she replied. She folded her hands
in her lap and was quiet until they reached the straight open road.
The meadows were alive with colorful wildflowers of orange and red
and blue, and prickly pear cacti. Mari also noticed long stretches of
land where there were no houses and few trees, but endless fences
and cattle everywhere.

"I thought there was oil everywhere in Texas," she murmured,
staring out at the landscape and the sparse houses.

"What do you think those big metal grasshoppers are?" he asked,
glancing at her as he sped down the road.

She frowned. "Oil wells? But where are the big metal things that
look like the Eiffel Tower?"

He laughed softly to himself. "My God. Eastern tenderfoot," he
chided. "You put up a derrick when you're hunting oil, honey, you
don't keep it on stripper wells. Those damned things cost money."

She smiled at him. "I'll bet you weren't born knowing that, either,
Mr. Jessup," she said.

"I wasn't." He leaned back and settled his huge frame comfortably.

He sure does look healthy for a dying man, Mari thought absently.

"I worked on rigs for years before I ever owned one."

"That's very dangerous work, isn't it?" she asked conversationally.

"So they say."

She studied his very Roman profile, wondering if anyone had ever painted him. Then she realized that she was staring and turned her attention to the landscape. It was spring and the trees looked misshapen and gloriously soft feathered with leaves.

"What kind of trees are those, anyway?" she asked.

"Mesquite," he said. "It's all over the place at the ranch, but don't ever go grabbing at its fronds. It's got long thorns everywhere."

"Oh, we don't have mesquite in Georgia," she commented, clasping her purse.

"No, just peach trees and magnolia blossoms and dainty little cattle farms."

She glared at him. "In Atlanta we don't have dainty little cattle farms, but we do have a very sophisticated tourism business and quite a lot of foreign investors."

"Don't tangle with me, honey," he advised with a sharp glance. "I've had a hard morning, and I'm just not in the mood for verbal fencing."

"I gave up obeying adults when I became one," she replied.

His eyes swept over her dismissively. "You haven't. Not yet."

"I'll be twenty-two this month," she told him shortly.

"I was thirty-five last month," he replied without looking her way. "And, to me, you'd still be a kid if you were four years older."

"You poor, old, decrepit thing," she murmured under her breath. It was getting harder and harder to feel sorry for him.

"What an interesting houseguest you're going to make, Miss Raymond," he observed as he drove down the interstate. "I'll have to arrange some razor-blade soup to keep your tongue properly sharpened."

"I don't think I like you," she said shortly.

He glared back. "I don't like women," he replied and his voice was as cold as his eyes.

She wondered if he knew why she'd come and decided that Aunt Lillian had probably told him everything. She averted her face to the window and gnawed on her lower lip. She was being deliberately antagonistic, and her upbringing bristled at her lack of manners. He'd asked Lillian to bring her out to Texas; he'd even paid for her ticket. She was supposed to cheer him up, to help him write his memoirs, to make his last days happier. And here she was being rude and unkind and treating him like a bad-tempered old tyrant.

"I'm sorry," she said after a minute.

"What?"

"I'm sorry," she repeated, unable to look at him. "You let me come here, you bought my ticket, and all I've done since I got off the plane is be sarcastic to you. Aunt Lillian told me all about it, you know," she added enigmatically, ignoring the puzzled expression on his face. "I'll do everything I can to make you glad you've brought me here. I'll help you out in every way I can. Well," she amended, "in most ways. I'm not really very comfortable around men," she added with a shy smile.

He relaxed a little, although he didn't smile. His hand caressed the steering wheel as he drove. "That's not hard to understand," he said after a minute, and she guessed that her aunt had told him about her strict upbringing. "But I'm the last man on earth you'd have to worry about in that particular respect. My women know the score, and they aren't that prolific these days. I don't have any interest in girls your age. You're just a baby."

Annoying, unnerving, infuriating man, she thought uncharitably, surprised by his statement. She looked toward him hesitantly, her eyes quiet and steady on his dark face. "Well, I've never had any interest in bad-tempered old men with oil wells," she said with dry humor. "That ought to reassure you as well, Mr. Jessup, sir."

"Don't be cheeky," he murmured with an amused glance. "I'm not that old."

"I'll bet your joints creak," she said under her breath.

He laughed. "Only on cold mornings," he returned. He pulled into the road that led to Three Forks and slowed down long enough to turn and stare into her soft blue eyes. "Tell you what, kid, you be civil to me and I'll be civil to you, and we'll never let people guess what we really think of each other. Okay?"

"Okay," she returned, eager to humor him. Poor man!

His green eyes narrowed. "Pity, about your age and that experience," he commented, letting his gaze wander over her face. "You're uncommon. Like your aunt."

"My aunt is the reincarnation of General Patton," she said. She wondered what experience he meant. "She could win wars if they'd give her a uniform."

"I'll amen that," he said.

"Thanks for driving up to get me," she added. "I appreciate it."

"I didn't know how you'd feel about a strange cowboy," he said gently. "Although we don't know each other exactly, I knew that Lillian's surely mentioned me and figured you'd be a bit more comfortable."

"I was." She didn't tell him how Lillian had described him as Attila the Hun in denim and leather.

"Don't tell her we've been arguing," he said unexpectedly as he put the car back in gear and drove up to the house. "It'll upset her. She stammered around for a half hour and even threatened to quit before she got up the nerve to suggest your visit."

"Bless her old heart." Mari sighed, feeling touched. "She's quite a lady, my aunt. She really cares about people."

"Next to my grandmother, she's the only woman that I can tolerate under my roof."

"Is your grandmother here?" she asked as they reached a huge cedarwood house with acres of windows and balconies.

"She left last week, thank God," he said heavily. "One more day of her and I'd have left and so would Lillian. She's too much like me. We only get along for short stretches."

"I like your house," she remarked as he opened the door for her.

"I don't, but when the old one burned down, my sister was going with an architect who gave us a good bid." He glared at the house. "I thought he was a smart boy. He turned out to be one of those innovative New Wave builders who like to experiment. The damned bathrooms have sunken tubs and Jacuzzis, and there's an indoor stream... Oh, God, what a nightmare of a house if you sleepwalk! You could drown in the living room or be swept off into the river."

She couldn't help laughing. He sounded horrified. "Why didn't you stop him?" she asked.

"I was in Canada for several months," he returned. He didn't elaborate. This strange woman didn't need to know that he'd gone into the wilderness to heal after Caroline's betrayal and that he hadn't cared what replaced the old house after lightning had struck and set it afire during a storm.

"Well, it's not so bad," she began but was interrupted when Lillian exploded out of the house, arms outstretched. Mari ran into them, feeling safe for the first time in weeks.

"Oh, you look wonderful," Lillian said with a sigh. "How are you? How was the trip?"

"I'm fine, and it was very nice of Mr. Jessup to come and meet me," she said politely. She turned, nodding toward him. "Thanks again. I hope the trip didn't tire you too much?"

"What?" he asked blankly.

"I told Mari how hard you'd been working lately, boss," Lillian said quickly. "Come on, honey, let's go inside!"

"I'll bring the bag," Ward said curiously and followed them into the rustic but modern house.

Mari loved it. It was big and rambling and there was plenty of room everywhere. It was just the house for an outdoorsman, right down to the decks that overlooked the shade trees around the house.

"I think this place is perfect for Ward, but for heaven's sake, don't tell him that! And please don't let on that you know about his condition," Lillian added, her eyes wary. "You didn't say anything about it?" she asked, showing Mari through the ultramodern upstairs where her bedroom overlooked the big pool below and the flat landscape beyond, fenced and cross-fenced with milling cattle.

"Oh, no, Scout's honor," Mari said. "But how am I going to help him write his memoirs?"

"We'll work up to it in good time," Lillian assured her. "He, uh, didn't ask why you came?"

Mari sighed. "He seemed to think I'd asked to come. Odd man, he thought I was afraid of him. Me, afraid of men, isn't that a scream? Especially after what Beth and I did at that all-night department store."

"Don't ever tell him, please," Lillian pleaded. "It would…upset him. We mustn't do that," she added darkly. "It could be fatal!"

"I won't, truly I won't," Mari promised. "He sure is healthy looking for a dying man, isn't he?"

"Rugged," Lillian said. "Real rugged. He'd never let on that he was in pain."

"Poor brave man," Mari said with a sigh. "He's so tough."

Lillian grinned as she turned away.

"Did his sister like this house?" Mari asked later after she'd unpacked and was helping Lillian in the kitchen.

"Oh, yes," Lillian confided to her niece. "But the boss hates it!"

"Is his sister like him?" Mari asked.

"To look at, no. But in temperament, definitely," the older woman told her. "They're both high-strung and mean tempered."

"You mentioned that he had a male secretary," Mari reminded her as she rolled out a piecrust.

"Yes. David Meadows. He's young and very efficient, but he doesn't like being called a secretary." Lillian grinned. "He thinks he's an administrative assistant."

"I'll have to remember that."

"I don't know what the boss would do without him, either," Lillian continued as she finished quartering the apples for the pie. Another apple pie might soften him up a little, she was thinking. "David keeps everything running smoothly around here, from paying the accounts to answering the phone and scheduling appointments. The boss stays on the road most of the time, closing deals. The oil business is vast these days. Last week he was in Saudi Arabia. Next week he's off to South America."

"All that traveling must get tiresome," Mari said, her blue eyes curious. "Isn't it dangerous for him in his condition?"

For a moment Lillian looked hunted. Then she brightened. "Oh, no, the doctor says it's actually good for him. He takes it easy, and it keeps his mind off things. He never talks about it, though. He's a very private person."

"He seems terribly cold," Mari remarked thoughtfully.

"Camouflage," Lillian assured her. "He's warm and gentle and a prince of a man," she added. "A prince! Now, get this pie fixed, girl. You make the best pies I've ever tasted, even better than my own.''

"Mama taught me," Mari said gently. "I really miss her sometimes. Especially in the autumn. We used to go up into the mountains to see the leaves. Dad was always too busy, but Mama and I were adventurous. It's been eight years since she died. And only one since Dad went. I'm glad I still have you."

Lillian tried not to look touched, but she was. "Get busy," she said gruffly, turning away. "It isn't good to look back."

That was true, Mari thought, keeping her own thoughts on the present instead of the past. She felt sad about Ward Jessup—even if he was a dreadful oilman. She'd heard her aunt talk about him for so many years that she felt as if she knew him already. If only she could make it through the week without making him angry or adding to his problems. She just wanted to help him, if he'd let her.

Mari was just going into the other room to call him when her attention was caught by the stream running through the room, lit by underwater colored lights. It was eerie and beautiful indoor "landscaping," with plants everywhere and literally a stream running through the middle of the living room, wide enough to swim in.

Not paying much attention to where she was going, Mari backed along the carpet, only half aware of footsteps, and suddenly collided with something warm and solid.

There was a terribly big splash and a furious curse. When she turned around, she felt herself go pale.

"Oh, Mr. Jessup, I'm sorry," she wailed, burying her cheeks in her hands.

He was very wet. Not only was he soaked, but there was a lily pad on top of his straight black hair that had been slicked down by all the water. He was standing, and though the water came to his chin, he looked very big and very angry. As he sputtered and blinked, Mari noticed that his green eyes were exactly the shade of the lily pad.

"Damn you..." he began as he moved toward the carpeted "shore" with a dangerous look on his dark face. At that moment nobody would have guessed that he was a dying man. As quick as lightning he was out of the water, dripping on the carpet. Suddenly Mari forgot his delicate condition and ran like hell.

"Aunt Lillian!"

Mari ran for the kitchen as fast as her slender legs could carry her, a blur in jeans and a white sweatshirt as she darted down the long hall toward the relative safety of the kitchen.

Behind her, soggy footsteps and curses followed closely.

"Aunt Lillian, help!" she cried as she dashed through the swing door.

She forgot that swing doors tend to swing back when forcibly opened by hysterical people. It slammed back into a tall, wet, cursing man. There was an ominous thud and the sound of shattering ceramic pieces.

Lillian looked at her niece in wide-eyed shock. "Oh, Mari," she said. Her ears told her more than she wanted to know as she stared at the horrified face of her niece. "Oh, Mari."

"I think Mr. Jessup may need a little help, Aunt Lillian," Mari began hesitantly.

"Prayer might be more beneficial at the moment, dear," Aunt Lillian murmured nervously. She wiped her hands on her printed apron and cautiously opened the swing door to peer into the dining room.

Ward Jessup was just sitting up among the ruins of his table setting, china shards surrounding him. His suit was wet, and there was a puddle of water under him as he tugged his enormous frame off the floor. His eyes were blazing in a face that had gone ruddy in anger. He held on to a chair and rose slowly, glaring at Lillian's half-hidden face with an expression that told her there was worse to come.

"She's really a nice girl, boss," Lillian began, "once you get to know her."

He brushed back his soaked hair with a lean, angry hand, and his chest rose and fell heavily. "I have a meeting just after supper," he said. "I sent the rest of my suits to the cleaner's this afternoon. This is the last suit I had. I didn't expect to go swimming in it."

"We could dry it and I could...press it," Lillian suggested half-heartedly, pretty sure that she couldn't do either.

"I could forget the whole damned thing, too," he said curtly. He glared at Lillian. "Nothing is going to make up for this, you know."

She swallowed. "How about a nice freshly baked apple pie with ice cream?"

He tilted his head to one side and pursed his lips. "Freshly baked?"

"Freshly baked."

"With ice cream?"

"That's right," she promised.

He shrugged his wet shoulders. "I'll think about it." He turned and sloshed off down the hall.

Lillian leaned back against the wall and stared at her transfixed niece. "Honey," she said gently, "would you like to tell me what happened?"

"I don't know," Mari burst out. "I went in to call him to the table, and I started looking at that beautiful artificial stream, and the next thing I knew, he'd fallen into it. I must have, well, backed into him."

"How you could miss a man his size is beyond me." Lillian shook her head and grabbed a broom and dustpan from the closet.

"I had my back to him, you know."

"I wouldn't ever do that again after this if I were you," the older woman advised. "If it wasn't for that apple pie, even I couldn't save you!"

"Yes, ma'am," Mari said apologetically. "Oh, Aunt Lillian, that poor, brave man." She sighed. "I hope he doesn't get a chill because of me. I'd never be able to live with myself!"

"There, there," Lillian assured her, "he's tough, you know. He'll be fine. For now, I mean," she added quickly.

Mari covered her face with her hands in mingled relief and suppressed amusement. Ward Jessup was quite a man. How sad that he had such little time left. She didn't think she'd ever forget the look on his face when he climbed out of the indoor stream, or the excited beat of her heart as she'd run from him. It was new to be chased by a man, even an ill one, and exhilarating to be uninhibited in one's company. She'd been shy with men all her life, but she didn't feel shy with Ward. She felt...*feminine.* And that was as new to her as the rapid beat of her heart.

Chapter 3

"I didn't mean to knock you into the pool," Mari told Ward the minute he entered the dining room.

He stopped in the doorway and stared at her from his great height. His hair was dry now, thick and straight against his broad forehead, and his wet clothes had been exchanged for dry jeans and a blue plaid shirt. His green eyes were a little less hostile than they had been minutes before.

"It isn't a pool," he informed her. "It's an indoor stream. And next time, Miss Raymond, I'd appreciate it if you'd watch where the hell you're going."

"Yes, sir," she said quickly.

"I told you not to let him put that stream in the living room," Lillian gloated.

He glared at her. "Keep talking and I'll give you an impromptu swimming lesson."

"Yes, boss." She turned on her heel and went back into the kitchen to fetch the rest of the food.

"I really am sorry," Mari murmured.

"So am I," he said unexpectedly, and his green eyes searched hers quietly. "I hope I didn't frighten you."

She glanced down at her shoes, nervous of the sensations that his level gaze prompted. "It's hard to be afraid of a man with a lily pad on his head."

"Stop that," he grumbled, jerking out a chair.

"You might consider putting up guardrails," she suggested dryly as she sat down across from him, her blue eyes twinkling with the first humor she'd felt in days.

"You'd better keep a life jacket handy," he returned.

She stuck her tongue out at him impulsively and watched his thick eyebrows arch.

He shook out his napkin with unnecessary force and laid it across his powerful thighs. "My God, you're living dangerously," he told her.

"I'm not afraid of you," she said smartly and meant it.

"That isn't what your Aunt Lillian says," he observed with narrowed eyes.

She stared at him blankly. "I beg your pardon?"

"She says you're afraid of men," he continued. He scowled at her puzzled expression. "Because of what happened to you and your friend," he prompted.

She blinked, wondering what her aunt had told him about that. After all, having your purse pinched by an overweight juvenile delinquent wasn't really enough to terrify most women. Especially when she and Beth had run the offender down, beaten the stuffing out of him, recovered the purse and sat on him until the police got there.

"You know, dear," Lillian blustered as she came through the door, shaking her head and smiling all at once. She looked as red as a beet, too. "The horrible experience you had!"

"Horrible?" Mari asked.

"Horrible!" Lillian cried. "We can't talk about it now!"

"We can't?" Mari parroted blankly.

"Not at the table. Not in front of the boss!" She jerked her head curtly toward him two or three times.

"Have you got a crick in your neck, Aunt Lillian?" her niece asked with some concern.

"No, dear, why do you ask? Here! Have some fried chicken and some mashed potatoes!" She shoved dishes toward her niece and began a monologue that only ended when it was time for dessert.

"I think something's wrong with Aunt Lillian," Mari confided to

Ward the moment Lillian started back into the kitchen for the coffeepot.

"Yes, so do I," he replied. "She's been acting strangely for the past few days. Don't let on you know. We'll talk later."

She nodded, concerned. Lillian was back seconds later, almost as if she was afraid to leave them alone together. How strange.

"Well, I think I'll go up to bed," Mari said after she finished her coffee, glancing quickly at Aunt Lillian. "I'm very tired."

"Good idea," Ward said. "You get some rest."

"Yes," Lillian agreed warmly. "Good night, dear."

She bent to kiss her aunt. "See you in the morning, Aunt Lillian," she murmured and glanced at Ward. "Good night, Mr. Jessup."

"Good night, Miss Raymond," he said politely.

Mari went quietly upstairs and into her bedroom. She sat by the window and looked down at the empty swimming pool with its wooden privacy fence and the gently rolling, brush-laden landscape, where cattle moved lazily and a green haze heralded spring. Minutes later there was a stealthy knock at the door, and Ward Jessup came into the room, scowling.

"Want me to leave the door open?" he asked hesitantly.

She stared at him blankly. "Why? Are you afraid I might attack you?"

He stared back. "Well, after the experience you had, I thought…"

"What experience?" she asked politely.

"The man at the shopping center," he said, his green eyes level and frankly puzzled as he closed the door behind him.

"Are you afraid of me because of that?" she burst out. "I do realize you may be a little weak, Mr. Jessup, but I promise I won't hurt you!"

He gaped at her. "What?"

"You don't have to be afraid of me," she assured him. "I'm not really as bad as Aunt Lillian made me sound, I'm sure. And it's only a red belt, after all, not a black one. I only sat on him until the police came. I hardly even bruised him—"

"Whoa," he said curtly. He cocked his dark head and peered at her. "You sat on him?"

"Sure," she agreed, pushing her hair out of her eyes. "Didn't she tell you that Beth and I ran the little weasel down to get my purse back and beat the stuffing out of him? Overweight little juvenile delinquent, he was lucky I didn't skin him alive.''

"You weren't attacked?" he persisted.

"Well, sort of." She shrugged. "He stole my purse. He couldn't have known I was a karate student."

"Oh, my God," he burst out. His eyes narrowed, his jaw tautened. "That lying old turkey!"

"How dare you call my aunt a turkey!" she returned hotly. "After all she's doing for you?"

"What, exactly, is she doing for me?"

"Well, bringing me here, to help you write your memoirs before…the end," she faltered. "She told me all about your incurable illness—"

"Incurable illness?" he bellowed.

"You're dying," she told him.

"Like hell I am," he said fiercely.

"You don't have to act brave and deny it," she replied hesitantly. "She told me that you wanted young people around to cheer you up. And somebody to help you write your memoirs. I'm going to be a novelist one day," she added. "I want to be a writer."

"Good. You can practice with your aunt's obituary," he muttered, glaring toward the door.

"You can't do that to a helpless old lady," she began.

"Watch me." He was heading for the door, his very stride frightening.

"Oh, no! You can't!" She ran after him, got in front of him and plastered herself against the door. "You'll have to go through me."

"Suits me, Joan of Arc," he grumbled, catching her by the waist. He lifted her clear off the floor until she was unnervingly at eye level with him. "You sweet little angel of mercy, you."

"Put me down or I'll…I'll put you down," she threatened.

He stared amusedly into her blue eyes under impossibly thick lashes. "Will you? Go ahead. Show me how you earned that red belt."

She tried. She used every trick her instructor had taught her, and all it accomplished was to leave her dangling from his powerful hands, panting into his mocking smile.

"Had enough?" she huffed.

"Not at all. Aren't you finished yet?" he asked politely.

She aimed one more kick, which he blocked effortlessly. She sagged in his powerful hold. Lord, he was strong! "Okay," she said, sighing wearily. "Now I'm finished."

"Next time," he told her as he put her back on her feet, leaving his hands tightly around her waist, "make sure your intended victim didn't take the same course of study. My belt is black. Tenth degree."

"Damn you!" she cursed sharply.

"And we'll have no more of that in this house," he said shortly, emphasizing the angry remark with a reproachful slap to her bottom, nodding as she gasped in outrage. "You've been working in that garage for too long already, if that's any example of what you're being taught."

"I'm not a child!" she retorted. "I'm an adult!"

"No, you aren't," he replied, jerking her against him with a mocking smile. "But maybe I can help you grow up a little."

He bent his head and found her lips with a single smooth motion, pressing her neck back against his muscular shoulder with the fierce possessiveness of his hard mouth.

Mari thought that in all her life nothing so unexpected had ever happened to her. His lips were warm and hard and insistent, forcing hers open so that he could put the tip of his tongue just under them, his breath tasting of coffee and mint, the strength of his big body overwhelming her with its hard warmth.

For an instant she tried to struggle, only to find herself enveloped in his arms, wrapped up against him so tightly that she could hardly breathe. And everywhere her face turned, his was there, his mouth provocative, sensuous, biting at hers, doing the most intimate things to it.

Her legs felt funny. They began to tremble as they came into sudden and shocking contact with his. Her heart raced. Her body began to ache with heat and odd longings. Her breath caught somewhere in her chest, and her breasts felt swollen. Because these new sensations frightened her, she tried to struggle. But he only held her tighter, not brutally but firmly, and went on kissing her.

His fingers were in her hair, tugging gently, strong and warm at her nape as they turned her face where he wanted it. His mouth pressed roughly against hers and opened softly, teaching hers. Eventually the drugging sweetness of it took the fight out of her. With a tiny sigh she began to relax.

"Open your mouth, Mari," he murmured in a deep, rough whisper, punctuating the command with a sensual brushing of his open lips against hers.

She obeyed him without hearing him, her body with a new heat, her hands searching over his arms to find hard muscle and warm strength through the fabric. She wanted to touch his skin, to experience every hard line of him. She wanted to open his shirt and touch his chest and see if the wiry softness she could feel through it was thick hair....

Her abandon shocked her back to reality. Her eyes opened and she tugged at his arms, only vaguely aware of the sudden, fierce hunger in his mouth just before he felt her resistance. He lifted his head, taking quick, short breaths, and by the time her eyes opened, he was back in control.

He was watching her, half amused, half mocking. He lifted his mouth, breathing through his nose, and let her move away.

"You little virgin," he accused in a tone that she didn't recognize. "You don't even know how to make love."

Her swollen lips could barely form words. She had to swallow and try twice to make herself heard. "That wasn't fair," she said finally.

"Why not?" he asked. "You tried to kick me, didn't you?"

"That isn't the way...a gentleman gets even," she said, still panting.

"I'm no gentleman," he assured her, smiling even with those cold green eyes. The smile grew colder as he realized how close he'd come to letting her knock him off balance physically. She was dangerous. Part of him wanted her off the property. But another part was hungry for more of that innocently ardent response he'd won from her. His own emotions confused him. "Haven't you realized yet why you're here, Georgia peach?" he asked mockingly. And when she shook her head, he continued, half amused. "Aunt Lillian is match-making. She wants you to marry me."

Mari's pupils dilated. "Marry you!"

His back stiffened. She didn't have to make it sound like the rack, did she? He glared down at her. "Well, plenty have wanted to, let me tell you," he muttered.

"Masochists," she shot back, humiliated by her aunt, his attitude and that unexpectedly ardent attack just minutes before. "Anyway," she said salvaging her pride, "Aunt Lillian would never—"

"She did." He studied her with a cold smile. "But I'm too old for you and too jaded. And I don't want to risk my heart again. So go home. Fast."

"It can't be fast enough to suit me. Honest," she told him huskily as she tried to catch her breath. "I don't want to wake up shackled to a man like you."

"How flattering of you."

"I want a partner, not a possessor," she said shakily. "I thought I knew something about men until just now. I don't know anything at all. And I'll be delighted to go back home and join a convent!"

"Was it that bad?" he taunted.

"You scare me, big man," she said and meant it. She backed away from him. "I'll stick to my own age group from now on, thanks. I'll bet you've forgotten more about making love than I'll ever learn."

He smiled slowly, surprised by her frankness. "I probably have. But you're pretty sweet all the same."

"Years too young for a renegade like you."

"I could be tempted," he murmured thoughtfully.

"I couldn't. You'd seduce me and leave me pregnant, and Aunt Lillian would quit, and I'd have to go away and invent a husband I didn't have, and our child would grow up never knowing his father…" she burst out.

His eyes widened. He actually chuckled. "My God, what an imagination."

"I told you I wanted to be a writer," she reminded him. "And now, since you're not dying, would you mind leaving me to pack? I think I can be out of here in ten minutes."

"She'll be heartbroken," he said unexpectedly.

"That's not my problem."

"She's your aunt. Of course it's your problem," he returned. "You can't possibly leave now. She'd—"

"Oh!"

The cry came from downstairs. They looked at each other and both dived for the door, opening it just in time to find Lillian on her back on the bottom step, groaning, one leg in an unnatural position.

Mari rushed down the stairs just behind Ward. "Oh, Aunt Lillian!" she wailed, staring at the strained old face with its pasty complexion. "How could you do this to me?"

"To you?" Lillian bit off, groaning again. "Child, it's my leg!"

"I was going to leave—" Mari began.

"Leave the dishes for you, no doubt." Ward jumped in with a warning glance in Mari's direction. "Isn't that right, Miss Raymond?" Fate was working for him as usual, he mused. Now he'd have a little time to find out just why this woman disturbed him so much. And to get her well out of his system, one way or another, before she left. He had to prove to himself that Mari wasn't capable of doing to him what Caroline had done. It was a matter of male pride.

Mari swallowed, wondering whether to go along with Ward. He did look pretty threatening. And huge. "Uh, that's right. The dishes. But I can do them!" she added brightly.

"It looks like…you may be doing them…for quite a while, if you…don't mind," Lillian panted between groans while Wade rushed to the telephone and dialed the emergency service number.

"You poor darling." Mari sighed, holding Lillian's wrinkled hand. "What happened?"

"I missed Ward and wondered if he might be…if you might be…" She cleared her throat and stared at Mari through layers of pain. "You didn't say anything to him?" she asked quickly. "About his… condition?"

Mari bit her tongue. *Forgive me for lying, Lord,* she thought. She crossed her fingers behind her. "Of course not," she assured her aunt with a blank smile. "He was just telling me about the ranch."

"Thank God." Lillian sank back. "My leg's broken, you know," she bit off. She glanced up as Ward rejoined them, scowling down at her. She forced a pitiful smile. "Well, boss, I guess you'll have to send for your grandmother," she said slyly.

He glared at her. "Like hell! I just got her off the place! Anyway, why should I?" he continued, bending to hold her other hand. "Your niece won't mind a little cooking, will she?" he added with a pointed glance at Mari.

Mari shifted restlessly. "Well, actually—"

"Of course she won't." Lillian grinned and then grimaced. "Will you, darling? You need to…recuperate." She chose her words carefully. "From your bad experience," she added, jerking her head toward Ward, her eyes pleading with her niece. "You know, at the shopping center?"

"Oh. That bad experience." Mari nodded, glancing at Ward and touching her lower lip where it was slightly swollen.

A corner of his mouth curved up and his eyes twinkled. "It wasn't that bad, was it?" he murmured.

"It was terrible!" Lillian broke in.

"You said it," Mari agreed blithely, her blue eyes accusing. "Besides, I thought you couldn't wait to push me out the door."

"You want her to leave?" Lillian wailed.

"No, I don't want her to leave," Ward said with suffering patience. He lifted his chin and stared down his straight nose at Mari, then smiled. "I've got plans for her," he added in a tone that was a threat in itself.

That was what bothered Mari. Now she was trapped by Lillian's lies and Ward's allegiance to his housekeeper. She wondered what on earth she was going to do, caught between the two of them, and she wondered why Ward Jessup wanted her to stay. He hated women most of the time, from what Lillian had divulged about him. He wasn't a marrying man, and he was a notorious womanizer. Surely he wouldn't try to seduce her. Would he?

She stared at him over Lillian's supine form with troubled eyes. He had an unscrupulous reputation. She wasn't so innocent that she hadn't recognized that evident hunger in his hard mouth just before she'd started fighting him.

But his green eyes mocked her, dared her, challenged her. She'd stay, he told himself. He'd coax her into it. Then he could find some way to make her show her true colors. He was betting there was a little of Caroline's makeup in her, too. She was just another female despite her innocence. She was a woman, and all women were unscrupulous and calculating. If he could make her drop the disguise, if he could prove she was just like all the other she-cats, he could rid himself of his unexpected lust. Lust, of course, was all it was. He forgave Lillian for her fall. It was going to work right in with his plans. Yes, it was.

Chapter 4

Lillian was comfortably settled in a room in the small Ravine hospital. The doctor had ordered a series of tests—not because of her broken leg but because of her blood pressure reading taken in the emergency room.

"Will she be all right, do you think?" Mari asked Ward as they waited for the doctor to speak to them. For most of the evening they'd been sitting in this waiting room. Ward paced and drank black coffee while Mari just stared into space worriedly. Lillian was her last living relative. Without the older woman she'd be all alone.

"She's tough," Ward said noncommittally. He glared at his watch. "My God, I hate waiting! I almost wish I smoked so that I'd have something to help kill the time."

"You don't smoke?" Mari said with surprise.

"Never could stand the things," he muttered. "Clogging up my lungs with smoke never seemed sensible."

Her eyebrows lifted. "But you drink."

"Not to excess," he returned, glancing down at her. "I like whiskey and water once in a blue moon, and I'll take a drink of white wine. But I won't do it and drive." He grinned. "All those commercials got to me. Those crashing beer glasses stick in my mind."

She smiled back a little shyly. "I don't drink at all."

"I guess not, tenderfoot," he murmured. "You aren't old enough to need to."

"My dad used to say that it isn't the age, it's the mileage."

His eyebrows arched. "How much mileage do you have, lady?" he taunted. "You look and feel pretty green to me."

Her face colored furiously, and she hated that knowing look on his dark face. "Listen here, Mr. Jessup—"

"Mr. Jessup." His name was echoed by a young resident physician, who came walking up in a white coat holding a clipboard. He shook hands with Ward and nodded as he was introduced tersely to Mari.

"She'll be all right," he told the two brusquely. "But I'd like to keep her one more day and run some more tests. She's furious, but I think it's for the best. Her blood pressure was abnormally high when we admitted her and it still is. I think that she might have had a slight stroke and that it caused her fall."

Mari had sudden horrible visions and went pale. "Oh, no," she whispered.

"I said, I *think*," the young doctor emphasized and then smiled. "She might have lost her balance for a number of reasons. That's why I want to run the tests. Even a minor ear infection or sinusitis could have caused it. I want to know for sure. But one thing's certain, and that's her attitude toward the high blood pressure medication she hasn't been taking."

Ward and Mari exchanged puzzled glances. "I wasn't aware that she had high blood pressure medication," Ward said.

"I guessed that," the young doctor said ruefully. "She was diagnosed a few weeks ago by Dr. Bradley. She didn't even get the prescription filled." He sighed. "She seems to look upon it as a death sentence, which is absurd. It's not, if she just takes care of herself."

"She will from now on," Mari promised. "If I have to roll the pills up in steak and trick them into her."

The young resident grinned from ear to ear. "You have pets?"

"I used to have a cat," Mari confided. "And the only way I could get medicine into him was by tricking him. Short of rolling him up in a towel."

Ward glared at her. "That's no way to treat a sick animal."

She lifted her thin eyebrows. "And how would you do it?"

"Force his mouth open and shove the pills down his throat, of course,'' he said matter-of-factly. ''Before you say it,'' he added when her mouth opened, ''try rolling a half-ton bull in a towel!''

The young doctor covered his mouth while Mari glared up at the taciturn oilman.

''I'll get the pills into her, regardless,'' Mari assured the doctor. She glanced at Ward Jessup. ''And it won't be by having them forced down her throat like a half-ton bull!''

''When will you know something?'' Ward asked.

''I'll have the tests by early afternoon, and I'll confer with Dr. Bradley. If you can be here about four o'clock, I'll have something to tell you,'' the young man said.

''Thank you, Doctor…?''

''Jackson,'' he replied, smiling. ''And don't worry too much,'' he told Mari. ''She's a strong-willed woman. I'd bet on her.''

They stopped by Lillian's room and found her half sedated, fuming and glaring as she sat propped up in bed.

''Outrageous!'' Lillian burst out the minute they entered the room. ''They won't give back my clothes. They're making me spend the night in this icebox, and they won't feed me or give me a blanket!''

''Now, now.'' Mari laughed gently and bent to kiss the thin face. ''You're going to be fine. They said so. They just want to run a few more tests. You'll be out of here in no time.''

That reassured the older woman a little, but her beady black eyes went to Ward for reassurance. He wouldn't lie to her. Not him. ''Am I all right?'' she asked.

''You might have had a stroke,'' he said honestly, ignoring Mari's shocked glare. ''They want to find out.''

Lillian sighed. ''I figured that. I sure did. Well,'' she said, brightening, ''you two will have to get along without me for a day or so.'' That seemed to cheer her up, too. Her eyes twinkled at the thought of them alone together in the house.

Ward could read her mind. He wanted to wring her neck, too, but he couldn't hurt a sick lady. First he had to get her well.

''I'll take good care of baby sister, here,'' he said, nodding toward Mari, and grinned.

Lillian's face fell comically. ''She's not that young,'' she faltered.

"Aunt Lillian!" Mari said, outraged. "Remember my horrible experience!"

"Oh, that." Lillian nibbled her lip. "Oh. That!" She cleared her throat, her eyes widened. "Well…"

"I'll help her get over it," Ward promised. He glanced down at Mari. "She's offered to help me get some of my adventures in the oil business down on paper. Wasn't that nice? And on her vacation, too," he added.

Lillian brightened. *Good.* They weren't talking about his "fatal illness" or her "brutal attack." With any luck they wouldn't stumble onto the truth until they were hooked on each other! She actually smiled. "Yes, how sweet of you, Mari!"

Although Mari felt like screaming, she smiled at her aunt. "Yes. Well, I thought it would give me something interesting to do. In between cooking and cleaning and such."

Lillian frowned. "I'm really sorry about this," she said, indicating her leg.

"Get well," Ward said shortly. "Don't be sorry. And one more thing. Whether or not this fall was caused by your blood pressure, you're taking those damned pills from now on. I'm going to ride herd on you like a fanatical ramrod on a trail drive. Got that?"

"Yes, sir, boss," Lillian said, pleased by his concern. She hadn't realized she mattered so much to anyone. Even Mari seemed worried. "I'll be fine. And I'll do what they tell me."

"Good for you," Ward replied. He cocked his head. "They said it could have been an ear infection or sinusitis, too. So don't go crazy worrying about a stroke. Did you black out before you went down?" he persisted.

Lillian sighed. "Not completely. I just got real dizzy."

He smiled "That's reassuring."

"I hope so. Now, you two go home," Lillian muttered. "Let me sleep. Whatever they gave me is beginning to work with a vengeance." She closed her eyes as they said their goodbyes, only to open them as they started to leave. "Mari, he likes his eggs scrambled with a little milk in them," she said. "And don't make the coffee too weak."

"I'll manage," Mari promised. "Just get well. You're all I have."

"I know." Lillian sighed as they closed the door behind them. "That's what worries me so."

But they didn't hear that troubled comment. Mari was fuming all the way to the car.

"You shouldn't have told her what the doctor said." She glowered at him as they drove out of the parking lot.

"You don't know her very well," he returned. He pulled into the traffic without blinking. Ravine had grown in the past few years, and the traffic was growing with it, but speeding cars didn't seem to bother him.

"She's my aunt. Of course I know her!"

"She isn't the kind of woman you nurse along," he shot back. "Any more than I'm that kind. I like the truth, even if it hurts, and so does she. You don't do people any favors by hiding it. You only make the impact worse when it comes out. God, I hate lies. There's nothing on earth I hate more."

He probably had a good reason for that attitude, but Mari wasn't going to pry into his privacy by asking.

At least now she understood Aunt Lillian's matchmaking frenzy. If the older woman had expected to die, she might also have worried about Mari's future. But to try to give Mari to a man like the one beside her was almost criminal! The very thought of being tied to that ex-drill rigger made her blanche. He frightened her in a way no other man ever had. It wasn't fear of brutality or even of rough behavior. It was fear of involvement, of being led on and dumped, the way Johnny Greenwood had teased her and taken her places, and then when she was drunk on loving him, he'd announced his engagement to someone else.

Ward Jessup wasn't the man for marriage, but he wouldn't mind amusing himself with a woman and then dropping her. He seemed to hate women, to be spoiling for revenge on the entire sex. She remembered him saying that he could only tolerate his grandmother and Lillian under his roof, and that said it all. She'd have to be very careful not to fall under his spell. Because he was just playing, and she didn't even know the first thing about his game.

She went to her room as soon as they were back at Three Forks, and although she hated her vulnerability, she actually locked her bedroom door. Not that he'd try anything, she assured herself. But, just in case, a little precaution wouldn't hurt.

The next morning she was awake at dawn. Rather than lie in bed and worry about Aunt Lillian, she got up, dressed in jeans and a yellow pullover and went to cook the beast's breakfast.

She did love this house, indoor waterway and all. It seemed to catch and scatter light so that the darkest corner was bright and cheery. The kitchen reflected the rest of the house. It was spacious and cheerful and contained every modern appliance known to man.

She started the coffee maker and fried bacon. By the time the aroma of coffee was filling the kitchen, she had biscuits in the oven and was setting the big, elegant dining room table.

"What the hell are you doing that for?" Ward Jessup asked from the doorway. "I don't mind eating in the kitchen."

She jumped, turning in time to see him shrug into a chambray shirt. His chest was…incredible. She couldn't help but stare. Despite her age and her exposure to men at the garage where she worked, she'd never in her life seen anything like Ward Jessup without his shirt. Talk about masculine perfection! His chest was as tanned as his face. Broad, rippling with muscle, tapering to his belt, it had a perfect wedge of dark, thick hair that made Mari's jaw drop.

"Close your mouth, honey, you'll catch flies that way," he said, then chuckled, torn between exasperation and honest flattery at her rapt and explicit stare.

She turned back to her table setting with trembling fingers, hating her youth and inexperience, hating the big man who was making fun ot it. "Excuse me. I'm not used to men…half dressed like that."

"Then you should have seen me ten minutes ago, sprout, before I got up. I sleep in the raw."

Now Mari was sure she was blushing. She pursed her lips as she put silverware at their places.

He came up behind her so that she could feel the heat of his big body and took her gently by the shoulders. "That wasn't fair, was it?" he murmured.

"No," she agreed, "considering what a beautiful breakfast I just fixed you."

His lips tugged into a smile. "Do I smell bacon?"

"And biscuits and an omelette and hash brown potatoes and hot coffee," she continued, glancing up at him.

"Then what are you standing here for?" he asked. "Feed me!"

She was rapidly becoming convinced that his appetite was the great love of his life. Food could stop his temper dead, keep him from teasing and prevent homicide, as that apple pie had done after she'd knocked him into the water. It was useful to have such a weapon, when dealing with such a formidable enemy, she thought as she went to put the platters on the table.

He ate without talking, and he didn't sit and read a newspaper, as her father always had done in her youth. She watched him curiously.

His eyebrows shot up. "Something bothering you?"

"Not really." She laughed self-consciously. "It's just that the only man I've ever had breakfast with was my father, and he read his paper all through it."

"I don't read at the table," he said. He finished his last mouthful of biscuit, washed it down with coffee and poured himself a second cup from the carafe. Then he sat back in his chair and stared straight into Mari's eyes. "Why does my chest disturb you?"

She tingled from her head to her toes at the unexpected question and felt a wave of heat wash over her. Some old lines about fighting fire with fire shot into her mind. "Because it's beautiful, in a purely masculine way," she blurted out.

He pondered that for a minute before he smiled into his coffee. "You don't lie well, do you?"

"I think it's a waste of time," she replied. She got to her feet. "If you're through, I'll clear the table."

She started to pick up his plate. His big hand, and it was enormously big, caught her wrist and swallowed it, staying her beside him.

"Have you ever touched a man, except to shake hands?" he asked quietly.

"I'm not a shrinking violet," she said, flustered. "I'm almost twenty-two years old, and I have been kissed a few times!"

"Not enough, and not by anyone who knew how." He pulled her closer, feeling her resistance, but he stopped short of dragging her down onto his lap. "Why are you afraid of me?"

"I am not!" she retorted.

His fingers on her wrist were softly caressing. She reacted to him in a way that shocked him. In all the years, with all the women, he'd never felt such response. She was innocent, despite her denials. He'd have bet an oil well on it.

"Calm down," he said softly, feeling so masculine that he could have swallowed a live rattler. He even smiled. "I won't hurt you."

She flushed even more and jerked away from him, but he was much too strong. "Please," she bit off. "Let me go. I don't know how to play this kind of game."

His thumb found her moist palm and rubbed it in a new and exciting way, tracing it softly, causing sensations that went far beyond her hand. "I stopped playing games a long time ago, and I never played them with virgins," he said quietly. "What are you afraid of, Mari?" He spoke her name softly, and she tingled like a schoolgirl.

"You hate women," she said in a voice barely above a whisper. She met his green eyes levelly. "I don't think there's any real feeling in you, any deep emotion. Sometimes you look at me as if you hate me."

He hadn't realized that. He stared down at their hands, hers so pale against his deeply tanned one. "I got burned once, didn't your aunt tell you?"

"I got burned once, too," she replied, "and I don't want to—"

"Again," he finished for her, looking up unexpectedly. "Neither do I."

"Then why don't you let go of my hand?" she asked breathlessly.

He drew it relentlessly to his hard mouth and brushed at it with soft, moist strokes that made her go hot all over. "Why don't you stop me?" he countered. He pried open her palm and touched his tongue to it, and she caught her breath and gasped.

He looked up, his eyes suddenly hotly green and acquisitive, and she felt the first tug of that steely hand on hers with a sense of fantasy. Her eyes were locked into his possessive gaze, her body throbbed with new longings, new curiosities.

"I'm going to teach you a few things you haven't learned," he said, his voice like velvet as he drew her relentlessly down toward him. "And I think it's going to be an explosive lesson for both of us. I feel like a volcano when I touch you..."

Her lips parted as her eyes dropped to his hard, hungry mouth. She could almost see it, feel it, the explosive desire that was going to go up like fireworks when he put his hard mouth on hers and began to touch her.

She almost cried out, the hunger was so formidable. Silence closed in on them. She could hear his breathing, she could feel her heartbeat shaking her. In slow motion she felt his hard thighs ripple as she was tugged down onto them, she felt the power and strength of his hands, smelled the rich fragrance of his cologne, stared into eyes that wanted her.

She parted her lips in breathless anticipation, aching for him. Just as his hand went to her shoulder, to draw her head down, the front door opened with a loud bang.

Chapter 5

"Good morning," a pleasant auburn-haired young man was saying before Mari was completely composed again. He seemed to notice nothing, equally oblivious to Mari's flushed face and Ward's uneven breathing.

"Good morning, David," Ward said in what he hoped was a normal voice. From the neck down he had an ache that made speech difficult. "Have some coffee before we start to work."

"No, thank you, sir," the young man said politely. "Actually, I came to ask for a little time off," he added with a sheepish grin. "You see...I've gotten married."

Ward gaped at him. His young secretary had always seemed such a levelheaded boy, with a head full of figures. As it turned out, the figures weren't always the numerical kind.

"Married?" Ward croaked.

"Well, sir, it was kind of a hurried-up thing," David said with a grin. "We eloped. She's such a sweet girl. I was afraid somebody else would snap her up. And I wondered, well, if I could just have a couple of weeks. If you could do without me? If you have to replace me, I'll understand," he added hesitantly.

"Go ahead," Ward muttered. "I'll manage." He shifted in the chair. "What would you like for a wedding present?"

David brightened immediately. "Two weeks off," came the amused reply.

"All right, you've got it. I'll hold your job for the time being. Now get out of here. You know weddings give me indigestion," he added for good measure and then spoiled the whole thing by smiling.

David shook his hand with almost pathetic eagerness. "Thank you, sir!"

"My pleasure. See you in two weeks."

"Yes, sir!" David grinned at Mari, to whom he hadn't even been introduced, and beat a path out the door before he could be called back. He knew his boss pretty well.

"That tears it," Ward grumbled. "What in hell will I do about the mail?"

She stared at him, stunned by his lack of feeling. "He just got married."

"So what?" he demanded. "Surely the only time he really needs to be with her is after dark."

"You male chauvinist!"

"What are you so keyed up about, honey?" he taunted irritably. "Frustrated because I couldn't finish what I started before he walked in on us?"

What good would it do to argue? she asked herself as she noisily loaded up the dirty plates and utensils and took them out to the kitchen without a single word.

He followed her a few minutes later, looking half out of humor and a little guilty.

Standing in the doorway he filled it with his big, tall frame. His hair looked rakish, falling over his broad forehead, and he was so handsome that she had to fight to keep from staring at him all over again.

"I've got to ride over and see about my rig on Tyson Wade's place," he said quietly. "Can you handle the phone?"

"Sure," she told him, walking over to the wall phone. "This is the receiver," she began, pointing to it, speaking in a monotone. "When it rings, you pick it up and talk right in here—"

"Oh, for God's sake," he burst out. "What I meant was that it rings all day long, with everything from stock options to social invitations to notices of board meetings!"

She pushed back her bangs. "I've worked in offices since I was eighteen," she told him.

He cocked his head. "Can you type?"

"How ever do you think I'll manage all the housekeeping and cooking as well as looking after your appointments and answering mail and waiting on Aunt Lillian all at once?" she demanded.

His eyebrows arched. "Well, if you aren't capable of it, I'll hire a cook and a maid and a nurse and a secretary..."

Mari could only imagine how her aunt would react to that. She glared at him. "And break Aunt Lillian's old heart by importing a lot of strangers to keep us apart?"

He laughed in spite of himself. "I guess it would," he confessed. His green eyes narrowed, and there was a light in them that disturbed her as he ran his gaze slowly over her slender body. "God forbid anything should keep us apart."

"Don't you have an oil well to check on?"

"Several, in fact," he agreed. He folded his arms. "But at the moment I'd rather look at you."

"And I'd rather you didn't," she said curtly, averting her eyes to the dishwater.

"I like the way you react to me, Mari," he said softly. "I like the way your body starts to tremble when I come close. If I'd started kissing you a few minute ago, we'd still be doing it. I don't even know if I could stop. And that being the case," he added, leveling with her, "I think you'd better practice ways to discourage me. Lillian won't be around much when she comes back until her leg heals. So you and I are going to get a bit of each other's company. I'd just as soon manage your little visit without showing you how good I am in bed."

His blatant speech shocked her. She turned, soapy hands poised over the sink, and stared at him. "Are you?" she asked without thinking.

He nodded slowly, holding her gaze, his face dead serious. "A man doesn't have to be emotionally involved to make love well. I've had years of practice. But it's never meant much, except physically. It never will. So you keep that in mind, sprout, okay?"

"Okay," she replied, all eyes.

His eyes narrowed at her expression. "Haven't you ever discussed these things with a man?"

"My parents didn't discuss things like that," she replied. "Most of the girls I've known had a distorted view of it because they did it with so many people. I...find the thought of it distasteful, somehow. Sleeping with someone, well, it's intimate, isn't it? Like us-ing someone's toothbrush, only more so. I couldn't...just do that, without loving."

She sounded so hopelessly naive. He searched her face and realized with a start that he'd never made love to a virgin. Not one. Not ever. And the thought of touching her in all the ways that he'd touched other women produced a shocking reaction from his body—one he was grateful that she wouldn't recognize.

"What an unusual attitude," he said involuntarily.

"That isn't the word most people use," she replied, her eyes dull and lackluster. "Men avoid me like the plague, except to do typing and answer phones. I'm what's known as an oddball."

"Because you don't sleep around?" he asked, stunned.

"Exactly. Didn't you know that the pill has liberated women?" she explained. "They're allowed the same freedom as men. They can sleep around every night without any consequences. Of course, they sacrifice a few things along the way that the liberals don't mention. Things like that deep-seated guilt that all the permissive ideals in the world won't change."

He stared at her. "My God, you are a fanatic, aren't you?" he mused.

She smiled slowly. "How would you like marrying a woman and hearing all about her old lovers? Meeting them occasionally and wondering if you measured up? How would you like to have a pregnant wife and wonder if the baby was really yours? I mean, if she sleeps around before marriage, what's to keep her from doing it afterward? If promiscuity is okay, isn't adultery okay as well?"

Everything she was saying disturbed him. Caroline had slept around. Not only with him, but, as he'd later found out, with at least two of his business acquaintances. He frowned at the thought. Yes, he'd have wondered. And he'd only just realized it.

"But I'm just a prude," she announced dryly. "So don't mind me.

I'll grow into happy spinsterhood and die with the reputation that Elizabeth I had.''

"Unless you marry," he said involuntarily.

She laughed ruefully. "Men don't marry women they haven't slept with. Not these days." She turned back to the dishes, oblivious to the brief flash of pain that crossed the face of the man behind her. "I'm not into self-pity, but I do face facts," she continued calmly. "I'm not pretty, I'm just passable. I'm too thin, and I don't know how to flirt. And, as you yourself said, I'm a greenhorn when it comes to intimacy. All that adds up to happy spinsterhood." She gazed thoughtfully out the window over the sink. "I'll grow prize roses," she mused aloud. "Yes, that's what I'll do. And zinnias and crape myrtle and petunias and lantana and hibiscus."

He wasn't listening anymore. He was staring at the back of her head. Her hair was very dark and sleek, and he wished she'd left it long, the way it was in the photograph he'd seen. She wasn't a beauty, that was true. But she had a pretty good sense of humor, and she didn't take herself or anyone else too seriously. She had guts and she told the truth. Damn her.

He didn't like his attraction to her. He didn't like how she could make him tremble all over like a boy when he started to kiss her. He didn't want her knowing it, either. The whole point of this exercise was to *exorcise*. He had to get rid of this lunatic obsession he felt.

"I'm going," he said shortly, shouldering himself away from the doorjamb. "I'll be back by three-thirty to go to the hospital with you."

"I'll phone meanwhile," she said.

"Do what you please." He stormed off, leaving her curious and speechless. What an odd man. What a dangerous man.

She spent the rest of the day working herself into exhaustion so that she wouldn't dwell on what had happened at breakfast.

When they got to the hospital, Lillian was sitting on the side of her bed, dressed.

"It's about time," she began hotly. "Get me out of here! They've put on a cast and decided it was infected sinuses that made me fall.

They've given me some tablets they say will lower my blood pressure, and if you don't spring me, I'll jump out a window!''

''With that?'' Ward asked, nodding toward the heavy plaster walking cast on one of her legs.

''With that,'' she assured him. ''Tell him I'm serious about this, Mari,'' she added.

Mari was trying not to laugh. ''You look pretty serious.''

''I can see that. Where's the doctor?''

''He'll be here any minute,'' Lillian began.

''I'll go find him,'' Ward returned, walking quickly out into the hall, moving lightly for a man his size.

''How's it going?'' Lillian asked, all eyes.

''How's what going?'' Mari asked with assumed innocence.

''You were alone all last night!'' she hissed. ''Did he try anything?''

Mari lifted her eyebrows and pursed her lips. ''Well, he did try to call somebody on the phone, but he couldn't get them.''

Lillian looked pained. ''I mean, did he make a pass at you?''

''No,'' Mari lied. It was only a white lie, just enough to throw the bloodhound off the scent.

The older woman looked miserable. It didn't bode well that Ward was so irritable, either. Maybe her matched pair had been arguing. Lillian had to get out of here and do a little stage-managing before it was too late and her whole plan went down the tube!

Ward was back minutes later, looking as unapproachable as he had since he'd driven up to the house at three-thirty with a face like a thunderhead.

''I found him. He says you're okay, no stroke,'' he told Lillian. ''You can leave. I've signed you out. Let's go.''

''But we need a wheelchair...'' Mari began.

He handed her Lillian's purse, lifted the elderly woman easily in his arms and carried her out the door, his set features daring anyone to question or stop him.

Back at Three Forks Lillian's room was on the ground floor, and despite all the protests she immediately returned to the kitchen and started supper.

"Do you want to go back to the hospital?" Ward demanded, hands on hips, glaring. "Get into bed!"

"I can cook with a broken leg," she returned hotly. "It isn't my hands that don't work, and I've never yet used my toes!"

He sighed angrily. "Mari can do that."

"Mari's answering your letters," he was pointedly reminded. "She can't do everything. And with David gone…"

"Damn David," he muttered darkly. "What a hell of a time to get married!"

Lillian glared at him until he muttered something rough under his breath and strode off toward his den.

Mari was inside the paneled room, working away at the computer. She was trying to erase a mistake and was going crazy deciphering the language of the computer he'd shown her. The word processing program was one of the most expensive and the most complicated. She couldn't even get it to backspace.

"I can't do anything with your aunt," he grumbled, slamming the door. "She's sitting on a stool making a pie."

"No wonder you can't do anything with her," she commented innocently. "Your stomach won't let you."

He glared at her. "How's it going?"

She sighed. "Don't you have a typewriter?"

"What year do you think this is?" he demanded. "What kind of equipment have you got at that garage where you work?"

"A manual typewriter," she said.

His head bent forward. "A what?"

"A manual type—"

"That's what I thought you said. My God!"

"Well, until they hired me, one of the men was doing all the office work. They thought the manual typewriter was the latest thing. It did beat handwriting all the work orders," she added sweetly.

"I work with modern equipment," he told her, gesturing toward the computer. "That's faster than even an electronic typewriter, and you can save what you do. I thought you knew how to use it."

"I know how to turn it on," she agreed brightly.

He moved behind her and peered over her shoulder. "Is that all you've done so far?"

"I've only been in here an hour," she reminded him. "It took me that long to discover what to stuff into the big slots."

"Diskettes," he said. "Program diskettes."

"Whatever. Anyway, this manual explains how to build a nuclear device, not how to use the word processing program," she said, pushing the booklet away. "Or it might as well. I don't understand a word of it. Could you show me how it works?" She looked up at him with eyes the color of a robin's egg.

He actually forgot what he was saying. She had a way of looking at him that made his blood thaw, like the sun beating down on an icy pond. He could imagine how a colt felt on a spring morning with the breeze stirring and juicy grass to eat and a big pasture to run in.

"Could you?" she prompted, lost in his green eyes.

His big hand touched the side of her face tentatively, his thumb moving over her mouth, exploring its soft texture, mussing her lipstick, sensitizing her lips until they parted on a caught breath.

"Could I what, Mari?" he asked in a tone that curled her toes inside her shoes.

Her head was much too far back. It gave him access to her mouth. She saw the intent in his narrowing eyes, in his taut stance. Her body ached for his touch. She looked up at him helplessly, his willing victim, wanting his mouth on hers with a passion that overwhelmed her.

He bent slowly, letting his gaze fall to her parted lips. She could smell the heady fragrance of his cologne now because he was so close. There was mint and coffee on his breath, and he had strong white teeth; she could see them where his chiseled lips parted in anticipation of possession. Her breasts throbbed, and she noticed a tingling, yearning sensation there.

"Your skin is hot," he whispered, tracing her cheek with his fingers as he tilted his face across hers and moved even closer. "I can feel it burning."

Her hands were on his arms now. She could feel the powerful muscles through the white shirt that he'd worn with a tie and jacket when they went to pick up Lillian. But the jacket and tie were gone, and the shirt was partially unbuttoned, and now the overwhelming sight of him filled Mari's world. Her short nails pressed into his skin, bending against those hard muscles as his lips brushed over hers.

"Bite me," he whispered huskily and then incited her to do it, teasing her mouth, teaching her.

She knew nothing, but she wanted so desperately to please him so that he wouldn't stop. This was magic, and she wanted more.

Her mouth opened and she nipped at his firm lower lip, nibbling it, feeling its softness. He laughed softly deep in his throat, and she felt his hand move from her cheek to her shoulder, down her arm to her waist. While he played with her mouth, his fingers splayed out and then moved up, and the thin fabric of her flowery shirtwaist dress was no barrier at all as he found her rib cage and began to tease it.

This was explosive. Mari trembled a little because she was catching fire. He hadn't been kidding when he told her he was a good lover. She hadn't dreamed of the kind of sensations that he was showing her. She hadn't realized how vulnerable she was. Her mind was telling her that it was a game, that he didn't mean it. He'd said so. But her body was enthralled by new feelings, new pleasures, and it wouldn't let her stop.

"Oh," she whispered unsteadily when his tongue began to taste the soft inner surface of her lips.

"Open my shirt," he whispered against her warm mouth. He drew her hands to the remaining buttons and coaxed them until they had the fabric away from him.

She put her hands against hard muscle and thick hair and gasped at the contact. She'd never touched a man this way, and he knew it and was excited by it.

He bit her lower lip with a slow, ardent pressure that was arousing. "Draw your nails down to my belt," he murmured against her parted mouth.

She did, amazed at the shudder of his big body, at the soft groan her caress produced. She drew away slightly so that she could see his face, could see the lazy, smoldering desire in his green eyes.

"I like it," he told her with a husky laugh.

She did it again, lowering her eyes this time to watch his muscles ripple with pleasure as she stroked them, to watch his flat stomach draw in even more with a caught breath. It was exciting to arouse him. It gave her a sense of her femininity that she'd never experienced.

Meanwhile, his hand was moving again, this time up her rib cage. Not blatant but subtle in its caress, teasing lightly, provocative. It reached the outer edges of her breast even as her nails were tenderly scoring him, and his fingers lifted to touch around her nipple.

She shuddered, looking up at him with the residue of virginal fear in her wide blue eyes. Her hand went to his hairy wrist and poised there while she tried to choose between pleasure and guilt.

"Have you ever done this before?" he asked, his lips against hers.

"No," she confessed.

Odd, how protective that made him feel. And how much a man. He brushed his lips gently over hers. "Lillian isn't fifty feet away," he whispered. "And we won't do anything horribly indiscreet. But I'm as excited by this as you are, and I don't want to stop just yet. I want to touch you and feel your reaction and let you feel mine. Mari," he murmured, tracing a path up her soft breast, "I've never been the first. Not in any way, even this. Let me teach you. I promise you, there's not the slightest danger. Not right now."

"Oh, but I shouldn't..." She was weakening and her voice betrayed her.

"Don't feel guilty," he whispered over her mouth. "This is love play. Women and men have indulged themselves this way since the beginning of time. I'm human. So are you. There's no shame in being hungry."

He made it sound natural. It was the seducer's basic weapon, but Mari was too outmatched to care. She arched toward his fingers because she couldn't help herself. That maddening tracing of his fingers was driving her to her limits. She wanted his hand to flatten on her body. She wanted him to touch her...there!

His teeth nibbled at her lower lip, catching it in a soft tug just as his fingers closed on an erect nipple and tightened gently.

She cried out. The sound would have penetrated the walls and door, but he caught it in his mouth and muffled it, half mad with unexpected arousal. Her cries and her trembling were driving him over the edge.

Somehow he had her on the sofa, flat on her back with his heavy body half covering her. Her dress was coming undone, she could feel the air on her bare skin, and her bra was all too loose, and his hand was...there.

She shuddered and her eyes opened, hazy with passion. Her mouth was swollen, her cheeks red, her upward gaze full of rapt wonder.

His big hand flattened over her soft breast, feeling the tip rub abrasively on his palm as he caressed her. His thumb circled it roughly, and she shuddered all over, her breath sighing out unsteadily like his own.

She wanted him to kiss her some more, but his eyes were on her dress now. He peeled it slowly away from the breast he was touching, moving her bra up so that he could see the pink and mauve contrast and that taut little nub. It was as if he'd never looked at a woman before. She was beautiful. Sweetly curving and high, and not too big or too little. Just right.

She felt as if she were watching from a distance. Her eyes wandered over his absorbed expression, seeing the veiled pleasure there, the wonder. If she was awed by him, so was he awed by her. He was touching her like some priceless treasure, taking his time, lovingly tracing every texture.

He took the nipple between his thumb and forefinger and felt its hardness. He looked up into her fascinated eyes. "If I put my mouth on you, you'll cry out again," he whispered softly. "And Lillian might mistake the sound and come hopping."

She was trembling. She wanted it. Her body arched sinuously. She reached up, shyly, and cupped his face, gently tugging at it.

"I won't...cry out," she whispered, biting her lower lip to make sure.

"Say 'taste me,'" he whispered back, searching her eyes.

She blushed feverishly and turned her face into his throat to hide her embarrassment.

"Virgin," he breathed, trembling himself with the newness of it. "Oh, God, I want to have you so much!"

She thought she knew what he meant, but just then he took her breast into his warm mouth, and she had to chew her lip almost through to keep from screaming at the incredible sensation.

Her hands released his face, and she clenched them over her head.

Writhing helplessly, she was caught up in the throes of something so powerful that it stopped her breath in her throat. She twisted up toward him, her body shuddering, her breast on fire with the feel of his mouth.

With a rough groan he suddenly rolled away from her and sat up with his face in his hands, shuddering, bent over as if in agony.

She lay there without moving, shaking all over with reaction and frustration, too weak from desire to even cover herself.

After a minute he took a deep, steadying breath and looked down at her. If she expected mockery or amusement, she was surprised. Because he wasn't smiling.

His dark green eyes ran over her like hands, lingering on all the places where his mouth had been, devouring her. He drew the bra slowly back down and reached around her for the hooks, fastening them. Then he pulled the edges of her dress together and buttoned them. He didn't speak until he was through.

"Do you understand why I stopped?" he asked gently. Yes, there was that. There was tenderness in every line of his face, in his voice, in the fingers that brushed her cheek.

"Yes," she returned slowly. "I think so."

"I didn't frighten you?"

That seemed to matter very much. She felt suddenly old and venerable and deeply possessive. "No," she said.

He tugged gently on a strand of damp hair. "Did I please you?" he persisted and this time he smiled but without mockery.

"As if you couldn't tell," she murmured, lowering her face so that he couldn't see it.

"If we ever make love completely, it will have to be in a sound-proof room," he said at her ear. "You'd scream the house down."

"Ward!" she groaned and buried her face in his chest.

"No." He shuddered, moving her away, and he looked pale all of a sudden.

Her eyes questioned his. All these feeling were very new to her.

He drew in a harsh breath, holding her hands in his. "Men are very easy to arouse," he told her without embarrassment. "When they get to fever pitch, it takes very little to fan the fire. Right now

I'm beyond fever pitch," he mused with a faint laugh, "and if you touch me that way again, we're both going to be in a lot of trouble."

"Oh," she returned, searching his eyes. "Does it hurt?" she whispered softly.

"A little," he replied. He brushed back her hair. "How about you?"

"Wow." She laughed shakily. "I never dreamed that could happen to me."

He felt incredible. New. Reborn. He touched her face lightly as if he were dreaming. Bending over her, he took her mouth softly under his and kissed her. It was different from any other kiss in his life. When he let her go, he had to stand up or lay her down.

"You'd better get back to work," he said and gestured toward the computer. "And, no, I'm not going to try to teach you. My body won't let me that close without making impossible demands on both of us so you'll have to muddle through alone." He laughed angrily. "Damn it, are you a witch?"

She stood up, smoothing her dress and hair. "Actually, until about five minutes ago, I thought I was Lady Dracula."

"Now you know better, don't you?" He stood watching her, his mouth slightly swollen, his shirt open, his hands on his narrow hips. The sight of him still took her breath away.

She went quickly back to the computer and sat down, keeping her eyes on the screen. "I'll get these finished before supper, if I can," she promised.

He smiled to himself. It took him a minute to leave her, his mind grappling furiously with the conflict between his desire and his calculating mind that insisted she was only interested in what he had—his ranch, his oil, his money.

Women had never wanted him for himself; why should Mari be different? But why had she reacted with such sweet ardor unless she'd wanted him as desperately as he'd wanted her? That kind of fever was hard to fake. No, he thought. No, she'd wanted him. But was she really that unmaterialistic? The only women he'd let himself get close to were his mother and Caroline, both of whom had been self-centered opportunists. How could he trust this one? She bothered him terribly. He no longer felt any confidence in his own judgment. He left the room scowling.

Chapter 6

Mari was so shaken by what had happened with Ward that she had eventually needed to escape from the den. She was afraid everything they'd done would show on her face, and Lillian had sharp eyes. She also wondered if Ward would tease her. That would be the last straw, to have a worldly man like that make fun of her for a physical reaction she couldn't help.

She needn't have worried. Ward was nowhere in sight, and Lillian was muttering furiously as she hobbled around the kitchen with a crutch under one arm.

"I wish you'd let me do that," Mari scolded. She picked up the plate of ham that Lillian was trying to take to the table and carried it in for her. "You shouldn't be trying to lift things, Aunt Lillian. You know what the doctor said."

"Yes, but it's pretty hard asking people for help," the older woman said irritably. She glanced at Mari. "He's gone."

Mari tried to look innocent. "He?"

"The boss. He decided to fly down to South America. Just like that." She snapped her fingers while Mari tried not to let her eyes reflect the shock she felt.

"He left tonight?" Mari asked blankly. It didn't seem possible. She'd been talking with him—among other things—less than two hours ago.

"Yep. He sure did. Bag and baggage. Imagine, getting a flight out of here that quickly. He'll go on a commercial flight from San Antonio, you see.'' She added, ''Flew himself over to the airport, he did.''

Mari cleared her throat. ''You said a few days ago that he'd have to go to South America.''

''Yes. But I didn't expect him to leave in the middle of my first night back home,'' Lillian said hotly.

''He knows I'm here,'' she returned and impulsively hugged the older woman. ''I'll take care of you.''

Lillian sighed miserably. ''Nothing is working the way it was meant to,'' she grumbled. ''Nothing!''

Now was her chance to perfect her acting ability. ''Whatever do you mean, Aunt Lillian?'' she asked with a smile.

Lillian actually flushed. ''Nothing. Not a thing. Here, set the table and help me get the food in here. There'll be a lot for just the two of us, seeing the boss and his appetite are missing, but we can freeze the rest, I suppose.''

''Did you take your pill?'' Mari asked.

Lillian glowered at her. Then she grinned. ''Yep.''

''Good for you,'' Mari returned. ''Now I'll get to keep you for a lot longer.''

Lillian started to speak, and then she just laughed. But her eyes were troubled when she hobbled back out to the kitchen.

Mari wandered around by herself during the next few days, when she wasn't helping Lillian, enjoying the spaciousness of the ranch and the feeling of being self-sufficient. It must have been very much like this a hundred years before, she thought as she gazed out at the level horizon, when bad men and cattlemen and refugees from the Confederacy had come through on the long trails that led north and south and west.

It was so quiet. Nothing like the noisy bustle of Atlanta. Mari felt at peace here, she felt safe. But she missed Ward in ways that she never would have expected. She'd only really known him for a matter of days, but even that made no difference to her confused emotions. She could close her eyes and feel his hard mouth, his hands holding her, touching her. It had been the most exquisite thing that she'd ever experienced, being in his arms that day. She wanted it again, so much.

But even wanting it, she realized how dangerous it was to let him that close a second time. He only wanted her, he'd admitted that. He didn't believe in marriage. Apparently, he'd had a rough time with a woman at some point in his life, and he'd been soured. Aunt Lillian had mentioned that his mother ran away with another man, leaving Ward and Belinda to be raised by their grandmother. So she couldn't really blame him for his attitude. But that didn't make her own emotions any easier to handle.

She found herself watching the driveway and looking out the window, waiting. When the phone rang, and it did constantly, she ran to answer it, sure that it would be him. But it never was. Five days passed, and despite the fact that she enjoyed Aunt Lillian's company, she was restless. It was almost the end of her vacation. She'd have to leave. What if she never saw him again before she had to go?

"Missing the boss?" Lillian asked one evening, eyeing her niece calculatingly over the chicken and stuffing the younger woman wasn't touching.

Mari actually jumped. "No. Of course not."

"Not even a little?"

Mari sighed as she toyed with a fresh roll. "Maybe a little."

Lillian smiled. "That's nice. Because he's just coming up the driveway."

Mari couldn't stop herself. She leaped up from the table and ran to the front door, threw it open and darted out onto the porch. She caught herself just before she dashed down the steps toward him. She hadn't realized until that moment just how deeply involved she already was. Boys had never paid her much attention. Surely it was just the newness of being touched and kissed. Wasn't it?

She held on to the porch railing, forcing herself not to take one more step.

He got out of the Chrysler, looking as out of humor as when he'd left, a flight bag slung over one shoulder. Striking in a deep-tan vested suit and creamy Stetson, he closed the door with a hard slam, turned and started for the steps. Then he spotted Mari and stood quite still, just looking.

She was wearing a gauzy sea-green blouse with beige slacks, and she looked young and very pretty and a little lonely. His heart shot up into his throat, and all the bad temper seeped out.

"Well, hello, little lady," he said, moving up the steps, and he was actually smiling.

"Hello." She forced herself to look calm. "Did you have a good trip?"

"I guess so."

He stopped just in front of her, and she could see new lines in his face, dark circles under his eyes. Had he been with some woman? Her eyes narrowed curiously.

"Do I look that bad?" he taunted.

"You look tired," she murmured.

"I am. I did two weeks' business in five days." He searched her big, soft blue eyes quietly. "Miss me?"

"I had lots to do," she hedged. "And the phone hasn't stopped."

"That's not surprising." He let the bag fall to the porch and took her face in his big hands, tilting it up to his curious green eyes. "Dark circles," he murmured, running his thumbs gently under her eyes. "You haven't slept, have you?"

"You look like you haven't, either," she returned. There was a note in her voice that surprised and secretly delighted him.

"I never mix business with women," he whispered lazily. "It's bad policy. I haven't been sleeping around with any of those gorgeous, dark-eyed Latins."

"Oh." She felt embarrassed and lowered her shocked eyes to his chest. "That's none of my business, after all," she began.

"Wouldn't you like it to be?" he asked softly. He leaned toward her, nuzzling her face so that she lifted it helplessly and met his quiet, steady gaze. "Or would you rather pretend that what we did the night I left meant nothing at all to you?"

"It meant nothing at all to you," she countered. "You even said so, that you…"

He stopped the soft tirade with his mouth. His arm reached across her back, pillowing her head, and his free hand spread on her throat, smoothing its silky softness as he ravished the warm sweetness of her parted lips. He was hungry, and he didn't lift his head for a long time, not until he felt her begin to tremble, not until he heard the soft gasp and felt the eager ardor of her young mouth.

He was breathing through his nose, heavily, and his eyes frightened her a little. "You haunted me, damn you," he said roughly, spearing his fingers into her thick dark hair. "In my sleep I heard you cry out..."

"Don't hurt me," she whispered shakily, her eyes pleading with him. "I'm not experienced enough, I'm not...old enough...to play adult games with men."

That stopped him, softened him. The harsh light went out of his eyes, and he searched her delicate features with growing protectiveness.

"I'll never hurt you," he whispered and meant it. He kissed her eyes closed. "Not that way or in bed. Oh, God, Mari, you make me ache like a teenager!"

Her nails bit into his arms as he started to lean toward her again, and just as his lips touched hers in the prelude to what would have become a violently passionate exchange, they heard the soft, heavy thud of Lillian's cast as she headed toward them.

"Cupid approaches," he muttered, a subtle tremor in the hands that gently put her away from him. "She'd die if she knew what she just interrupted."

Mari stared at him, a little frightened by her lack of resistance, by the blatant hunger that she'd felt.

"Passion shouldn't be frightening to you," he said gently as the thuds grew closer. "It's as natural as breathing."

She shifted, watching him lift his bag without moving his eyes from her. "It's very new," she whispered.

"Then it's new for both of us," he said just before Lillian opened the door. "Because I've never felt this with another woman. And if that shocks you, it should. It damned well shocks me. I thought I'd done it all."

"Welcome home, boss." Lillian beamed, holding the door back. "You look good. Doesn't he, Mari?" Flushed face on the girl, and the boss looked a little flustered. Good. Good. Things were progressing. Absence worked after all.

"I feel pretty good, too," he returned, putting an affectionate arm around Lillian. "Been behaving?"

"Yes, sir. Pills and all." Lillian glared at her niece. "It's pretty hard not to take pills when you're threatened with being rolled in a towel."

He laughed warmly, glancing over at Mari. "Good girl."

"I should get medals for this," Mari returned, her eyes searching his, searching his face, quiet and curious and puzzled.

He hugged Lillian. "No doubt. What's for dinner? I'm starved."

"Finally," Lillian said with a grin. "Things are back to normal. You should see all the food I've saved up."

"Don't just stand there, both of you, go fetch it," he said, looking starved. "I'll die if I don't eat soon!"

Lillian responded to his order, producing an abundance of hearty food. While Ward dug in, Mari watched him with pure admiration. She'd never seen a human being put it away with such pleasure. He didn't seem to gain an ounce, for all his appetite. But then he was on the run most of his life, which probably explained his trim but masculine build.

He finished the last of the dressing and sat back with a heavy sigh to sip his second cup of coffee while Lillian, despite offers of help and threats, pushed a trolley of dirty dishes out to the kitchen and dishwasher.

"She won't slow down," Mari said. "I've tried, but she won't let me take over. I called the doctor, but he said as long as she was taking her medicine and didn't overdo standing on that cast, she'd be okay. I do at least get her to sit down, and I help when she lets me."

"Good thing her room's on the ground floor," he remarked.

"Yes."

He studied her over the rim of his coffee cup, his eyes narrow and quiet and full of green flames. There was no amusement in them now, no mockery. Just frank, blatant desire.

She looked back because it was beyond her powers of resistance not to. He held her in thrall, his darkening eyes full of promised pleasure, exquisite physical delight. Her body recognized that look, even if her brain didn't, and began to respond in frightening ways.

"I should bring in the dessert," she said as she rose, panicked.

"I don't want dessert," he said deeply.

She thought she knew what he did want, and she almost said so, but she dropped back down into her chair and put more sugar in her already oversweet coffee.

"Keep that up, and you can take rust off with it." He nodded toward her efforts with the sugar bowl.

She flushed. "I like it sweet."

"Do you?" He reached over and stilled her hand, his fingers lightly caressing it. While he held her eyes, he took the spoon away from her and linked his fingers slowly with hers in a light, caressing pressure that made her want to scream with frustrated hunger.

She couldn't help it. Her fingers contracted, too, convulsively, and she looked at him with aching desire.

His face went hard. "Suppose we go over those phone messages?" he asked.

"All right."

They both knew it was only an excuse, a reason to be alone together in the den to make love. Because that was surely what was going to happen. Being apart and then experiencing this explosive togetherness had taken its toll on them. He stood up and drew her along with him, and she could feel the throbbing silence that grew as they walked down the hall.

"Don't you want dessert?" Lillian called after them but not very heartily. She was grinning too much.

"Not right now," Ward replied. He looked down at Mari as he opened the door to the den, and there were blazing fires in his steady, possessive eyes.

Mari felt her lips part as she looked up at him. She started past him, feeling the warmth of his big body, the strength and power of it, and smelling his spicy cologne. She could hardly wait to be alone with him.

Just as he started to follow her into the room, into the secret silence of it, the heady atmosphere was shattered by a loud knock at the front door.

He cursed under his breath, whirling with such unexpected violence that Mari felt sorry for whoever was out there.

He opened the door and glared out. "Well?" he demanded.

"Well, you invited me, didn't you?" came an equally curt reply in a voice as deep and authoritative as Ward's. "You called me from the airport and said come over and we'd work out that second lease. So here I am. Or did you forget?"

"No."

"Do you want to serve my coffee on the damned porch?"

Ward tried not to grin, but he couldn't help it. Honest to God, Ty Wade was just like him.

"Oh, hell, come in," he muttered, holding the door open.

A tall, whipcord-lean man entered the house, Stetson in hand. He was as homely as leftover bacon, and he had eyes so piercing and coldly gray that Mari almost backed away. And then he saw her and smiled, and his face changed.

"Marianne, this is my neighbor, Tyson Wade," Ward told her curtly.

Ty nodded without speaking, glancing past Mari to where Lillian was standing in her cast. "What did you do, kick him?" he asked Lillian, nodding toward Ward.

Lillian laughed. "Not quite. How are Erin and the twins?"

"Just beautiful, thanks," Ty said with a quiet smile.

"Give them my best," Lillian said. "Coffee?"

"Just make it, I'll come and get the tray," Ward said firmly.

Lillian grumbled off toward the kitchen while Mari searched for words.

"I think I'll turn in," she said to Ward. "If you still want me to help with the office work, I need to get some sleep so that I can start early."

Ward looked harder than usual. Mari couldn't know that seeing Ty and the change marriage had made in him had knocked every amorous thought right out of his head. Ty spelled commitment, and Ward wanted none of it. So why in hell, he was asking himself, had he been coming on to a virgin?

"Sure," he told Mari. "You do that. If you don't mind, try to get your aunt into bed, too, could you? She's going to make a basket case of me if she doesn't start resting. Tell her that, too. Play on her conscience, girl."

Mari forced a smile. "I'll try. Nice to meet you, Mr. Wade," she told Ty and went after Lillian.

"Imagine, Tyson Wade in this very house," Lillian said with a sigh as she fixed a tray. "It's been a shock, seeing those two actually talk. They've been feuding as long as I've worked here. Then Mr. Wade got married and just look at him."

"He seems very much a family man," Mari commented.

"You should have seen him before." Lillian grinned. "He made the boss look like a pussycat."

"That bad?"

"That bad. Bad enough, in fact, to make the boss get rid of a half-wolf, half-shepherd dog he loved to death. It brought down some of Ty's cattle, and he came over here to 'discuss it' with the boss." She turned, grinning at her niece. "The very next day that dog was adopted into a good home. And the boss had to see his dentist. Tyson Wade was a mean man before Miss Erin came along. Ah, the wonder of true love." She gave Mari a sizing-up look and grinned even more when the younger woman blushed. "Well, let's get to the dishes, if you're determined to get in my way."

Mari was and she did, quickly shooing Lillian out. Then she disappeared herself before Ward came for the coffee tray. She'd had enough for one night.

Breakfast was an ordeal, Ward was cold all of a sudden, not the amorous, very interested man of the day before. Mari felt cold and empty and wondered what she'd done to make him look at her with those indifferent eyes. She was beginning to be glad that her vacation was almost over.

He followed her into the office and started opening mail. It had piled up in his absence, and he frowned over the amount waiting for him.

"Can you take dictation?" he asked Mari without looking up.

"Yes."

"Okay. Get a pad and pen out of the desk drawer and let's get started."

He began to dictate. The first letter was in response to a man who owed Ward money. The man had written Ward to explain that he'd had a bad month and would catch up on his payments as soon as he could. Instead of an understanding reply, Ward dictated a scorching demand for full payment that ended in a threatened lawsuit.

Mari started to speak, but the look he gave her was an ultimatum. She forced back the words and kept her silence.

Each letter was terse, precise and without the least bit of compassion. She began to get a picture of him that was disappointing and disillusioning. If there was any warmth in him, she couldn't find it in business. Perhaps that was why he was so wealthy. He put his own success above the problems of his creditors. So he had money. And apparently not much conscience. But Mari had one, and the side of him that she was seeing disturbed her greatly.

Finally Ward was finished dictating the letters, but just as she started to type them, the phone rang. Ward answered it, his face growing darker with every instant.

It was a competitor on the phone, accusing him of using underhanded methods to get the best of a business deal. He responded with language that should have caused the telephone company to remove his phone and burn it. Mari was the color of a boiled lobster when he finished and hung up.

"Something bothering you, honey?" he chided.

"You're ruthless," she said quietly.

"Hell, yes, I am," he returned without embarrassment. "I grew up the butt of every cruel tongue in town. I was that Jessup boy, the one whose mother was the easiest woman around and ran off with Mrs. Hurdy's husband. I was that poor kid down the road that never had a decent family except for his battle-ax of a grandmother." His green eyes glowed, and she wondered if he'd ever said these things to anyone else. "Success is a great equalizer, didn't you know? The same people who used to look down their noses at me now take off their hats and nod these days. I'm on everybody's guest list. I get recognized by local civic groups. I'm always being mentioned in the newspapers. Oh, I'm a big man these days, sprout." His face hardened. "But I wasn't always. Not until I had money. And how I get it doesn't bother me. Why should I be a good old boy in business? Nobody else is."

"Isn't Mr. Wade?" she fished.

"Mr. Wade," he informed her, "is now a family man, and he's missing his guts. His wife removed them, along with his manhood and his pride."

She stood. "What a terrible thing to say," she burst out. "How can you be so coldhearted? Don't you realize what you're doing to yourself? You're shriveling up into an old Scrooge, and you don't seem to realize it."

"I give to charity," he said arrogantly.

"For appearances and to get ahead," she replied hotly. "Not because you care. You don't, do you? You don't really care about one living soul."

His chin lifted and his eyes sparkled dangerously. "I care about my grandmother and my sister. And maybe Lillian."

"And nobody else," she said, hurt a bit by his admission that he didn't feel a thing for her.

"That's right," he said coldly. "Nobody else."

She stood there with her hands clenched at her sides, hurting in ways that she'd never expected she could. "You're a real prince, aren't you?" she asked.

"I'm a rich one, too," he returned, smiling slowly. "But if you had any ideas about taking advantage of that fact, you can forget them. I like my money's worth. And I'm not suited to wedding cake and rice."

When what he had said finally broke through the fog and she realized what he was accusing her of, she had to bite her tongue to keep from crying. So that was what he thought—that she was nothing but a gold digger, out to set herself up for life on his fortune.

"I know," she said with an icy look. "And that's good because most women who are looking for a husband want one who doesn't have to be plugged into a wall socket to warm up!"

"Get out of my office," he said shortly. "Since you're here to visit your aunt, go do it and keep the hell out of my way! When I want a sermon, I'll get it in church!"

"Any minister who got you into church would be canonized!" she told him bluntly and ran out of the room.

She didn't tell Lillian what had happened. Shortly thereafter Ward stormed out, slamming the door behind him. He didn't come back

until well after bedtime. Mari hadn't gone back into the den, and by
the time she crawled into bed, she was already planning how to tell
Aunt Lillian that she'd have to return to Georgia.

It wouldn't be easy to leave. But now that she'd had a glimpse of
the real man, the character under the veneer, she was sure that she
was doing the right thing. Ward Jessup might be a rich man with a
fat wallet. But he was ice-cold. If she had any sanity left, she'd get
away from him before her addiction got so bad that she'd find excuses
to stay just to look at him.

That remark about not caring for anyone except family had hurt
terribly. She did understand why he was the way he was, but it didn't
help her broken heart. She'd been learning to love him. And now she
found that he had nothing at all to give. Not even warmth. It was the
worst blow of all. Yes, she'd have to go home now. Aunt Lillian was
coping beautifully, taking her medicine and even resting properly. At
least Ward would take care of the older woman. He cared about *her*.
He'd never care about Mari, and it was high time she faced facts.

Chapter 7

Mari had a miserable day. She kept out of Ward's way, and she didn't go back into the den. Let him get a temporary secretary, she thought furiously, if he couldn't manage his dirty work alone. She wasn't going to do it for him.

"Talk about unarmed conflict," Lillian muttered as Mari went out the back door in a lightweight jacket and jeans.

"He started it," Mari said irritably. "Or didn't you know how he did business?"

Lillian's expression said that she did. "He's a hard man to understand sometimes," she said, her voice gentle, coaxing. "But you can't imagine the life he's had, Mari. People aren't cold without reason. Very often it's just a disguise."

"His is flawless."

"So is yours," Lillian said with a warm smile. "Almost. But don't give up on him yet. He might surprise you."

"He won't have time. Have you forgotten that I have to go home in two more days?"

The older woman looked worried. "Yes, I know. I had hoped you might stay a little longer."

"You're feeling better," she returned. "And he doesn't want me here. Not anymore. I'm not even sure I'd stay if I was asked." She opened the door. "I'm going to look at the horses."

She walked out without another word, crestfallen and miserable.

She stuck her hands in the pockets of her jacket and walked aimlessly along the fence until she came in sight of the barn.

There he was, sitting astride a huge chestnut-colored horse, his working clothes making him look even bigger than usual, his Stetson cocked over one eye. Watching her.

She stopped in her tracks, glaring at him. He urged the horse into a slow trot and reined in beside her, resting his crossed hands on the pommel. The leather creaked as he shifted in the saddle and pushed back his hat.

"Are we still speaking?" he asked, his tone half amused.

"Can someone run me to the bus station in the morning?" she asked, ignoring the question. "My vacation is up the day after to-morrow. I have to get back to Atlanta."

He stared at her for a long moment before he spoke. "How are you going to explain that decision to Lillian?" he asked, carefully choosing his words. "You're supposed to think I'm dying, aren't you? You're supposed to be helping me write my memoirs."

"I don't think my stomach is strong enough," she replied.

His green eyes glittered at her. "Stop that. I'm trying to make friends with you."

"I tried to make friends with a gerbil once," she commented. "I stuck my hand down into its cage to let it have a nice sniff, and it tried to eat my little finger."

"You're making this difficult," he grumbled, tilting his hat back over his eyes.

"No, you are," she corrected. "I'm doing my best to relieve you of my gold-digging, sermonizing presence."

He sighed heavily, searching her eyes. "I've never had to justify myself to anyone," he told her. "I've never wanted to." He studied the pommel as if he hadn't seen one before, examining it as he spoke. "I don't want you to go, Mari."

Her heart ran away. "Why not?"

He shrugged and smiled faintly. "Maybe I've gotten used to you." He looked up. "Besides, your aunt will never get over it if you leave right now. All her plans for us will be ruined."

"That's a foregone conclusion as far as I'm concerned," she said, her voice curt. She clenched her hands in her pockets. "I wouldn't have you on a stick, roasted."

He had to work to keep from grinning. "Wouldn't you?"

"I'm going home," she repeated.

He tilted his hat back again. "You don't have a job."

"I do so. I work at a garage!"

"Not anymore." He did grin this time. "I called them last week and told them that you had to quit to take care of your sick aunt and her 'dying' employer."

"You what!"

"It seemed like the thing to do at the time," he said conversationally. "They said they were real sorry, and it sure was lucky they'd just had a girl apply for a job that morning. I'll bet they hired her that very day."

She could hardly breathe through her fury. She felt as if her lungs were on fire. "You...you...!" She searched for some names she'd heard at the garage and began slinging them at him.

"Now, shame on you," he scolded, bending unexpectedly to drag her up to sit in the saddle in front of him. "Sit still!" he said roughly, controlling the excited horse with one hand on the reins while the other was on Mari.

"I hate you," she snapped.

He got the gelding under control and wheeled it, careful not to jerk the reins and unseat them both. The high-strung animal took gentle handling. "Care to prove that?" he asked.

She didn't ask what he meant. There was no time. She was too busy trying to hold on to the pommel. She hadn't realized how far off the ground that saddle was until she was sitting in it. Behind her, she felt the warm strength of his powerful body, and if she hadn't been so nervous, she might have felt the tense set of it in the saddle.

He rode into a small grove of oak and mesquite trees and dismounted. Before she knew it, she was out of the saddle and flat on her back in the lush spring grass with Ward's hard face above her.

"Now," he said gently, "suppose you show me how much you hate me?"

His dark head bent, and she reached up, unthinking, to catch his thick hair and push him away. But it only gave him an unexpected opening, and she caught her breath as his full weight came down over her body, crushing her into the leaves and grass.

"Better give in, honey, or you could sink down all the way to China," he commented wickedly. His hands were resting beside her head, and somehow he'd caught hers in them. He had her effectively pinned, without any effort at all, and was just short of gloating about it. He wasn't trying to spare her his formidable weight, either, and she could just barely breathe.

She panted, struggling, until she felt what her struggles were accomplishing and reluctantly subsided. She contented herself with glaring up at him from a face the color of pickled beets.

"Coward," he chided.

She was very still, barely breathing. His hands were squeezing hers, but with a caressing pressure not a brutal one. The look in his eyes was slowly changing from faint amusement to dark passion. If she hadn't recognized the look, his body would have told her as he began to move subtly over hers, sensually, with a practiced expertness that even her innocence recognized.

"Yes, that makes you tremble, doesn't it?" he breathed, watching her as his hips caressed hers.

"Of course...it does," she bit off. "I've never...felt this way with anyone else."

"Neither have I," he whispered, bending to brush his hard mouth over her soft one. "I told you that when I got home, and I meant it. Never like this, not with anyone..." His eyes closed, his heavy brows drawing together as he slowly fitted his mouth to hers.

She wanted to protest, but she couldn't move, let alone speak, and his mouth was making the most exquisite sensations in places far removed from her lips. With a shaky little sigh she opened her mouth a little to taste his and felt him stiffen. She felt that same tautness in her legs, her arms, even in her stomach, sensations that she'd never experienced.

His hard fingers flexed, linking with hers caressingly, teasing as he explored her mouth first with his lips and then with the slightest probing of his tongue.

She hadn't been kissed that way before, and her eyes opened, puzzled.

He lifted his head a little, searching her face with green eyes that were dark and mysterious and as full of answers as her blue ones were full of questions.

"You can trust me this once," he whispered, sensing her apprehension in the smooth as silk young body that wouldn't give an inch to the dominance of his. "Even if I went half mad with wanting, I wouldn't risk trying to make love to you within sight of the barn."

He couldn't have been less convincing, but she did trust him. She searched his eyes, feeling the warm weight of him, smelling the leathery scent that clung to him, and she began to relax despite the unknown intimacy of the embrace.

"You've never felt a man this way, have you?" he asked quietly. "It's all right. You're old enough to leave chaste kisses and daydreams behind. This is the reality, little Mari," he whispered, shifting his hips as he looked down into her wide, awed eyes. "This is what it's really like when a man and a woman come together in passion. It isn't neat and quiet and uncomplicated. It's hot and wild and complex."

"Is it part of the rules to warn the victim?" she asked in a husky whisper.

"It is when the victim is as innocent as you," he returned. "I don't want a virgin sacrifice, you see," he added, bending again to her mouth. "I want a full-blooded woman. A woman to match me."

At that moment she almost felt that she could. Her body was throbbing, blazing with fire and fever, and instead of shrinking from the proof of his desire for her, she lifted her body up to his, gave him her mouth and her soft sighs.

Ward felt the hunger in her slender body, and it fostered an oddly protective impulse in him. He, who was used to taking what he wanted without regret or shame, hesitated.

His mouth gentled, slowed and became patiently caressing. He found that she followed where he led, quickly learning the tender lessons that he gave her without words. He let go of her hands and felt them go instinctively to his shirt, pressing over the hard, warm muscles, searching. His heart pounded furiously against breasts whose softness he could feel under him. He wanted to strip off his shirt and give himself to her young hands, he wanted to strip off her own shirt and put his mouth on those tender breasts and look at them and watch her blush. It was then that he realized just how urgent the situation was becoming.

His body was taking over. He could feel himself grinding down against her, forcing her hips into intimate contact with his, he could feel his own taut movements. His mouth felt hot. Hers felt like velvet, feverish and swollen from the hungry probing of his own.

He lifted his head, surprised to find himself breathing in gasps, his arms trembling slightly as they held him poised over her. Her eyes were misty, half closed, her lips parted and moist, her body submissive. His.

She drew in a slow, lazy breath, looking up at him musingly, so hungry for him that she hadn't the strength to refuse him anything he wanted. From the neck down she was throbbing with sweet pulses, experiencing a pleasure that she'd never known before.

"No," he whispered roughly. "No. Not like this."

He rolled away from her, shuddering a little before he sat up and breathed roughly. He brushed back his hair with fingers that were almost steady but held a fine tremor.

Mari was just realizing what had happened, and she stared at him with slowly dawning comprehension. So that was what happened. That was why women didn't fight or protest. It wasn't out of fear of being overpowered. It was because of the sweet, tender pleasure that came from being held intimately, kissed and kissed until her mind got lost in her body's pleasure. He could have had her. But he stopped.

"Surprised?" He turned his head, staring down at her with dark green eyes that still held blatant traces of passion. "I told you I wouldn't take advantage, didn't I?"

"Yes. But I forgot."

"Fortunately for you I didn't." He got to his feet and stretched lazily, feeling as if he'd been beaten, but he wasn't letting her see that. He grinned down at her. "Men get good at pulling back. It comes from years of practice dating virgins," he added in a wicked whisper as he extended a hand to her.

She sat up, flushed, ignoring his outstretched hand as she scrambled to her feet. "I can't imagine that many of them were still virgins afterward," she muttered with a shy glance.

"Oh, some of them had great powers of resistance," he admitted. "Like you."

"Sure," she said shakily, pushing back her damp hair. "Some great resistance. If you hadn't stopped…"

"But I did," he interrupted. He picked up his hat from where he'd tossed it and studied the crown before he put it back on his head. "And for the time being you can forget going back to Georgia," he added with a level gaze. "Lillian needs you. Maybe I need you, too. You've given me a new perspective on things."

"I've butted in and made a spectacle of myself, you mean," she said, her eyes quietly curious on his hard, dark face.

"If I'd meant that, I'd have said it," he returned. "You're a breath of fresh air in my life, Mari. I was getting set in my wicked ways until you came along. Maybe you were right about my attitude toward money. So why don't you stay and reform me?"

"I can't imagine anyone brave enough to try," she said. She lifted her face. "And besides all that, how dare you cost me my job!"

"You can't work in a garage full of men anymore," he said blandly. "Remember your horrible nightmares about the assault?" he added. "Men make you nervous. Lillian said so."

"Those men wouldn't make anyone nervous. All they did was work on cars and go home to their wives," she informed him. "Not one of them was single."

"How sad for you. What wonderful luck that Lillian found me dying and sent for you." He grinned. "It isn't every girl who gets handed a single, handsome, rich bachelor on a platter."

"I am not a gold digger," she shot at him.

"Oh, hell, I know that," he said after a minute, studying her through narrowed eyes. "But I had to have some kind of defense, didn't I? You're a potent little package, honey. A fish on the hook does fight to the bitter end."

His words didn't make much sense to her, but Mari was a little dazed by everything that had happened. She just stared at him, puzzled.

"Never mind," he said, taking her hand. "Let's go back. I've got a few odds and ends to take care of before lunch. Do you like to ride?''

"I think so," she admitted.

"You can have your own horse next time," he promised. "But for now I think we'll walk back. I'm just about out of self-control, if you want the truth. I can't handle you at a close proximity right now."

That was embarrassing and flattering, and she hid a smile. But he saw it and gathered her close to his side, leading the horse by the reins with one hand and holding her with the other. The conversation on the way back was general, but the feel of Ward's strong arm had Mari enthralled every step of the way.

He went off to make some business calls. Lillian took one look at Mari's face and began humming love songs. Mari, meanwhile, went up to her room to freshen up and took time to borrow one of the outside lines to call Atlanta. Her boss at the garage was delighted to hear from her and immediately burst into praise of her unselfishness to help that "poor dying man in Texas." How fortunate, he added brightly, that a young woman about Mari's age had just applied for a job the morning poor Mr. Jessup had called him. Everything had worked out just fine, hadn't it, and how did she like Texas?

She mumbled something about the weather being great for that time of year, thanked him and hung up. Poor Mr. Jessup, indeed!

Ward had to go out on business later in the day, and he wasn't back by supper time. Lillian and Mari ate alone, and after Mari had finished helping in the kitchen, she kissed her aunt good night and went upstairs. She was torn between disappointment and relief that Ward hadn't been home since that feverish interlude. It had been so sweet that she'd wanted it again and that could be dangerous. Each time it got harder to stop. Today she hadn't been able to do anything except follow where he led, and it was like some heady alcoholic beverage—she just couldn't get enough of him. She didn't really know what to do anymore. Her life seemed to be tangled up in complications.

She laid out a soft pink gown on the bed—a warm but revealing one with a low neckline—and fingered it lovingly. It had been an impulse purchase, something to cheer her up on a depressing Saturday when she had been alone. It was made of flannelette, but it was lacy and expensive, and she loved the way it felt and clung to the slender lines of her body.

She ran a bath in the big Jacuzzi and turned on the jets after filling the tub with fragrant soap that was provided, along with anything else a feminine guest might need, in the pretty blue-tiled bathroom. To Mari, who lived in a small efficiency apartment in Atlanta, it was really plush. She frowned as she stripped off her clothing and climbed into the smooth tub with its relaxing jets of water surging around her. The apartment rent was due in a week or so, and she hadn't paid it yet. She'd have to send a check. She also wished that she'd brought more clothes with her. She hadn't counted on being here for life, but it looked as if Ward wasn't in any hurry to let her go.

Too, there was Lillian, who was behaving herself only as long as her niece was around to make her. If Mari left, what would happen to the older woman? With Ward away on business so often, it was dangerous for Lillian to be left alone now. Perhaps Ward had considered that, and it was why he wanted Mari to stay. The real reason, anyway. He didn't seem to be dying of love for her, although his desire was apparent. He wanted her.

With all her turbulent thoughts and the humming sound of the Jacuzzi, she didn't hear the door to her room open or hear it close again. She didn't hear the soft footfalls on the carpet, or the soft sound that came from a particularly male voice as Ward saw her sitting up in the tub with her pretty pink breasts bare and glistening with soap and water.

She happened to glance up then and saw him. She couldn't move. His green eyes were steady and loving on the soft curves of her body, and with horror she felt the tips of her breasts harden under his intent scrutiny.

He shook his head when she started to lift her hands to them. "No," he said gently, moving toward her. "No, don't cover them, Mari."

She could hardly get her breath. Although she'd never let anyone see her like this in all her life, she couldn't stop him. Mari couldn't seem to move at all. He towered over her, still and somber, and as she watched, he began to roll up the sleeves of the white shirt that was open halfway down his chest. He'd long ago shed his jacket and tie, although he was still wearing dress boots and suit trousers. He looked expensive and very masculine and disturbing, and as he bent beside the tub, she caught the scent of luxurious cologne.

"You mustn't!" she began frantically.

But he picked up the big fluffy sponge she'd soaped and shook his head, smiling faintly. "Think of it as a service for a special, tired guest," he whispered amusedly, although his eyes were frankly possessive. "Lie back and enjoy it."

She started to protest again, but he didn't pay the least attention. One lean hand moved behind her neck to support her in the bubbling water while the other slowly, painstakingly, drew the sponge over every soft line and curve of her body.

She hadn't realized how many nerve endings she had, but he found every single one. In a silence that throbbed with new sensation, he bathed her, pausing now and again to put the sponge down and touch her, experience the softness of her skin with the added silkiness of soap and water making it vibrantly alive.

Her eyes were half closed, languorous, as his fingers brushed lightly over her small, high breasts and found every curve and hardness, every sensual contrast, every texture, as if she fascinated him.

She trembled a little when he turned off the Jacuzzi and let the water out of the tub, especially when he began to sponge away the last traces of soap, and her body was completely revealed to him.

He lifted his dark, quiet eyes to hers and searched them, finding apprehension, fear, awe and delight in their blue depths. "I've never bathed a woman before," he said softly. "Or bathed with one. In some ways I suppose I'm pretty old-fashioned."

She was breathing unsteadily. "I've never let anyone look at me before," she said in a hesitant tone.

"Yes. I know." He helped her out of the tub and removed a warmed towel from the rail. It was fluffy and pink, and warm against her skin as he slowly dried her from head to toe. This time she could feel his hands in a new way, and she clutched at his broad shoulders when he reached her hips and began to touch her flat stomach. She felt a rush of sensation that was new and shocking.

"Ward?" she whispered.

He knelt in front of her, discarding the towel and all pretense as he held her hips and pressed his mouth warmly against her stomach.

She cried out. It was a high-pitched, helpless cry, and it made his blood surge like a flood through his veins. His fingers flexed and his mouth drew over her stomach with agonizing slowness, moving up with relentless hunger to her soft, smooth breasts.

She held him there, held his hard, moist mouth over the tip of one, felt him take her inside, warming her. He touched her then in a way she'd never expected, and her breath drew in harshly and she shivered.

"Shhhh," he whispered at her breast. "It's all right. Don't fight me."

She couldn't have. She shuddered and trembled, crying as he made the most exquisite sensations felt in the nether reaches of her slender body. Her nails dug into him and she couldn't help it.

"Marianne," he whispered, shifting his mouth over hers. He stopped his delicate probing and lifted her in his arms. She felt the soft shock of his footsteps as he carried her to the bed, felt the mattress sink under their combined weights.

His mouth moved slowly back down her to her stomach, her thighs, and then she did fight him, fought the newness and the strangeness and the frank intimacy.

He lifted his head and slid back up to look at her shocked face. "All right," he said gently. "If you don't want it, I won't force you."

Her face was creamy pink now, fascinated. He looked down at her body, smoothing over it with a lean, very dark hand, savoring its soft vulnerability.

"This is so new," he whispered. "I never realized how soft a woman's body really was, how exquisitely formed. I could get drunk just on the sight of you."

She was trembling all over but not from the soft chill of the room. She felt reckless under his intense gaze.

He looked up into her eyes. "You aren't protected, are you?" he asked softly.

It took a minute for her to realize what he was asking, and it made the situation take on alarming, very adult implications. To him this was familiar territory. But Mari was a pioneer.

"No," she whispered unsteadily. "I'm not."

"It's just as well," he murmured, bending to her mouth. "I think...it might spoil things right now to force that kind of total intimacy on you." His hand smoothed tenderly over her breast as he probed at her trembling lips. "Don't you want to touch me like this?"

She did, but she couldn't say it. Her hands went slowly to his shirt and slid under it, finding the exciting abrasion of thick chest hair over warm muscle a heady combination. His mouth moved hungrily against hers at the first tentative touch, and one hand went between them to rip the fabric completely out of the way and give her total access.

His harsh breathing disturbed her, but she was intoxicated by the intimacy they were sharing. Impulsively she moved her hands and arched upward letting her breasts tease his chest, feeling the sudden acceleration of his heartbeat with wonder.

He poised over her, lifting his head. His eyes were dark with passion, his chest shuddering with it. "Do that again," he said roughly.

She did, on fire with hunger, wanting something more than the teasing, wanting him. She felt his chest tremble, and she looked down at his darkness against her paler flesh with a sense of wonder.

"Yes, look at it," he whispered, his voice harsh, shaken as he stared, too. "Look at the differences. Dark against light, muscle against softness. Your breasts are like bread and honey."

As he spoke, he eased down. His heavy body surged against hers as he fitted it over her bareness, and her pupils dilated helplessly at the warm ecstasy of his full weight over her.

"Give me your mouth now," he whispered, bending. "Let me feel you completely."

It was a kiss like nothing she'd ever imagined in her life. She held him tenderly, her hands smoothing his thick, dark hair, her body throbbing its whole length where she could feel the powerful muscles of his body taut and smooth.

He tasted of coffee, and there was a new tenderness in him, in the lips that delicately pushed at hers so that his tongue could enter the soft, sweet darkness of her mouth. She felt it touch hers, tangle with it, and she gave herself up to a sensation that was all mystery and delight.

His hands smoothed down her sides, her back, savoring the smooth suppleness of her skin. He ached like hell, and he could have cursed himself for causing this, for forgetting how naive she was. She wanted him and, God, he wanted her! But he could make her pregnant. And part of her would hate him forever if he forced this on her. It wasn't going to be good for her. She was so much a virgin...

His cheek slid against hers, and he rolled onto his side, holding her protectively to him, feeling her breasts crush softly against his chest.

"Hold me," he whispered. "Just hold me until we stop trembling."

"I want you," she whimpered, beyond thought, beyond pride. She bit his shoulder. "I want you."

"I know. But we can't." His cheek nuzzled hers, and his lips touched her tear-streaked face tenderly. He hadn't realized she was crying until then. He drew a breath. "Are you all right?" he asked softly.

"I ache," she sobbed.

"I could satisfy you," he whispered. "Without going all the way."

She sensed that. Her eyes searched his in wonder. "No," she said after a minute. "I won't do that to you." She touched his face, fascinated by the look the words produced. "I'm sorry. I should have said something a long time ago. I should have asked you to stop."

"But it was too sweet, wasn't it?" he asked, his voice quiet and deep as he touched her face with fingers that were possessive and gentle. "So sweet, like making love with every part of us. I've never in my life experienced anything like it. Not even sex was ever this good."

That shocked her, and her eyes mirrored it. "Not...even sex?"

He shook his head. "With you I think it would be lovemaking, not sex. I don't think you and I could accept something as coldly clinical as that."

She was so tempted. She wanted him desperately. Everybody did it these days, didn't they? Maybe she wouldn't get pregnant. She loved him. Loved him!

But he saw the uncertainty in her eyes and mistook it for fear. For God's sake, where was his brain, anyway? She was a virgin. Lillian was right downstairs. Was he crazy? He ignored the feverish hunger of his body and managed to smile reassuringly as he slowly drew away from her to sit up with a hard sigh.

"No more, honey," he said heavily and managed to laugh. "I'm too old for this kind of playing."

Playing? She stared at him helplessly as he forced his staggered brain to function and found her gown. He put her into it with a minimum of fuss and then lifted her long enough to turn down the covers. He put her under them, smoothing them over her breasts.

He couldn't tell her that his own vulnerability and weakness had shocked him. He hadn't planned this, he hadn't expected to be drawn into such a long, intimate loving. It had been loving, of a kind. He scowled, watching her, fascinated by her innocence, her helpless re-action to his touch. He'd come to her room, in fact, to tell her that he wanted to get on a friendly footing with her, to stop the intimacy that could all too easily overwhelm both of them. But the sight of her in that tub had wiped every sane thought right out of his mind. Now he looked at her and saw commitment and the loss of his pre-cious freedom. He saw all the old wounds, the helplessness of his attraction to that tramp who'd taken him in.

With a rough curse he got to his feet, running an angry hand through his hair.

"You needn't look at me that way," she bit off, close to tears again but for a totally different reason. "As if I were a fallen woman. I didn't walk into your bathroom and start staring at you."

"I didn't mean for that to happen," he said curtly.

She softened a little at the confession. He looked as shaken as she felt. "It's all right," she replied, fumbling with the coverlet. "I didn't, either."

"I'm old enough to know better, though," he murmured, feeling venerable and protective as he stared down at her. He put his hands in his pockets with a long sigh. "I came up here to see if we might get on a different footing. A friendly footing, without all these phys-ical complications." He laughed softly. "I suppose you noticed how well I succeeded."

"Yes," she murmured tongue in cheek. She recalled everything she'd let him do and went scarlet, dropping her embarrassed eyes.

"None of that," he chided. "You're a woman now, not a little girl. Nothing we did would make you pregnant."

"I know that!" she burst out, feverishly avoiding his mocking gaze.

"I just wanted to reassure you." He stretched lazily, very masculine with his shirt unbuttoned and his hair mussed. Very disturbing, watching her that way. "No one will ever know what we did in here," he added. "Just you and me. That makes it a very private thing, Mari."

"Yes." She glanced up and then down again. "I hope you don't think I do that with just anyone."

"I don't think that at all." He bent and brushed his lips gently over her forehead. "It's very exciting being the first," he whispered. "Even in this way."

Her face felt hot as she looked up into lazy, warm eyes. "I'm glad it was with you."

"Yes. So am I." He searched her eyes gently and started to lean toward her, but his survival instincts warned him against it. Instead, he stood up with a smile and went to the door. "Good night, honey. Sleep well."

"You, too."

He closed the door without looking back, and Mari stared at it for a long time before she drew a shuddering sigh and turned out the light.

Chapter 8

Mari hardly slept. She felt his hands all through the night, along with a new and curious kind of frustration that wouldn't subside. Every time she thought about Ward, her body began to throb. These new feelings frightened her because they were so unexpected. She didn't know what to do. The urge to cut and run was very strong.

Lillian was hobbling around putting platters on the table for breakfast. She looked up, smiling, as Mari came into the room dressed in jeans and a pullover burgundy knit blouse.

"Good morning, glory," Lillian said brightly. "Isn't it a beautiful day?"

It was, in fact, but Lillian seemed to be overjoyed at something besides the great outdoors. "Yes," Mari returned. She glanced at the empty chair at the head of the table.

"He'll be back in a minute," the older woman said knowingly. "Looks like a storm cloud this morning, he does. All ruffled and absentminded. Been staring up that staircase ever since he came downstairs, too," she added wickedly.

Mari darted into the kitchen. "I'll help you get breakfast on the table," she said quickly, avoiding that amused gaze. At least Lillian was enjoying herself. Mari wasn't. She was afraid.

She and Lillian had started eating before Ward came back. He looked tired, but his face brightened when he spotted Mari. He smiled without really wanting to and tossed his hat onto a side table before he sprawled into a chair. His jeans were dusty and his blue checked shirt was a little disheveled.

"I've washed up," he told Lillian before she could open her mouth. "I had to help get a bull out of a ditch."

"How did he get into the ditch?" Mari asked curiously.

Ward grinned. "Trying to jump a fence to get to one of my young heifers. Amazing how love affects the mind, isn't it?"

Mari flushed. Lillian giggled. Ward leaned back in his chair, enjoying the view, watching Mari try to eat scrambled eggs with forced enjoyment.

"Don't you want something to eat, boss?" Lillian asked.

"I'm not really hungry," he said without realizing what he was giving away to the old woman, who beamed at him. "But I'll have some toast and coffee, I guess. Sleep well, Mari?" he asked as Lillian handed him the carafe.

Mari lifted her eyes. "Of course," she said, bluffing. "Did you?"

He shook his head, smiling faintly. "Not a wink."

She got lost in his green gaze and felt the force of it all the way to her toes. It took several seconds to drag her eyes down to her plate, and even then her heart ran wild.

Ward watched her with evident enjoyment, caught up in the newness of having a woman react that way to his teasing. Everything was new with Marianne. Just ordinary things, like sharing breakfast, took on new dimensions. He found that he liked looking at her. Especially now since he knew exactly what she looked like under her clothes. His eyes darkened in memory. God, how exquisite she was!

Mari felt his intent stare all through her body. She could have made a meal of him, too, with her eyes. He looked so good. For all his huge size he was lithe and graceful, and she loved the way he moved. He was as sensuous a man as she'd ever known, a very masculine presence with a disturbing effect on her senses. She didn't think her feet would ever touch the ground again. Just being near him set her on fire. She wanted to get up and touch him, put her mouth on his, feel his arms crushing her to every inch of that long, elegant body. Her fingers trembled on her fork, and she flushed with embarrassment when he noticed her nervousness.

"Come for a ride with me," Ward said suddenly.

She looked up at him. "Now?"

He shrugged. "Lillian can answer the phone. There's nothing pressing for today. Why not?"

"No reason at all," Lillian agreed quickly. "Go ahead. I'll handle the home front."

Mari submitted before she could begin to protest. Why pretend? She wanted to be alone with him, and he knew it. Her blue eyes searched his green ones longingly, everything plain and undisguised in her oval face. He felt explosive. Young. A boy again with a special girl.

He threw down his napkin and got to his feet, hoping his helpless urgency didn't show too much. "Let's go," he bit off.

Mari followed him. She barely heard Lillian's voice behind her saying something about having fun. Her eyes were on Ward's strong back, her body moving as if she were a sleepwalker. She was on fire for him. Whatever happened now happened. She loved him. If he wanted her, she wasn't going to stop him. He had to feel something for her, too. He had to care just a little!

He saddled two horses in stark silence, his hands deft and firm as he pulled cinches tight and checked bridles.

When he helped her into the saddle, his eyes were dark and possessive, his hand lingering when she was seated. "You look good on a horse, honey," he said quietly.

She looked down at him and smiled, feeling the warmth of his chest against her leg. "Do I?" she asked gently, her voice soft with longing.

"I want you, Marianne," he said half under his breath. "I've thought about nothing else all night. So go slow, will you? I want to talk today. Just talk. I want to get to know you."

That was flattering and a little surprising. Maybe even disappointing. But she had to keep it from showing so she kept smiling. "I'd like that," she said.

He didn't answer her. He felt the same hunger she did, but he was more adept at hiding his yearnings. He didn't want to frighten her off, not before he made a stab at establishing a relationship with her. He didn't know how she was going to react to what he had in mind, but he knew they couldn't go on like this. Things had to be settled—

today. Business was going to suffer if he kept on mooning over that perfect young body. Physical attraction was a damnable inconvenience, he thought angrily. He'd thought he was too old to be this susceptible. Apparently he was more vulnerable than he'd ever realized.

He swung into the saddle and led the way down the long trail that ran around the ranch. His men were out working with the cattle, getting them moved to summer pasture, doing all the little things around the ranch that contributed to the huge cow-calf operation. Fixing machines. Planting feed. Cleaning out stalls. Checking supplies. Making lists of chores. It was a big task, running a ranch even this size, but Ty Wade's, which adjoined it, was huge by comparison. The oil business was Ward's main concern, but he did like the idea of running cattle, as his grandfather had done so many years before. Perhaps it got into a man's blood. Not that he minded sinking wells under his cattle. He had one or two on his own property, and Tyson Wade's spread was proving to be rich in the black gold. His instincts hadn't failed him there, and he was glad. Ty would never have let him live it down if he'd been wrong and the oil hadn't been there. As it was, the discovery on that leased land had saved Ty from some hard financial times. It had worked out well all the way around.

Mari glanced at him, curious about that satisfied look on his hard, dark face. She wondered what thoughts were giving him such pleasure.

He laughed out loud, staring ahead. "Those old instincts never seem to let me down," he murmured. "I think I could find oil with my nose."

"What?"

He looked over at her. "I was thinking about that oil I found on Ty Wade's place. It was a hell of a gamble, but it sure paid off."

So. It was business that made him feel so good, not her company. "Is business the only pleasure in your life?" she asked gently.

He shrugged. "The only lasting one, I guess." He stared toward the horizon. "There were some pretty hard times around here when I was a kid. Oh, we always had plenty of food, you know—that's one of the advantages of living on a ranch. But we didn't have much in the way of material things. Clothes were all secondhand, and I wore boots with holes in the soles for most of my childhood. That wasn't so bad, but I got ragged a lot about my mother.''

She could imagine that he had. ''I guess I was pretty lucky,'' she said. ''My parents were good to me. We always got by.''

He studied her quietly. ''I'll bet you were a tomboy.''

She laughed, delighted. ''I was. I played sandlot baseball and climbed trees and played war. There was only one other girl on my street, and she and I had to be tough to survive with all the boys. They didn't pull their punches just because we were girls. We had a good time growing up all the same.''

He fingered the reins as they rode along to the musical squeak of saddle leather. ''I liked playing cowboys and Indians,'' he recalled. ''Had my own horse.''

''Which were you?''

He chuckled. ''Mostly I was the Indian. I had a Cherokee ancestor, they say.''

''You're very dark,'' she agreed.

''Honey, that's sun, not inherited. I spent a lot of time working rigs when I was younger, and I still help out on occasion. The heat's easier stripped to the waist.''

She'd noticed how dark his skin was when he'd stripped off his shirt the night before and let her touch him. Her eyes went involuntarily to the hard muscles of his torso and lingered there.

''You don't do much sunbathing, do you?'' he asked unexpectedly, and his eyes told her that he was remembering how pale she was.

Her face colored. ''No. There's no beach nearby, and I live upstairs in an apartment building. I don't have any place to sunbathe.''

''It isn't good for the skin. Mine's like leather,'' he commented. ''Yours is silky soft....''

She urged her mount ahead, embarrassed because she knew what he was seeing in his mind.

His mount fell into easy step beside her. ''Don't be shy with me,'' he said gently. ''There's nothing to be ashamed of.''

''I guess I seem grass green to you,'' she commented.

''Sure you do,'' he replied and smiled. ''I like it.''

Her eyes went to the flat horizon beyond, to the scant trees and the long fence lines and the red coats of the cattle. ''I never had many boyfriends,'' she told him, remembering. ''My dad was very strict.''

''What was he like?''

''Oh, very tall and stubborn. And terrific,'' she added. ''I had great parents. I loved them both. Losing Mama was hard, but having both of them gone is really rough. I never missed having brothers or sisters until now.''

''I suppose it makes you feel alone.''

''I've felt that way for a long time,'' she said. ''My father wasn't really an affectionate man, and he didn't like close ties. He thought it was important that I stand alone. Perhaps he was right. I got used to being by myself after Mama died.''

He studied her averted features. ''At least I had Grandmother and Belinda,'' he said. ''Although with Grandmother it's been a fight all the way. She's too much like me.''

She remembered him saying that the only women he cared about where those two. ''What is your sister like?'' she asked.

He grinned. ''Like Grandmother and me. She's another hardheaded Jessup.''

''Does she look like you?'' she asked curiously.

''Not a lot. Same green eyes, but she's prettier, and we're built differently.''

She glared at him. ''I do realize that.''

''No. She's small. Petite,'' he clarified. ''I suppose I take after my father. He was a big man.''

''An oilman?''

He nodded. ''Always looking for that big strike.'' His eyes suddenly had a faraway look. ''Right out there is where we found him, in that grove of trees.'' He gestured to the horizon. ''Hell of a shock. There was hardly a mark on him. He looked like he was asleep.''

''I'm sorry.''

''It was a long time ago.'' He turned his horse, leaving her to follow where the trail led down to the river and a grove of trees. He dismounted, tying his horse to a small tree growing on a grassy knoll. He helped Mari down and tied hers nearby.

''Funny, I never thought of Texas being like this,'' she mused as she watched the shallow river run over the rocks and listened to its serene bubbling. "It's so bare except for occasional stands of timber. Along the streams, of course, there are more trees. But it's not at all what I expected. It's so…big."

"Georgia doesn't look like this?" he asked.

She watched him stretch out on the leaves under a big live oak tree, his body relaxed as he studied her. "Not a lot, no. We don't have mesquite trees," she said. "Although around Savannah we do have huge live oaks like these. Near Atlanta we have lots of dogwoods and maples and pines, but there's not so much open land. There are always trees on the horizon, except in south Georgia. I guess southwest Georgia is a lot like here. I've even seen prickly pear cactus growing there, and there are diamondback rattlers in that part of the state. I had a great aunt there when I was a child. I still remember visiting her."

He drew up a knee and crossed his arms, leaning back against the tree. "Homesick yet?"

"Not really," she confessed shyly. "I always wanted to visit a real ranch. I guess I got my wish." She turned. "Do you think Aunt Lillian will be all right now?"

"Yes, I do." He laughed. "She's having a hell of a good time with us. You haven't told her that we know the truth about each other?"

"No," she said. "I didn't want to disappoint her. But we really ought to tell her."

"Not yet." He let his darkening eyes run down her body, and his blood began to run hot. "Come here."

She gnawed her lower lip. "I don't think that's a good idea," she began half convincingly.

"Like hell you don't," he returned. "You didn't sleep last night any more than I did, and I'll bet your heart is doing the same tango mine is."

It was, but she was apprehensive. Last night it had been so difficult to stop.

"You want me, Marianne," he said under his breath. "And God knows, I want you. We're alone. No prying eyes. No one to see or hear what we do together. Make love with me."

Her mind kept saying no. So why did her legs carry her to him?

She couldn't hear reason through the wild slamming of her heart at her throat. She needed him like water in the desert, like warmth in the cold.

He opened his arms, and she went down into them. Coming home. Feeling his big body warm and close to hers, his arms protecting, his eyes possessive.

He rolled over, taking her with him until she was lying on her back under the shade of the big tree with its soft green leaves blowing in the warm breeze.

As she watched, his hand went to his shirt. He flicked open the buttons until his chest was bare, and then his hand went to the hem of her blouse. She caught his wrist, but it didn't even slow him down. He slid his hand under it and around to the back, easily undoing the catch of her bra.

"Why bother with that thing?" he whispered, sliding his hand around to tease the side of her breast. "It just gets in my way."

Her body trembled at the lazy brushing of his fingers. "Why can't I fight you?" she whispered huskily.

"Because what we give each other defies reason," he whispered. He looked down at her mouth as his fingers brushed closer and closer to the hard, aching tip of her breast. "Little virgin, you excite me beyond bearing, do you know that? I can feel what this does to you. Here…"

His forefinger touched the hard tip and she gasped, shuddering under him, her eyes huge and frightened.

"My God, you can't imagine what it does to me," he said curtly. "Feeling that and knowing that I'm causing it. Knowing how hungry you are for me. If I took you right now, you'd scream, Marianne. You'd writhe and cry out, and I wouldn't be able to hold back a damned thing because you've already got me so aroused I don't know where I am."

As he spoke, he moved, letting her feel the proof of the statement as his weight settled against her. His big hand smoothed up, cupping her warm breast, and his mouth opened, taking her lips with it in a silence that shattered her resistance.

Her body lifted toward him as he slid both hands under it, taking her breasts, savoring them with his warm, calloused hands. His mouth was taking a wild toll of hers, crushing against her parted lips, tasting the sweetness of them in a blazing hunger.

Her hips shifted and he groaned huskily. Her eyes opened, looking curiously up into his.

"What you feel is getting worse by the minute," he whispered huskily. "If you start moving your hips, I'm going to lose control. Are you willing to take that risk?"

She almost was. Her body was crying out for fulfillment. She wanted his hands on all of her. She wanted his clothes out of the way so that she could touch his skin. She wanted to smooth her fingers down the hard muscles of his back and thighs and feel him in the most intimate embrace of all.

He groaned at the look in her eyes. His hand found hers, pulling it to his body, pressing it flat against him, letting her experience him.

She trembled and jerked away from that intimacy, and it brought him to his senses. He rolled over, bringing up his legs, covering his eyes with his forearms. He stiffened, groaning harshly.

"I'm sorry," she whispered, biting her lip. "Ward, I'm sorry!"

"Not your fault," he managed roughly. His teeth clenched. "God, it hurts!"

She sat up, helpless. She didn't know what to do, what to say. It must be horrible for him, and it was her fault, and she didn't know how to ease that obvious pain.

He jackknifed to a sitting position, bent over his drawn-up legs, breathing unsteadily. His hands were clenched together, and the knuckles went white. He shuddered and let out an uneven breath.

"I never realized...it hurt men like that," she faltered. "I'm so sorry!"

"I told you it's not your fault," he said curtly. He didn't look at her. He couldn't yet. His body was still in torment, but it was easing just a little. He sat quietly, waiting for the ache to go away. She was potent. He wondered if he was ever going to be able to stand up again. Damn his principles and damn hers!

"If I were modern and sophisticated..." she began angrily.

"That's what we're going to talk about in a minute," he said.

She stared at his downbent head, absently fumbling to close her bra and pull down her blouse. Together they were an explosive pair.

She loved him beyond bearing. Did he, could he, feel the same way? Her heart flew up into the sun. Was he going to ask her to marry him?

She scrambled to her feet, feeling nervous and shy and on the edge of some monumental discovery. "What are we going to talk about?" she asked, her eyes bright, her smile shy and soft.

He looked up, catching his breath at the beauty in her face. "I want you."

"Yes, I know."

He smiled slowly. "I guess you do, honey," he said, reminding her of that forbidden touch that made her blush.

She lowered her eyes to the ground, watching an ant make its way across a twig. "Well?"

"We can't go on like this," he said, getting slowly to his feet. He stopped just in front of her, near the edge of the river. "You realize that, don't you?"

"Yes," she said miserably.

"And one of these days I'm going to go off my head. It could have happened just now. Men aren't too reliable when their bodies start getting that involved," he added quietly. "I'm just like any other man in passion. I want fulfillment."

She swallowed. This was it. She looked up. "So. What do you want to do about it?" she asked gently.

He stuck his hands into his pockets and searched her eyes with a weary sigh. "I'll set you up in an apartment for a start," he said, his voice reluctant but firm. "I'll open an expense account for you, give you whatever you need. Lillian can be told that you've got a job in the city. Not Ravine, obviously. Maybe in Victoria. That's not too far away for me to drive, and it's big enough that people won't be too curious."

She stared at him. "But it's so far from the ranch..." she began, wondering how they were going to stay married with that kind of arrangement.

"Far enough to keep people from making remarks," he said. "I don't want to expose you to gossip."

"Gossip?" She blinked. Wasn't he proposing?

"You know how I feel about my freedom," he said curtly. "I

can't give that up. But you'll have a part of my life that I've never shared with anyone else. You'll never want for anything. And there won't be another woman. Not ever. Just you. I'll manage enough time to keep us both happy when we're together.''

It was all becoming clear now. His hard face and his determined eyes gave her all the information she needed.

''You're asking me to be your mistress.'' She almost choked on the word, but she had to be sure.

He nodded, confirming her worst fears. ''That's all I can give you, Marianne. That's all I have to give. Marriage isn't something I want. I've had a taste of commitment that left me half demented. I'll never risk it again.''

''And you think that I can be satisfied with this kind of arrangement?'' she asked in a ghost of her normal voice.

''You'll be satisfied, all right,'' he said, his voice sensual and low. ''I'll satisfy you to the roots of your hair, little virgin.''

''And...Aunt Lillian?''

He shifted uncomfortably. Somehow this was all leaving a bad taste in his mouth. It had seemed the right thing, the only thing, to do when he'd worked it out last night. But now it sounded and felt cheap.

''Lillian will never have to know,'' he said shortly.

''And what if I get pregnant?'' she asked blatantly. ''Nothing is foolproof.''

He drew in a slow breath. Children. He hadn't realized that children might come of such a liaison. He studied her, wondering absently if they might have a son together. His body surged in a new and unexpected way. His reaction shocked him.

''Pregnant.'' He said the word aloud, savoring it.

''It does happen,'' she reminded him, going colder by the second. ''Or hasn't the problem ever arisen before?'' she added, wondering how many women had come and gone in his life.

''I've never been desperate enough to compromise a virgin before,'' he said quietly, searching her eyes. ''I've never wanted anything the way I want you.''

She pulled herself erect. ''I'm sorry,'' she said stiffly. ''Sorry that you think so little of me that you could make a proposition like that.

I guess I've given you every reason to think I'd accept, and I'm sorry for that, too. I never realized how…how easy it would make me seem to you.''

His face fell. He could feel his heart sinking. "Cheap?" he asked softly. "Marianne, that's the last thing I think of you!"

"Do tell?" She laughed through building tears. "I'll bet you've made that little speech until it's second nature to you! I'll bet you've even forgotten the names of the women you've had in your bed!''

His lips parted on a caught breath. This wasn't working out the way he'd envisioned. Nothing was going right. There were tears in her eyes, for God's sake.

"Marianne, don't…'' he began, reaching for her.

"Don't you touch me, Ward Jessup,'' she sobbed, sidestepping. "I've made an awful fool of myself, and I guess you had every reason to ask me what you did, but I don't want to be any rich man's kept woman, thanks.''

"Look here—'' He started toward her again.

Instinctively her hands went out, and she pushed jerkily at his chest. Ordinarily it wouldn't have moved him. But the riverbank was slick, and his boots went out from under him. He went over backward with a horrible splash.

Mari didn't stay around to see how wet he was. She ran for her horse, fumbled for the reins from around the trunk of the tree and struggled into the saddle through a blur of tears.

Ward stood up, dripping wet, watching her ride away. He didn't think he'd ever in his life felt so miserable or so stupid. It had seemed like a good idea, that proposition. He didn't want marriage, he didn't. For God's sake, why did women have to have so much permanence? Why couldn't they just enjoy themselves like men did? Then he thought about Mari "enjoying'' herself with another man, and his face went ruddy with bad temper. He didn't understand himself lately. But the sight of her riding away, almost certainly to a speedy departure from the ranch, made him feel hollow inside.

Mari rode home feeling just as hollow herself. She should have been flattered, she supposed, at such a generous offer. But she only felt cheap. Stupid, she told herself. You let him do whatever he wants and then get angry at him for making the obvious assumption. She hated herself for giving in, for giving him license to such intimacy. Her body had betrayed her, hungry for pleasure, and she'd lost her reason somewhere along the way. Now she was going to have to leave here. All because she hadn't been sensible. All because she loved him too much to deny herself the ecstasy of his lovemaking.

"You've got a lot to answer for," she told her body angrily. She could have died of shame. Now he'd be sure that she was an idiot.

What was she going to tell Lillian? Her heart sank. The older woman would be heartbroken. Mari closed her eyes, feeling the tears burn them. Why had she ever come here? It had begun so sweetly, only to end in such tragedy. Well, she'd made her bed. Now she'd have to try to lie in it. That wouldn't be much comfort in the lonely years ahead. Leaving Ward Jessup behind would hurt more than anything else ever had. She'd loved him too much, and now she was going to lose him because of it. Because he didn't want commitment and she did.

Perhaps she should have said yes, she thought miserably. Then she thought about how she'd feel, being kept, being used and then abandoned. No. It was better to never know him that way than to have a taste of him and lose him. It would only make things worse, and she'd never respect herself again. Oddly enough, she had a feeling that he wouldn't have respected her, either. Pride would get her through, she promised herself. Yes. She still had that, even if her heart was shattered. She lifted her face and dried the tears on her sleeve. She had to think up some good excuse to go back to Georgia. Something that would give Lillian a reason to think she'd be back, which would keep her on the mend. Her eyes narrowed in deep thought as she approached the ranch house.

Chapter 9

Mari thought she had it down pat when she left her horse with one of the men at the stable and went into the house to tell Lillian she was leaving.

The older woman was sitting down in the living room, looking smug while she thumbed through a magazine.

Mari paused in the hall, took a deep breath and went into the room determinedly. "Well," she said brightly, "I've got a terrific assignment!"

"You've what?" Lillian asked, staring at her niece.

"Mr. Jessup is sending me to Atlanta to get some information on a distant relative of his," she continued, pretending for all she was worth. "You know, to go into his memoirs. It will give me a chance to see about my rent at the apartment and get some more clothes, too."

Lillian had stiffened, but she relaxed all at once with a smile. "Just for a few days, I guess?" she probed.

"That's right." Mari sighed, laying it on thick. "Isn't he just the nicest man? What a pity he's got so little time." She peeked at Lillian out of the corner of one eye. "There's not much sense in getting attached to a dying man, you know."

Lillian hadn't considered that. She gnawed her lip thoughtfully. "He's not a goner yet," she said. "He could get well." She warmed to her topic. "That's right. They could find a treatment that would work and save him!"

"That would be lovely. He's so macho, you know," Mari said with a forced smile.

"Isn't he, though? You two seem to be spending quite a lot of time together these days, too," she added. "Exchanging some very interesting looks as well."

Mari lowered her eyes demurely. "He's very handsome."

"You're very pretty." Lillian put the magazine aside. "When are you going to Atlanta?"

"This very afternoon!" Mari enthused. "I want to hurry and get back," she added.

Lillian fell for it, hook, line and sinker. "Is he going to let you fly there?" she asked.

"No, I'm, uh, taking the bus. Hate flying, you know. Just do it when I have to." Actually, she didn't have the price of a ticket, thanks to her lost job and small savings account. It would take all she had to pay her rent, and then she'd have to pray that she could find another job. Damn Ward Jessup!

"Bus?" Lillian began, giving her suspicious looks.

"He'll come after me, of course," she said. "We might drive back...."

The older woman brightened. Lots of opportunities if they had to stop overnight. Of course, they wouldn't do anything reckless. She knew Mari wouldn't.

"Do you need some help packing?" she asked Mari.

"No, thanks, dear, I can do it. And I'd better get busy!" She blew Aunt Lillian a kiss. "You'll be all right until I get back?" she added, hesitating.

"Of course," Lillian huffed. "I just have a broken leg. I'm taking those stupid pills."

"Good." Mari went upstairs and quickly threw things into her bag. She called the bus station to ask about an outgoing bus and was delighted to find that she had an hour to get to the station. She grabbed her bag and rushed back down the staircase just in time to watch a wet, angry, coldly polite Ward Jessup come in the front door.

"I told Aunt Lillian about the job, Mr. Jessup," she said, loud enough for Lillian to hear. "My goodness, what happened to you? You're all wet!"

Ward glared at her. "So I am, Miss Raymond," he returned. His gaze went to the bag in her hand. Well, he'd expected it, hadn't he? What did she think he'd do, propose marriage?

Mari went the rest of the way down the staircase, keeping her features calm when she felt like throwing herself at his wet boots and begging him to let her stay. She did have a little pride left. Anyway, he was the one who should be ashamed of himself, going around propositioning good girls.

"Boss, you'd better get into some dry clothes," Lillian fussed.

"I will in a minute." He glared at Mari. "When do you leave?"

"In an hour. Can you get somebody to run me to the bus station? After all, the research trip," she raised her voice, "was your idea."

"Tell Billy I said to drive you," he said curtly, and his eyes cut into hers.

"I'll do that," she replied, struggling to maintain her tattered pride. Her hands clutched the bag. "See you."

He didn't reply. Lillian was getting suspicious.

"Aren't you going to drive her?" Lillian asked him.

"He's soaking wet, poor thing," Mari reminded her. "You wouldn't want him to get worse."

"No, of course not!" Lillian said quickly. "But should you go alone, Mari, with your bad experience."

"She's tough," Ward told his housekeeper, and his eyes were making furious statements in the privacy of the hallway. "She'll get by."

"You bet I will, big man," she assured him. "Better luck next time," she added under her breath. "Sorry I wasn't more... cooperative."

"Don't miss your bus, honey," he said in a tone as cold as snow.

She smiled prettily and went past him to kiss Lillian goodbye.

Lillian frowned as she returned the hug. "Are you sure nothing's wrong?"

"Not a thing," Mari said and smiled convincingly. "He's just trying not to show how hurt he is that I'm leaving," she added in a whisper.

"Oh," Lillian said, although she was feeling undercurrents.

"See you soon," Mari promised. She walked straight past Ward, who was quietly dripping on the hall carpet, his fists clenched by his side. "So long, boss," she drawled. "Don't catch cold, now."

"If I die of pneumonia, I hope your conscience hurts you," he muttered.

She turned at the doorway. "It's more likely that pneumonia would catch you and die. You're dripping on the carpet."

"It's my damned carpet. I'll drip on it if I please."

She searched his hard eyes, seeing nothing welcoming or tender there now. The lover of an hour ago might never have been. "I'll give Georgia your regards."

"Have you got enough money for a bus ticket?" he asked.

She glared at him. "If I didn't have it," she said under her breath, "I'd wait tables to get it! I don't want your money!"

He was learning that the hard way. As he tried to find the right words to smooth over the hurt, to stop her until he could sort out his puzzling, disturbing new feelings, she whirled and went out the door.

"She sure is in a temper." Lillian sighed as she hobbled out of the living room and down the hall. "Sure is going to be lonesome around here without her." She stopped and turned, her eyes full of regret and resignation. "I guess you know what I told her."

"I know," he said curtly. "Everything."

She shrugged. "I was getting older. She was alone. I just wanted her to have somebody to care about her. I'm sorry. I hope both of you can forgive me. I'll write Mari and try to explain. No sense trying to talk to her right now." She knew something had gone badly wrong between them, and the boss didn't look any more eager to discuss it than Mari had. "I hope you'll forgive me."

"I already have."

She looked up with a wan smile. "She's not a bad girl. You…will let her come back if I straighten things out and stop trying to play cupid?"

He studied her quietly. "You heard what was said out here, didn't you?"

She stared at the floor. "I got ears that hear pins falling. I was all excited about it, I thought you two were… Well, it's not my business to arrange people's lives, and I've only just realized it. I'll mind my own business from now on.'' She looked up. ''She'll be all right, won't she? Thanks to us, she doesn't even have a job now.''

He was dying inside, and that thought didn't help one bit. He didn't want her to go, but he was going to have to let her.

''She'll be all right,'' he said, for his own benefit as well as Lillian's. Of course she'd be all right. She was tough. And it was for the best. He didn't want to get married.

What if she went back and married someone else? His heart skipped a beat and he scowled.

''Can she come back, at least to visit?'' Lillian asked sadly.

''Of course she can!'' he grumbled. ''She's your niece.''

Lillian managed a smile. ''Thanks for letting her come. You could have fired me.''

''Not on your life—I'd starve to death.'' He smiled halfheartedly. ''I'd better change.''

A truck started up, and they both looked toward the window as Mari went past sitting beside Billy in the ranch truck.

Ward's face hardened. He turned on his heel without a word and went up the staircase. Lillian sighed, watching him. Well, the jig was up and no harm done. Or was there? He did look frustrated. She turned and went toward the kitchen. Maybe things might work out better than she had expected. She hummed a little, remembering the explosive force of that argument she'd overheard. And then she smiled. Where there was smoke, there was fire, her daddy used to say.

A week later, back in Atlanta, Mari was just getting over bouts of crying. Her small savings account was enough to pay the rent for the next month, thank goodness. She had bought groceries and cleaned her apartment and done her best not to think about what had happened in Texas.

Getting a job was the big problem, and she haunted the unemployment office for secretarial positions. There just weren't any available, but when there was an opening for a beginning bank clerk, she jumped at it. She hated figures and adding numbers, but it wasn't a good time to be choosy. She reported for work at a big bank in downtown Atlanta, and began the tedious process of learning to use computers and balance accounts.

After Mari was settled in Aunt Lillian called to make sure she'd made it home all right.

"I'm sorry, girl," the older woman said gruffly. "I never meant to cause you any hurt. I just wanted someone to look after you when I was gone. Now that I know I'm going to live, of course, I can do it by myself."

Mari was touched by her aunt's concern, even though she felt as if part of her had died. "I'll be okay," Mari promised brightly. "I'm sorry I had to leave so suddenly. I guess you figured out that we'd had a big argument."

"Hard to miss, the way you were going at each other before you left," Lillian said. "I knew the jig was up when he asked if you had the bus fare. He said you both knew I'd been spinning tales."

"We knew almost from the beginning," Mari said with a sigh. "We played along because we both think so much of you. But no more cupid, all right? You're much too tall to pass for the little guy, and you'd look pretty funny in a diaper carrying a bow and arrow."

Lillian actually laughed. "Guess I would, at that." She paused. "The boss left an hour ago for Hawaii. He said it was business, but he wasn't carrying any briefcase. He looked pretty torn up."

That would have been encouraging if Mari hadn't known him so well, but she didn't allow herself to feel hopeful. She wanted to tell Lillian just what the scalawag had offered to do, but she didn't want to crush all her aunt's illusions. He had been pretty good to Lillian, after all. He could afford to be. It was only eligible women he seemed to have it in for.

"He'll be back in form in no time," Mari told her aunt. "He'll proabably find some new woman to make passes at in Hawaii."

"He made a pass?" Lillian sounded almost girlish with glee.

Mari groaned, realizing what she'd given away. "Well, that was what you wanted, wasn't it?" she asked miserably. "You got your wish, but it wasn't commitment he had in mind."

"No man in his right mind ever wants to make a commitment," the other woman assured her. "They have to be led into it."

"I don't want to lead your boss anywhere except maybe into quicksand," Mari said darkly.

"You will come and see me again, won't you?" Lillian probed gently. "When you get over being mad at him?"

"Someday maybe."

"How about a job? Do you have any prospects yet?"

"Finally," Mari sighed. "I started working in the accounts department of a bank this morning."

"Good girl. I knew you'd bounce back quickly. I love you, Marianne."

Mari smiled in spite of herself. "I love you, too, Aunt Lillian. Take care of yourself. Please take your pills."

"I will, I promise. Good night."

Mari hung up and stared at the receiver. So the boss had gone to Hawaii. How nice for him. Balmy breezes, blooming flowers, beautiful women doing the hula. Well, he wouldn't be depressed for long or even missing the one that got away. Thank goodness she'd had sense enough to refuse his proposition. At least she still had her pride and her self-respect.

"And they'll keep you very warm on winter nights, too," Mari muttered to herself before she went to bed.

The bank job was interesting, at least, and she met some nice people. She liked Lindy and Marge, with whom she worked, and there was even a nice young assistant vice president named Larry, who was single and redheaded and just plain nice. She began to have coffee and sweet rolls with him in the mornings the second week she was at the bank. Little by little she was learning to live without the shadow of Ward Jessup.

Or she told herself she was. But the memory of him haunted her. She could close her eyes and feel the warm, hard crush of his mouth, the tantalizing seduction of his big hands. It had been so beautiful between them, so special. At no time in her life had she felt more secure or safe than she had with him. Despite his faults he was more man than she'd ever known. She found that love forgave a lot. She missed him terribly. Sometimes just seeing the back of a dark-headed tall man would be enough to make her heart jump. Or if she heard a deep masculine voice. Or if she saw Texas license plates on a car.

She began to wonder if she was going to survive being away from him.

She called Lillian the third week, just to see how her aunt was getting along, she told herself. But it wasn't Lillian who answered the phone.

When she heard Ward's deep voice, her heart ran away. She hadn't realized how shattering it was going to be to talk to him. She'd assumed Lillian would answer.

"Hello?" he repeated impatiently.

Mari took a calming breath. "Is Aunt Lillian there, please?" she asked formally.

There was a long pause. She couldn't know that hearing her voice had made a similar impact on him.

"Hello, Mari," he said quietly. "Are you all right?"

"I'm very well, thank you. How is Aunt Lillian?"

"She's fine. It's her church social night. Billy ran her over there in the pickup. She'll be home around nine, I guess. Have you got a job?"

That was no business of his, especially seeing as how he'd caused her to lose the one she had in the first place. But hearing his voice had done something to her pride.

"Yes, I'm working at a bank," she told him, mentioning its name. "It's big and convenient to where I live. I work with nice people, and I'm making a better salary there than at the garage. You needn't worry about me."

"But I do," he said quietly. "I worry about you a lot. And I miss you," he added curtly, the words so harsh that they sounded quite involuntary.

She closed her eyes, gripping the receiver. "Do you?" she asked unsteadily, trying to laugh. "I can't imagine that."

"Someday soon I may work on making you imagine it," he said, his voice deep and slow and sensuous.

"I thought I'd told you already that I am not in the market for a big bank account and my own luxury apartment in Victoria, Texas," she returned, hating the unsteadiness that would tell him how much that hateful proposition had hurt her.

He said something rough under his breath. "Yes, I know that," he said gruffly. "I wish you were here. I wish we could talk. I made the biggest mistake of my life with you, Marianne. But I think it might help if you understood why."

Mistake. So now that was all he felt about those magical times they'd had. It had all been just a mistake. And he was sorry.

Tears burned her eyes, but she kept her voice steady. "There's no need to explain," she said gently. "I understand already. You told me how much you loved your freedom."

"It wasn't altogether just that," he returned. "You said Lillian had told you about what happened to me, about the woman I planned to marry."

"Yes."

He sighed heavily. "I suppose she and my mother colored my opinion of women more than I'd realized. I've seen women as nothing more than gold-digging opportunists for most of my adult life. I've used them that way. Anything physical came under the heading of permissible pleasure with me, and I paid for it like I paid for business deals. But until you came along, I never had a conscience. You got under my skin, honey. You're still there."

She imagined that he hadn't told anyone what he was telling her. And while it was flattering, it was disturbing, too. He was explaining why he'd made that "mistake" and was trying to get them back on a friendly footing. She remembered him saying the night he'd come to her room that he'd had that intention even then. It was like lighting a match to the paper of her hopes. An ending.

"Don't let me wear on your conscience, Ward," she said quietly. "You can't help the way you are. I'm a puritan. An old-fashioned prude. I won't change, either, even if the whole world does. So I guess I'll be like Aunt Lillian when I'm her age. Going to church socials and playing cupid for other women..." Her voice broke. "Listen, I have to go."

"No," he ground out. "Marianne, listen to me!"

"Goodbye, Ward."

She hung up before he could hear the tears that were falling hotly down her cheeks, before the break in her voice got worse. She went to bed without calling back. He'd tell Lillian she'd called, she knew, but she couldn't bear the risk that he might answer the phone again. Her heart was in tatters.

She went to work the next morning with her face still pale and her eyes bloodshot from the night before. She sat at her desk mechanically, answering the phone, going over new accounts, smiling at customers. Doing all the right things. But her mind was still on Ward and the sound of his voice and the memory of him that was eating her alive.

It would get better, wouldn't it? It had to! She couldn't go on like this, being haunted by a living ghost, so much in love that she could barely function as a human being. She'd never understood the idea of a couple being halves of the same whole until she met Ward. Now it made perfect sense because she felt as if part of her was missing.

When a long shadow fell across her desk just before lunchtime, she didn't even look up.

"I'll be with you in just a minute," she said with a forced smile as she finished listing a new account. And then she looked up and her body froze.

Ward stared down at her like a blind artist who could suddenly see again. His green eyes found every shadow, every line, every curve of her face in the stark, helpless silence that followed. Around them was the buzz of distant voices, the tap of fingers on keyboards, the ringing of telephones. And closer there was the rasp of Mari's hurried breathing, the thump of her heart shaking the silky pink blouse she was wearing with her gray skirt.

Ward was wearing a suit—a very elegant three-piece beige one that made him look even taller than he actually was. He had a creamy dress Stetson in one big hand, and his face looked thinner and drawn. His green eyes were as bloodshot as hers, as if he hadn't slept well. She thought as she studied him that he was the handsomest man she'd ever seen. If only he wasn't such a cold-blooded snake.

She stiffened defensively, remembering their last meeting. "Yes, sir?" she said with cold politeness. "May I help you?"

"Cut that out," he muttered. "I've had a long flight and no breakfast, and I feel like hell."

"I would like to point out that I work here," she informed him. "I have no time to socialize with old acquaintances. If you want to open an account, I'll be delighted to assist you. That's what I do here. I open accounts.''

"I don't want to open an account," he said through his teeth.

"Then what do you want?" she asked.

"I came to take you home—where you belong." He searched her puzzled eyes. "Your boss will be sorry you have to leave, but he'll understand. You can come with me right now."

She blinked. Somewhere along the line she was sure that she'd missed something.

"I can what?" she asked.

"Come with me right now," he repeated. He turned the Stetson in his hands. "Don't you remember my condition? I'm dying, remember. I have something vaguely terminal, although medical science will triumph in plenty of time to save me."

"Huh?" she said blankly. None of this was getting through to her. She just stared at him.

"You're going to help me write my memoirs, remember?" he persisted.

"You aren't dying!" she burst out, coming to her senses at last.

"Shhhhh!" he said curtly, glancing stealthily around. "Somebody might hear you!"

"I can't quit! I just started working here the week before last!"

"You have to quit," he insisted. "If I go home without you, Lillian is going to starve me to death. She's getting her revenge in the kitchen. Small portions. Desserts without sugar. Diet foods." He shuddered. "I'm a shadow of my former self."

She glared at him. "Poor old thing," she said with poisonous sweetness.

He glared back. "I am not old. I'm just hitting my prime."

"That's nothing to do with me," she assured him. "I hope you didn't come all the way to Atlanta just to make this little scene!"

"I came to take you back with me," he replied. His eyes took on a determined hardness. "And, by God, I'm taking you back. If I have to pick you up bodily and carry you out of here in a fireman's lift."

Her heart jumped, but she didn't let him see how he was disturbing her. "I'll scream my head off," she said shortly.

"Good. Then everyone will think you're in pain, and I'll tell them

I'm taking you to the hospital for emergency treatment.'' He glared at her. "Well?"

He had a stubborn streak that even outmatched her own. She weighed the possibilities. If he carried her out by force, she'd lose all credibility with her colleagues. If she fought him in front of everyone, Ward would get all the sympathy, and Mari would look like a heartless shrew. He had her over a barrel.

"Why?" she asked, her voice quiet and defeated. "Why not just let me stay here?"

He searched her eyes. "Your aunt misses you," he said gruffly.

"She could call me collect and talk to me," she replied. "There's no reason at all for me to go back to Texas and complicate my life and yours."

"My life is pretty boring right now, if you want to know the truth." He sighed, watching her. "I don't even enjoy foreclosing on people anymore. Besides all that, my cousin Bud's come to stay, and he's driving me out of my mind."

Cousin Bud was a familiar name. He was the one Ward's fiancée had wound up marrying for a brief time. She couldn't imagine Ward actually welcoming the man as a guest.

"I'm surprised that you let him," she confessed.

He stared at her. "So you know all about that, too?"

She flushed, dropping her eyes to the desk. "Aunt Lillian mentioned it."

He sighed heavily. "Well, he's family. My grandmother worships him. I couldn't say no without having her jump all over me—and maybe even rush home to defend him. She's having a good time at Belinda's. No reason to disturb her."

She knew about old Mrs. Jessup as well, and she almost smiled at his lack of enthusiasm for his grandmother's company.

"If you've already got one houseguest, you surely don't need another one."

He shrugged. "There's plenty of room. My secretary quit," he added, studying his hat. "I sure could use some help in the office. You could almost name your own salary."

"You forced me to leave Texas in the first place," she shot back, glaring up at him. "You did everything but put me on the bus! You propositioned me!"

His cheeks had a sudden flush, and he looked away. "You can't actually like this job," he said shortly. "You said you hated working with numbers."

"I like eating," she replied. "It's hard to eat when you aren't making money."

"You could come home with me and make money," he said. "You could live with your aunt and help me keep Cousin Bud from selling off cattle under my nose."

"Selling off cattle?"

His powerful shoulders rose and fell. "He owns ten percent of the ranch. I had a weak moment when he was eighteen and made him a graduation present of it. The thing is, I never know which ten percent he happens to be claiming at the moment. It seems to change quarterly." He brushed at a speck of dust on his hat. "Right now, he's sneaking around getting statistics on my purebred Santa Gertrudis bull."

"What could I do about Cousin Bud—*if* I went with you?" she asked reasonably.

"You could help me distract him," he said. "With you in the office, he couldn't very well get to any statistics. He couldn't find out where I keep that bull unless he found it on the computer. And you'd be watching the computer."

It was just an excuse, and she knew it. For reasons of his own it suited him to have her at the ranch. She didn't flatter herself that it was out of any abiding love. He probably did still want her, but perhaps it was more a case of wanting to appease Lillian. She frowned, thinking.

"Is my aunt all right?" she asked.

He nodded. "She's fine. I wouldn't lie to you about that. But she's lonesome. She hasn't been the same since you left." Neither had he, he thought, but he couldn't tell her. Not yet. She didn't trust him at all, and he couldn't really blame her.

She fiddled with a pencil, considering Ward's offer. She could tell him to go away and he would. And she'd never see him again. She could go on alone and take up the threads of her life. What a life it would be. What a long, lonely life.

"Come with me, Mari," he said softly. "This is no place for you."

She didn't look up. "I meant what I said before I left. If I come back, I don't...I don't want you to...to..."

He sighed gently. "I know, I know. You don't have to worry," he told her. "I won't proposition you. You have my word on that."

She shifted. "Then I'll go."

He forced back a smile. "Come on, then. I've got the tickets already."

She lifted her eyebrows. "Were you that confident?"

"Not confident at all," he replied. "But I figured I could always put my Stetson in one of the seats if you refused."

She did smile faintly at that. "I always heard that a real Texan puts his hat on the floor and his boots on the hat rack."

He lifted a tooled leather boot and studied it. "Yep," he said. "I guess I'd put my boots in the extra seat, at that. But I'd rather have you in it."

She got to her feet and put her work aside. "I need to see Mr. Blake, my boss."

"I'll wait." He wasn't budging.

After Mari had apologetically informed her boss of her departure, she picked up her purse, waved at her new friends and went quietly out the door with Ward. It felt odd, and she knew it was foolhardy. But she was too vulnerable still to refuse him. She only hoped that she could keep him from knowing just how vulnerable she was.

He drove her back to her apartment and then wandered around the living room while she packed.

His fingers brushed the spines of the thick volumes in her small bookcase. *"The Tudors of England,"* he murmured, "ancient Greece, Herodotus, Thucydides—quite a collection of history."

"I like history," she commented. "It's interesting reading about how other people lived in other times."

"Yes, I think so, too," he agreed. "I prefer Western history myself. I have a good collection of information on the Comanche and the cowboy period in south Texas, from the Civil War up to the 1880s."

She took her bag into the living room, watching the way he filled the room. He was so big. So masculine. He seemed to dwarf everything.

"We don't really know a lot about each other, do we?" he asked as she joined him. He turned, hands in his pockets, spreading the fabric of his trousers close against the powerful muscles of his legs.

"Getting to know women isn't one of your particular interests, from what I've heard," she returned quietly. "At least, not in any intellectual way."

"I explained why," he reminded her, and his green eyes searched her blue ones. "It isn't easy learning to trust people."

She nodded. "I suppose not." She wanted to ask him why he seemed to be so interested in where she lived, but she was too shy. "I'm packed."

He glanced toward her suitcase. "Enough for a little while?"

"Enough for a week or so," she said. "You didn't say how long I was to stay."

He sighed heavily. "That's something we'll leave for later. Right now I just want to go home." He looked around him. "It's like you," he said finally. "Bright. Cheerful, Very homey."

She hadn't felt bright and cheerful and homey in recent weeks. She'd felt depressed and miserable. But it fascinated her that her apartment told him so much.

"It doesn't have an indoor stream," she commented.

He smiled slowly. "No, it doesn't. Good thing. With my batting average so far, I guess I'd be in it by now, wouldn't I?"

She cleared her throat, feeling embarrassed. "I didn't mean to push you in the river."

"Didn't you? It seemed like it at the time." He searched her eyes quietly. "I meant what I said, Marianne. I won't make any more insulting propositions."

"I appreciate that. I'm just sorry that I gave you such a poor opinion of me," she added, admitting her own guilt. "I shouldn't have let things go on the way they did."

He moved closer, lifting his hands to her shoulders, lightly holding her in front of him. "What we did together was pretty special," he said hesitantly. ''I couldn't have stopped it any more than you could. Let's try not to look back. That part of our relationship is over.''

He sounded final, and she felt oddly hurt. She stared at his vest, watching the slow rise and fall of his chest.

''Yes,'' she murmured.

He looked down at her silky dark hair, smelled the soft floral scent that clung to her, and his heart began to throb. It had been so long since he'd held her, kissed her. He wanted to, desperately, but he'd just tied his own hands by promising not to start anything.

''Do you like kittens?'' he asked unexpectedly.

Her eyes came up, brightly blue and interested. ''Yes. Why?''

''We've got some,'' he said with a grin. ''Lillian found an old mama cat squalling at the back door in a driving rain and couldn't help herself. The very next morning we had four little white kittens with eyes as blue as—'' he searched hers with a disturbing intensity ''—as yours.''

''You let her keep the kittens?'' she asked softly.

He shifted restlessly. ''Well, it was raining,'' he muttered. ''The poor little things would have drowned if I'd put them outside.''

She wasn't buying that. Odd, how well she'd come to know him in the little time she'd spent on his ranch. ''And...?'' she prodded with raised eyebrows.

He almost smiled at the knowing look on her face. She knew him, warts and all, all right. ''Cousin Bud's got one hell of an allergy to little kitties.''

He was incorrigible. She burst out laughing. ''Oh, you black-hearted fiend, you!'' she groaned.

''I like little kitties,'' he said with mock indignation. ''If he doesn't, he can leave, can't he? I mean, I don't lock him in at night or anything.''

If love was knowing all about someone—the good things and the bad—and loving them just the same, then it sure did apply here, she mused silently. ''Ward Jessup,'' she said, sighing, ''you just won't leave Bud alone, will you?''

''Sure I will, if he'll go home and leave my bull alone,'' he returned. ''My God, you don't know how hard I fought to get that critter into my breeding program. I outbid two of the richest Texans in cattle to get him!''

"And now Cousin Bud wants him. What for?'' she asked.

"Beats me.'' He sighed. "Probably for his advertising agency.''

She sat down on the sofa. "He wants your bull for an ad agency?'' she asked dubiously.

His eyebrows rose while his brain began to grasp what she was thinking. "Ad agency...oh, no, hell, no, he isn't going to use the bull to pose for male underwear commercials! He wants to sell it to finance expanding his advertising agency!''

"Well, don't glare at me, it sounded like he wanted to make a male model out of it,'' she defended herself.

He sighed heavily. "Woman, you're going to be my undoing,'' he said. And probably she would if he let himself think too hard about just why he'd come all this way after her. But missing her was just part of the torturous process. Now he had to prove to himself that he could have her around and not go off his head anymore. He still wanted her for certain, but marriage wouldn't suit him any more than being his mistress would suit her. So they'd be...friends. Sure. Friends. Lillian would stop starving him. There. He had noble motives. He just had to get them cemented in his mind, that was all.

"Can't you just tell Cousin Bud to go home?'' she asked curiously.

"I have!'' he grumbled. "Lillian has, too. But every time we get him to the front door, he calls up my grandmother and she raises hell with Lillian and me for not offering him our hospitality.''

"She must like him a lot,'' she mused.

"More than she likes me, I'm afraid,'' he returned. He whirled his Stetson in his hands. "I'll give you one of the kittens if you want it.''

"Bribery,'' she said in a stage whisper and actually grinned.

He grinned back. She was pretty that way. "Sure it is,'' he said shamelessly. He glanced around her small apartment. "Will they let you keep a cat here?''

"I guess so. I haven't ever asked.'' So he was already planning for her to come back here, she thought miserably.

He shrugged. "You might not want to come back here, though,'' he said unexpectedly. He smiled slowly. "You might like working for me. I'm a good boss. You can have every Sunday off, and I'll only keep you at the computer until nine every night.''

''You old slave driver!''

He didn't laugh as she'd expected him to. He just stared at her. ''Am I old to you?'' he asked softly as if it really mattered.

Watch it, girl, she warned herself. Take it easy, don't let the old devil fox you. ''No,'' she said finally. ''I don't think you're that old.''

''To a kid like you I guess I seem that way,'' he persisted, searching her blue eyes with his darkening green ones.

She didn't like remembering how much older she felt because of his searching ardor. She dropped her eyes to the floor. ''You said the past was over. That we'd forget it.''

He shifted his booted feet. ''I guess I did, honey,'' he agreed quietly. ''Okay. If that's how you want it.''

She looked up unexpectedly and found a strange, haunting look on his dark face. ''It's an impasse, don't you think?'' she asked him. ''You don't want a wife, and I don't want an unattached temporary lover. So all that's really left is friendship.''

He clutched the hat tighter. ''You're making it sound cheap,'' he said in a faintly dangerous tone. He didn't like what she was saying.

''Isn't it?'' she persisted, rising to her feet. He still towered over her, but it gave her a bit of an advantage. ''You'd get all the benefits of married life with none of the responsibility. And what would I get, Ward? A little notoriety as the boss's mistress, and after you got tired of me, I'd be handed some expensive parting gift and left alone with my memories. No respectability, no self-respect, tons of guilt and loneliness. I think that's a pretty poor bargain.''

''You little prude,'' he said curtly. ''What do you know about grown-up problems, you with your spotless conscience? It's so easy, isn't it, all black and white. You tease a man with your body until he's crazy for it, you try to trap him into a marriage he doesn't want, you take whatever you can get and walk out the door. What does the man have out of all that?''

His attitude shocked her. She hadn't realized just how poisoned he was against the female sex until he made that bitter statement.

''Is that what she did to you?'' she asked gently. ''Did she tease you beyond endurance and then marry someone else because what you gave her wasn't enough?''

His face grew harder than she'd ever seen it. He'd never talked about it, but she was forcing his hand.

''Yes,'' he said curtly. ''That's precisely what she did. And if I'd been fool enough to marry her, she'd have cut my throat emotionally and financially, and she wouldn't even have looked back to see if I was bleeding to death on her way to the bank!''

She moved closer to him, hating that hurt in his eyes, that disillusionment that had drawn his face muscles taut. ''Shall I tell you what most women really want from marriage? They want the closeness of caring for one man all their lives. Looking after him, caring about him, doing little things for him, loving him…sharing good times and bad. A good marriage doesn't have a lot to do with money, from what I've seen. But mutual trust and caring about each other makes all the difference. Money can't buy those.''

He felt himself weakening and hated it. She was under his skin, all right, and it was getting worse all the time. He wanted her until he ached, and it didn't stop with his body. She stirred him inside, in ways no other woman ever had. Except Caroline. Caroline. Would he ever forget?

''Pretty words,'' he said bitterly, searching her eyes.

''Pretty ideals,'' she corrected. ''I still believe in those old virtues. And someday I'll find a man who believes in them, too.''

''In some graveyard, maybe.''

''You are so cynical!'' she accused, exasperated.

''I had good teachers,'' he retorted, slamming his Stetson down on his head to cock it arrogantly over one eye. ''Are you ready?''

''I'm ready,'' she muttered, sounding every bit as bad-tempered as he did.

He took her bag in one hand and opened the apartment door with the other. She followed him out, locked the door with a sigh and put the key in her purse. Her life was so unpredictable these days. Just like the man beside her.

The commercial flight seemed longer than it actually was. Mari had found a few magazines to read at the huge Atlanta Hartsfield International Airport, and it was a good thing that she had because

Ward pulled his hat over his eyes and folded his arms and he hadn't said one word to her yet. The flight attendants were already serving their lunch, but Ward only glanced up, refusing food. Mari knew, as she nibbled at ham and cheese on a bun, that he had to be furious or sick. He never refused food for any other reason.

Mari was sorry that they'd quarreled. She shouldn't have been because, if he was angry, at least he wouldn't be making passes at her. But if he stayed angry, it was going to make working for him all that much harder, and she'd promised, God knew why, to do his secretarial work. Now she couldn't imagine what had possessed her to agree. At the time it had seemed a wonderful idea. Of course, she'd had some crazy idea that he'd cared a little in order to come all that way to get her. Now it was beginning to seem as if he hated himself for the very thought. Mari was miserable. She should have said no. Then she remembered that she had, and that, ultimately, she had little choice in the matter.

She sighed over her food, glancing at him under the hat. "Aren't you hungry?" she offered.

"If I was hungry, I'd be eating, wouldn't I?" he muttered indistinctly.

She shrugged. "Then go right ahead and starve if you want to. I couldn't care less."

He lifted the brim of the hat and glared at her. "Like hell you couldn't," he retorted. "You and your pristine little conscience would sting for months."

"Not on your account," she assured him as she finished the ham. "After all, you're starving yourself. I haven't done anything."

"You've ruined my appetite," he said curtly.

Her eyebrows arched. "How did I do that, pray tell? By mentioning the word marriage? Some people don't mind getting married. I expect to do it myself one of these days. You see, I don't have your blighted outlook. I think you get out of a relationship what you put into it."

His green eyes narrowed, glittering. "And just what would you plan to put into one?"

"Love, laughter and a lot of pillow talk," she said without hesitation. "I expect to be everything my husband will ever want, in and out of bed. So you just go right ahead and have affairs, Mr. Jessup, until you're too old to be capable of it, and then you can live alone and count your money. I'll let my grandchildren come and visit you from time to time.''

He seemed to swell all over with indignation. "I can get married any time I want to," he said shortly. "Women hound me to death to marry them!"

Her mouth made a soft whistle. "Do tell? And here you are pushing forty and still single…"

"I'm pushing thirty-six, not forty!"

"What's the difference?" she asked reasonably.

He opened his mouth to answer, glared fiercely at her and then jerked his hat down over his eyes with a muttered curse. He didn't speak to her again until the plane landed in Texas.

"Are you going to ignore me the rest of the way?" Mari said finally when they were in the Chrysler just a few minutes outside of Ravine.

"I can't carry on a civilized conversation without having you blow up at me," he said gruffly.

"I thought it was the other way around." She picked a piece of lint off her sleeve. "You're the one doing all the growling, not me. I just said that I wanted to get married and have babies."

"Will you stop saying that?" He shifted angrily in the seat. "I'll get hives just thinking about it."

"I don't see why. They'll be my babies, not yours."

He was grinding his teeth together. He'd just realized something that he hadn't considered. Cousin Bud was young and personable and hungry to settle down. He'd take one look at this sweet innocent and be hanging by his heels, trying to marry her. Bud wasn't like Ward; he was carefree and his emotions were mostly on the surface. He didn't have scars from Caroline, and he wasn't afraid of love. In fact, he seemed to walk around in a perpetual state of it. And here was Ward, bringing him the perfect victim. The only woman Ward had ever wanted and hadn't got. Bud might be the one… Suddenly he slammed on the brakes.

"What!" Mari burst out, gasping as she grasped the dash. "What is it?"

"Just a rabbit," he muttered with a quick glance in her direction. "Sorry."

She stared at him. She hadn't seen any rabbit, and he sure was pale. What was wrong with him?

"Are you all right?" she asked cautiously, her voice soft with helpless concern.

It was the concern that got to him. He felt vulnerable with her. That evidence of her soft heart wound strands around him, binding him. He didn't want marriage or ties or babies! But when he looked at her, he felt such sweet longings, such exquisite pleasure. It had nothing to do with sex or carefree lust. It was...disturbing.

"Yes," he said quietly. "I'm all right."

A little farther down the road he suddenly pulled into a shallow farm road that was little more than ruts in the grass. It went beyond a closed fence, through a pasture, toward a distant grove of trees.

"My grandfather's place," he said as he turned off the engine. "My father was born out there, where you see those trees. It was a one-room shack in those days, and my grandmother once fought off a Comanche raiding party with an old Enfield rifle while my grandfather was up in Kansas on a trail drive."

He got out of the car and opened her door. "I know the owner," he said when she was standing beside him. "He doesn't mind if I come here. I like to see the old place sometimes."

He didn't ask if she wanted to. He just held out his big hand. Without hesitation she placed her slender one in it and felt tingly all over as his fingers closed warmly around it.

She felt small beside him as they walked. He opened and closed the gate, grinning at her curious stare.

"Any cattleman knows the value of a closed fence," he remarked as he grasped her hand once more and began to walk along the damp ruts. It had rained recently and there were still patches of mud. "In the old days a rancher might very well shoot a greenhorn who left a gate open and let his cattle get out."

"Were there really Indian raids around here?" she asked.

"Why, sure, honey," he said, smiling down at her. "Comanche, mostly, and there were Mexican bandidos who raided the area, too. Cattle rustling was big business back then. It still is in some areas.

Except now they do it with big trucks, and in the old days they had to drive the herd out of the country or use a running iron.''

She glanced up curiously. "What's a running iron?"

"A branding iron with a curved tip," he said. "It was used to alter brands so a man could claim another man's cattle. Here.'' He let go of her hand and found a stick and drew a couple of brands in the dirt, explaining how a running iron could be used to add an extra line or curve to an existing brand and change its shape entirely.

"That's fascinating!" she said.

"It's also illegal, but it happened quite a lot.'' He put the stick down and stuck his hands in his pockets, smiling as he looked around at feathery mesquite and live oak trees and open pasture. "God, it's pretty here," he said. "Peaceful, rustic... I never get tired of the land. I guess it's that damned Irish in my ancestry.'' He glanced down. "My grandmother, now, says it's British. But just between us, I don't think O'Mara is a British name, and that was my great-grandmother's maiden name.''

"Maybe your grandmother doesn't like the Irish," she suggested.

"Probably not since she was jilted by a dashing Irishman in the war.''

"Which war?" Mari asked cautiously.

"I'm afraid to ask,'' he said conspiratorially. "I'm not quite sure just how old she is. Nobody knows.''

"How exciting," she said with a laugh.

He watched her with a faint smile, fascinated by the change in her when she was with him. That pale, quiet woman in the bank bore no resemblance to this bright, beautiful one. He scowled, watching her wander through the wooded area where the old ramshackle ranch house sagged under the weight of age and rotting timbers and rusting tin. She made everything new and exciting, and the way she seemed to light up when he was near puzzled him, excited him. He wondered if she might care about him. Love him...

She whirled suddenly, her face illuminated with surprised delight. "Ward, look!"

There were pink roses by the steps. A profusion of vines bore pink roses in tight little clusters, and their perfume was everywhere.

"Aren't they beautiful!" she enthused, bending to smell them. "What a heavenly aroma!"

"Legend has it that my father's grandmother, Mrs. O'Mara, brought those very roses from Calhoun County, Georgia, and nursed them like babies until they took hold here. She carried them across the frontier in a pot. In a Conestoga wagon, and saved them from fire, flood, swollen river crossings, robbers, Indians and curious little children. And they're still here. Like the land," he mused, staring around with eyes full of pride. "The land will be here longer than any of us and very little changed despite our meddling."

She smiled. "You sound just like a rancher."

He turned. "I am a rancher."

"Not an oilman?"

He shrugged. "I used to think oil was the most important thing in the world. Until I got plenty of it. Now I don't know what's the most important thing anymore. My whole life seems to be upside down lately." He stared straight at her. "I was a happy man until you came along."

"You were a vegetable until I came along," she replied matter-of-factly. "You thought robbing people was all right."

"Why, you little devil," he said in a husky undertone, and his eyes went a glittering green. "You little devil!"

She laughed because there was as much mischief as threat in that look. She started running across the meadow, a picture in her full gray skirt and pretty pink blouse, with her dark hair gleaming in the sun. He ran after her in time to catch the colorful glimmer of something moving just in front of her in the grass.

"Mari!" he called out, his voice deep and cutting and full of authority. "Stop!"

She did, with one foot in midair, because he sounded so final. She didn't look down. With her inborn terror of snakes, she knew instinctively what he was warning her about.

"Don't move, baby," he breathed, stopping himself just within reach of a fallen limb from one of the oaks. "Don't move, don't breathe. It's all right. Just stand perfectly still...."

He moved with lightning speed picking up a heavy branch and swinging his arm down, slamming. There was a feverish rattling, like bacon sizzling in a pan, and then only a bloody, writhing, coiling mass on the ground.

She was numb with unexpressed terror, her eyes huge at the thing on the ground that, only seconds ago, could have taken her life. She started to speak, to tell him how grateful she was, when he caught her up in his arms and brought his hard mouth down bruisingly on hers.

She couldn't breathe, couldn't move. He was hurting her, and she hardly noticed. His mouth was telling her things words couldn't. That he was afraid for her, that he was glad she was safe, that he'd take care of her. She let him tell her that way, glad of his strength. Her arms curled around his broad shoulders, and she sighed under his warm, hungry mouth, savoring its rough ardor.

"My God," he whispered unsteadily, his mouth poised over hers, his eyes dark in a face that was pale under its tan, his breath rough. "My God, one more step and it would have had you!"

"I'm all right, thanks to you." She managed to smile through the shaking relief, her fingers traced his rough cheek, his mouth. "Thank you."

He lifted her against his body, as rugged as any frontier man would have been, his face mirroring pride and masculinity. "Thank me, then," he whispered, opening his mouth as he bent to her lips. "Thank me..."

She did, so hungrily that he had to put her away from him or let her feel how easily she could arouse him. He held her by the waist, breathing unsteadily, watching her flushed face.

"We agreed that wouldn't happen again," he said.

She nodded, searching his eyes.

"But the circumstances were...unusual," he continued.

"Yes," she whispered, her eyes falling to his hard mouth with languorous remembered pleasure. "Unusual."

"Stop looking at me like that, or it won't end with kisses," he threatened huskily. "You felt what you were doing to me."

She averted her eyes and moved away. Sometimes she forgot how experienced he was until he made a remark like that and emphasized it. She had to remember that she was just another woman. He felt responsible for her, that was why he'd reacted like that to the snake. It wasn't anything personal.

"Well, thanks for saving me," she said, folding her arms over her breasts as she walked back to the car, and carefully she avoided looking at the dead snake as she went.

"Watch where you put your feet, will you?" he asked from behind her. "One scare like that is enough."

Scare for which one of us? she wanted to ask. But she was too drained to say it. Her mouth ached for his. She could hardly bear to remember that she'd inflicted this torment on herself by letting him bring her out here. How was she going to bear days or weeks of it, of being near him and being vulnerable and having no hope at all for a future that included him?

Chapter 10

Ward was quiet the rest of the way to the ranch, but he kept watching Mari and the way he did it was exciting. Once he reached across the space between them and found her hand. He kept it close in his until traffic in Ravine forced him to let go, and Mari found her heart doing spins.

She didn't know how to handle this new approach. She couldn't quite trust him yet, and she wasn't altogether sure that he didn't have some ulterior motive for bringing her back. After all, he wasn't hampered by emotions as she was.

Lillian came quickly out to meet them, looking healthy and fit and with a healed leg.

"Look here," she called to Mari and danced a jig. "How's that for an improvement?" She laughed gaily.

"Terrific!" Mari agreed. She ran forward to embrace the older woman warmly. "It's good to see you again."

"He's been horrible," Lillian whispered while Ward was getting the bag out of the car. "Just horrible. He moped around for days after you left and wouldn't eat at all."

"He should have foreclosed on somebody, then," Mari said matter-of-factly. "That would have cheered him up."

Lillian literally cackled. "Shame on you," she said with a laugh.

"What's all the humor about?" Ward asked as he joined them, his expression tight and mocking.

"Your appetite," Mari volunteered tongue in cheek.

Lillian had turned to go back inside. Ward leaned down, holding Mari's eyes. "You know more about that than most women do, honey," he said in a seductive undertone. "And if you aren't careful, you may learn even more."

"Don't hold your breath," she told him, rushing away before she fell under the spell of his mocking ardor.

"Where's Bud?" Ward asked as they entered the hall.

"Did somebody call me?" came a laughing voice from the study.

The young man who came out to greet them was a total surprise for Mari. She'd been expecting Ward's cousin to be near his own age, but Bud was much younger. He was in his late twenties, at a guess, and lithe and lean and handsome. He had Ward's swarthy complexion, but his eyes were brown instead of green and his hair was lighter than his cousin's. He was a striking man, especially in the leather and denim he was wearing.

"Have you been sneaking around after my bull again?" Ward demanded.

"Now, Cousin," Bud said soothingly, "how would I find him in there?" He jerked his hand toward the study and shuddered. "It would take a team of secretaries a week just to find the desk!"

"Speaking of secretaries," Ward said, "this is my new one. Marianne Raymond, this is Bud Jessup. My cousin."

"Ah, the much-talked-about niece," Bud murmured, winking at Mari. "Hello, Georgia peach. You sure do your home state proud."

Ward didn't like Bud's flirting. His eyes told his cousin so, which only made Bud more determined than ever.

"Thank you," Mari was saying, all smiles. "It's nice to meet you at last."

"Same here," Bud said warmly, moving forward.

"Here, son," Ward said, tossing the bag at him. "You can put that in the guest room, if you don't mind. I'm sure Mari would like to see the study." Before anybody could say anything else, Ward had taken Mari by the arm and propelled her none too gently into the study.

He slammed the door behind them, bristling with masculine pride, and turned to glare at her. "He's not marrying material," he told her immediately, "so don't take him too seriously. He just likes to flirt."

"Maybe I do, too," she began hotly.

He shook his head, moving slowly toward her. "Not you, honey," he replied. "You aren't the flirting kind. You're no butterfly. You're a little house wren, all feathered indignation and quick eyes and nesting instinct."

"You think you know a lot about me, don't you?" She faltered on the last word because she was backing away from him and almost fell over a chair. He kept coming, looming over her with threatening eyes and sheer size.

"I know more than I ever expected to," he agreed, coming closer. "Stop running. We both know it's me you really want, not Bud."

She drew herself up, glaring at him. "You conceited…"

He moved quickly, scooping her up in his arms, holding her off the floor, his eyes wavering between amusement and ardor. "Go ahead, finish it," he taunted.

She could have if he hadn't been so close. His breath was minty and it brushed her lips when he breathed, warm and moist. He made her feel feminine and vulnerable, and when she looked at his hard mouth, she wanted to kiss it.

"Your office," she swallowed, "is a mess."

"So am I," he whispered huskily, searching her eyes. "So is my life. Oh, God, I missed you!"

That confession was her undoing. She looked up at him and couldn't look away, and her heart felt like a runaway engine. Her head fell back onto his shoulder, and she watched him lower his dark head.

"Open your mouth when I put mine over it," he breathed against her lips. "Taste me…"

Her breath caught. She was reaching up, she could already feel the first tentative brushing of his warm lips when a knock at the door made them both jump.

He lifted his head with a jerky motion. "What is it?" he growled.

Mari trembling in his arms, heard a male voice reply, "Lillian's got coffee and cake in the dining room, Cousin! Why don't you come and have some refreshment?"

"I'd like to have him, fricasseed," Ward muttered under his breath as Bud's laughing voice became dimmer along with his footsteps.

"I'd like some coffee," she said hesitantly even though she was still shaking with frustrated reaction and her voice wobbled.

He looked down into her eyes. "No, you wouldn't," he said huskily. "You'd like me. And I'd like you, right there on that long sofa where we almost made love the first time. And if it hadn't been for my meddling, jealous cousin, that's where we'd be right now!"

He put her down abruptly and moved away. "Come on, we'll have coffee." He stopped at the door with his hand on the knob. "For now," he added softly. "But one day, Marianne, we'll have each other. Because one day neither one of us is going to be able to stop."

She couldn't look at him. She couldn't even manage a defiant stare. It was the truth. She'd been crazy to come here, but there was no one to blame but herself.

From that first meeting, Cousin Bud seemed determined to drive Ward absolutely crazy. He didn't leave Mari alone with the older man for a second if he could help it. He found excuse after excuse to come into the office when she was typing things for Ward, and if she ever had to find Ward to ask a question, Bud would find them before they said two words to each other. Mari wondered if it might just be mischief on Bud's part, but Ward treated the situation as if he had a rival.

That in itself was amazing. Ward seemed possessive now, frankly covetous whenever Mari was near him. He shared things with her. Things about the ranch, about his plans for it, the hard work that had gone into its success. When he came home late in the evening, it was to Mari that he went, seeking her out wherever she might be, to ask for coffee or a sandwich or a slice of cake. Lillian took this new attitude with open delight, glad to have her former position usurped when she saw the way he was looking at her puzzled niece.

Bud usually managed to weasel in, of course, but there eventually came a night when he had business out of town. Ward came in about eight o'clock, covered in dust and half starved.

"I sure could use a couple of sandwiches, honey," he told Mari gently, pausing in the living room doorway. Lillian had gone to bed, and curled up on the sofa in her jeans and a yellow tank top, Mari was watching the credits roll after an entertainment special.

"Of course," she said eagerly and got up without bothering to look for her shoes.

He was even taller when she was barefoot, and he seemed amused by her lack of footwear.

"You look like a country girl," he remarked as she passed close by him, feeling the warmth of his big body.

"I feel like a country girl," she said with a pert smile. "Come on, big man, I'll feed you."

"How about some coffee to go with it?" he added as he followed her down the hall into the spacious kitchen.

"Easier done than said," she told him. She flicked the on switch of the small coffee machine, grinning at him when it started to perk. "I had it fixed and ready to start."

"Reading my mind already?" he teased. He pulled out a chair and sat down, sprawling with a huge stretch before he put his long legs out and rested his booted feet in another chair. "The days are getting longer, or I'm getting older," he said with a yawn. "I guess if I keep up this pace, before long you'll be pushing me around in a wheelchair."

"Not you," she said with loving amusement. "You're not the type to give up and get old before your time. You'll still be chasing women when you're eighty-five."

He sobered with amazing rapidity, his green eyes narrowing in his handsome face as he studied her graceful movements around the kitchen. "Suppose I told you that you're the only woman I'll want to chase when I'm eighty-five, Marianne?" he asked gently.

Her heart leaped, but she wasn't giving in to it that easily. He'd already come too close once and hurt her. She'd been deliberately keeping things light since she'd come back to the ranch, and she wasn't going to be trapped now.

She laughed. "Oh, I guess I'd be flattered."

"Only flattered?" he mused.

She finished making the sandwiches and put them down on the table. "By that time I expect to be a grandmother many times over," she informed him as she went back to pour the coffee. "And I think my husband might object."

He didn't like thinking about Marianne with a husband. His face darkened. He turned his attention to the sandwiches and began to eat.

"I have to go over to Ty Wade's place tomorrow," he murmured. "Want to come and meet Erin and the babies?"

She caught her breath. "Me? But won't I be in the way if you're going to talk business?"

He shook his head, holding her soft blue eyes. "You'll never be in my way, sweetheart," he said with something very much like tenderness in his deep voice. "Not ever."

She smiled at him. The way he was looking at her made her feel trembly all over. He was weaving subtle webs around her, but without the wild passion he'd shown her at the beginning of their turbulent relationship. This was new and different. While part of her was afraid to trust it, another part was hungry for it and for him.

"How about it?" he asked, forcing himself to go slow, not to rush her. He'd already had to face the fact that he wasn't going to be able to let her go. Now it was a question of making her see that he didn't have ulterior motives, and she was as hard to trust as he was.

"I'd like to meet Mrs. Wade," she said after a minute. "She sounds like quite a lady."

He laughed under his breath. "If you'd known Ty before she came along, you'd think she was quite a lady," he agreed with a grin. "It took one special woman to calm down that cougar. You'll see what I mean tomorrow."

The next afternoon Mari climbed into the Chrysler beside Ward for the trip over to the Wades' place. Ward was wearing slacks with a striped, open-necked green shirt, and she had on a pretty green pantsuit with a gaily striped sleeveless blouse. He'd grinned when he noticed that their stripes matched.

Erin Wade opened the door, a picture in a gaily flowing lavender caftan. She looked as if she smiled a lot, and she was obviously a beauty when she was made up, with her long black hair and pretty green eyes. But she wasn't wearing makeup. She looked like a country girl, clean and fresh.

"Hello!" she said enthusiastically. "I'm glad you brought her, Ward. Hello, I'm Erin, and you have to be Marianne. Come in and see my boys!"

"I'm glad to meet you, too." Marianne grinned. "I've heard legends about you already."

"Have you, really?" Erin laughed. She was beautiful even without makeup, Marianne thought, the kind of beauty that comes from deep within and makes even homely women bright and lovely when it shows. "Well, Ty and I got off to a bad start, but we've come a long way in very little time. I don't think he has many regrets about getting married. Not even with twin boys."

"I can just see him now, changing a diaper." Ward chuckled.

Erin's green eyes widened. "But you can," she said. "Follow me."

Sure enough, there he was, changing a diaper. It looked so touching, the big, tough rancher Marianne had met before bending over that tiny, smiling, kicking baby on the changing table in a bedroom decorated with teddy bear wallpaper and mobiles.

"Oh, hello, Jessup," he murmured, glancing over his shoulder as he put the last piece of adhesive in place around the baby's fat middle. "Matthew was wet, I was just changing him," he told Erin. He glanced toward a playpen, where another baby was standing on unsteady little fat legs with both chubby hands on the rail, biting delightedly on the plastic edging. "Jason's hungry, I think. He's been trying to eat the playpen for the past five minutes."

"He's teething," Erin said, leaning over to pick him up and cuddle him while he cooed and patted her shoulder and chanted, "Da, Da, Da, Da."

Ty grinned mockingly at his frowning wife. "She hates that," he told the guests. "Most babies say Mama first. Both of them call me instead of her."

"Don't gloat." Erin stuck her tongue out at him. "You just remember who got up with them last night and let you sleep."

He winked at her, with torrents of love pouring on her from his light eyes. Marianne glanced up at Ward and found him watching her with the oddest look on his face. His green eyes went slowly down to her flat stomach and back up again, and she blushed because she knew what he was thinking. *Exactly* what he was thinking. She could read it in the sudden flare of his eyes, in the set of his face. She went hot all over with the unexpected passion that boiled up so suddenly and had to turn away to get herself under control again.

"How about some coffee?" Erin asked them, handing Jason to his dad. "Ward, if you'll bring the playpen, the boys can come with us."

Ward, to his credit, tried to figure out how the device folded up, but he couldn't seem to fathom it. Ty chuckled. "Here, if Marianne will hold the boys, I'll do it."

"Surely!" She took them, cooing to them both, loving their little chubby smiling faces and the way they tried to feel every inch of her face and hair as she carried them into the living room.

"Oh, how sweet," she cooed, kissing fat cheeks and heads that had just a smattering of hair. The twins had light eyes like their father, but they were green.

"Thank God they both take after Erin and not me," Ty said with a sigh as he set up the playpen and took the boys from Marianne to put them back in.

"You're not that bad," Ward remarked, cocking his head. "I've seen uglier cactus plants, in fact."

Ty glared at him. "If you want that second damned lease, you'd better clean up your act, Jessup."

Ward grinned. "Can I help it if you go asking for insults?"

"Watch it," Ty muttered, turning back to help Erin with the coffee service.

The men talked business, and Marianne and Erin talked babies and clothes and fashion. It was the most enjoyable afternoon Marianne had spent in a long time and getting to cuddle the babies was a bonus. She was reluctant to leave.

"Ward, you'll have to bring her back to see me," Erin insisted. "I don't have much company, and I do love to talk clothes."

"I will," Ward promised. He shook hands with Ty, and they said their goodbyes. As they drove away, Ty had one lean arm around Erin, looking as if he were part of her.

"That marriage will outlast this ranch," she murmured, watching the landscape turn gray with a sudden shower. It seemed chilly in the car with that wetness beating on the hood and windshield. "They seem so happy."

"They are," he agreed. He glanced at her and slowly pulled the truck off onto one of the farm roads, pulling up under a huge live oak tree before cutting the engine. "Would you like to guess why I stopped?" he asked, his voice slow and tender as he looked at her. "Or do you know?"

Chapter 11

No, Marianne thought, she didn't really have to wonder why he'd parked the car. His face gave her the answer. So did the heavy, quick rise and fall of his chest under the green-striped shirt. He looked so handsome that she could hardly take her eyes off him, and the sheer arrogance in his narrowed eyes was intimidating.

But she wasn't sure she wanted a sweet interlude with him. Her defenses were weak enough already. Suppose he insisted? Could she resist him if she let herself fall in that heady trap?

"I don't think this is a good idea," she began as he unfastened his seat belt and then hers.

"Don't you?" he asked. "Even after the way you went scarlet when I stared at your waistline in the twins' room? You knew what I was thinking, Marianne," he whispered, reaching for her. "You knew."

He lifted her across him, finding her mouth even as he eased her down against his arm with her head at the window. Outside rain was streaming down the glass, making a quick tattoo on the hood and the roof, as driving as the passion that began to take over Mari's blood.

He bit at her soft lips, tender little nips that made her want him. His big hand smoothed over her blouse, under it, finding the softness of her breast in its silky casing.

"Lie still," he whispered when her body jerked under that gentle probing. "It's been a long time since we've enjoyed each other like this. Too long."

He kissed her wide eyes shut and found the catch that bared her to his warm, hard fingers. She couldn't let this happen, she kept telling herself. It was just a game to him, he didn't mean it. Any minute now he was going to let that seat down and turn her in his arms....

With a wounded cry she pulled out of his arms so suddenly that he was startled into releasing her. She fumbled the door open, deaf to his sharp exclamation, and ran out into the rain.

The long grass beat against her slacks as she ran, not really sure why she was running or where she was trying to go. Seconds later it didn't matter because he'd caught her and dragged her down onto the ground in the wet grass with him.

"Never run from a hunter," he breathed roughly, turning her under him as he found her mouth with his. The rain beat down on them, drenching them, making their bodies as supple as silk-covered saplings, binding them as if there had been no fabric at all in the way.

It was new and exciting to lie like this, to kiss like this, feeling the warm, twisting motions of Ward's big body against hers, their clothes wet and their skin sensitive.

"We might as well have no clothes on at all," he breathed into her open, welcoming mouth, his voice husky with passion. "I can feel you. All of you."

His hands were sliding down her body now, exploring, experiencing her through the wet thinness of fabric, and it was like feeling his hands on her skin.

She moaned as she slid her own hands against his hard-muscled back, his chest, his hips. She didn't understand what was happening, how this passion had crept up on her. But she was lost now, helpless. He could do anything he liked, and she couldn't stop him. She was on fire despite the drenching rain, reaching up toward him, sliding her wet body against his in the silence of the meadow with the rain slicking their hair as it slicked their skin.

He eased his full weight onto her, devouring her mouth with his. His hands smoothed under her back, sensuously pressing her up against him.

Her body throbbed, burned, with the expertness of his movements. Yes, he knew what to do and how to do it. He knew...too much!

"Tell me to stop," he challenged under his breath, probing her lips with his tongue. "Tell me to let you go. I dare you."

"I can't," she whimpered, and her eyes stung with tears as she clung to his broad, wet shoulders. "I want you. Oh, I want you!"

His lips were all over her face. Tender, seeking, gentling, his breath catching in his throat at her devastating submission. He was trembling all over with the force of this new sensation. He wanted to protect her. Devour her. Warm her. Hold her until he died, just like this.

His big hands framed her face as he touched it softly with his lips. "I want to give you a baby," he whispered shakily. "That's what you saw in my face at Wade's, and it made you go red all over. You saw, didn't you?"

"Yes," she whispered back, her body trembling.

He searched her wide eyes, his own blazing with hunger. "I could take you, Marianne," he said very quietly. "Right here. Right now. I could have you, and no one would see us or hear us."

She swallowed, closing her eyes. Defeated. She knew that. She could feel how capable he was of it, and her body trembled under his fierce arousal. She wanted him, too. She loved him more than her honor.

"Yes," she whispered, so softly that he could barely hear.

He didn't move. He seemed to stop breathing. She opened her eyes and saw his face above her, filled with such frank exultation that she blinked incomprehensibly.

"Baby," he breathed softly, bending. He kissed her with such aching tenderness that her eyes stung, tasting her lips, smoothing his lips over her cheeks, her forehead, her nose, her eyes. "Baby, sweet, sweet baby. You taste of roses and gardenias, and I could lie here doing this for all my life."

That didn't sound like uncontrollable passion. It didn't even sound like lust. She reached up and touched his face, his chin.

He kissed the palm of her hand, smiling down at her through wildly exciting shudders. "Do you know how wet you are?" he said with a gentle smile, glancing down at her blouse, which was plastered against breasts that no longer had the shelter of a bra.

"So are you," she replied unsteadily and managed to smile back. What good was pride now when she'd offered herself to him?

He touched her taut nipples through the cloth. "No more embarrassment?" he asked quietly.

"You know what I look like," she whispered.

"Yes." He opened her blouse, no longer interested in the rain that had slowed to a sprinkle, and his eyes feasted on her soft skin before he bent and tasted it warmly with his mouth.

Mari lifted softly toward his lips, savoring their sweet touch, so much a part of him that nothing seemed wrong anymore.

"You're so sweet," he whispered. He drew his cheek across her breasts, his eyes closed, savoring her. "For the rest of my life, I'll never touch another woman like this. I'll never lie with another woman, taste another woman, want another woman."

That was how she felt, too, about other men. She closed her eyes, smoothing his wet hair as he brushed his mouth over her pulsating, trembling body. She loved him so much. If this was all he could give her, it would be enough. Fidelity would do. She couldn't leave him again.

"I'll never want another man," she replied quietly.

He laid his cool cheek against her and sighed, holding her as she held him, with the wind blowing softly and the rain coming down like droplets of silk over them.

Then he moved away, gently rearranging her disheveled clothing. He brushed back her damp hair, kissed her tenderly one last time and carried her in his arms back to the car with her face pressed wetly into his warm throat.

"The car," she faltered. "We'll get the seats wet."

"Hush, baby," he whispered, brushing a kiss against her soft mouth as he put her into the passenger seat and fastened her seat belt. "It doesn't matter. Nothing matters now."

He got in beside her, found her warm hand and linked her fingers with his. He managed to start the car and drive it all the way home with one free hand.

Lillian took one look at them, and her eyebrows shot up.

"Not one word," Ward cautioned as he led Marianne inside. "Not one single word."

Lillian sighed. "Well, at least now you're getting wet together," she murmured with a smile as she wandered back toward the kitchen. "I guess that's better than mildewing alone."

Marianne smiled gently at Ward and went upstairs to change her clothing. He disappeared a few minutes later after an urgent telephone call and drove off by himself with only a wink and a smile for Mari. She walked around in a daze, dodging Lillian's hushed questions, waiting for him to come home. But when bedtime came, he still wasn't back.

Mari went up to her room and paced the floor, worrying, wondering what to do. She couldn't leave, not after this afternoon. He wanted her and she wanted him. Maybe he couldn't offer her marriage, but she'd just settle for what he could give her. He had to care a little. And she loved him enough for both of them.

Why hadn't he gone ahead, she wondered, when he had the chance this afternoon? Why had he stopped? Was he just giving her time to make up her mind, to be sure she could accept him this way? That had to be it. Well, it was now or never.

She put on her one seductive gown, a pretty white one with lots of lace and long elegant sleeves. She brushed out her dark hair until it was smooth and silky and dabbed on perfume. Then, looking in the mirror, she stared into her troubled blue eyes and assured herself that she was doing the right thing.

An hour later she heard Ward drive up. He came up the stairs, pausing at her door. Seconds later he started away, but Mari was already on her feet. She opened the door breathlessly and looked up at him.

He was wearing a dark pair of slacks with a patterned gray shirt open at the throat. His creamy dress Stetson was held in one hand. The other worried his hair. He stared at Mari with eyes that devoured her.

"Dangerous, baby, wearing something like that in front of me," he said softly and smiled.

She swallowed her pride. "I want you," she whispered shakily.

He smiled down at her. "I know. I want you, too."

She opened the door a little wider, her hands unsteady.

He cocked an eyebrow. "Is that an invitation to be seduced?"

She swallowed again. "I don't think I quite know how to seduce you. So I think you'll have to seduce me."

His smile widened. "What about precautions, little temptress?"

She blushed to her toes. She hadn't expected resistance. "Well," she began, peeking up at him, "can't you take care of that?"

His white teeth showed under his lips. "No."

Her blush deepened. "Oh."

He tossed his hat onto the hall table and went inside the room, gently closing the door behind him. "Now, come here." He drew her in front of him, holding her by both shoulders, his face gentle and almost loving. "What do you think I want, Marianne?"

"You've made what you want pretty obvious," she replied sadly.

"What you think I want," he corrected. His eyes went over her like hands, enjoying the exciting glimpses of her silky skin that he was getting through the gossamer-thin fabric of her gown. "And you're right about that. I could make a banquet of you in bed. But not tonight."

She turned her head a bit, looking up at him. "Are you too tired?" she asked innocently.

He grinned. "Nope."

None of this was getting through to her. "I don't understand," she said softly.

"Yes, I gathered that." He reached into his pocket and drew out a box. It was black and velvety and small. He opened it and handed it to her.

The ring was a diamond. A big, beautiful diamond in a setting with lots of little diamonds in rows encircling the large stone. Beside it was a smaller, thinner matching diamond band.

"It's an engagement ring," he explained. "It goes on the third finger of your left hand, and at the wedding I'll put the smaller one on your finger beside it."

She was hearing things. Surely she was! But the ring looked real. She couldn't stop staring at it.

"You don't want to get married," she told him patiently, her eyes big and soft. "You hate ties. You hate women. They're all deceitful and greedy."

He traced a slow, sensuous pattern down her silky cheek, smiling softly. "I want to get married," he said. "I want you to share your life with me."

It was the way he put it. She burst into tears. They rolled down her cheeks in a torrent, a sob broke from her throat. He became a big, handsome blur.

"Now, now," he murmured gently. He bent to kiss the tears away. "It's all right."

"You want to marry me?" she whispered unsteadily.

"Yes," he said, smiling.

"Really?"

"Really." He brushed back her hair, his green eyes possessive on her oval face. "I'd be a fool to let go of a woman who loves me as much as you do."

She froze in place. Was he fishing? Was he guessing? Did he know? If he did, how?

"You told me this afternoon," he said gently, pulling her to him. "You offered yourself to me with no strings. You'd never make an offer like that to a man you didn't love desperately. I knew it. And that's why I stopped. It would have been cheap, somehow, to have our first time on the ground without doing things properly."

"But...but..." she began, trying to find the right words.

"But how do I feel?" he probed softly, touching her lips with a faintly unsteady index finger. "Don't you know?"

His eyes were telling her. His whole face was telling her. But despite her rising excitement, she had to have it all. The words, too.

"Please tell me," she whispered.

He framed her face and lifted it to his darkening eyes, to his firm, hungry mouth. "I love you, Marianne," he breathed against her mouth as he took it. "And this is how much..."

It took him a long time to show her how much. When he was through, they were lying on the bed with her gown down to her waist, and he looked as if he were going to die trying to stop himself from going the whole way. Fortunately, or unfortunately, Lillian had guessed what was going on and was trying to knock the door down.

"It's bedtime, boss," she called loudly. "It's late. She's a growing girl. Needs her sleep!"

"Oh, no, that's not what I need at all," Marianne said with such tender frustration that Ward laughed through his own shuddering need.

"Okay, aunt-to-be," he called back. "Give me a minute to say good-night and I'll be right out."

"You're getting married?" Lillian shouted gleefully.

"That's about the size of it," he answered, smiling down at Mari. "Aren't you just overjoyed with your meddling now?"

"Overjoyed doesn't cover it," Lillian agreed. "Now, speaking as your future aunt-in-law, come out of there! Or wait until supper tomorrow night and see if you get fed! We're going to do this thing right!"

"I was just about to do this thing right," he whispered to Mari, his eyes softly mocking. "Wasn't I?"

"Yes." She laughed. "But we can't admit that."

"We can't?" He sighed. "I guess not."

He got up reluctantly, rebuttoning the shirt that her darting fingers had opened over a chest that was aching for her hands. "Pretty thing," he murmured, watching her pull the gown up again.

"You're pretty, too, so there," she teased.

"Are you coming out, or am I coming in?" Lillian was sounding militant.

Ward glowered at the door. "Can't I even have a minute to say good-night?"

"You've been saying good-night for thirty minutes already, and that's enough," she informed him. "I'm counting! One, two, three…"

She was counting loudly. Ward sighed at Mari. "Good night, baby," he said reluctantly.

She blew him a kiss. "Good night, my darling."

He took one last look and opened the door on "…Fourteen!"

Mari laid back against the pillows, listening to the pleasant murmur of voices outside the door as she stared at her ring.

"Congratulations and good night, dear!" Aunt Lillian called.

"Good night and thank you!" Mari called back.

"Oh, you're very welcome!" Ward piped in.

"Get out of here," Lillian muttered, pushing him down the hall.

Alone in her room Mari was trying to convince herself that she wasn't dreaming. It was the hardest thing she'd ever done. He was hers. They were going to be married. They were going to live together and love each other and have children together. She closed her eyes reluctantly, tingling all over with the first stirrings of possession.

Chapter 12

The next morning Mari was sure it had all been a beautiful dream until she looked at the ring on her finger. When she went down to breakfast, she found a new, different Ward waiting for her.

He went to her without hesitation, bending to brush a tender kiss against her smiling lips.

"It was real after all," he murmured, his green eyes approving her cool blue knit sundress. "I thought I might have dreamed it."

"So did I," she confessed. Her hands smoothed hesitantly over the hard, warm muscles of his chest. It felt wonderful to be able to do that, to feel so much a part of him that it no longer was forbidden to touch him, to look at him too long. "Are you really mine now?" she murmured aloud.

"Until I die," he promised, bringing her close against him. He sighed into her hair, rocking her against the powerful muscles of his body. "I never thought this would happen. I didn't think I'd ever be able to love or trust a woman again after Caroline. And then you came along, pushing me into indoor streams, backing me into corners about my business sense, haunting me with your soft innocence. You got under my skin that first night. I've spent the rest of the time trying to convince myself that I was still free when I knew all along that I was hopelessly in love with you."

She burrowed closer, tingling all over at that sweet, possessive note in his deep voice. "I was so miserable in Atlanta," she confessed. "I missed you every single day. I tried to get used to being alone."

"I shouldn't have propositioned you," he said with a sigh, lifting his head to search her eyes with his. "But I still thought I could stop short of a commitment. God knows how I'd have coped with the conscience I didn't even have until you came along. Every time Ty Wade was mentioned, I got my back up, thinking how he'd changed." He touched her face with wonder in his whole look. "And now I know how and why, and I think he must have felt this way with his Erin when he realized what he felt for her."

She sighed softly, loving him with her eyes. "I know I felt like part of me was missing when I left here. It didn't get any better, either."

"Why do you think I came after you?" he murmured dryly. "I couldn't stand it here without you. Not that I admitted that to myself in any great rush. Not until that rattler almost got you, and I had to face it. If anything had happened to you, I wouldn't have wanted to live," he added on a deep, husky note that tugged at her heart.

"I feel that way, too," she whispered, searching his eyes. "Can we really get married?"

"Yes," he whispered back, bending his head down. "And live together and sleep together and raise a family together..."

Her lips opened for him, welcoming and warm, just for a few seconds before Lillian came in with breakfast and knowing grins. Ward glowered at her.

"All your fault," he told her. "I could have gone on for years living like a timber wolf but for you."

"No need to thank me," she said with a big smile. "You're welcome."

She vanished back into the kitchen, laughing, as Ward led Mari to the table, shaking his head with an exasperated chuckle.

The wedding was a week later, and old Mrs. Jessup and Belinda had come home just for the occasion. They sat on either side of Lillian, who was beaming.

"Nice girl," Belinda whispered. "She'll make a new man of him."

"I think she has already." Old Mrs. Jessup grinned. "Spirited little thing. I like her, too."

"I always did," Lillian said smugly. "Good thing I saw the shape he was getting in and brought her out here. I knew they'd be good for each other."

"It isn't nice to gloat," Belinda reminded her.

"Amen," Mrs. Jessup harrumphed. "Don't I seem to remember that you introduced that Caroline creature to him in the first place?"

Lillian was horrified. "That wasn't me! That was Belinda!"

Mrs. Jessup's eyes widened as she glared past Lillian at the restless young woman on the other side. "Did you?"

"It was an accident," Belinda muttered. "I meant to introduce her to Bob Whitman, to get even for jilting me. Ward kind of got in the way. I never meant for her to go after my poor brother."

"It's all in the past now anyway," Lillian said, making peace. "He's got the right girl, now. Everything will be fine."

"Yes." Old Mrs. Jessup sighed, glancing past Lillian again. "If only Belinda would settle down. She goes from boyfriend to boyfriend, but she never seems to get serious."

Lillian pursed her lips, following the older woman's gaze to Belinda, who was sighing over Mari's wedding gown as she walked down the aisle accompanied by the organ music. She'd have to see what she could do....

The wedding ceremony was short and beautiful. Mari thought she'd never seen a man as handsome as her Ward, and when the minister pronounced them husband and wife, she cried softly until Ward kissed away the tears.

Lillian, not Belinda, caught the wedding bouquet and blushed like a schoolgirl when everyone giggled. The guests threw rice and waved them off, and Mari caught a glimpse of tall, slender Ty Wade with his Erin just on the fringe of the guests.

"Alone at last." Ward grinned, glancing at her.

"I thought they'd never leave," she agreed with a wistful sigh. "Where are we going? I didn't even ask."

"Tahiti," he said with a slow smile. "I booked tickets the day after you said yes. We're flying out of San Antonio early tomorrow morning."

"What about tonight?" she asked curiously and flushed at the look on his face.

"Let me worry about tonight," he murmured softly.

He held her hand as he drove, and an hour later he drove up to a huge, expensive hotel in the city.

He'd reserved the bridal suite, and it was the most incredible sight Mari had ever seen. The bed was huge, dominating the bedroom. She stood in the doorway just staring at it while Ward paid the bellhop and locked the door.

"It's huge," she whispered.

"And strategically placed, did you notice?" he murmured with a laugh, suddenly lifting her clear of the floor in her neat white linen traveling suit.

"Yes, I did notice," she said huskily, clinging to him. "You looked so handsome."

"You looked so lovely." He bent to her mouth and started walking. "I love you to distraction, did I tell you?"

"Several times."

"I hope you won't mind hearing it again frequently for the next hour or so," he murmured against her eager mouth and laid her gently down on the bed.

Mari had expected ardor and passion, and she had experienced a tiny measure of apprehension. But he made it so natural, so easy. She relaxed even as he began to undress her, his hands and mouth so deeply imprinted on her memory that she accepted them without the faintest protest.

"This is familiar territory for us, isn't it?" he breathed as he moved back beside her after stripping off his own clothing. "Up to this point, at least," he added at her rapt, faintly shocked visual exploration of him. "But you know how it feels to have my eyes and my hands and my mouth on you. You know that I won't hurt you. That there's nothing to be afraid of."

She looked back up into his eyes. "I couldn't be afraid of you."

"I won't lose control right away," he promised, bending slowly to her mouth. "Give yourself to me now, Mari. Remember how it was on the ground, with the rain soaking us, and give yourself to me the way you offered then."

She felt all over again the pelting rain, the sweetness of his hands, the wild fever of his mouth claiming hers in the silence of the meadow. She reached up to him, suddenly on fire with the unaccustomed removal of all barriers, physical and moral, and she gave herself with an abandon that frankly startled him.

''Shhh,'' she whispered when he tried to draw back at the last minute, to make it gentle, to keep from hurting her. But she reached up to his hips and softly drew them down again, lifting, and a tiny gasp was the only sound she made as she coaxed his mouth back to hers. ''Now,'' she breathed into his devouring lips. ''Now, now...''

''Mari,'' he groaned. His body surged against hers, his arms became painfully strong, his hands biting into her hips, his mouth trembling as his body trembled. He was part of her. She was part of him. Locking together, loving, linking...

''Mari!''

She went with him on a journey as exquisitely sweet as it was incredibly intimate, yielding to his strength, letting him guide her, letting him teach her. She used muscles she hadn't realized she possessed, she whispered things to him that would shock her later. She wound herself around him and lost all her inhibitions in a wild, fierce joining that ripped the veil of mystery from the sweetest expression of shared love. Even the first time it was still a kind of pleasure that she hadn't known existed.

She stretched lazily, contentedly, and snuggled close to him under the lightweight sheet, nuzzling against his matted chest with a face radiant with fulfillment.

''I love you,'' he said softly as if the words still awed him. He smoothed her hair tenderly. ''I always will.''

''I love you just as much.'' She smoothed her hand over his chest. ''Cousin Bud wasn't at the wedding.'' She frowned. Her mind had been curiously absent for a week. She lifted up. ''Ward, Bud hasn't been at the house!''

''Not for a week,'' he agreed complacently, grinning. ''Not since that day I took you to see Ty and Erin.''

''But this is horrible! I didn't notice!''

''That's all right, sweetheart, I don't mind,'' he said, drawing her back down.

"Where is he?"

"Oh, I sent him on a little trip," he murmured at her temple. "I told him that bull he wanted was out to stud at a cattle ranch in Montana, and he went up there looking."

"Looking?" she frowned.

"Well, honey, I didn't exactly tell him which ranch it was on. Just the state. There are a lot of ranches in Montana."

"You devil!" she accused, digging him in the ribs.

He pulled her over him, smiling from ear to ear. "All's fair, don't they say? Cousin Bud always did cramp my style." He coaxed her mouth down to his and kissed it softly. "I didn't want him on my case until I had you safely married to me."

"You couldn't have been jealous?"

"I've always been jealous," he confessed, tugging a strand of her hair playfully. "You were mine. I didn't want him trying to cut me out. Don't worry, he'll figure it out eventually."

"I shouldn't ask," she mumbled. "Figure what out?"

"That the bull is still on my ranch, just where I had him all along."

"What are you going to tell Cousin Bud?"

"That I misplaced him," he said easily. "Don't worry, he'll believe me. After all, he didn't think I was serious about you, either, and look how I fooled him!"

She would have said something else, but he was already rolling her over on the big bed and kissing the breath out of her. So she just closed her eyes and kissed him back. Outside it was raining softly, and Mari thought she'd never heard a sweeter sound.

THE PRINCESS BRIDE

For Matt and Elisha

Chapter 1

Tiffany saw him in the distance, riding the big black stallion that had already killed one man. She hated the horse, even as she admitted silently how regal it looked with the tall, taciturn man on its back. A killer horse it might be, but it respected Kingman Marshall. Most people around Jacobsville, Texas, did. His family had lived on the Guadalupe River there since the Civil War, on a ranch called Lariat.

It was Spring, and that meant roundup. It was nothing unusual to see the owner of Lariat in the saddle at dawn lending a hand to rope a stray calf or help work the branding. King kept fit with ranch work, and despite the fact that he shared an office and a business partnership with her father in land and cattle, his staff didn't see a lot of him.

This year, they were using helicopters to mass the far-flung cattle, and they had a corral set up on a wide flat stretch of land where they could dip the cattle, check them, cut out the calves for branding and separate them from their mothers. It was physically demanding work, and no job for a tenderfoot. King wouldn't let Tiffany near it, but it wasn't a front row seat at the corral that she wanted. If she could just get his attention away from the milling cattle on the wide, rolling plain that led to the Guadalupe River, if he'd just look her way...

She stood up on a rickety lower rung of the gray wood fence, avoiding the sticky barbed wire, and waved her creamy Stetson at him. She was a picture of young elegance in her tan jodphurs and sexy pink silk blouse and high black boots. She was a debutante. Her father, Harrison Blair, was King's business partner and friend, and if she chased King, her father encouraged her. It would be a marriage made in heaven. That is, if she could find some way to convince King of it. He was elusive and quite abrasively masculine. It might take more than a young lady of almost twenty-one with a sheltered, monied background to land him. But, then, Tiffany had confidence in herself; she was beautiful and intelligent.

Her long black hair hung to her waist in back, and she refused to have it cut. It suited her tall, slender figure and made an elegant frame for her soft oval face and wide green eyes and creamy complexion. She had a sunny smile, and it never faded. Tiffany was always full of fire, burning with a love of life that her father often said had been reflected in her long-dead mother.

"King!" she called, her voice clear, and it carried in the early-morning air.

He looked toward her. Even at the distance, she could see that cold expression in his pale blue eyes, on his lean, hard face with its finely chiseled features. He was a rich man. He worked hard, and he played hard. He had women, Tiffany knew he did, but he was nothing if not discreet. He was a man's man, and he lived like one. There was no playful boy in that tall, fit body. He'd grown up years ago, the boyishness burned out of him by a rich, alcoholic father who demanded blind obedience from the only child of his shallow, runaway wife.

She watched him ride toward her, easy elegance in the saddle. He reined in at the fence, smiling down at her with faint arrogance. He was powerfully built, with long legs and slim hips and broad shoulders. There wasn't an ounce of fat on him, and with his checked red shirt open at the throat, she got fascinating glimpses of bronzed muscle and thick black hair on the expanse of his sexy chest. Jeans emphasized the powerful muscles of his legs, and he had big, elegant hands that hers longed to feel in passion. Not that she was likely to. He treated her like a child most of the time, or at best, a minor irritation.

"You're out early, tidbit," he remarked in a deep, velvety voice with just a hint of Texas drawl. His eyes, under the shade of his wide-brimmed hat, were a pale, grayish blue and piercing as only blue eyes could be.

"I'm going to be twenty-one tomorrow," she said pertly. "I'm having a big bash to celebrate, and you have to come. Black tie, and don't you dare bring anyone. You're mine, for the whole evening. It's my birthday and on my birthday I want presents—and you're it. My big present."

His dark brows lifted with amused indulgence. "You might have told me sooner that I was going to be a birthday present," he said. "I have to be in Omaha early Saturday."

"You have your own plane," she reminded him. "You can fly."

"I have to sleep sometimes," he murmured.

"I wouldn't touch that line with a ten-foot pole," she drawled, peeking at him behind her long lashes. "Will you come? If you don't, I'll stuff a pillow up my dress and accuse you of being the culprit. And your reputation will be ruined, you'll be driven out of town on a rail, they'll tar and feather you..."

He chuckled softly at the vivid sparkle in her eyes, the radiant smile. "You witch," he accused. "They'd probably give me a medal for getting through your defenses."

She wondered how he knew that, and reasoned that her proud parent had probably told him all about her reputation for coolness with men.

He lit a cigarette, took a long draw from and blew it out with faint impatience. "Little girls and their little whims," he mused. "All right, I'll whirl you around the floor and toast your coming of age, but I won't stay. I can't spare the time."

"You'll work yourself to death," she complained, and she was solemn now. "You're only thirty-four and you look forty."

"Times are hard, honey," he mused, smiling at the intensity in that glowering young face. "We've had low prices and drought. It's all I can do to keep my financial head above water."

"You could take the occasional break," she advised. "And I don't mean a night on the town. You could get away from it all and just rest."

"They're full up at the Home," he murmured, grinning at her exasperated look. "Honey, I can't afford vacations, not with times so hard. What are you wearing for this coming-of-age party?" he asked to divert her.

"A dream of a dress. White silk, very low in front, with diamanté straps and a white gardenia in my hair." She laughed.

He pursed his lips. He might as well humor her. "That sounds dangerous," he said softly.

"It will be," she promised, teasing him with her eyes. "You might even notice that I've grown up."

He frowned a little. That flirting wasn't new, but it was disturbing lately. He found himself avoiding little Miss Blair, without really understanding why. His body stirred even as he looked at her, and he moved restlessly in the saddle. She was years too young for him, and a virgin to boot, according to her doting, sheltering father. All those years of obsessive parental protection had led to a very immature and unavailable girl. It wouldn't do to let her too close. Not that anyone ever got close to Kingman Marshall, not even his infrequent lovers. He had good reason to keep women at a distance. His upbringing had taught him too well that women were untrustworthy and treacherous.

"What time?" he asked on a resigned note.

"About seven?"

He paused thoughtfully for a minute. "Okay." He tilted his wide-brimmed hat over his eyes. "But only for an hour or so."

"Great!"

He didn't say goodbye. Of course, he never had. He wheeled the stallion and rode off, man and horse so damned arrogant that she felt like flinging something at his tall head. He was delicious, she thought, and her body felt hot all over just looking at him. On the ground he towered over her, lean and hard-muscled and sexy as all hell. She loved watching him.

With a long, unsteady sigh, she finally turned away and remounted her mare. She wondered sometimes why she bothered hero-worshiping such a man. One of these days he'd get married and she'd just die. God forbid that he'd marry anybody but herself!

That was when the first shock of reality hit her squarely between the eyes. Why, she had to ask herself, would a man like that, a mature man with all the worldly advantages, want a young and inexperienced woman like herself at his side? The question worried her so badly that she almost lost control of her mount. She'd never questioned her chances with King before. She'd never dared. The truth of her situation was unpalatable and a little frightening. She'd never even considered a life without him. What if she had to?

As she rode back toward her own house, on the property that joined King's massive holdings, she noticed the color of the grass. It was like barbed wire in places, very dry and scant. That boded ill for the cattle, and if rain didn't come soon, all that new grass was going to burn up under a hot Texas sun. She knew a lot about the cattle business. After all, her father had owned feedlots since her youth, and she was an only child who worked hard to share his interests. She knew that if there wasn't enough hay by the end of summer, King was going to have to import feed to get his cattle through the winter. The cost of that was prohibitive. It had something to do with black figures going red in the last column, and that could mean disaster for someone with a cow-calf operation the size of King's.

Ah, well, she mused, if King went bust, she supposed that she could get a job and support him. Just the thought of it doubled her over with silvery laughter. King's pride would never permit that sort of help.

Even the Guadalupe was down. She sat on a small rise in the trees, looking at its watery width. The river, like this part of Texas, had a lot of history in it. Archaeologists had found Indian camps on the Guadalupe that dated back seven thousand years, and because of that, part of it had been designated a National Historic Shrine.

In more recent history, freight handlers on their way to San Antonio had crossed the river in DeWitt County on a ferryboat. In Cuero, a nice drive from Lariat, was the beginning of the Chisolm Trail. In nearby Goliad County was the small town of Goliad, where Texas patriots were slaughtered by the Mexican army back in 1836, just days after the bloodbath at the Alamo. Looking at the landscape, it was easy to imagine the first Spanish settlers, the robed priests founding missions, the Mexican Army with proud, arrogant Santa Anna at its fore, the Texas patriots fighting to the last breath, the pioneers and the settlers, the Indians and the immigrants, the cowboys and cattle barons and desperadoes. Tiffany sighed, trying to imagine it all.

King, she thought, would have fitted in very well with the past.

Except that he had a blasé attitude toward life and women, probably a result of having too much money and time on his hands. Despite his hard work at roundup, he spent a lot of time in his office, and on the phone, and also on the road. He was so geared to making money that he seemed to have forgotten how to enjoy it. She rode home slowly, a little depressed because she'd had to work so hard just to get King to agree to come to her party. And still haunting her was that unpleasant speculation about a future without King.

Her father was just on his way out the door when she walked up from the stables. The house was stucco, a big sprawling yellow ranch house. It had a small formal garden off the patio, a swimming pool behind, a garage where Tiffany's red Jaguar convertible and her father's gray Mercedes-Benz dwelled, and towering live oak and pecan trees all around. The Guadalupe River was close, but not too close, and Texas stretched like a yellow-green bolt of cloth in all directions to an open, spacious horizon.

"There you are," Harrison Blair muttered. He was tall and gray-headed and green-eyed. Very elegant, despite his slight paunch and his habit of stooping because of a bad back. "I'm late for a board meeting. The caterer called about your party…something about the cheese straws not doing."

"I'll give Lettie a ring. She'll do them for her if I ask her nicely," she promised, grinning as she thought of the elderly lady who was her godmother. "King's coming to my party. I ran him to ground at the river."

He looked over his glasses at her, his heavily lined face vaguely reminiscent of an anorexic bassett hound; not that she'd ever have said anything hurtful to her parent. She adored him. "You make him sound like a fox," he remarked. "Careful, girl, or you'll chase him into a hollow stump and lose him."

"Not me," she laughed, her whole face bright with young certainty. "You just wait. I'll be dangling a diamond one of these days. He can't resist me. He just doesn't know it yet."

He only shook his head. She was so young. She hadn't learned yet that life had a way of giving with one hand, only to take back with the other. Oh, well, she had plenty of years to learn those hard lessons. Let her enjoy it while she could. He knew that King would never settle for a child-woman like his beautiful daughter, but it was something she was going to have to accept one of these days.

"I hope to be back by four," he said, reaching down to peck her affectionately on one cheek. "Are we having champagne? If we are, I hope you told the caterer. I'm not breaking out my private stock until you get married."

"Yes, we are, and yes, I told them," she assured him. "After all, I don't become twenty-one every day."

He studied her with quiet pride. "You look like your mother," he said. "She'd be as proud of you as I am."

She smiled faintly. "Yes." Her mother had been dead a long time, but the memories were bittersweet. The late Mrs. Blair had been vivacious and sparkling, a sapphire in a diamond setting. Her father had never remarried, and seemed not to be inclined toward the company of other women. He'd told Tiffany once that true love was a pretty rare commodity. He and her mother had been so blessed. He was content enough with his memories.

"How many people are we expecting, by the way?" he asked as he put on his Stetson.

"About forty," she said. "Not an overwhelming number. Just some of my friends and some of King's." She grinned. "I'm making sure they're compatible before I railroad him to the altar."

He burst out laughing. She was incorrigible and definitely his child, with her keen business sense, he told himself.

"Do you reckon they'll have a lot in common?"

She pursed her pretty lips. "Money and cattle," she reminded him, "are always a good mix. Besides, King's friends are almost all politicians. They pride themselves on finding things in common with potential voters."

He winked. "Good thought."

She waved and went to call Lettie about doing the cheese straws and the caterers to finalize the arrangements. She was a good hostess, and she enjoyed parties. It was a challenge to find compatible people and put them together in a hospitable atmosphere. So far, she'd done well. Now it was time to show King how organized she was.

The flowers and the caterer had just arrived when she went down the long hall to her room to dress. She was nibbling at a chicken wing on the way up, hoping that she wouldn't starve. There was going to be an hors d'oeuvres table and a drinks bar, but no sit-down dinner. She'd decided that she'd rather dance than eat, and she'd hired a competent local band to play. They were in the ballroom now, tuning up, while Cass, the housekeeper, was watching some of the ranch's lean, faintly disgusted cowboys set up chairs and clear back the furniture. They hated being used as inside labor and their accusing glances let her know it. But she grinned and they melted. Most of them were older hands who'd been with her father since she was a little girl. Like her father, they'd spoiled her, too.

She darted up the staircase, wild with excitement about the evening ahead. King didn't come to the house often, only when her father wanted to talk business away from work, or occasionally for drinks with some of her father's acquaintances. To have him come to a party was new and stimulating. Especially if it ended the way she planned. She had her sights well and truly set on the big rancher. Now she had to take aim.

Chapter 2

Tiffany's evening gown was created by a San Antonio designer, who also happened to own a boutique in one of the larger malls there. Since Jacobsville was halfway between San Antonio and Victoria, it wasn't too long a drive. Tiffany had fallen in love with the gown at first sight. The fact that it had cost every penny of her allowance hadn't even slowed her down. It was simple, sophisticated, and just the thing to make King realize she was a woman. The low-cut bodice left the curve of her full breasts seductively bare and the diamanté straps were hardly any support at all. They looked as if they might give way any second, and that was the charm of the dress. Its silky white length fell softly to just the top of her oyster satin pumps with their rhinestone clips. She put her long hair in an elaborate hairdo, and pinned it with diamond hairpins. The small silk gardenia in a soft wave was a last-minute addition, and the effect was dynamite. She looked innocently seductive. Just right.

She was a little nervous as she made her way down the curve of the elegant, gray-carpeted staircase. Guests were already arriving, and most of these early ones were around King's age. They were successful businessmen, politicians mostly, with exquisitely dressed wives and girlfriends on their arms. For just an instant, Tiffany felt young and uneasy. And then she pinned on her finishing-school smile and threw herself into the job of hostessing.

She pretended beautifully. No one knew that her slender legs were unsteady. In fact, a friend of one of the younger politicians, a bachelor clerk named Wyatt Corbin, took the smile for an invitation and stuck to her like glue. He was good-looking in a tall, gangly redheaded way, but he wasn't very sophisticated. Even if he had been, Tiffany had her heart set on King, and she darted from group to group, trying to shake her admirer.

Unfortunately he was stubborn. He led her onto the dance floor and into a gay waltz, just as King came into the room.

Tiffany felt like screaming. King looked incredibly handsome in his dark evening clothes. His tuxedo emphasized his dark good looks, and the white of his silk shirt brought out his dark eyes and hair. He spared Tiffany an amused glance and turned to meet the onslaught of two unattached, beautiful older women. His secretary, Carla Stark, hadn't been invited—Tiffany had been resolute about that. There was enough gossip about those two, already, and Carla was unfair competition.

It was the unkindest cut of all, and thanks to this redheaded clown dancing with her, she'd lost her chance. She smiled sweetly at him and suddenly brought down her foot on his toe with perfect accuracy.

"Ouch!" he moaned, sucking in his breath.

"I'm so sorry, Wyatt," Tiffany murmured, batting her eyelashes at him. "Did I step on your poor foot?"

"My fault, I moved the wrong way," he drawled, forcing a smile. "You dance beautifully, Miss Blair."

What a charming liar, she thought. She glanced at King, but he wasn't even looking at her. He was talking and smiling at a devastating blonde, probably a politician's daughter, who looked as if she'd just discovered the best present of all under a Christmas tree. No thanks to me, Tiffany thought miserably.

Well, two could play at ignoring, she thought, and turned the full effect of her green eyes on Wyatt. Well, happy birthday to me, she thought silently, and asked him about his job. It was assistant city clerk or some such thing, and he held forth about his duties for the rest of the waltz, and the one that followed.

King had moved to the sofa with the vivacious little blonde, where he looked as if he might set up housekeeping. Tiffany wanted to throw back her head and scream with outrage. Whose party was this, anyway, and which politician was that little blonde with? She began scanning the room for unattached older men.

"I guess I ought to dance with Becky, at least once," Wyatt sighed after a minute. "She's my cousin. I didn't have anyone else to bring. Excuse me a second, will you?"

He left her and went straight toward the blonde who was dominating King. But if he expected the blonde to sacrifice that prize, he was sadly mistaken. They spoke in whispers, while King glanced past Wyatt at Tiffany with a mocking, worldly look. She turned her back and went to the punch bowl.

Wyatt was back in a minute. "She doesn't mind being deserted," he chuckled. "She's found a cattle baron to try her wiles on. That's Kingman Marshall over there, you know."

Tiffany looked at him blankly. "Oh, is it?" she asked innocently, and tried not to show how furious she really was. Between Wyatt and his cousin, they'd ruined her birthday party.

"I wonder why he's here?" he frowned.

She caught his hand. "Let's dance," she muttered, and dragged him back onto the dance floor.

For the rest of the evening, she monopolized Wyatt, ignoring King as pointedly as if she'd never seen him before and never cared to again. Let him flirt with other women at her party. Let him break her heart. He was never going to know it. She'd hold her chin up if it killed her. She smiled at Wyatt and flirted outrageously, the very life and soul of her party, right up to the minute when she cut the cake and asked Wyatt to help her serve it. King didn't seem to notice or care that she ignored him. But her father was puzzled, staring at her incomprehensibly.

"This party is so boring," Tiffany said an hour later, when she felt she couldn't take another single minute of the blonde clinging to King on the dance floor. "Let's go for a ride."

Wyatt looked uncomfortable. "Well...I came in a truck," he began.

"We'll take my Jag."

"You've got a Jaguar?"

She didn't need to say another word. Without even a glance in King's direction, she waved at her father and blew him a kiss, dragging Wyatt along behind her toward the front door. Not that he needed much coaxing. He seemed overwhelmed when she tossed him the keys and climbed into the passenger seat of the sleek red car.

"You mean, I can drive this?" he burst out.

"Sure. Go ahead. It's insured. But I like to go fast, Wyatt," she said. And for tonight, that was true. She was sick of the party, sick of King, sick of her life. She hurt in ways she'd never realized she could. She only wanted to get away, to escape.

He started the car and stood down on the accelerator. Tiffany had her window down, letting the breeze whip through her hair. She deliberately pulled out the diamond hairpins and tucked them into her purse, letting her long, black hair free and fly on the wind. The champagne she'd had to drink was beginning to take effect and was making her feel very good indeed. The speed of the elegant little car added to her false euphoria. Why, she didn't care about King's indifference. She didn't care at all!

"What a car!" Wyatt breathed, wheeling it out onto the main road.

"Isn't it, though?" she laughed. She leaned back and closed her eyes. She wouldn't think about King. "Go faster, Wyatt, we're positively crawling! I love speed, don't you?"

Of course he did. And he didn't need a second prompting. He put the accelerator peddle to the floor, and twelve cylinders jumped into play as the elegant vehicle shot forward like its sleek and dangerous namesake.

She laughed, silvery bells in the darkness, enjoying the unbridled speed, the fury of motion. Yes, this would blow away all the cobwebs, all the hurt, this would...!

The sound of sirens behind them brought her to her senses. She glanced over the seat and saw blue bubbles spinning around, atop a police car.

"Oh, for heaven's sake, where did he come from!" she gasped. "I never saw the car. They must parachute down from treetops," she muttered, and then giggled at her own remark.

Wyatt slowed the car and pulled onto the shoulder, his face rapidly becoming the color of his hair. He glanced at Tiffany. "Gosh, I'm sorry. And on your birthday, too!"

"I don't care. I told you to do it," she reminded him.

A tall policeman came to the side of the car and watched Wyatt fumble to power the window down.

"Good God. *Wyatt?*" the officer gasped.

"That's right, Bill," Wyatt sighed, producing his driver's license. "Tiffany Blair, this is Bill Harris. He's one of our newest local policemen and a cousin of mine."

"Nice to meet you, officer—although I wish it was under better circumstances," Tiffany said with a weak smile. "I should get the ticket, not Wyatt. It's my car, and I asked him to go faster."

"I clocked you at eighty-five, you know," he told Wyatt gently. "I sure do hate to do this, Wyatt. Mr. Clark is going to be pretty sore at you. He just had a mouthful to say about speeders."

"The mayor hates me anyway," Wyatt groaned.

"I won't tell him you got a ticket if you don't." Bill grinned.

"Want to bet he'll find out anyway? Just wait."

"It's all my fault," Tiffany muttered. "And it's my birthday...!"

A sleek, new black European sports car slid in behind the police car and came to a smooth, instant stop. A minute later, King got out and came along to join the small group.

"What's the trouble, Bill?" he asked the policeman.

"They were speeding, Mr. Marshall," the officer said. "I'll have to give him a ticket. He was mortally flying."

"I can guess why," King mused, staring past Wyatt at a pale Tiffany.

"Nobody held a gun on me," Wyatt said gently. "It's my own fault. I could have refused."

"The first lesson of responsibility," King agreed. "Learning to say no. Come on, Tiffany. You've caused enough trouble for one night. I'll drop you off on my way out."

"I won't go one step with you, King...!" she began furiously.

He went around to the passenger side of the Jag, opened the door, and tugged her out. His lean, steely fingers on her bare arm raised chills of excitement where they touched. "I don't have time to argue. You've managed to get Wyatt in enough trouble." He turned to Wyatt. "If you'll bring the Jag back, I think your cousin is ready to leave. Sorry to spoil your evening."

"It wasn't spoiled at all, Mr. Marshall," Wyatt said with a smile at Tiffany. "Except for the speeding ticket, I enjoyed every minute of it!"

"I did, too, Wyatt," Tiffany said. "I...King, will you stop dragging me?"

"No. Good night, Wyatt. Bill."

A chorus of good-nights broke the silence as King led an unwilling, sullen Tiffany back to his own leather-trimmed sports car. He helped her inside, got in under the wheel and started the powerful engine.

"I hate you, King," she ground out as he pulled onto the highway.

"Which is no reason at all for making a criminal of Wyatt."

She glared at him hotly through the darkness. "I did not make him a criminal! I only offered to let him drive the Jaguar."

"And told him how fast to go?"

"He wasn't complaining!"

He glanced sideways at her. Despite the rigid set of her body, and the temper on that lovely face, she excited him. One diamanté strap was halfway down a silky smooth arm, revealing more than a little of a tip-tilted breast. The silk fabric outlined every curve of her body, and he could smell the floral perfume that wafted around her like a seductive cloud. She put his teeth on edge, and it irritated him beyond all reason.

He lit a cigarette that he didn't even want, and abruptly put it out, remembering belatedly that he'd quit smoking just last week. And he was driving faster than he normally did. "I don't know why in hell you invited me over here," he said curtly, "if you planned to spend the whole evening with the damned city clerk."

"Assistant city clerk," she mumbled. She darted a glance at him and pressed a strand of long hair away from her mouth. He looked irritated. His face was harder than usual, and he was driving just as fast as Wyatt had been.

"Whatever the hell he is."

"I didn't realize you'd even noticed what I was doing, King," she replied sweetly, "what with Wyatt's pretty little cousin wrapped around you like a ribbon."

His eyebrows arched. "Wrapped around me?"

"Wasn't she?" she asked, averting her face. "Sorry. It seemed like it to me."

He pulled the car onto the side of the road and turned toward her, letting the engine idle. The hand holding the steering wheel clenched, but his dark eyes were steady on hers; she could see them in the light from the instrument panel.

"Were you jealous, honey?" he taunted, in a tone she'd never heard him use. It was deep and smooth and low-pitched. It made her young body tingle in the oddest way.

"I thought you were supposed to be my guest, that's all," she faltered.

"That's what I thought, too, until you started vamping Wyatt whats-his-name."

His finger toyed with the diamanté strap that had fallen onto her arm. She reached to tug it up, but his lean, hard fingers were suddenly there, preventing her.

Her eyes levered up to meet his quizzically, and in the silence of the car, she could hear her own heartbeat, like a faint drum.

The lean forefinger traced the strap from back to front, softly brushing skin that had never known a man's touch before. She stiffened a little, to feel it so lightly tracing the slope of her breast.

"They...they'll miss us," she said in a voice that sounded wildly high-pitched and frightened.

"Think so?"

He smiled slowly, because he was exciting her, and he liked it. He could see her breasts rising and falling with quick, jerky breaths. He could see her nipples peaking under that silky soft fabric. The pulse in her throat was quick, too, throbbing. She was coming-of-age tonight, in more ways than one.

He reached beside him and slowly, blatantly, turned off the engine before he turned back to Tiffany. There was a full moon, and the light of it and the subdued light of the instrument panel gave him all the illumination he needed.

"King," she whispered shakily.

"Don't panic," he said quietly. "It's going to be delicious."

She watched his hand move, as if she were paralyzed. It drew the strap even further off her arm, slowly, relentlessly, tugging until that side of her silky bodice fell to the hard tip of her nipple. And then he gave it a whisper of a push and it fell completely away, baring her pretty pink breast to eyes that had seen more than their share of women. But this was different. This was Tiffany, who was virginal and young and completely without experience.

That knowledge hardened his body. His lean fingers traced her collarbone, his eyes lifted to search her quiet, faintly shocked face. Her eyes were enormous. Probably this was all new to her, and perhaps a little frightening as well.

"You're of age, now. It has to happen with someone," he said.

"Then...I want it to happen...with you," she whispered, her voice trembling, like her body.

His pulse jumped. His eyes darkened, glittered. "Do you? I wonder if you realize what you're getting into," he murmured. He bent toward her, noticing her sudden tension, her wide-eyed apprehension. He checked the slow movement, for an instant; long enough to whisper, "I won't hurt you."

She leaned back against the leather seat as he turned toward her, her body tautening, trembling a little. But it wasn't fear that motivated her. As she met his smoldering eyes, she slowly arched her back, to let the rest of the bodice fall, and saw the male desire in his dark eyes as they looked down at what the movement had uncovered.

"Your breasts are exquisite," he said absently, that tracing hand moving slowly, tenderly, down one tip-tilted slope, making her shudder. "Perfect."

"They ache," she whispered on a sob, her eyes half closed, in thrall to some physical paralysis that made her throb all over with exquisite sensations.

"I can do something about that," he mused with a brief smile.

His forefinger found the very tip of one small breast and traced around it gently, watching it go even harder, feeling it shudder with the tiny consummation. He heard the faint gasp break from her lips and looked up at her face, at her wide, misty eyes.

"Yes," he said, as if her expression told him everything. And it did. She wanted him. She'd let him do anything he wanted to do, and he felt hot all over.

She moved against the seat, her body in helpless control now, begging for something, for more than this. Her head went back, her full lips parting, hungry.

He slid his arm under her neck, bringing her body closer to his, his mouth poised just above hers. He watched her as his hand moved, and his lean fingers slowly closed over her breast, taking its soft weight and teasing the nipple with his thumb.

She cried softly at the unexpected pleasure, and bit her lower lip in helpless agony.

"Don't do that," he whispered, bending. "Let me..."

His hard lips touched hers, biting softly at them, tracing them warmly from one side to the other. His nose nuzzled against hers, relaxing her, gentling her, while his hand toyed softly with her breast. "Open your mouth, baby," he breathed as his head lowered again, and he met her open mouth with his.

She moaned harshly at the wild excitement he was arousing in her. She'd never dreamed that a kiss could be so intimate, so sweetly exciting. His tongue pushed past her startled lips, into the soft darkness of her mouth, teasing hers in a silence broken only by the sounds of breathing, and cloth against cloth.

"King," she breathed under his lips. Her hands bit into his hair, his nape, tugging. "Hard, King," she whispered shakily, "hard, hard...!"

He hadn't expected that flash of ardor. It caused him to be far rougher than he meant to. He crushed her mouth under his, the force of it bending her head back against his shoulder. His searching hand found first one breast, then the other, savoring the warm silk of their contours, the hard tips that told him how aroused she was.

He forgot her age and the time and the place, and suddenly jerked her across him, his hands easing her into the crook of his arm as he bent his head to her body.

"Sweet," he whispered harshly, opening his mouth on her breast. "God, you're sweet...!"

She cried out from the shock of pleasure his mouth gave her, a piercing little sound that excited him even more, and her body arched up toward him like a silky pink sacrifice. Her hands tangled in his thick black hair, holding him there, tears of mingled frustration and sweet anguish trailing down her hot cheeks as the newness of passion racked her.

"Don't...stop," she whimpered, her hands contracting at his nape, pulling him back to her. "Please!"

"I wonder if I could," he murmured with faint self-contempt as he gave in to the exquisite pleasure of tasting her soft skin. "You taste of gardenia petals, except right...here," he whispered as his lips suddenly tugged at a hard nipple, working down until he took her silky breast into his mouth in a warm, soft suction that made her moan endlessly.

His steely fingers bit into her side as he moved the dress further down and shifted her, letting his mouth press warmly against soft skin, tracing her stomach into the soft elastic of her briefs, tracing the briefs to her hips and waist and then back up to the trembling softness of her breasts.

She found the buttons of his jacket, his silk shirt, and fumbled at them, whimpering as she struggled to make them come apart. She wanted to touch him, experience him as he was experiencing her. Without a clue as to what he might want, she tugged at the edges until he moved her hand aside and moved the fabric away for her. She flattened her palm against thick hair and pure man, caressing him with aching pleasure.

"Here," he whispered roughly, moving her so that her soft breasts were crushed against the abrasive warmth of his chest.

He wrapped her up tight, then, moving her against his hair-roughened skin in a delirium of passion, savoring the feel of her breasts, the silkiness of her skin against him. His body was demanding satisfaction, now, hard with urgent need. His hand slid down her back to her spine and he turned her just a little so that he could press her soft hips into his, and let her know how desperately he wanted her.

She gasped as she felt him in passion, felt and understood the changed contours of his body. Her face buried itself in his hot throat and she trembled all over.

"Are you shocked, Tiffany?" he whispered at her ear, his voice a little rough as if he weren't quite in control. "Didn't you know that a man's body grows hard with desire?"

She shivered a little as he moved her blatantly against him, but it didn't shock her. It delighted her. "It's wicked, isn't it, to do this together?'' she whispered shakily. Her eyes closed. ''But no, I'm not shocked. I want you, too. I want...to be with you. I want to know how it feels to have you...''

He heard the words with mingled joy and shock. His whirling mind began to function again. *Want. Desire. Sex.* His eyes flew open. She was only twenty-one, for God's sake! And a virgin. His business partner's daughter. What the hell was he doing?

He jerked away from her, his eyes going helplessly to her swollen, taut breasts before he managed to pull her arms from around his neck and push her back in her seat. He struggled to get out of the car, his own aching body fighting him as he tried to remove himself from unbearable temptation in time.

He stood by the front fender, his shirt open, his chest damp and throbbing, his body hurting. He bent over a little, letting the wind get to his hot skin. He must be out of his mind!

Tiffany, just coming to her own senses, watched him with eyes that didn't quite register what was going on. And then she knew. It had almost gone too far. He'd started to make love to her, and then he'd remembered who they were and he'd stopped. He must be hurting like the very devil.

She wanted to get out of the car and go to him, but that would probably make things even worse. She looked down and realized that she was nude to the hips. And he'd seen her like that, touched her...

She tugged her dress back up in a sudden flurry of embarrassment. It had seemed so natural at the time, but now it was shameful. She felt for the straps and pulled the bodice up, keeping her eyes away from her hard, swollen nipples. King had suckled them...

She shuddered with the memory, with new knowledge of him. He'd hate her now, she thought miserably. He'd hate her for letting him go so far, for teasing him. There were names for girls who did that. But she hadn't pulled away, or said no, she recalled. He'd been the one to call a halt, because she couldn't.

Her face went scarlet. She smoothed back her disheveled hair with hands that trembled. How could she face her guests now, like this? Everyone would know what had happened. And what if Wyatt should come along in the Jaguar...?

She looked behind them, but there was no car in sight. And then she realized that they were on King's property, not hers. Had he planned this?

After another minute, she saw him straighten and run a hand through his sweaty hair. He rebuttoned his shirt and tucked it back into his trousers. He did the same with his evening jacket and straightened his tie.

When he finally turned back to get into the car, he looked pale and unapproachable. Tiffany glanced at him as he climbed back in and closed the door, wondering what to say.

"I'll drive you home," he said tersely. "Fasten your seat belt," he added, because she didn't seem to have enough presence of mind to think of it herself.

He started the car without looking at her and turned it around. Minutes later, they were well on the way to her father's house.

It was ablaze with lights, although most of the cars had gone. She looked and saw the Jaguar sitting near the front door. So Wyatt was back. She didn't know what kind of car he was driving, so she couldn't tell if he'd gone or not. She hoped he had, and his cousin with him. She didn't want to see them again.

King pulled up at the front door and stopped, but he didn't cut the engine.

She reached for the door handle and then looked back at him, her face stiff and nervous.

"Are you angry?" she asked softly.

He stared straight ahead. "I don't know."

She nibbled her lower lip, and tasted him there. "I'm not sorry," she said doggedly, her face suddenly full of bravado.

He turned then, his eyes faintly amused. "No. I'm not sorry, either."

She managed a faint smile, despite her embarrassment. "You said it had to happen eventually."

"And you wanted it to happen with me. So you said."

"I meant it," she replied quietly. Her eyes searched his, but she didn't find any secrets there. "I'm not ashamed."

His dark eyes trailed down her body. "You're exquisite, little Tiffany," he said. "But years too young for an affair, and despite tonight's showing, I don't seduce virgins."

"Is an affair all you have to offer?" she asked with new maturity.

He pursed his lips, considering that. "Yes, I think it is. I'm thirty-four. I like my freedom. I don't want the commitment of a wife. Not yet, at least. And you're not old enough for that kind of responsibility. You need a few years to grow up."

She was grown up, but she wasn't going to argue the point with him. Her green eyes twinkled. "Not in bed, I don't."

He took a deep breath. "Tiffany, there's more to a relationship than sex. About which," he added shortly, "you know precious little."

"I can learn," she murmured.

"Damned fast, judging by tonight," he agreed with a wicked smile. "But physical pleasure gets old quickly."

"Between you and me?" she asked, her eyes adoring him. "I don't really think it ever would. I can imagine seducing you in all sorts of unlikely places."

His heart jumped. He shouldn't ask. He shouldn't... "Such as?" he asked in spite of himself.

"Sitting up," she breathed daringly. "In the front seat of a really elegant European sports car parked right in front of my house..."

His blood was beating in his temple. She made him go hot all over with those sultry eyes, that expression...

"You'd better go inside," he said tersely.

"Yes, I suppose I had," she murmured dryly. "It really wouldn't do, would it, what with the risk of someone coming along and seeing us."

It got worse by the second. He was beginning to hurt. "Tiffany..."

She opened the door and glanced back at his hard, set face. He was very dark, and she loved the way he looked in evening clothes. Although now, she'd remember him with his shirt undone and her hands against that sexy, muscular chest.

"Run while you can, cattle baron," she said softly. "I'll be two steps behind."

"I'm an old fox, honey," he returned. "And not easy game."

"We'll see about that," she said, smiling at him. "Good night, lover."

He caught his breath, watching her close the door and blow him a kiss. He had to get away, to think. The last thing he wanted was to find himself on the receiving end of a shotgun wedding. Tiffany was all too tempting, and the best way to handle this was to get away from her for a few weeks, until they both cooled off. A man had to keep a level head, in business and in personal relationships.

He put the car in gear and drove off. Yes, that was what he should do. He'd find himself a nice business trip. Tiffany would get over him. And he'd certainly get over her. He'd had women. He'd known this raging hunger before. But he couldn't satisfy it with a virgin.

He thought about her, the way she'd let him see her, and the aching started all over again. His face hardened as he stepped down on the accelerator. Maybe a long trip would erase that image. Something had to!

Tiffany went back into the house, breathless and worried that her new experiences would show. But they didn't seem to. Wyatt came and asked where she and King had been and she made some light, outrageous reply.

For the rest of the evening, she was the belle of her own ball. But deep inside she was worried about the future. King wasn't going to give in without a fight. She hoped she had what it took to land that big Texas fish. She wanted him more than anything in the whole world. And she wasn't a girl who was used to disappointments.

Chapter 3

"Well, King's left the country," Harrison Blair murmured dryly three days after Tiffany's party. "You don't seem a bit surprised."

"He's running scared," she said pertly, grinning up at her father from the neat crochet stitches she was using to make an afghan for her room. "I don't blame him. If I were a man being pursued by some persistent woman, I'm sure that I'd run, too."

He shook his head. "I'm afraid he isn't running from you," he mused. "He took his secretary with him."

Her heart jumped, but she didn't miss a stitch. "Did he? I hope Carla enjoys the trip. Where did they go?"

"To Nassau. King's talking beef exports with the minister of trade. But I'm sure Carla took a bathing suit along."

She put in three more stitches. Carla Stark was a redhead, very pretty and very eligible and certainly no virgin. She wanted to throw her head back and scream, but that would be juvenile. It was a temporary setback, that was all.

"Nothing to say?" her father asked.

She shrugged. "Nothing to say."

He hesitated. "I don't want to be cruel," he began. "I know you've set your heart on King. But he's thirty-four, sweetheart. You're a very young twenty-one. Maturity takes time. And I've been just a tad overprotective about you. Maybe I was wrong to be so strict about young men."

"It wouldn't really have mattered," she replied ruefully. "It was King from the time I was fourteen. I couldn't even get interested in boys my own age."

"I see."

She put the crochet hook through the ball of yarn and moved it, along with the partially finished afghan, to her work basket. She stood up, pausing long enough to kiss her father's tanned cheek. "Don't worry about me. You might not think so, but I'm tough."

"I don't want you to wear your heart out on King."

She smiled at him. "I won't!"

"Tiff, he's not a marrying man," he said flatly. "And modern attitudes or no, if he seduces you, he's history. He's not playing fast and loose with you."

"He already told me that himself," she assured him. "He doesn't have any illusions about me, and he said that he's not having an affair with me."

He was taken aback. "He did?"

She nodded. "Of course, he also said he didn't want a wife. But all relationships have these little minor setbacks. And no man really wants to get married, right?"

His face went dark. "Now listen here, you can't seduce him, either!"

"I can if I want to," she replied. "But I won't, so stop looking like a thundercloud. I want a home of my own and children, not a few months of happiness followed by a diamond bracelet and a bouquet of roses."

"Have I missed something here?"

"Lettie said that's how King kisses off his women," she explained. "With a diamond bracelet and a bouquet of roses. Not that any of them last longer than a couple of months," she added with a rueful smile. "Kind of them, isn't it, to let him practice on them until he's ready to marry me?"

His eyes bulged. "What ever happened to the double standard?"

"I told you, I don't want anybody else. I couldn't really expect him to live a life of total abstinence when he didn't know he was going to marry me one day. I mean, he was looking for the perfect woman all this time, and here I was right under his nose. Now that he's aware of me, I'm sure there won't be anybody else. Not even Carla.''

Harrison cleared his throat. "Now, Tiffany…"

She grinned. "I hope you want lots of grandchildren. I think kids are just the greatest things in the world!"

"Tiffany…"

"I want a nice cup of tea. How about you?"

"Oolong?"

She grimaced. "Green. I ran out of oolong and forgot to ask Mary to put it on the grocery list this week."

"Green's fine, then, I guess."

"Better than coffee," she teased, and made a face. "I won't be a minute."

He watched her dart off to the kitchen, a pretty picture in jeans and a blue T-shirt, with her long hair in a neat ponytail. She didn't look old enough to date, much less marry.

She was starry-eyed, thinking of a home and children and hardly considering the reality of life with a man like King. He wouldn't want children straight off the bat, even if she thought she did. She was far too young for instant responsibility. Besides that, King wouldn't be happy with an impulsive child who wasn't mature enough to handle business luncheons and the loneliness of a home where King spent time only infrequently. Tiffany would expect constant love and attention, and King couldn't give her that. He sighed, thinking that he was going to go gray-headed worrying about his only child's upcoming broken heart. There seemed no way to avoid it, no way at all.

Tiffany wasn't thinking about business lunches or having King home only once in a blue moon. She was weaving dreams of little boys and girls playing around her skirts on summer days, and King holding hands with her while they watched television at night. Over and above that, she was plotting how to bring about his downfall. First things first, she considered, and now that she'd caught his eye, she had to keep it focused on herself.

She phoned his office to find out when he was coming back, and wrangled the information that he had a meeting with her father the following Monday just before lunch about a stock transfer.

She spent the weekend planning every move of her campaign. She was going to land that sexy fighting fish, one way or another.

She found an excuse to go into Jacobsville on Monday morning, having spent her entire allowance on a new sultry jade silk dress that clung to her slender curves as if it were a second skin. Her hair was put up neatly in an intricate hairdo, with a jade clip holding a wave in place. With black high heels and a matching bag, she looked elegant and expensive and frankly seductive as she walked into her father's office just as he and King were coming out the door on their way to lunch.

"Tiffany," her father exclaimed, his eyes widening at the sight of her. He'd never seen her appear quite so poised and elegant.

King was doing his share of looking, as well. His dark eyebrows dove together over glittering pale eyes and his head moved just a fraction to the side as his gaze went over her like seeking hands.

"I don't have a penny left for lunch," she told her father on a pitiful breath. "I spent everything in my purse on this new dress. Do you like it?" She turned around, her body exquisitely posed for King's benefit. His jaw clenched and she had to repress a wicked smile.

"It's very nice, sweetheart," Harrison agreed. "But why can't you use your credit card for lunch?"

"Because I'm going to get some things for an impromptu picnic," she replied. Her eyes lowered demurely.

"You could come to lunch with us," Harrison began.

King looked hunted.

Tiffany saw his expression and smiled gently. "That's sweet of you, Dad, but I really haven't time. Actually, I'm meeting someone. I hope he likes the dress," she added, lowering her head demurely. She was lying her head off, but they didn't know it. "Can I have a ten-dollar bill, please?"

Harrison swept out his wallet. "Take two," he said, handing them to her. He glared at her. "It isn't Wyatt, I hope," he muttered. "He's too easily led."

"No. It's not Wyatt. Thanks, Dad. See you, King."

"Who is it?"

King's deep, half-angry voice stopped her at the doorway. She turned, her eyebrows lifted as if he'd shocked her with the question. "Nobody you know," she said honestly. "I'll be in by bedtime, Dad."

"How can you go on a picnic in that dress?" King asked shortly.

She smoothed her hand down one shapely hip. "It's not *that* sort of picnic," she murmured demurely. "We're going to have it on the carpet in his living room. He has gas logs in his fireplace. It's going to be so romantic!"

"It's May," King ground out. "Too hot for fires in the fireplace."

"We won't sit too close to it," she said. "Ta, ta."

She went out the door and dived into the elevator, barely able to contain her glee. She'd shaken King. Let him stew over that lie for the rest of the day, she told herself, and maybe he'd feel as uncomfortable as she'd felt when he took his secretary to Nassau!

Of course there was no picnic, because she wasn't meeting anyone. She stopped by a fish and chips place and got a small order and took it home with her. An hour later, she was sprawled in front of her own fireplace, unlit, with a trendy fashion magazine. Lying on her belly on the thick beige carpet, in tight-fitting designer jeans and a low-cut tank top, barefoot and with her long hair loose, she looked the picture of youth.

King's sudden appearance in the doorway shocked her. She hadn't expected to be found out, certainly not so quickly.

"Where is he?" he asked, his hands in his slacks pocket. He glanced around the spacious room. "Hiding under the sofa? Behind a chair?"

She was frozen in position with a small piece of fish in her hand as she gaped at him.

"What a tangled web we weave," he mused.

"I wasn't deceiving you. Well, maybe a little," she acknowledged. Her eyes glared up at him. "You took Carla to Nassau, didn't you? I hope you had fun."

"Like hell you do."

He closed the door behind him abruptly and moved toward her, resplendent in a gray suit, his black hair catching the light from the ceiling and glowing with faint blue lights.

She rolled over and started to get up, but before she could move another inch, he straddled her prone figure and with a movement so smooth that it disconcerted her, he was suddenly full-length over her body on the carpet, balancing only on his forearms.

"I suppose you'll taste of fish," he muttered as he bent and his hard mouth fastened roughly on her lips.

She gasped. His hips shifted violently, his long legs insistent as they parted her thighs and moved quickly between them. His hands trapped her wrists, stilling her faint instinctive protest at the shocking intimacy of his position.

He lifted his mouth a breath away and looked straight into her eyes. One lean leg moved, just briefly, and he pushed forward against her, his body suddenly rigid. He let her feel him swell with desire, and something wickedly masculine flared in his pale, glittering eyes as new sensations registered on her flushed face.

"Now you know how it happens," he murmured, dropping his gaze to her soft, swollen mouth. "And how it feels when it happens. Draw your legs up a little. I want you to feel me completely against you there."

"King!"

He shifted insistently, making her obey him. She felt the intimacy of his hold and gasped, shivering a little at the power and strength of him against her so intimately.

"Pity, that you don't have anybody to compare me with," he mused deeply as his head bent. "But that might be a good thing. I wouldn't want to frighten you…"

His mouth twisted, parting her lips. It was so different from the night of her party. Then, she'd been the aggressor, teasing and tempting him. Now, she was very much on the defensive. He was aroused and insistent and she felt young and uncertain, especially when he began to move in a very seductive way that made her whole body tingle and clench with sensual pleasure.

He heard the little gasp that escaped the lips under his hard mouth, and his head lifted.

He searched her eyes, reading very accurately her response to him. "Didn't you know that pleasure comes of such intimacy?" he whispered.

"Only from…books," she confessed breathlessly. She shivered as he moved again, just enough to make her totally aware of her body's feverish response to that intimate pressure.

"Isn't this more exciting than reading about it?" he teased. His mouth nibbled at her lips. "Open them," he whispered. "Deep kisses are part of the process."

"King, I'm not…not…sure…"

"You're sure," he whispered into her mouth. "You're just apprehensive, and that's natural. They told you it was going to hurt, didn't they?"

She swallowed, aware of dizziness that seemed to possess her.

His teeth nibbled sensually at her lower lip. "I'll give you all the time you need, when it happens," he murmured lazily. "If I can arouse you enough, you won't mind if I hurt you a little. It might even intensify the pleasure."

"I don't understand."

His open mouth brushed over hers. "I know," he murmured. "That's what excites me so. Slide your hands up the back of my thighs and hold me against you."

"Wh…what?"

His mouth began to move between her lips. "You wore that dress to excite me. All right. I'm excited. Now satisfy me."

"I…but I…can't…" she gasped. "King!"

His hands were under her, intimate, touching her in shocking ways.

"Isn't this what you wanted? It's what you implied when you struck that seductive pose and invited me to ravish you right there on the floor of your father's office."

"I did not!"

His thumbs pressed against her in a viciously arousing way, so that when he pushed down with his hips, she lifted to meet them, groaning harshly at the shock of delight that was only the tip of some mysterious iceberg of ecstasy.

"Tell me that again," he challenged.

She couldn't. She was burning up, dying, in anguish. A stranger's hands fought her tank top and the tiny bra under it, pushing them out of the way only seconds before those same hands tugged at his shirt and managed to get under it, against warm muscle and hair.

While he kissed her, she writhed under him, shivering when she felt his skin against her own. Delirious with fevered need, she slid her hands down his flat belly and even as he dragged his mouth from hers to protest, they pressed, trembling, against the swollen length of him through the soft fabric.

He moaned something, shuddered. He rolled abruptly onto his side and drew her hand back to him, moving it softly on his body, teaching her the sensual rhythm he needed.

"Dear God," he whispered, kissing her hungrily. "No, baby, don't stop," he groaned when her movements slowed. "Touch me. Yes. Yes. Oh, God, yes!"

It was fascinating to see how he reacted to her. Encouraged, she moved closer and her mouth pressed softly, sensually, against the thick hair that covered his chest. He was shaking now. His body was strangely vulnerable, and the knowledge inhibited her.

He rolled onto his back, the very action betraying his need to feel her touch on him. He lay there, still shivering, his eyes closed, his body yielding to her soft, curious hands.

She laid her cheek against his hot skin, awash in new sensations, touches that had been taboo all her life. She was learning his body as a lover would.

"Tell me what to do," she whispered as she drew her cheek against his breastbone. "I'll do anything for you. Anything!"

His hand held hers to him for one long, aching minute. Then he drew it up to his chest and held it there while he struggled to breathe.

Her breasts felt cool as they pressed nakedly into his rib cage where his shirt was pulled away. Her eyes closed and she lay there, close to him, closer to him than she'd ever been.

"Heavens, that was exciting," she choked. "I never dreamed I could touch you like that, and in broad daylight, too!"

That raw innocence caught him off guard. Laughter bubbled up into his chest, into his throat. He began to laugh softly.

"Do hush!" she chided. "What if Mary should hear you and walk in?"

He lifted himself on an elbow and looked down at her bare breasts. "She'd get an eyeful, wouldn't she?" He traced a taut nipple, arrogantly pleased that she didn't object at all.

"I'm small," she whispered.

He smiled. "No, you're not."

She looked down to where his fingers rested against her pale skin. "Your skin is so dark compared to mine…"

"Especially here, where you're so pale," he breathed. His lips bent to the soft skin he was touching, and he took her inside his mouth, gently suckling her.

She arched up, moaning harshly, her fists clenched beside her head as she tried to deal with the mounting delight of sensation.

He heard that harsh sound and reacted to it immediately. His mouth grew insistent, hot and hungry as it suckled hard at her breast. Her body clenched and suddenly went into a shocking spasm that she couldn't control at all. It never seemed to end, the hot, shameful pleasure he gave her with that intimate caress.

She clutched him, breathless, burying her hot face in his neck while she fought to still her shaking limbs, the faint little gasps that he must certainly be able to hear.

His mouth was tender now, calming rather than stirring. He pressed tender, brief kisses all over her skin, ending only reluctantly at her trembling lips.

Her shamed eyes lifted to his, full of tears that reflected her overwhelmed emotions.

He shook his head, dabbing at them with a handkerchief he drew from his slacks pocket. "Don't cry," he whispered gently. "Your breasts are very, very sensitive. I love the way you react to my mouth on them." He smiled. "It's nothing to worry about."

"It's…natural?" she asked.

His hand smoothed her dark hair. "For a few women, I suppose," he said. He searched her curious eyes. "I've never experienced it like this. I'm glad. There should be at least one or two firsts for me, as well as for you."

"I wish I knew more," she said worriedly.

"You'll learn." His fingers traced her nose, her softly swollen lips. "I missed you."

Her heart felt as if it could fly. She smiled. "Did you, really?"

He nodded. "Not that I wanted to," he added with such disgust that she giggled.

He propped himself on an elbow and stared down at her for a long time, his brows drawn together in deep thought.

She could feel the indecision in him, along with a tension that was new to her. Her soft eyes swept over his dark, lean face and back up to meet his curious gaze.

"You're binding me with velvet ropes," he murmured quietly. "I've never felt like this. I don't know how to handle it."

"Neither do I," she said honestly. She drew a slow breath, aware suddenly of her shameless nudity and the coolness of the air on her skin.

He saw that discomfort and deftly helped her back into her clothes with an economy of movement that was somehow disturbing.

"You make me feel painfully young," she confessed.

"You are," he said without hesitation. His pale eyes narrowed. "This is getting dangerous. I can't keep my hands off you lately. And the last thing on earth I'll ever do is seduce my business partner's only daughter."

"I know that, King," she said with an odd sort of dignity. He got to his feet and she laid down again, watching him rearrange his own shirt and vest and jacket and tie. It was strangely intimate.

He knew that. His eyes smiled, even if his lips didn't.

"What are we going to do?" she added.

He stared down at her with an unnerving intensity. "I wish to God I knew."

He pulled her up beside him. His big hands rested warmly on her shoulders. "Wouldn't you like to go to Europe?" he asked.

Her eyebrows lifted. "What for?"

"You could go to college. Or have a holiday. Lettie could go with you," he suggested, naming her godmother. "She'd spoil you rotten and you'd come back with a hefty knowledge of history."

"I don't want to go to Europe, and I'm not all that enthralled with history."

He sighed. "Tiffany, I'm not going to sleep with you."

Her full, swollen lips pouted up at him. "I haven't asked you to."

She lowered her eyes. "But I'm not going to sleep with anyone else. I haven't even thought about anyone else since I was fourteen."

He felt his mind whirling at the confession. He scowled deeply. He was getting in over his head and he didn't know how to stop. She was too young; years too young. She didn't have the maturity, the poise, the sophistication to survive in his world. He could have told her that, but she wouldn't have listened. She was living in dreams. He couldn't afford to.

He didn't answer her. His hands were deep in his pockets and he was watching her worriedly, amazed at his own headlong fall into ruin. No woman in his experience had ever wound him up to such a fever pitch of desire by just parading around in a silk dress. He'd accused her of tempting him, but it wasn't the whole truth. Ever since the night of her birthday party, he hadn't been able to get her soft body out of his mind. He wanted her violently. He just didn't know what to do about it. Marriage was out of the question, even more so was an affair. Whatever else she was, she was still his business partner's daughter.

"You're brooding," she murmured.

He shrugged. "I can't think of anything better to do," he said honestly. "I'm going away for a while," he added abruptly. "Perhaps this will pass if we ignore it."

So he was still going to fight. She hadn't expected anything else, but she was vaguely disappointed, just the same.

"I can learn," she said.

His eyebrow went up.

"I know how to be a hostess," she continued, as if he'd challenged her. "I already know most of the people in your circle, and in Dad's. I'm not fifteen."

His eyes narrowed. "Tiffany, you may know how to be a hostess, but you haven't any idea in hell how to be a wife," he said bluntly.

Her heart jumped wildly in her chest. "I could learn how to be one."

His face hardened. "Not with me. I don't want to get married. And before you say it," he added, holding up a hand, "yes, I want you. But desire isn't enough. It isn't even a beginning. I may be the first man you've ever wanted, Tiffany, but you aren't the first woman I've wanted."

Chapter 4

The mocking smile on his face made Tiffany livid with jealous rage. She scrambled to her feet, her face red and taut.

"That wasn't necessary!" she flung at him.

"Yes, it was," he replied calmly. "You want to play house. I don't."

Totally at a loss, she knotted her hands at her sides and just stared at him. This sort of thing was totally out of her experience. Her body was all that interested him, and it wasn't enough. She had nothing else to bargain with. She'd lost.

It was a new feeling. She'd always had everything she wanted. Her father had spoiled her rotten. King had been another impossible item on her list of luxuries, but he was telling her that she couldn't have him. Her father couldn't buy him for her. And she couldn't flirt and tease and get him for herself. Defeat was strangely cold. It sat in the pit of her stomach like a black emptiness. She didn't know how to handle it.

And he knew. It was in his pale, glittering eyes, in that faint, arrogant smile on his hard mouth.

She wanted to rant and rave, but it wasn't the sort of behavior that would save the day. She relaxed her hands, and her body, and simply looked at him, full of inadequacies and insecurities that she'd never felt before.

"Perhaps when I'm Carla's age, I'll try again," she said with torn pride and the vestiges of a smile.

He nodded with admiration. "That's the spirit," he said gently.

She didn't want gentleness, or pity. She stuck her hands into her jeans pockets. "You don't have to leave town to avoid me," she said. "Lettie's taking me to New York next week," she lied, having arranged the trip mentally in the past few minutes. Lettie would do anything her godchild asked, and she had the means to travel wherever she liked. Besides, she loved New York.

King's eyes narrowed suspiciously. "Does Lettie know she's going traveling?"

"Of course," she said, playing her part to the hilt.

"Of course." He drew in a heavy breath and slowly let it out. His body was still giving him hell, but he wasn't going to let her know it. Ultimately she was better off out of his life.

"See you," she said lightly.

He nodded. "See you."

And he left.

Late that autumn, Tiffany was walking down a runway in New York wearing the latest creation of one David Marron, a young designer whose Spanish-inspired fashions were a sensation among buyers. The two had met through a mutual friend of Lettie's and David had seen incredible possibilities in Tiffany's long black hair and elegance. He dressed her in a gown that was reminiscent of lacy Spanish noblewomen of days long past, and she brought the house down at his first showing of his new spring line. She made the cover of a major fashion magazine and jumped from an unknown to a familiar face in less than six months.

Lettie, with her delicately tinted red hair and twinkling brown eyes, was elated at her accomplishment. It had hurt her deeply to see Tiffany in such an agony of pain when she'd approached her godmother and all but begged to be taken out of Texas. Lettie doted on the younger woman and whisked her away with a minimum of fuss.

They shared a luxurious Park Avenue apartment and were seen in all the most fashionable places. In those few months, Tiffany had grown more sophisticated, more mature—and incredibly more withdrawn. She was ice-cold with men, despite the enhancement of her beauty and her elegant figure. Learning to forget King was a full-time job. She was still working on it.

Just when she was aching to go home to her father where her chances of seeing King every week were excellent, a lingerie company offered her a lucrative contract and a two-week holiday filming commercials in Jamaica.

"I couldn't turn it down," she told Lettie with a groan. "What's Dad going to say? I was going to help him with his Christmas party. I won't get home until Christmas Eve. After we get back from Jamaica, I have to do a photo layout for a magazine ad campaign due to hit the stands next spring."

"You did the right thing," Lettie assured her. "My dear, at your age, you should be having fun, meeting people, learning to stand alone." She sighed gently. "Marriage and children are for later, when you're established in a career."

Tiffany turned and stared at the older woman. "You never married."

Lettie smiled sadly. "No. I lost my fiancé in Vietnam. I wasn't able to want anyone else in that way."

"Lettie, that's so sad!"

"One learns to live with the unbearable, eventually. I had my charities to keep me busy. And, of course, I had you," she added, giving her goddaughter a quick hug. "I haven't had a bad life."

"Someday you have to tell me about him."

"Someday, I will. But for now, you go ahead to Jamaica and have a wonderful time filming your commercial."

"You'll come with me?" she asked quickly, faintly worried at the thought of being so far away without any familiar faces.

Lettie patted her hand. "Of course I will. I love Jamaica!"

"I have to call Dad and tell him."

"That might be a good idea. He was complaining earlier in the week that your letters were very far apart."

"I'll do it right now."

She picked up the receiver and dialed her father's office number, twisting the cord nervously while she waited to be put through.

"Hi, Dad!" she said.

"Don't tell me," he muttered. "You've met some dethroned prince and you're getting married in the morning."

She chuckled. "No. I've just signed a contract to do lingerie commercials and we're flying to Jamaica to start shooting."

There was a strange hesitation. "When?"

"Tomorrow morning."

"Well, when will you be back?" he asked.

"In two weeks. But I've got modeling assignments in New York until Christmas Eve," she said in a subdued tone.

"What about my Christmas party?" He sounded resigned and depressed. "I was counting on you to arrange it for me."

"You can have a New Year's Eve party for your clients," she improvised with laughter in her voice. "I'll have plenty of time to put that together before I have to start my next assignment. In fact," she added, "I'm not sure when it will be. The lingerie contract was only for the spring line. They're doing different models for different seasons. I was Spring."

"I can see why," he murmured dryly. "My daughter, the model." He sighed again. "I should never have let you get on the plane with Lettie. It's her fault. I know she's at the back of it."

"Now, Dad..."

"I'm having her stuffed and hung on my wall when she comes back. You tell her that!"

"You know you're fond of Lettie," she chided, with a wink at her blatantly eavesdropping godmother.

"I'll have her shot!"

She grimaced and Lettie, reading her expression, chuckled, unabashed by Harrison Blair's fury.

"She's laughing," she told him.

"Tell her to laugh while she can." He hesitated and spoke to someone nearby. "King said to tell you he misses you."

Her heart jumped, but she wasn't leaving herself open to any further humiliation at his hands. "Tell him to pull the other one," she chuckled. "Listen, Dad, I have to go. I'll phone you when we're back from Jamaica."

"Wait a minute. Where in Jamaica, and is Lettie going along?"

"Of course she is! We'll have a ball. Take care, Dad. Bye!"

He was still trying to find out where she was going when she hung up on him. He glanced at King with a grimace.

The younger man had an odd expression on his face. It was one Harrison couldn't remember ever seeing there before.

"She's signed a contract," Harrison said, shoving his hands into his pockets as he glared at the telephone, as if the whole thing had been its fault.

"For what?" King asked.

"Lingerie commercials," his partner said heavily. "Just think, my sheltered daughter will be parading around in sheer nighties for the whole damned world to see!"

"Like hell she will. Where is she?" King demanded.

"On her way to Jamaica first thing in the morning. King," he added when the other man started to leave. "She's of age," he said gently. "She's a woman. I don't have the right to tell her how to live her own life. And neither do you."

"I don't want other men ogling her!"

Harrison just nodded. "I know. I don't, either. But it's her decision."

"I won't let her do it," King said doggedly.

"How do you propose to stop her? You can't do it legally. I don't think you can do it any other way, either."

"Did you tell her what I said?"

Harrison nodded again. "She said to pull the other one."

Pale blue eyes widened with sheer shock. It had never occured to him that he could lose Tiffany, that she wouldn't always be in Harrison's house waiting for him to be ready to settle down. Now she'd flown the coop and the shoe was on the other foot. She'd discovered the pleasure of personal freedom and she didn't want to settle down.

He glanced at Harrison. "Is she serious about this job? Or is it just another ploy to get my attention?"

The other man chuckled. "I have no idea. But you have to admit, she's a pretty thing. It isn't surprising that she's attracted a modeling agency."

King stared out the window with narrowed, thoughtful eyes. "Then she's thinking about making a career of it."

Harrison didn't tell him that her modeling contract might not last very long. He averted his eyes. "She might as well have a career. If nothing else, it will help her mature."

The other man didn't look at him. "She hasn't grown up yet."

"I know that. It isn't her fault. I've sheltered her from life—perhaps too much. But now she wants to try her wings. This is the best time, before she has a reason to fold them away. She's young and she thinks she has the world at her feet. Let her enjoy it while she can."

King stared down at the carpet. "I suppose that's the wise choice."

"It's the only choice," came the reply. "She'll come home when she's ready."

King didn't say another word about it. He changed the subject to business and pursued it solemnly.

Meanwhile, Tiffany went to Jamaica and had a grand time. Modeling, she discovered, was hard work. It wasn't just a matter of standing in front of a camera and smiling. It involved wardrobe changes, pauses for the proper lighting and equipment setup, minor irritations like an unexpected burst of wind, and artistic temperament on the part of the cameraman.

Lettie watched from a distance, enjoying Tiffany's enthusiasm for the shoot. The two weeks passed all too quickly, with very little time for sight-seeing.

"Just my luck," Tiffany groaned when they were back in New York, "I saw the beach and the hotel and the airport. I didn't realize that every free minute was going to be spent working or resting up for the next day's shoot!"

"Welcome to the world of modeling." Lettie chuckled. "Here, darling, have another celery stick."

Tiffany grimaced, but she ate the veggie platter she was offered without protest.

At night, she lay awake and thought about King. She hadn't believed his teasing assertion that he'd missed her. King didn't miss people. He was entirely self-sufficient. But how wonderful if it had been true.

That daydream only lasted until she saw a tabloid at the drugstore where she was buying hair care products. There was a glorious color photo of King and Carla right on the front page of one, with the legend, "Do wedding bells figure in future for tycoon and secretary?"

She didn't even pick it up, to her credit. She passed over it as if she hadn't seen it. But she went to bed that evening, she cried all night, almost ruining her face for the next day's modeling session.

Unrequited love took its toll on her in the weeks that followed. The one good thing about misery was that it attracted other miserable people. She annexed one Mark Allenby, a male model who'd just broken up with his long-time girlfriend and wanted a shoulder to cry on. He was incredibly handsome and sensitive, and just what Tiffany needed for her shattered ego.

The fact that he was a wild man was certainly a bonus.

He was the sort of person who'd phone her on the spur of the moment and suggest an evening at a retro beatnik coffeehouse where the patrons read bad poetry. He loved practical jokes, like putting whoopee cushions under a couple posing for a romantic ad.

"I can see why you're single," Tiffany suggested breathlessly when she'd helped him outrun the furious photographer. "And I'll bet you never get to work for *him* again," she indicated the heavyset madman chasing them.

"Yes, I will." He chuckled. "When you make it to my income bracket, you don't have to call photographers to get work. They call you." Mark turned and blew the man a kiss, grabbed Tiffany's hand, and pulled her along to the subway entrance nearby.

"You need a makeover," he remarked on their way back to her apartment.

She stopped and looked up at him. "Why?"

"You look too girlish," he said simply, and smiled. "You need a more haute couture image if you want to grow into modeling."

She grimaced. "I'm not sure I really do, though. I like it all right. But I don't need the money."

"Darling, of course you need the money!"

"Not really. Money isn't worth much when you can't buy what you want with it," she said pointedly.

He pushed back his curly black hair and gave her his famous inscrutable he-man stare. "What do you want that you can't buy?"

"King."

"Of which country?"

She grinned. "Not royalty. That's his name. Kingman. Kingman Marshall."

"The tycoon of the tabloids?" he asked, pursing his chiseled lips. "Well, well, you do aim high, don't you? Mr. Marshall has all the women he wants, thank you. And if you have anything more serious in mind, forget it. His father taught him that marriage is only for fools. Rumor has it that his mother took his old man for every cent he had when she divorced him, and that it drove his father to suicide."

"Yes, I know," she said dully.

"Not that Marshall didn't get even. You probably heard about that, too."

"Often," she replied. "He actually took his mother to court and charged her with culpability in his father's suicide in a civil case. He won." She shivered, remembering how King had looked after the verdict—and, more importantly, how his mother had looked. She lost two-thirds of her assets and the handsome gigolo that she'd been living with. It was no wonder that King had such a low opinion of marriage, and women.

"Whatever became of the ex-Mrs. Marshall?" he asked aloud.

"She overdosed on drugs and died four years ago," she said.

"A sad end."

"Indeed it was."

"You can't blame Marshall for treating women like individually wrapped candies," he expounded. "I don't imagine he trusts anything in skirts."

"You were talking about a makeover?" she interrupted, anxious to get him off the subject of King before she started screaming.

"I was. I'll take you to my hairdresser. He'll make a new woman of you. Then we'll go shopping for a proper wardrobe."

Her pale eyes glittered with excitement. "This sounds like fun."

"Believe me, it will be," he said with a wicked grin. "Come along, darling."

They spent the rest of the day remaking Tiffany. When he took her out that night to one of the more fashionable nightspots, one of the models she'd worked with didn't even recognize her. It was a compliment of the highest order.

Lettie was stunned speechless.

"It's me," Tiffany murmured impishly, whirling in her black cocktail dress with diamond earrings dripping from her lobes. Her hair was cut very short and feathered toward her gamine face. She had just a hint of makeup, just enough to enhance her high cheekbones and perfect bone structure. She looked expensive, elegant, and six years older than she was.

"I'm absolutely shocked," Lettie said after a minute. "My dear, you are the image of your mother."

Tiffany's face softened. "Am I, really?"

Lettie nodded. "She was so beautiful. I always envied her."

"I wish I'd known her," she replied. "All I have are photographs and vague memories of her singing to me at night."

"You were very young when she died. Harrison never stopped mourning her." Her eyes were sad. "I don't think he ever will."

"You never know about Dad," Tiffany remarked, because she knew how Lettie felt about Harrison. Not that she was gauche enough to mention it. "Why don't you go out with us tonight?"

"Three's a crowd, dear. Mark will want you to himself."

"It isn't like that at all," Tiffany said gently. "He's mourning his girlfriend and I'm mourning King. We have broken hearts and our work in common, but not much else. He's a friend—and I mean that quite sincerely."

Lettie smiled. "I'm rather glad. He's very nice. But he'll end up in Europe one day in a villa, and that wouldn't suit you at all."

"Are you sure?"

Lettie nodded. "And so are you, in your heart."

Tiffany glanced at herself in the mirror with a quiet sigh. "Fine feathers make fine birds, but King isn't the sort to be impressed by sophistication or beauty. Besides, the tabloids are already predicting that he's going to marry Carla."

"I noticed. Surely you don't believe it?"

"I don't believe he'll ever marry anyone unless he's trapped into it," Tiffany said honestly, and her eyes were suddenly very old. "He's seen nothing of marriage but the worst side."

"It's a pity about that. It's warped his outlook."

"Nothing will ever change it." She smiled at Lettie. "Sure you won't come with us? You won't be a crowd."

"I won't come tonight. But ask me again."

"You can count on it."

Mark was broody as he picked at his mint ice cream.

"You're worried," Tiffany murmured.

He glanced at her wryly. "No. I'm distraught. My girl is being seen around town with a minor movie star. She seems smitten."

"She may be doing the same thing you're doing," she chided. "Seeing someone just to numb the ache."

He chuckled. "Is that what I'm doing?"

"It's what we're both doing."

He reached his hand across the table and held hers. "I'm sorry we didn't meet three years ago, while I was still heart-whole. You're unique. I enjoy having you around."

"Same here. But friendship is all it can ever be."

"Believe it or not, I know that." He put down his spoon. "What are you doing for Christmas?"

"I'll be trying to get back from a location shoot and praying that none of the airline pilots go on strike," she murmured facetiously.

"New Year's?"

"I have to go home and arrange a business party for my father." She glanced at him and her eyes began to sparkle. "I've had an idea. How would you like to visit Texas?"

His eyebrows arched. "Do I have to ride a horse?"

"Not everyone in Texas rides. We live in Jacobsville. It's not too far from San Antonio. Dad's in business there."

"Jacobsville." He fingered his wineglass with elegant dark fingers that looked very sexy in the ads he modeled for. "Why not? It's a long way from Manhattan."

"Yes, it is, and I can't bear to go home alone."

"May I ask why?"

"Of course. My own heartbreaker lives there. I told you about him. I ran away from home so that I could stop eating my heart out over him. But memories and heartache seem to be portable," she added heavily.

"I could attest to that myself." He looked up at her with wickedly twinkling black eyes. "And what am I going to be? The competition?"

"Would you mind?" she asked. "I'll gladly do the same for you anytime you like. I need your moral support."

He paused thoughtfully and then he smiled. "You know, this might be the perfect answer to both our headaches. All right. I'll do it." He finished his wine.

"I've been asked to fill a lot of roles. That's a new one." He lifted his glass and took a sip. "What the hell. I'll tangle with Kingman Marshall. I don't want to live forever. I'm yours, darling. At least, for the duration of the party," he added with a grin.

She lifted her own glass. "Here's to pride."

He answered the toast. As she drank it, she wondered how she was going to bear seeing King with Carla. At least she'd have company and camouflage. King would never know that her heart was breaking.

Chapter 5

Tiffany and Mark boarded the plane with Lettie the day before New Year's Eve. Tiffany looked sleek and expensive in a black figure-hugging suit with silver accessories and a black-and-white striped scarf draped over one shoulder. Mark, in a dark suit, was the picture of male elegance. Women literally sighed when he walked past. It was odd to see a man that handsome in person, and Tiffany enjoyed watching people react to him.

Lettie sat behind them and read magazines while Mark and Tiffany discussed their respective assignments and where they might go next.

It wasn't as long a flight as she'd expected it to be. They walked onto the concourse at the San Antonio airport just in time for lunch.

Tiffany had expected her father to meet them, and sure enough, he was waiting near the gate. Tiffany ran to him to be hugged and kissed warmly before she introduced Mark.

Harrison scowled as he shook hands with the young man, but he gathered his composure quickly and the worried look vanished from his features. He greeted Lettie warmly, too, and led the three of them to the limousine near the front entrance.

"Mark's staying with us, Dad," Tiffany said. "We're both working for the same agency in Manhattan and our holidays coincided."

"We'll be glad to have you, Mark," Harrison said with a forced warmth that only Tiffany seemed to notice.

"How is King?" Lettie asked.

Harrison hesitated with a lightning glance at Tiffany. "He's fine. Shall we go?"

Tiffany wondered why her father was acting so peculiarly, but she pretended not to be interested in King or his feelings. Only with Mark.

"Did you manage to get the arrangements finalized?" Harrison asked his daughter.

She grinned. "Of course. Long distance isn't so long anymore, and it wasn't that hard. I've dealt with the same people for years arranging these 'do's' for you. The caterer, the flowers, the band, even the invitations are all set."

"You're sure?" Harrison murmured.

She nodded. "I'm sure."

"You didn't forget to send an invitation to King and Carla?" her father added.

"Of course not! Theirs were the first to go out," she said with magnificent carelessness. "I wouldn't forget your business partner."

Harrison seemed to relax just a little.

"What's wrong?" she asked, sensing some problem.

"He's out of town," he said reluctantly. "Rather, they're out of town, and not expected back until sometime next week. Or so King's office manager said. I hadn't heard from him, and I wondered why he was willing to forgo the party. He never misses the holiday bash. Or, at least, he never has before."

Tiffany didn't betray her feelings by so much as the batting of an eyelash how much that statement hurt. She only smiled. "I suppose he had other plans and wasn't willing to change them."

"Perhaps so," he said, but he didn't look convinced.

Mark reached beside him and caught Tiffany's hand in his, pressing it reassuringly. He seemed to sense, as her father did, how miserable she felt at King's defection. But Mark asked Harrison a question about a landmark he noticed as they drove down the long highway that would carry them to Jacobsville, and got him off on a subject dear to his heart. By the time they reached the towering brick family home less than an hour later, Mark knew more about the siege at the Alamo than he'd ever gleaned from books.

Tiffany was too busy with her arrangements to keep Mark company that day or the next, so he borrowed a sedan from the garage and set about learning the area. He came back full of tidbits about the history of the countryside, which he seemed to actually find fascinating.

He watched Tiffany directing the traffic of imported people helping with the party with amused indulgence.

"You're actually pretty good at this," he murmured. "Where did you learn how to do it?"

She looked surprised. "I didn't. It just seemed to come naturally. I love parties."

"I don't," he mused. "I usually become a decoration."

She knew what he meant. She learned quickly that very few of the parties models attended were anything but an opportunity for designers to show off their fashions in a relaxed setting. The more wealthy clients who were present, the better the opportunity to sell clothes. But some of the clients found the models more interesting than their regalia. Tiffany had gravitated toward Mark for mutual protection at first. Afterward, they'd become fast friends.

"You won't be a decoration here," she promised him with a smile. "What do you think?"

She swept her hand toward the ballroom, which was polished and packed with flowers and long tables with embroidered linen tablecloths, crystal and china and candelabras. Buffets would be set up there for snacks, because it wasn't a sit-down dinner. There would be dancing on the highly polished floor to music provided by a live band, and mixed drinks would be served at the bar.

"It's all very elegant," Mark pronounced.

She nodded absently, remembering other parties when she'd danced and danced, when King had been close at hand to smile at her and take her out onto the dance floor. She hadn't danced with him often, but each time was indelibly imprinted in her mind. She could close her eyes and see him, touch him. She sighed miserably. Well, she might as well stop looking back. She had to go on, and King wanted no part of her. His absence from this most special of all parties said so.

"I think it'll do," she replied after a minute. She gave him a warm smile. "Come on and I'll show you the way I've decorated the rest of the house."

Tiffany wore a long silver-sequined dress for the party, with a diamond clip in her short hair. She'd learned how to walk, how to move, how to pose, and even people who'd known her for years were taken aback at her new image.

Mark, at her side, resplendent in dark evening dress, drew feminine eyes with equal magnetism. His Italian ancestry was very evident in his liquid black eyes and olive complexion and black, black hair. One of Tiffany's acquaintances, a pretty little redhead named Lisa, seemed to be totally captivated by Mark. She stood in a corner by herself, just staring at him.

"Should I take pity on her and introduce you?" she asked Mark in a teasing whisper.

He glanced toward the girl, barely out of her teens, and she blushed as red as her hair. Seconds later, she rushed back toward her parents. He chuckled softly.

"She's very young," he mused. "A friend?"

She shook her head. "Her parents are friends of my father's. Lisa is a loner. As a rule, she doesn't care as much for dating as she does for horses. Her family has stables and they breed racehorses."

"Well, well. All that, and no beaux?"

"She's shy with men."

His eyebrows arched. He looked at the young woman a second time, and his eyes narrowed as they caught her vivid blue ones and held them relentlessly. Lisa spilled her drink and blushed again, while her mother fussed at the skirt of her dress with a handkerchief.

"How wicked," Tiffany chided to Mark.

"Eyes like hers should be illegal," he murmured, but he was still staring at Lisa just the same. He took Tiffany's arm and urged her toward the group. "Introduce me."

"Don't...", she began.

"I'm not that much a rake." He calmed her. "She intrigues me. I won't take advantage. I promise." He smiled, although his eyes were solemn.

"All right, then." She stopped at Mrs. McKinley's side. "Will it stain?" she asked gently.

"Oh, I don't think so," the older woman said with a smile. "It was mostly ice. Lisa, you remember our Tiffany, don't you?" she added.

Lisa looked up, very flustered as her eyes darted nervously from Mark's to Tiffany. "H...hi, Tiffany. Nice to see you."

"Nice to see you, Lisa," Tiffany replied with a genuine smile. "I'm sorry about your dress. Have you met Mark Allenby? He works with me. We're both represented by the same modeling agency in New York. You might have seen him in the snack food commercials with the puppet...?"

"G...good Lord, was that you?" Lisa choked. "I thought he...you...looked familiar, Mr. Allenby!"

He smiled lazily. "Nice of you to remember it, Miss McKinley. Do you dance?"

She looked as if she might faint. "Well, yes..."

He held out a hand. "You'll excuse me?" he said to Tiffany and Lisa's parents.

Lisa put her hand into his and let him lead her onto the dance floor. Her eyes were so full of dreams and delight that Mark couldn't seem to stop looking down at her.

"He dances beautifully," Mrs. McKinley said.

"Not bad," her gruff husband agreed. "Is he gay?"

"Mark?" Tiffany chuckled. "Not a chance. He's quite a success story, in fact. His parents are Italian. He came to this country as a baby and his father held down two jobs while his mother worked as a waitress in a cafeteria. He makes enough to support both of them now, and his three young sisters. He's very responsible, loyal, and not a seducer of innocents, just in case you wondered."

Mrs. McKinley colored. "I'm sorry, but he was an unknown quantity, and it's very easy to see the effect he has on Lisa."

"I wouldn't worry," she said gently. "He's just broken up with his long-time girlfriend and his heart hurts. He's not in the market for an affair, anyway."

"That's a relief," the older woman said with a smile. "She's so unworldly."

Because she'd been as sheltered as Tiffany herself had. There were great disadvantages to that overprotection in today's world, Tiffany thought miserably. She stared into her champagne and wondered why King had declined the invitation to the party. Perhaps he was making the point that he could do nicely without Tiffany. If so, he'd succeeded beyond his wildest dreams.

She got through the long evening on champagne and sheer willpower. Mark seemed to be enjoying himself immensely. He hardly left Lisa all evening, and when she and her parents got ready to leave, he held onto her hand as if he couldn't bear to let it go.

They spoke in terse, quiet tones and as she left, her blue eyes brightened considerably, although Mrs. McKinley looked worried.

"I'm going over there tomorrow to see their horses. You don't mind?" he asked Tiffany as the other guests were preparing to leave.

She stared up at him curiously. "She's very young."

"And innocent," he added, his hands deep in his pockets. "You don't need to tell me that. I haven't ever known anyone like her. She's the sort of girl I might have met back home, if my parents hadn't immigrated to America."

She was startled. "I thought you were grinding your teeth over your girlfriend?"

He smiled vaguely. "So did I." His head turned toward the front door. "She's breakable," he said softly. "Vulnerable and sweet and shy." His broad shoulders rose and fell. "Strange. I never liked redheads before."

Tiffany bit her lower lip. She didn't know how to put into words what she was feeling. Lisa was the sort of girl who'd never get over having her hopes raised and then dashed. Did he know that?

"She dances like a fairy," he murmured, turning away, his dark eyes introspective and oblivious to the people milling around him.

Harrison joined his daughter at the door as the last guests departed.

"Your friend seems distracted," he murmured, his eyes on Mark, who was staring out a darkened window.

"Lisa affected him."

"I noticed. So did everybody else. He's a rake."

She shook her head. "He's a hardworking man with deep family ties and an overworked sense of responsibility. He's no rake."

"I thought you said he had a girlfriend."

"She dumped him for somebody richer," she said simply. "His pride was shattered. That's why he's here with me. He couldn't bear seeing her around town in all the nightspots with her new lover."

Harrison's attitude changed. "Poor guy."

"He won't hurt Lisa," she assured him, mentally crossing her fingers. She saw trouble ahead, but she didn't know quite how to ward it off.

He studied her face. "You're much more mature. I wouldn't have recognized you." He averted his eyes. "Pity King didn't get back in time for the party."

She froze over. "I didn't expect him, so it's no great loss."

He started to speak, and suddenly closed his mouth. He smiled at her. "Let's have a nightcap. Your friend can come along."

She took his arm with a grin. "That sounds more like you!"

The next day, Mark borrowed Harrison's sedan again and made a beeline for the McKinley place outside town. He was wearing slacks and a turtle-neck white sweater and he looked both elegant and expensive.

As Tiffany stood on the porch waving him off, a car came purring up the driveway. It was a black Lincoln. She fought down the urge to run. She didn't have to back away from King anymore. She was out of his reach. She folded her arms over the red silk blouse she was wearing with elegant black slacks and leaned against a post in a distinctive pose to wait for him. It surprised her just a little that he didn't have Carla with him.

King took the steps two at a time. He was wearing dark evening clothes, as if he'd just come from a party. She imagined he was still wearing the clothes he'd had on the night before. Probably he didn't keep anything to change into at Carla's place, she thought venomously, certain that it explained his state of dress.

"Well, well, what brings you here?" she drawled, without any particular shyness.

King paused at the last step, scowling as he got a good look at her. The change was phenomenal. She wasn't the young girl he'd left behind months before. She was poised, elegant, somehow cynical.

Her eyes were older and there was no welcome or hero-worship in them now. Her smile, if anything, was mocking.

"I came to see Harrison," he said curtly.

She waved a hand toward the front door. "Help yourself. I was just seeing Mark off."

He seemed suddenly very still. "Mark?"

"Mark Allenby. We work together. He came home with me for our holidays." She gave him a cool glance. "You've probably seen him in commercials. He's incredibly handsome."

He didn't say another word. He walked past her without speaking and went right into the house.

Tiffany followed a few minutes later, and found him with her father in the study.

Harrison glanced out the door as she passed it on her way to the staircase. "Tiffany! Come in here a minute, would you, sweetheart?"

He never called her pet names unless he wanted something. She wandered into the room as if King's presence made no difference at all to her. "What do you want, Dad?" she asked with a smile.

"King needs some papers from the safe at my office, and I promised I'd drive Lettie down to Floresville to visit her sister. Would you…?"

She knew the combination by heart, something her father had entrusted her with only two years before. But she sensed a plot here and she hesitated. King noticed, and his face froze over.

"You don't have anything pressing, do you?" Harrison persisted. "Not with Mark away?"

"I suppose not." She gave in. "I'll just get my jacket."

"Thanks, sweetheart!"

She only shrugged. She didn't even glance at King.

It was a short drive to the downtown office her father shared with King. It seemed a little strange to her that King didn't have the combination to Harrison's safe, since they were partners. She'd never really wondered why until now.

"Doesn't he trust you?" she chided as they went into the dark office together.

"As much as he trusts anyone," he replied. "But in case you

wondered, he doesn't have the combination to my safe, either. Our respective lawyers have both. It's a safeguard, of a sort.''

He turned on the lights and closed the door. The sprawling offices were vacant on this holiday and she was more aware than ever of being totally alone with him. It shouldn't have bothered her, knowing what she did about his relationship with Carla, but it did. It hadn't been long enough for her to forget the pleasure of his kisses, being in his arms.

She ignored her tingling nerves and went straight to the concealed safe, opening it deftly. ''What do you want out of here?'' she asked.

''A brown envelope marked Internet Proposals.''

She searched through the documents and found what he wanted. She closed the safe, replaced the painting that covered it, and handed the envelope to King.

''Is that all you needed me for?'' she asked, turning toward the door.

''Not quite.''

She hesitated a few feet away from him. Her eyes asked the question for her.

He wasn't smiling. The friendly man of years past was missing. His eyes were wary and piercing. He didn't move at all. He just stared at her until she felt her heartbeat accelerate.

She lifted her chin. ''Well?''

''Was it deliberate?''

She blinked. ''Was what deliberate?''

''Leaving us off the guest list for the New Year's Eve party.''

She felt an uncomfortable tension in the air. She frowned. ''You and Carla were invited,'' she said. ''I faxed the list of invitations straight to the printers. The two of you were the first two names on the list. In fact, they went straight to my father's secretary from the printer's, to be mailed. Carla knows Rita, Dad's secretary. I'm sure she knew that you were on the list.''

His eyes narrowed. ''She said that she checked the list. Our names weren't there.''

''Someone's lying,'' Tiffany said quietly.

He made a sound deep in his throat. ''I don't need two guesses for a name.''

"You think I did it. Why?"

He shrugged. "Spite?" he asked with a mocking smile. "After all, I sent you packing, didn't I?"

Months of conditioning kept her face from giving away any of her inner feelings. She pushed a hand into her jacket pocket and lifted an eyebrow. "You did me a favor, as it happens," she said. "You needn't worry, I'm no longer a threat to you. Mark and I are quite an item about town these days. We both work for the same agency. We see a lot of each other. And not only on the job."

His narrow gaze went over her, looking for differences. "You've changed."

Her shoulders rose and fell. "I've only grown up." Her smile never reached her eyes. "I have a bright future, they tell me. It seems that my body is photogenic."

Something flashed in his eyes and he turned away before she could see it. "I thought you were going on a holiday, not to find a job."

"I didn't have much choice," she said, turning back to the door. "There was nothing for me here."

His fist clenched at his side. He turned, about to speak, but she'd already opened the door and gone out into the hall.

He followed her, surprised to find her headed not for the exit, but for Rita's computer. She sat down behind the desk that her father's secretary used, turned on the computer, fed in a program, and searched the files for the invitation list. She found it and pulled it up on the screen. Sure enough, King's name wasn't on it. Neither was Carla's. But one of the agency models was a computer whiz and she'd been tutoring Tiffany on the side.

"I told you our names weren't there," he said gruffly from behind her.

"Oh, don't give up yet. Wait just a sec..." She put up another program, one designed to retrieve lost files, and set it searching. A minute later, she pulled up the deleted file and threw it up on the screen. There, at the top of the list, were King's and Carla's names.

King scowled. "How did you do that? I didn't see your hands typing on the keyboard."

"They didn't. This file was deliberately erased and replaced. I'm sure if I look for the fax, I'll discover that it's been redone as well."

She saved the file, cut off the computer, and got to her feet. She met his eyes coldly. "Tell Carla nice try. But next time, she'd better practice a little more on her technique."

She retrieved her purse and went out the door, leaving King to follow, deep in thought.

"Why do you think Carla tampered with the list?" he asked on the way home.

"She's a girl with aspirations. Not that I'm any threat to them," she added firmly. "I have a life in New York that I'm learning to love, and a man to shower affection on. You might tell her that, before she dreams up any new ideas to put me in a bad light."

He didn't answer her. But his hands tightened on the steering wheel.

She was out of the car before he could unfasten his seatbelt.

The house was empty, she knew, because Harrison was supposed to be out, and she was certain that Mark was still at Lisa's house. She didn't want King inside.

She paused on the lowest step. "I'll tell Dad you got the information you needed," she said firmly.

His narrow eyes went from her to the front of the house. "Is he in there waiting for you?" he asked coldly.

"If he is, it's nothing to do with you," she said solemnly. "As you said on that most memorable occasion, I wanted to play house and you didn't. For the record," she added with cold eyes, "I no longer want to play with you, in any manner whatsoever. Goodbye."

She went to the door, unlocked it, let herself in, and threw the bolt home after her. If he heard it, so much the better. She didn't want him within three feet of her, ever again!

Chapter 6

Tiffany went upstairs, almost shaking with fury at Carla's treacherous action, because certainly no one else could be blamed for the omission of those names on the guest list. Carla was playing to win and thought Tiffany was competition. It was funny, in a way, because King wanted no part of her. Why didn't Carla know that?

She went into her room and opened her closet. It was New Year's Day, and tomorrow she and Mark would have to fly back to New York and get ready to begin work again. It was going to be a hectic few weeks, with the Spring showings in the near future, and Tiffany was almost certain that she'd be able to land a new contract. She was young and photogenic and her agent said that she had great potential. It wasn't as heady a prospect as a life with King, but it would have to suffice. Loneliness was something she was just going to have to get used to, so she...

"Packing already?"

The drawled question surprised her into gasping. She whirled, a hand at her throat, to find King lounging in the doorway.

"How did you get in?" she demanded.

"Kitty let me in the back door. She's cleaning the kitchen." He closed the door firmly behind him and started toward Tiffany with a strange glitter in his pale blue eyes. "It isn't like you to run from a fight. You never used to."

"Maybe I'm tired of fighting," she said through a tight throat.

"Maybe I am, too," he replied curtly.

He backed her against the bed and suddenly gave her a gentle push. She went down onto the mattress and his lean, hard body followed her. He braced himself on his forearms beside her head and stared into her eyes at a breathless proximity.

"I'm expecting Mark..." She choked.

"Really? Kitty says he's at Lisa McKinley's house, and very smitten, too, from the look of them at the party last night." His hand smoothed away the lapels of her jacket. His big hand skimmed softly over her breast and his thumb lingered there long enough to make the tip go hard. He smiled when he felt it. "Some things, at least, never change."

"I don't know what you...oh!"

She arched completely off the bed when his mouth suddenly covered her breast. Even through two layers of cloth, it made her shiver with pleasure. Her hands clenched at her ears and her eyes closed as she gave in without even a struggle.

His hands slid under her clothing to the two fastenings at her back. He loosened them and his hands found the softness of her breasts. "Good God, it's like running my hands over silk," he whispered as his head lifted. "You feel like sweet heaven."

As he spoke, his hands moved. He watched her pupils dilate, her lips part on whispery little sighs that grew sharp when his thumbs brushed her hard nipples.

"The hell with it," he murmured roughly. He sat up, drawing her with him, and proceeded to undress her.

"King...you can't...!"

"I want to suckle you," he said quietly, staring into her shocked eyes as he freed her body from the clothes.

The words fanned the flames that were already devouring her. She didn't speak again. She sat breathing like a track runner while he tossed her jacket and blouse and bra off the bed. Then his hands at her rib cage arched her delicately toward him. He bent and his mouth slowly fastened on her breast.

There was no past, no present. There was only the glory of King's hard mouth on her body. She sobbed breathlessly as the pleasure grew to unbelievable heights.

He had her across his knees, her head falling naturally into the crook of his arm, while he fed on her breasts. The nuzzling, suckling pressure was the sweetest sensation she'd ever known. It had been so long since he'd held her like this. She was alive again, breathing again.

"Easy, darling," he whispered when she began to sob aloud. "Easy, now."

"King...!" Her voice broke. She sounded as frantic as she felt, her heartbeat smothering her, the pressure of his hands all of heaven as he held her to his chest.

"Baby..." He eased her onto the bed and slid alongside her, his face solemn, his eyes dark with feeling. His mouth found hers, held it gently under his while his hands searched out the places where she ached and began to soothe them...only the soothing made the tension worse.

She moaned, tears of frustration stinging her eyes as his caresses only made the hunger more unbearable.

"All right," he whispered, easing down against her. "It's too soon, Tiffany, but I'm going to give you what you want."

He shifted her and his hand moved slowly against her body. She stiffened, but he didn't stop. He kissed her shocked eyelids closed and then smothered the words of protest she tried to voice.

She had no control over her body, none at all. It insisted, it demanded, it was wanton as it sought fulfillment. Her eyes remained tightly closed while she arched and arched, pleading, whispering to him, pride shorn from her in the grip of a madness like none she'd ever experienced.

She opened her eyes all at once and went rigid as a flash of pleasure like hot lightning shot through her flesh. She looked at him in shock and awe and suddenly she was flying among the stars, falling, soaring, in a shuddering ecstasy that none of her reading had ever prepared her for.

Afterward, of course, she wept. She was embarrassed and shocked by this newest lesson in passion and its fulfillment. She hid her face against him, still shivering gently in the aftermath.

"I told you it was too soon," he whispered quietly. He held her close, his face nuzzling her throat. "I took it too far. I only meant to kiss you.'' His arms tightened. ''Don't cry. There's no reason to be upset.''

''Nobody...*ever*...'' She choked.

His thumb pressed against her swollen lips. ''I know.'' His mouth moved onto her wet eyelids and kissed the tears away slowly. ''And that was only the beginning,'' he whispered. ''You can't imagine how it really feels.''

He carried her hand to his body and shivered as he moved it delicately against him. ''I want you.''

She pressed her lips to his throat. ''I know. I want you, too.''

His teeth nipped her earlobe gently and his breath caught. ''Tiffany, your father is my business partner. There's no way we can sleep together without having him find out. It would devastate him. He doesn't really belong to this century.''

''I know.'' She grimaced slightly. ''Neither do I, I suppose.''

He lifted his head and looked down at her soft hand resting so nervously against his body. He smiled gently even through the pleasure of her touch. His hand pressed hers closer as he looked into her eyes hungrily. ''I'm starving,'' he whispered.

She swallowed, gathering her nerve. ''I could...?''

He sighed. ''No. You couldn't.'' He took her hand away and held it tightly in his. ''In my way, I'm pretty old-fashioned, too.'' He grimaced. ''I suppose you'd better come into town with me tomorrow and pick out a ring.''

Her eyelids fluttered. ''A what?''

''An engagement ring and a wedding band,'' he continued.

''You don't want to marry. You said so.''

He looked down at himself ruefully and then back at her flushed face. ''It's been several months,'' he said pointedly. ''I'm not a man to whom abstinence comes naturally, to put it modestly. I need a woman.''

''I thought you were having Carla,'' she accused.

He sighed heavily. ''Well, that's one of the little problems I've been dealing with since you left. She can't seem to arouse my... interest.''

Her eyes widened. This was news. ''I understood that any woman can arouse a man.''

"Reading fiction again, are we?" he murmured dryly. "Well, books and instruction manuals notwithstanding, my body doesn't seem to be able to read. It only wants you. And it wants you violently."

She was still tingling from her own pleasure. She grimaced.

"What?" he asked.

"I feel guilty. This was all just for me," she faltered, still a little embarrassed.

"I'll run around the house three times and have a cold shower," he murmured dryly. "No need to fret."

She laid back on the bed, watching him sketch her nudity with quick, possessive eyes. "You can, if you want to," she whispered with a wicked smile, never so sure of him as she was at the moment. "I'll let you."

His high cheekbones actually flushed. "With Kitty in the kitchen and aware that I'm up here?" He smiled mockingly and glanced at his watch. "I'd say we have about two minutes to go."

"Until what?"

"Until you have a phone call, or I have a phone call," he remarked. "Which will have strangely been disconnected the minute we pick up the receiver."

She giggled. "You're kidding."

"I'm not." He got up and rearranged his tie, staring down at her with pure anguish. "I want to bury myself in you!" he growled softly.

She flushed. "King!"

It didn't help that her eyes went immediately to that part of him that would perform such a task and she went even redder. She threw herself off the bed and began to fumble to put her clothing back on.

He chuckled. "All that magnificent bravado, gone without a whimper. What a surprise you've got in store on our wedding night," he murmured.

She finished buttoning her blouse and gave him a wry look. "You really are a rake."

"And you'll be glad about that, too," he added with a knowing look. "I promise you will."

She moved close to him, her eyes wide and eloquent. "It won't hurt after what we've done, will it?"

He hesitated. "I don't know," he said finally. "I'll be as careful and gentle as I can."

"I know that." She searched his eyes with a deep sadness that she couldn't seem to shake. "It's only because you want me that we're getting married, isn't it?"

He scowled. "Don't knock it. Sex is the foundation of any good marriage. You and I are highly compatible in that respect."

She wanted to pursue the conversation, but there was a sudden knock at the door.

"Yes, what is it, Kitty?" Tiffany called, distracted.

"Uh, there's a phone call for Mr. Marshall, Miss Tiffany," she called nervously.

"I'll take it downstairs, Kitty. Thanks!" he added with a roguish look in Tiffany's direction.

"You're welcome!" Kitty called brightly, and her footsteps died away.

"Your father puts her up to that," he mused.

"He's sheltered me."

"I know."

She pursed her lips and eyed him mischievously. "I've been saved up for you."

"I'll be worth the effort," he promised, a dark, confident gleam in his eyes.

"Oh, I know that." She went to open the door, pushing back her disheveled hair. "Are you coming to dinner tonight?"

"Is your male fashion plate going to be here?"

"I'm not sure. Lisa was very taken with him, and vice versa."

He smiled. "I started up here bristling with jealousy. I could have danced a jig when Kitty stopped me to tell me about your houseguest and Lisa."

"You were jealous?" she asked.

He lifted an eyebrow and his eyes slid over her like hands. "We both know that you've belonged to me since you've had breasts," he said blatantly. "I kept my distance, almost for too long. But I came to my senses in time."

"I hope you won't regret it."

"So do I," he said without thinking, and he looked disturbed.

"I'll try to make you glad," she whispered in what she hoped was a coquettish tone.

He grinned. "See that you do."

She opened the door and he followed her out into the hall.

Mark was more amused than anything when he discovered that his gal pal was engaged to her dream man. He and Lisa had found many things in common and a romance was blooming there, so he had only good wishes for Tiffany and her King. But there was something in the way King looked that made him uneasy. That man didn't have happily ever after in mind, and he wasn't passionately in love with Tiffany—and it showed. He wanted her; that was obvious to a blind man. But it seemed less than honest for a man to marry a woman only because of desire. Perhaps her father was the fly in the ointment. He couldn't see the dignified Mr. Blair allowing his only daughter to become the mistress of his business partner.

Of course! That had to be the reason for the sudden marriage plans. King had manipulated Tiffany so that she was done out of a fairy tale wedding, so that she was settling for a small, intimate ceremony instead. It was unkind and Mark wished he could help, but it seemed the only thing he could do for his friend was wish her the best and step aside. King didn't seem like a man who'd want a male friend in his virgin bride's life....

Life changed for Tiffany overnight. She went to one of the biggest jewelers in San Antonio with King, where they looked at rings for half an hour before she chose a wide antique gold wedding band in yellow and white gold, with engraved roses.

King hesitated. "Don't you want a diamond?" he asked.

"No." She wasn't sure why, but she didn't. She let the salesman try the ring on her finger. It was a perfect fit and she was enchanted with it.

King held her hand in his and looked down at it. The sentiment of the old-fashioned design made him strangely uneasy. It looked like an heirloom, something a wife would want to pass down to a child. His eyes met hers and he couldn't hide his misgivings. He'd more or less been forced into proposing by the situation, but he hadn't thought past the honeymoon. Here was proof that Tiffany had years, not months, of marriage in mind, while he only wanted to satisfy a raging hunger.

"Don't you like it?" she asked worriedly.

"It's exquisite," he replied with a determined smile. "Yes, I like it."

She sighed, relieved. "Don't you want to choose one?" she asked when he waved the salesman away.

"No," he said at once. He glanced down at her. "I'm not much on rings. I'm allergic to gold," he added untruthfully, thinking fast.

"Oh. Oh, I see." She brightened a little. It had hurt to think he didn't want to wear a visible symbol of his married status.

In no time at all, they were caught up in wedding arrangements. King didn't want a big society wed ding, and neither did Tiffany. They settled for a small, intimate service in the local Presbyterian church with friends and family. A minister was engaged, and although traditionally the groom was to provide the flowers, Tiffany made the arrangements for them to be delivered.

Her one regret was not being able to have the elegant wedding gown she'd always imagined that she'd have. Such a dress seemed somehow out of place at a small service. She chose to wear a modern designer suit in white, instead, with an elegant little hat and veil.

She wished that her long-time best friend hadn't married a military man and moved to Germany with him. She had no one to be maid or matron of honor. There again, in a small service it wouldn't be noticeable.

King became irritable and withdrawn as the wedding date approached. He was forever away on business or working late at the office, and Tiffany hoped this wasn't going to become a pattern for their married life. She was realistic enough to understand that his job was important to him, but she wanted a big part in his life. She hoped she was going to have one.

The night before the wedding, King had supper with Tiffany and her father. He was so remote even Harrison noticed.

"Not getting cold feet, are you?" Harrison teased, and tensed at the look that raced across the younger man's face before he could conceal it.

"Of course not," King said curtly. "I've had a lot on my mind lately, that's all."

Tiffany paused with her glass in midair to glance at King. She hadn't really noticed how taut his face was, how uneasy he seemed. He'd never spoken of marriage in anyone's memory. In fact, he'd been quite honest about his mistrust of it. He'd had girlfriends for as long as Tiffany could remember, but there had never been a reason to be jealous of any of them. King never let himself become serious over a woman.

"Don't drop that," King murmured, nodding toward the loose grip she had on the glass.

She put it down deliberately. "King, you do want to marry me, don't you?" she asked abruptly.

His eyes met hers across the table. There was no trace of expression in them. "I wouldn't have asked you if I hadn't meant to go through with it," he replied.

The phrasing was odd. She hesitated for a few seconds, tracing patterns on her glass. "I could work for a while longer," she suggested, "and we could put off the ceremony."

"We're getting married Saturday," he reminded her. "I already have tickets for a resort on Jamaica for our honeymoon. We're scheduled on a nonstop flight Saturday afternoon to Montego Bay."

"Plans can be changed," she replied.

He laughed humorlessly. "Now who's got cold feet?" he challenged.

"Not me," she lied. She smiled and drained her glass. But inside, butterflies were rioting in her stomach. She'd never been more unsure of her own hopes and dreams. She wanted King, and he wanted her. But his was a physical need. Had she pushed him into this marriage after all, and now he was going to make the most of it? What if he tired of her before the honeymoon was even over?

She stopped this train of thought. It was absurd to have so little faith in her own abilities. She'd vamped him at her twenty-first birthday party, to such effect that he'd come home from his business trip out of his mind over her. If she could make him crazy once, she could do it twice. She could make him happy. She could fit in his world. It was, after all, hers, too. As for Carla, and the complications she might provoke, she could worry about that later. If she could keep King happy at home, Carla wouldn't have a prayer of splitting them up.

Her covetous eyes went over him as if they were curious hands, searching out his chiseled mouth, his straight nose, the shape of his head, the darkness of his hair, the deep-set eyes that could sparkle or stun. He was elegant, devastating to look at, a physical presence wherever he went. He had power and wealth and the arrogance that went with them. But was he capable of love, with the sort of loveless background he'd had? Could he learn it?

As she studied him, his head turned and he studied her, his eyes admiring her beauty, her grace. Something altered in the eyes that swept over her and his eyes narrowed.

"Am I slurping my soup?" she asked with an impish grin.

Caught off guard, he chuckled. "No. I was thinking what a beauty you are," he said honestly. "You won't change much in twenty years. You may get a gray hair or two, but you'll still be a miracle."

"What a nice thing to say," she murmured, putting down her soup spoon. "You remember that, in about six years' time. I'll remind you, in case you forget."

"I won't forget," he mused.

Harrison let out a faint sigh of relief. Surely it was only prenuptial nerves eating at King. The man had known Tiffany for years, after all, there wouldn't be many surprises for them. They had things in common and they liked each other. Even if love was missing at first, he knew it would come. It would have to. Nothing short of it would hold a man like King.

Tiffany glanced at her father's somber expression and lifted an eyebrow. "It's a wedding, not a wake," she chided.

He jerked and then laughed. "Sorry, darling, I was miles away."

"Thinking about Lettie?" she teased.

He glared at her. "I was not," he snapped back. "If they ever barbecue her, I'll bring the sauce."

"You know you like her. You're just too stubborn to admit it."

"She's a constant irritation, like a mole at the belt line."

Tiffany's eyes widened. "What a comparison!"

"I've got a better one," he said darkly.

"Don't say it!"

"Spoilsport," he muttered, attacking his slice of apple pie as if it were armed.

King was listening to the byplay, not with any real interest. He was deeply thoughtful and unusually quiet. He glanced at Tiffany occasionally, but now his expression was one of vague concern and worry. Was he keeping something from her? Perhaps something was going on in his life that she didn't know about. If she could get him alone later, perhaps he'd tell her what it was.

But after they finished eating, King glanced quickly at his watch and said that he had to get back to the office to finish up some paperwork.

Tiffany got up from the table and followed him into the hallway. "I thought we might have a minute to talk," she said worriedly. "We're getting married tomorrow."

"Which is why I have to work late tonight," he replied tersely. "It's been a very long time since I've given myself a week off. Ask your father."

"I don't have to. I know how hard you work." She looked up at him with real concern. "There's still time to back out, if you want to."

His eyebrows shot up. "Do you want to?"

She gnawed the inside of her lip, wondering if that was what he wanted her to admit. It was so difficult trying to read his thoughts. She couldn't begin to.

"No," she said honestly. "I don't want to. But if you do…"

"We'll go through with it," he said. "After all, we've got plenty in common. And it will keep the business in the family."

"Yes, it will go to our children…" she began.

"Good God," he laughed without mirth, "don't start talking about a family! That's years away, for us." He scowled suddenly and stared at her. "You haven't seen a doctor, have you?"

"For the blood test," she reminded him, diverted.

"For birth control," he stated flatly, watching her cheeks color. "I'll take care of it for now. But when we get back from our honeymoon, you make an appointment. I don't care what you choose, but I want you protected.''

She felt as if he'd knocked her down and jumped on her feetfirst. ''You know a lot about birth control for a bachelor,'' she faltered.

''That's why I'm still a bachelor,'' he replied coldly. He searched her eyes. ''Children will be a mutual decision, not yours alone. I hope we've clarified that.''

''You certainly have,'' she said.

''I'll see you at the church tomorrow.'' His eyes went over her quickly. ''Try to get a good night's sleep. We've got a long day and a long trip ahead of us.''

''Yes, I will.''

He touched her hair, but he didn't kiss her. He laughed again, as if at some cold personal joke. He left her in the hallway without a backward glance. It was a foreboding sort of farewell for a couple on the eve of their wedding, and because of it, Tiffany didn't sleep at all.

Chapter 7

The next day dawned with pouring rain. It was a gloomy morning that made Tiffany even more depressed than she had been to start with. She stared at her reflection in the mirror and hardly recognized herself. She didn't feel like the old devil-may-care Tiffany who would dare anything to get what she wanted from life. And she remembered with chilling precision the words of an old saying: *Be careful what you wish for; you might get it.*

She made up her face carefully, camouflaging her paleness and the shadows under her eyes. She dressed in her neat white suit and remembered belatedly that she hadn't thought to get a bouquet for the occasion. It was too late now. She put on her hat and pulled the thin veil over her eyes, picked up her purse, and went out to join her father in the downstairs hall. The house seemed empty and unnaturally quiet, and she wondered what her late mother would have thought of this wedding.

Harrison, in an expensive dark suit with a white rose in his lapel, turned and smiled at his daughter as she came down the staircase.

"You look lovely," he said. "Your mother would have been proud."

"I hope so."

He came closer, frowning as he took her hands and found them ice-cold. "Darling, are you sure this is what you want?" he asked solemnly. "It's not too late to call it off, you know, even now."

For one mad instant, she thought about it. Panic had set in firmly. But she'd gone too far.

"It will work out," she said doggedly, and smiled at her father. "Don't worry."

He sighed impotently and shrugged. "I can't help it. Neither of you looked much like a happy couple over dinner last night. You seemed more like people who'd just won a chance on the guillotine."

"Oh, Dad," she moaned, and then burst out laughing. "Trust you to come up with something outrageous!"

He smiled, too. "That's better. You had a ghostly pallor when you came down the stairs. We wouldn't want people to mistake this ceremony for a wake."

"God forbid!" She took his arm. "Well," she said, taking a steadying breath, "let's get it over with."

"Comments like that are so reassuring," he muttered to himself as he escorted her out the door and into the white limousine that was to take them to the small church.

Surprisingly, the parking lot was full of cars when they pulled up at the curb.

"I don't remember inviting anyone," she ventured.

"King probably felt obliged to invite his company people," he reminded her. "Especially his executive staff."

"Well, yes, I suppose so." She waited for the chauffeur to open the door, and she got out gingerly, keenly aware that she didn't have a bouquet. She left her purse in the limo, in which she and King would be leaving for the airport immediately after the service. A reception hadn't been possible in the time allocated. King would probably have arranged some sort of refreshments for his office staff, of course, perhaps at a local restaurant.

Tiffany entered the church on her father's arm, and they paused to greet two of King's vice presidents, whom they knew quite well.

King was standing at the altar with the minister. The decorations were unsettling. Instead of the bower of roses she'd hoped for, she found two small and rather scruffy-looking flower arrangements gracing both sides of the altar. Carelessly tied white ribbons festooned the front pews. Family would have been sitting there, if she and King had any close relatives. Neither did, although Tiffany claimed Lettie as family, and sure enough, there she sat, in a suit, and especially a hat, that would have made fashion headlines. Tiffany smiled involuntarily at the picture her fashionable godmother made. Good thing the newspapers weren't represented, she thought, or Lettie would have overshadowed the bride and groom for splendor in that exquisite silk dress. And, of course, the hat.

The minister spotted Tiffany in the back of the church with her father and nodded to the organist who'd been hired to provide music. The familiar strains of the "Wedding March" filled the small church.

Tiffany's knees shook as she and her father made their way down the aisle. She wondered how many couples had walked this aisle, in love and with hope and joy? God knew, she was scared to death of what lay ahead.

And just when she thought she couldn't feel any worse, she spotted Carla in the front pew on King's side of the church. With disbelief, she registered that the woman was wearing a white lacy dress with a white veiled hat! As if she, not Tiffany, were the bride!

She felt her father tense as his own gaze followed hers, but neither of them were unconventional enough to make any public scene. It was unbelievable that King would invite his paramour here, to his wedding. But, then, perhaps he was making a statement. Tiffany would be his wife, but he was making no concessions in his personal life. When confronted by the pitiful floral accessories, and her lack of a bouquet, she wasn't particularly surprised that he'd invited Carla. She and her dress were the final indignity of the day.

King glanced sideways as she joined him, her father relinquishing her and going quickly to his own seat. King's eyes narrowed on her trim suit and the absence of a bouquet. He scowled.

She didn't react. She simply looked at the minister and gave him all her attention as he began the ceremony.

There was a flutter when, near the end of the service, he called for King to put the ring on Tiffany's finger. King searched his pockets, scowling fiercely, until he found it loose in his slacks' pocket, where he'd placed it earlier. He slid it onto Tiffany's finger, his face hardening when he registered how cold her hand was.

The minister finished his service, asked if the couple had any special thing they'd like to say as part of the ceremony. When they looked uneasy, he quickly pronounced them man and wife and smiled as he invited King to kiss the bride.

King turned to his new wife and stared at her with narrowed eyes for a long moment before he pulled up the thin veil and bent to kiss her carelessly with cold, firm lips.

People from the front pews surged forward to offer congratulations. Lettie was first. She hugged Tiffany warmly, acting like a mother hen. Tiffany had to fight tears, because her new status would take her away from the only surrogate mother she'd ever known. But she forced a watery smile and started to turn to her father when she saw a laughing Carla lift her arms around King's neck and kiss him passionately, full on the mouth.

The minister looked as surprised as Tiffany and her father did. Harrison actually started forward, when Lettie took his arm.

"Walk me to my car, Harrison," Lettie directed.

Seconds later, King extricated himself and shook hands with several of his executives. Tiffany gave Carla a look that could have fried an egg and deliberately took her father's free arm.

"Shall we go?" she said to her two elderly companions.

"Really, dear, this is most...unconventional," Lettie faltered as Tiffany marched them out of the church.

"Not half as unconventional as forgetting which woman you married," she said loudly enough for King, and the rest of the onlookers, to hear her.

She didn't look at him, although she could feel furious eyes stabbing her in the back.

She didn't care. He and his lover had humiliated her beyond bearing, and on her wedding day. She was tempted to go home with her father and get an annulment on the spot.

As she stood near the limousine with Harrison and Lettie, debating her next move, King caught her arm and parceled her unceremoniously into the limousine. She barely had time to wave as the driver took off.

"That was a faux pas of the highest order," he snapped at her.

"Try saying that with less lipstick on your mouth, darling," she drawled with pure poison.

He dug for a handkerchief and wiped his mouth, coming away with the vivid orange shade that Carla had been wearing.

"My own wedding," she said in a choked tone, her hands mangling her small purse, "and you and that…creature…make a spectacle of the whole thing!"

"You didn't help," he told her hotly, "showing up in a suit, without even a bouquet."

"The bouquet should have come from you," she said with shredded pride. "I wasn't going to beg for one. Judging by those flower arrangements you provided, if you'd ordered a bouquet for me, it would have come with dandelions and stinging nettle! As for the suit, you didn't want a big wedding, and a fancy gown would have been highly inappropriate for such a small ceremony."

He laughed coldly, glaring at her. "You didn't say you wanted a bouquet."

"You can give Carla one later and save her the trouble of having to catch mine."

He cursed roundly.

"Go ahead," she invited. "Ruin the rest of the day."

"This whole damned thing was your idea," he snapped at her, tugging roughly at his constricting tie. "Marriage was never in my mind, until you started throwing yourself at me! God knew, an affair was never an option."

She searched his averted profile sadly. As she'd feared, this had been, in many ways, a shotgun wedding. She mourned for the old days, when they were friends and enjoyed each other's company. Those days were gone forever.

"Yes. I know," she said heavily. She leaned back against the seat and felt as if she'd been dragged behind the car. She'd lost her temper, but it wasn't really his fault. He was as much a victim as she was, at the moment. "I don't know why I should have expected you to jump with joy," she said when she'd calmed a little. "You're right. I did force you into a marriage you didn't want. You have every right to be furious." She turned to him with dead eyes in a face like rice paper. "There's no need to go on with this farce. We can get an annulment, right now. If you'll just have the driver take me home, I'll start it right away."

He stared at her as if he feared for her sanity. "Are you out of your mind?" he asked shortly. "We've just been married. What the hell do you think it will say to my executives and my stockholders if I annul my marriage an hour after the ceremony?"

"No one has to know when it's done," she said reasonably. "You can fly to Jamaica and I'll go back to New York with Lettie until this all blows over."

"Back to modeling, I suppose?" he asked curtly.

She shrugged. "It's something to do," she said.

"You have something to do," he returned angrily. "You're my wife."

"Am I?" she asked. "Not one person in that church would have thought so, after you kissed Carla. In fact, I must say, her dress was much more appropriate than mine for the occasion, right down to the veil."

He averted his eyes, almost as if he were embarrassed. She leaned back again and closed her own eyes, to shut him out.

"I don't care," she said wearily. "Decide what you want, and I'll do it. Anything at all, except," she added, turning her head to stare at him with cold eyes, "sleep with you. That I will not do. Not now."

His eyebrows arched. "What the hell do you mean?"

"Exactly what I just said," she replied firmly. "You can get… that…from Carla, with my blessings." She almost bit through her lip telling the flat lie. Pride was very expensive. She closed her eyes again, to hide the fear that he might take her up on it. "I've been living in a fool's paradise, looking for happily ever after, dreaming of satin and lace and delicious nights and babies. And all I've got to show for it is a secondhand lust without even the gloss of friendship behind it and an absolute edict that I'm never to think of having a child."

He sat back in his own seat and stared straight ahead. Yes, he'd said that. He'd been emphatic, in fact, about not having children right away. He'd withdrawn from her in the past two weeks, so deliberately that he'd given the impression of a man being forced to do something he abhorred. He'd arranged a quick ceremony, but he hadn't let his secretary—Carla—arrange the flowers. He'd left that duty to another subordinate. He wondered what the hell had gone wrong. Only two sparse and not-very-attractive flower arrangements had graced the church and Tiffany had been denied a bouquet. He knew that it was deliberate, that Carla was somehow involved, but there was no way to undo the damage. By the time he saw the flowers it was far too late to do anything. Carla's dress and the kiss had been as much a surprise to him as it had to Tiffany. She wouldn't believe it, though. She was thinking of the things he'd denied her.

She'd been denied more than just flowers, at that. She hadn't had a photographer, a ring bearer, flower girls and attendants, a reception—she'd lacked all those as well. And to top it all off, it looked as if he'd wanted to kiss his secretary instead of his new bride, in front of the whole assembly.

His eyes sought her averted face again, with bitter regret. He'd fought marrying her from the start, hating his weakness for her, punishing her for it. This had been a travesty of a wedding, all around. She was bitter and wounded, and it was his fault. He studied her drawn countenance with haunted eyes. He remembered Tiffany all aglitter with happiness and the sheer joy of living, teasing him, laughing with him, tempting him, loving him. He could have had all that, just for himself. But he'd let his fears and misgivings cloud the occasion, and Tiffany had suffered for them.

He drew in a long breath and turned his eyes back to the window. This, he thought wearily, was going to be some honeymoon.

In fact, it was some honeymoon, but not at all the sort Tiffany had once dreamed about having. Montego Bay was full of life, a colorful and fascinating place with a long history and the friendliest, most welcoming people Tiffany could ever remember in her life.

They had a suite at an expensive resort on the beach, and fortunately it contained two rooms. She didn't ask King what he thought of her decision to sleep in the smaller of the two rooms; she simply moved in. She paid him the same attention she'd have paid a female roommate, and she didn't care what he thought about that, either. It was her honeymoon. She'd had no real wedding, but she was going to have a honeymoon, even if she had to spend it alone.

King had brought along his laptop with its built-in fax-modem, and he spent the evening working at the small desk near the window.

Tiffany put on a neat beige trouser suit and fixed her hair in a soft bun atop her head. She didn't even worry with makeup.

"I'm going to the restaurant to have supper," she announced.

He looked up from his monitor, with quiet, strangely subdued eyes. "Do you want company?"

"Not particularly, thanks." She went out the door while he was getting used to being an unwelcome tourist.

She sat alone at a table and ate a seafood salad. She had a piña colada with her meal, and the amount of rum it contained sent her head spinning.

She was very happy, all of a sudden, and when a steel band began to play to the audience, she joined in the fun, clapping and laughing with the crowd.

It wasn't until a tall, swarthy man tried to pick her up that she realized how her behavior might be misinterpreted. She held up her left hand and gave the man a smile that held just the right portions of gratitude and regret. He bowed, nonplussed, and she got up to pay her bill.

King was out on the patio when she returned, but he looked at her curiously when she stumbled just inside the closed door and giggled.

"What the hell have you been doing?" he asked.

"Getting soused, apparently," she said with a vacant smile. "Do you have any idea how much rum they put in those drinks?"

"You never did have a head for hard liquor," he remarked with a faint smile.

"A man tried to pick me up."

The smile turned into a cold scowl. He came back into the room slowly. He'd changed into white slacks and a patterned silk shirt, which was hanging open over his dark-haired chest. He looked rakish with his hair on his forehead and his eyes glittering at her.

"I showed him my wedding ring," she said to placate him. "And I didn't kiss him. It is, after all, my wedding day."

"A hell of a wedding day," he replied honestly.

"If I hadn't gone all mushy, we'd still be friends," she said with a sad little sigh as the liquor made her honest. "I wish we were."

He moved a little closer and his chest rose and fell roughly. "So do I,'' he admitted tersely. He searched her sad eyes. "Tiffany, I...didn't want to be married.''

"I know. It's all right,'' she said consolingly. "You don't have to be. When we get back, I'll go and see an attorney.''

He didn't relax. His eyes were steady and curious, searching over her slender body, seeking out all the soft curves and lines of her. "You shouldn't have grown up.''

"I didn't have much choice.'' She smothered a yawn and turned away. "Good night, King.''

He watched her go with an ache in his belly that wouldn't quit. He wanted her, desperately. But an annulment would be impossible if he followed her into her room. And she'd already said that she didn't want him. He turned back to the cool breeze on the patio and walked outside, letting the wind cool his hot skin. He'd never felt so restless, or so cold inside.

Tiffany awoke with a blinding headache and nausea thick in her throat. She managed to sit up on the side of the bed in her simple white cotton gown. It covered every inch of her, and she was glad now that she'd decided not to pack anything suggestive or glamorous. She looked very young in the gown and without her makeup, with her dark hair in a tangle around her pale face.

King knocked at the door and then walked in, hesitating in the doorway with an expression of faint surprise when he saw the way she looked. His brows drew together emphatically.

"Are you all right?'' he asked curtly.

"I have a hangover,'' she replied without looking at him. "I want to die.''

He breathed roughly. "Next time, leave the rum to the experts and have a soft drink. I've got some tablets in my case that will help. I'll bring you a couple. Want some coffee?''

"Black, please,'' she said. She didn't move. Her head was splitting.

When he came back, she still hadn't stirred. He shook two tablets into her hand and gave her a glass of water to swallow them with. She thanked him and gave back the glass.

"I'll bring the coffee in as soon as room service gets here,'' he said. "I don't suppose you want breakfast, but it would help not to have an empty stomach."

"I can't eat anything." She eased back down on the bed, curled up like a child with her eyes closed and a pillow shoved over her aching head.

He left her against his better judgment. A caring husband would have stayed with her, held her hand, offered sympathy. He'd fouled up so much for her in the past few weeks that he didn't think any overtures from him would be welcomed. She didn't even have to tell him why she'd had so much to drink the night before. He already knew.

Minutes later, he entered the room with the coffee and found Tiffany on the floor, gasping for breath. She couldn't seem to breathe. Her face was swollen. Red-rimmed eyes looked up at him with genuine panic.

"Good God." He went to the phone by her bed and called for a doctor, in tones that made threats if one wasn't forthcoming. Then he sat on the floor beside her, his expression one of subdued horror, trying to reassure her without a single idea what to do. She looked as if she might suffocate to death any minute.

The quick arrival of the doctor relieved his worry, but not for long.

Without even looking at King, the doctor jerked up the telephone and called for an ambulance.

"What did she eat?" the doctor shot at him as he filled a syringe from a small vial.

"Nothing this morning. She had a hangover. I gave her a couple of aspirins a few minutes ago..."

"Is she allergic to aspirin?" he asked curtly.

"I...don't know."

The doctor gave him a look that contained equal parts of contempt and anger. "You are her husband?" he asked with veiled sarcasm, then turned back to put the needle directly into the vein at her elbow.

"What are you giving her?" King asked curtly.

"Something to counteract an allergic reaction. You'd better go out and direct the ambulance men in here. Tell them not to lag behind."

King didn't argue, for once. He did exactly as he was told, cold all over as he took one last, fearful glance at Tiffany's poor swollen face. Her eyes were closed and she was still gasping audibly.

"Will she die?" King choked.

The doctor was counting her pulse. "Not if I can help it," he said tersely. "Hurry, man!"

King went out to the balcony and watched. He heard the ambulance arrive an eternity of seconds later. Almost at once ambulance attendants came into view. He motioned them up the stairs and into Tiffany's bedroom.

They loaded her onto a gurney and carried her out. Her color was a little better and she was breathing much more easily, but she was apparently unconscious.

"You can ride in the ambulance with her, if you like," the doctor invited.

King hesitated, not because he didn't want to go with her, but because he'd never been in such a position before and he was stunned.

"Follow in a cab, then," the other man rapped. "I'll ride with her."

He muttered under his breath, grabbed his wallet and key, locked the door, and went down to catch a cab at the front of the hotel. It was a simple exercise, there was always a cab waiting and a doorman to summon it.

Minutes later, he was pacing outside the emergency room waiting for the doctor to come out. Strange how quickly his priorities had changed and rearranged in the past few minutes. All it had taken was seeing Tiffany like that. He knew that as long as he lived, the sight of her on the floor would come back to haunt him. It had been so unnecessary. He'd never bothered to ask if she was allergic to anything. He hadn't wanted to know her in any intimate or personal way.

Now he realized that he knew nothing at all, and that his ignorance had almost cost her her life this morning. Nothing was as important now as seeing that she had the best care, that she got better, that she never had to suffer again because of a lack of interest or caring on his part. He might not have wanted this marriage, but divorce was not feasible. He had to make the best of it. And he would.

Chapter 8

But the thing that hadn't occurred to him was that Tiffany might not care one way or the other for his concern. When she was released from the hospital later that day, with a warning not to ever touch aspirin again in any form, her whole attitude toward her husband had changed. Every ounce of spirit seemed to have been drained out of her.

She was quiet, unusually withdrawn on the way back to the hotel in the taxi. Her paleness hadn't abated, despite her treatment. The swelling had gone, but she was weak. He had to help her from the taxi and into the hotel.

"I never asked if you had allergies," King said as he supported her into the elevator. He pushed the button for their floor. "I'm sorry this happened."

"The whole thing was my fault," she said wearily. "My head hurt so bad that it never occurred to me to question what you were giving me. I haven't had an aspirin since I was thirteen."

He studied her as she leaned back against the wall of the elevator, looking as if she might collapse any minute. "One way or another, you've had a hell of a wedding."

She laughed mirthlessly. "Yes, I have."

The elevator jerked to a stop and the doors opened. King abruptly swung her up into his arms and carried her to their room, putting her down only long enough to produce the key and open the door.

She let her head rest on his broad shoulder and closed her eyes, pretending that he loved her, pretending that he wanted her. She'd lived on dreams of him most of her life, but reality had been a staggering blow to her pride and her heart. They were married, and yet not married.

He carried her into the sitting room and deposited her gently on the sofa. "Are you hungry?" he asked. "Do you think you could eat something?"

"A cold salad, perhaps," she murmured. "With thousand island dressing, and a glass of milk."

He phoned room service, ordering that for her and a steak and salad and a beer for himself.

"I didn't know you ever drank beer," she mused when he hung up.

He glanced at her curiously. "We've lived in each other's pockets for as long as I can remember," he said. "Amazing, isn't it, how little we actually know about each other."

She pushed back her disheveled hair with a sigh and closed her eyes. "I don't think there's a drop of anything left in my poor stomach. I couldn't eat last night. I didn't even have breakfast this morning."

"And you don't need to lose weight," he stated solemnly. He scowled as he searched over her body. "Tiffany, you've dropped a few pounds lately."

"I haven't had much appetite for several months," she said honestly. "It wasn't encouraged when I was modeling. After I came home, and we...decided to get married, I was too busy to eat a lot. It's been a hectic few weeks."

He hadn't missed the hesitation when she spoke of their decision to marry. He hated the way she looked. The change in her was so dramatic that anyone who'd known her even a year before wouldn't recognize her.

His heavy sigh caught her attention.

"Do you want to go home?" she asked.

The sadness in her eyes hurt him. "Only if you do," he said. "There are plenty of things to see around here. We could go up and walk around Rose Hall, for example,'' he added, mentioning a well-known historical spot.

But she shook her head. "I don't feel like sight-seeing, King," she told him honestly. "Couldn't we go home?"

He hesitated. She was worn-out from the rushed wedding, the trip over here, her experience with the allergic reaction. He wanted to tell her that a night's sleep might make all the difference, but the sight of her face was enough to convince him that she'd do better in her own environment.

"All right," he said gently. "If that's what you want. We'll leave at the end of the week. I'll try to get tickets first thing in the morning."

She nodded. "Thank you."

Room service came with their orders and they ate in a strained silence. Tiffany finished her salad and coffee and then, pleading tiredness, got up to go to bed.

She started for her own room.

"Tiffany."

His deep voice stopped her at the doorway. She turned. "Yes?"

"Sleep with me."

Her heart jerked in her chest. Her eyes widened.

"No," he said, shaking his head as he got to his feet. "I don't want you that way yet, honey," he said softly, to lessen the blow of the statement. "You don't need to be alone tonight. It's a king-size bed, and you won't need to worry that I'll take advantage."

It was very tempting. He'd hardly touched her in almost a month. And although he didn't know it, any fear of having him take advantage of the situation was nonexistent. She sometimes felt that she'd have given six months of her life to have him throw her down onto the nearest available surface and ravish her to the point of exhaustion. She wondered what he'd say if she admitted that. Probably it would be just one more complication he didn't want. And there was still Carla, waiting back home.

"All right," she said after a minute. "If you don't mind..."

"Mind!" He bit off the word and turned away before she could see his strained face. "No," he said finally. "I don't...mind."

He was behaving very oddly, she mused as she showered and then put on another of her white embroidered gowns. The garment was very concealing and virginal, and there was a cotton robe that matched it, with colorful pastel embroidery on the collar and the hem, and even on the belt that secured it around her trim waist.

When she walked into the other room and approached King's, through the slightly open door she heard him talking on the telephone.

"...be home tomorrow," he was saying. "I'll want everything ready when I get to the office. Yes, we'll talk about that," he added in a cold, biting tone. "No, I wouldn't make any bets on it. You do that. And don't foul things up this time or it will be the last mistake you make on my payroll. Is that clear?"

He put down the receiver with an angry breath and ran a hand through his own damp hair. He was wearing an incredibly sexy black velour robe with silver trim. When he turned, Tiffany's knees went weak at the wide swath of hair-roughened chest it bared to her hungry eyes.

He was looking at her, too. The gown and robe should have been dampening to any man's ardor, because she looked as virginal as he knew she was. But it inflamed him. With her face soft in the lamplight, her eyes downcast, she made him ache.

"Which side of the bed do you want?" he asked curtly.

"I like the left, but it doesn't matter."

He waved her toward it. Trying not to notice that he was watching her obsessively, she drew off the robe and spread it across the back of a nearby chair before she turned down the covers and, tossing off her slippers, climbed under the sheet.

He looked at her with darkening, narrowed eyes. She could see his heartbeat, it was so heavy. While she watched, his hand went to the loop that secured the belt of his robe and loosened it, catching the robe over one arm to toss it aside. He stood there, completely nude, completely aroused, and let her look.

Her lips parted. It was a blatant, arrogant action. She didn't know what to do or say. She couldn't manage words. He was...exquisite. He had a body that would have made the most jaded woman swoon with pleasure. And, remembering the heated mastery of his lovemaking, her body throbbed all over. It was in her eyes, her flushed face, her shaking heartbeat.

"Take it off," he said in a husky soft tone. "I want to look at you."

She wasn't able to think anymore. She clammered out from under the sheet and onto her knees, struggling to throw off the yards of concealing cotton. At last, she tugged it over her head and threw it onto the floor. Her body was as aroused as his. He knew the signs.

He moved around the bed. As he came closer, he caught the rose scent of her. Forgotten was the rocky start to their honeymoon, the accusations, the sudden illness. He approached her like a predator.

She made a helpless little sound and abruptly reached beside her to sweep both pillows off the bed and onto the floor as she surged backward, flat on the sheet, her legs parted, her arms beside her head. She trembled there, waiting, a little afraid of the overwhelming masculinity of him, but hungry and welcoming despite it.

He came onto the bed, slowly, stealthily, as if he still expected her to bolt. One lean, powerful leg inserted itself between both of hers, his chest hovered above hers, his arms slid beside her, his fingers interlaced with her own and pinned them beside her ears.

"It's…pagan." She choked.

He understood. He nodded slowly, and still his eyes held hers, unblinking, as his leg moved against the inside of hers in a sinuous, sensual touch that echoed the predatory approach of his mouth to her parted lips.

It was like fencing, she thought half-dazed. His body teased her, his mouth teased her, every part of him was an instrument of seduction. It was nothing like their earlier lovemaking, when he'd kissed her, touched her, even pleasured her. This was the real thing, a prowling, tenderly violent stalking of the female by the male, a controlled savagery of pleasure that enticed but never satisfied, that aroused and denied all at the same time.

Her body shook as if with a fever and she arched, pleaded, pulled, twisted, trying to make him end it. The tension was at a level far beyond any that he'd ever subjected her to.

He touched her very briefly and then, finally—finally!—moved down into the intimacy that she'd begged for. But even as it came, it frightened her. She stiffened, her nails digging into his muscular arms, her teeth biting at her lower lip.

He stilled. His heart was beating furiously, but his eyes, despite their fierce need, were tender.

"First times are always difficult," he whispered. He held her eyes as he moved again, very gently. "Can you feel me, there?" he murmured wickedly, bending to brush his smiling lips against hers. They rested there as he moved again. "Talk to me."

"Talk?" She gasped as she felt him invading her. "Good... Lord...!"

"Talk to me," he chided, laughing as she clutched him. "This isn't a ritual of silence. We're learning each other in the most intimate way there is. It shouldn't be an ordeal. Look down my body while I'm taking you. See how it looks when we fit together like puzzle pieces."

"I couldn't!" she gasped.

"Why?" He stilled and deliberately lifted himself for a few seconds. "Look, Tiffany," he coaxed. "It isn't frightening, or sordid, or ugly. We're becoming lovers. It's the most beautiful thing a man and woman can share, especially when it's as emotional as it is physical. Look at us."

It was a powerful enticement, and it worked. But her shocked eyes didn't linger. They went quickly back to his, as if to seek comfort and reassurance.

"You're my wife," he whispered softly. He caught his breath as his next movement took him completely to the heart of her, and his eyes closed and he shivered.

Seeing him vulnerable like that seemed to rob her of fear and the slight discomfort of their intimate position. One of her hands freed itself and moved hesitantly to touch his drawn face, to sift through his thick, cool black hair. His eyes opened, as if the caress startled him.

It was incredible, to look at him and talk to him with the lights on while they fused in the most shocking way. But he didn't seem at all shocked. In fact, he watched her the whole time. When his hips began to move lazily against hers and the shock of pleasure lifted her tight against him, and she gasped, he actually laughed.

"For...shame!" She choked, shivering with each movement as unexpected pleasure rippled through her.

"Why?" he taunted.

"You laughed!"

"You delight me," he whispered, bending to nibble her lips as his movements lengthened and deepened. "I've never enjoyed it like this."

Which was an uncomfortable reminder that he was no novice. She started to speak, but as if he sensed what she was going to say, he suddenly shifted and she was overwhelmed by the most staggering pleasure she'd ever felt.

It possessed her. She couldn't even breathe. She arched up, helpless, her mouth open, her eyes dazed, gasping with each deliberate movement of his body. She was trying to grasp something elusive and explosive, reaching toward it with every thread of her being. It was just out of her reach, almost, almost, tantalizingly close...

"Oh...please!" she managed to say in a shuddering little cry.

He looked somber, almost violent in that instant. He said something, but she didn't hear him. Just as the tension abruptly snapped and she heard her own voice sobbing in unbearable pleasure, his face buried itself in her soft throat and his own body shuddered with the same sweet anguish.

For a long time afterward, his breathing was audible, raspy and unsteady at her ear. She gasped for air, but she was still clinging to him, as if she could retain just a fragment of that extraordinary wave of pleasure that had drowned her for endless seconds.

"It doesn't last," she whispered shakenly.

"It couldn't," he replied heavily. "The human body can only bear so much of it without dying."

Her hands spread on his damp shoulders with a sort of wonder at the feel of him so deep in her body. She moved her hips and felt the pleasure ripple through her unexpectedly.

She laughed at her discovery.

He lifted his dark head and his eyes, sated now, searched hers. "Experimenting?"

She nodded, and moved gently again, gasping as she found what she was searching for. But along with it came a new and unfamiliar stinging sensation and she stilled.

He brushed back her damp hair gently. "Your body has to get used to this," he murmured. "Right now, you need rest more than you need me." He moved very slowly and balanced himself on his hands. "Try to relax," he whispered. "This may be uncomfortable."

Which was an understatement. She closed her eyes and ground her teeth together as he lifted away from her.

He eased over onto his back with a heavy breath and turned his head toward her. "And now you know a few things that you didn't, before," he mused, watching her expressions. "Want a bath or just a wet cloth?"

The matter-of-fact question shouldn't have shocked her, but it did. Her nudity shocked her, too, and so did his. Without the anesthetic of passion, sex was very embarrassing. She got to her feet and gathered up her gown, holding it over her front.

"I...I think I'd like a shower," she stammered.

He got out of bed, completely uninhibited, and took the gown from her fingers, tossing it onto the bed. "None of that," he taunted softly. "We're an old married couple now. That means we can bathe together."

Her expression was complicated. "We can?"

"We can."

He led her into the bathroom, turned on the shower jets, and plopped her in before him.

It was an adventure to bathe with someone. She was alternately embarrassed, intrigued, amused, and scandalized by it. But she laughed with pure delight at this unexpected facet of married life. It had never occurred to her that she might take a shower with King, even in her most erotic dreams.

Afterward, they dried each other and he carried her back to bed, placing her neatly under the covers, nude, before he joined her and turned off the lights.

He caught her wandering hand and drew it to his hairy chest with a chuckle.

"Stop that," he murmured. "You're used up. No more for you tonight, or probably tomorrow, either."

She knew he was right, but she was still bristling with curiosity and the newness of intimacy.

His hand smoothed her soft hair. "We have years of this ahead of us," he reminded her quietly. "You don't have to rush in as if tonight was the last night we'd ever have together."

She lay against him without speaking. That was how it had felt, though. There was a sort of desperation in it, a furious seeking and holding. She didn't understand her own fears, except that she was fatally uncertain of Kingman Marshall's staying power. Carla still loomed in the background, and even if he'd found Tiffany enjoyable in bed, he was still getting used to a married status that he'd never wanted. She didn't kid herself that it was smooth sailing from now on. In fact, the intimacy they'd just shared might prove to be more of a detriment than an advantage in the cold light of day.

The worry slowly drifted away, though, as she lay in her husband's warm arms and inhaled the expensive scent of his cologne. Tomorrow would come, but for tonight, she could pretend that she was a much-loved wife with a long happy marriage ahead of her. King must know that she hadn't had time to see a doctor about any sort of birth control. But he apparently hadn't taken care of it as he'd said he would. He'd been too hungry for her to take time to manage it himself.

She thought of a child and her whole body warmed and flushed. He didn't want children, but she did, desperately. If he did leave her for Carla, she'd have a small part of him that the other woman could never take from her.

From pipe dreams to reality was a hard fall. But she woke alone the next day, with her gown tossed haphazardly on the bed with her. King was nowhere in sight, and it was one o'clock in the afternoon!

She put on the gown and her slippers and robe and padded slowly out into the sitting room of the suite. It was empty, too. Perturbed, she went across into her own room and found some white jeans and a red-and-blue-and-white jersey to slip into. She tied her hair back in a red ribbon, slipped on her sneakers, and started to go out and look for King when she saw the envelope on the dresser.

Her name was on the front in a familiar bold black slash. She picked up the envelope and held it, savoring for a moment the night before, because she knew inside herself that whatever was in that envelope was going to upset her.

She drew out a piece of hotel stationery and unfolded it.

Tiffany,
I've left your passport, and money for a return ticket and anything else you need in your purse. I've paid the hotel bill. An emergency came up back home. I meant to tell you last night that I had to leave first thing this morning, but it slipped my mind. I managed to get the last seat on a plane to San Antonio. We'll talk later.
King.

She read it twice more, folded it, and put it into the envelope. What sort of emergency was so pressing that a man had to leave his honeymoon to take care of it?

That was when something niggled at the back of her mind, and she remembered the snatch of conversation she'd overheard before they'd gone to bed. King had said that he'd be home tomorrow— today. She drew in a harsh breath. *Carla.* Carla had phoned him and he'd left his wife to rush home. She'd have bet her last dollar that there was no emergency at all, unless it was that he was missing his old lover. Apparently, she thought with despair, even the heated exchange of the night before hadn't been enough for him. And why should it? She was a novice, only a new experience for him. Carla was probably as expert as he was.

With wounded pride stiffening her backbone, she picked up the telephone and dialed the international code and her father's private office number.

"Hello?" he answered after a minute.

The sound of his voice was so dear and comforting that she hesitated a few seconds to choke back hurt tears. "Hi, Dad," she said.

"What the hell's going on?" he demanded. "King phoned me from the airport and said he was on his way into the city to sort out some union dispute at one of the branch offices. Since when do we have a union dispute?" he asked irritably.

"I don't know any more than you do," she said. "He left me a note."

He sighed angrily. "I could have dealt with a dispute, if there had been one. I've been doing it longer than he has, and I'm the senior partner."

He didn't have to say that. She already knew it. "I'm coming home tomorrow," she told him. "I, uh, sort of had a bout with some aspirin and I'm feeling bad. I was ready to leave, but there was only one seat available on the morning flight. We agreed that I'd follow tomorrow," she lied glibly.

It sounded fishy to Harrison, but he didn't say a word about it. "You're allergic to aspirin," he said pointedly.

"I know, but King didn't. I had a splitting headache and he gave me some. He had to take me to the hospital, but I'm fine now, and he knows not to give me aspirin again."

"Damnation!" her father growled. "Doesn't he know anything about you?"

"Oh, he's learning all the time," she assured him. "I'll talk to you tomorrow, Dad. Can you have the car meet me at the airport? I'm not sure if King will remember me, if he's involved in meetings." *Or with Carla,* she thought. King hadn't said anything about her coming home at all in his terse little note. She was going to be a surprise.

There was an ominous pause. "I'll remember you. Phone me when you get in. Take care, darling."

"You, too, Dad. See you."

He put down the receiver, got out of his chair, and made the door in two strides. He went past his secretary and down the hall to King's office, pushed open the door on a startled Carla, and slammed it back.

She actually gasped. "Mr....Mr. Blair, can I do something for you?"

"You can stop trying to sabotage my daughter's marriage, you black-eyed little pit viper," he said with furious eyes. "First you fouled up the flowers, then you wore a dress to the ceremony that even to the most unprejudiced person in the world looked like a wedding gown. You kissed the groom as if you were the bride, and now you've managed to get King back here on some tom fool excuse, leaving his bride behind in Jamaica!"

Carla's eyes almost popped. "Mr. Blair, honestly, I never meant..."

"You're fired," he said furiously.

She managed to get to her feet and her cheeks flamed. "Mr. Blair, I'm King's secretary," she said through her teeth. "You can't fire me!"

"I own fifty-one percent of the stock," he told her with pure contempt. "That means I can fire whom I damned well please. I said, you're fired, and that means you're fired."

She drew an indignant breath. "I'll file a complaint," she snapped back.

"Go right ahead," he invited. "I'll call the tabloids and give them a story that you'll have years to live down, after they do a little checking into your background."

It was only a shot in the dark, but she didn't know that. Her face went paper white. She actually shivered.

"Your severance pay will be waiting for you on the way out," he said shortly.

He went out the office door, almost colliding with King.

"I've just fired your damned secretary!" Harrison told King with uncharacteristic contempt. "And if you want a divorce from my daughter so you can go chasing after your sweet little paramour, here, I'll foot the bill! The two of you deserve each other!"

He shouldered past King and stormed away down the hall, back into his own office. The walls actually shook under the force with which he slammed the door.

King gave Carla a penetrating look. He walked into the office, and closed the door. Harrison had beaten him to the punch. He was going to fire Carla, but first he wanted some answers.

"All right," he said. "Let's have it."

"Have what?" she faltered. She moved close to him, using every wile she had for all she was worth. "You aren't going to let him fire me, are you?" she teased, moving her hips gently against his body. "Not after all we've been to one another?"

He stiffened, but not with desire, and stepped back. "What we had was over long before I married Tiffany."

"It never had to be," she cooed. "She's a child, a little princess.

What can she be to a man like you? Nothing more than a new experience.''

"You phoned and said there was a labor dispute," he reminded her. "I can't find a trace of it."

She shrugged. "Tom said there were rumors of a strike and that I'd better let you know. Ask him, if you don't believe me." She struck a seductive pose. "Are you going to let him fire me?" she asked again.

He let out a harsh breath. Harrison was breathing fire. Apparently he'd got the wrong end of the stick and Carla had done nothing to change his mind.

"You've made an enemy of him," King told her. "A bad one. Your behavior at the wedding is something he won't forget."

"You will," she said confidently. "You didn't want to marry her. You didn't even check about the flowers or a silly bouquet, because you didn't care, and she embarrassed you by wearing a suit to get married in." She made a moue of distaste. "It was a farce."

"Yes, thanks to you." He stuck his hands into his pockets and glowered at her. He wondered how far out of his mind he'd been to get involved with this smiling boa constrictor. She'd been exciting and challenging, but now she was a nuisance. "I'll see what I can do about getting you another job. But not here," he added quietly. "I'm not going against Harrison."

"Is that why you married her?" she asked. "So that you could be sure of inheriting the whole company when he dies?"

"Don't be absurd."

She shrugged. "Maybe it's why she married you, too," she said, planting a seed of doubt. "She'll have security now, even if you divorce her, won't she?"

Divorce. Harrison had said something about a divorce. "I have to talk to Harrison," he said shortly. "You'll work your two weeks notice, despite what he said, and I'll see what's going at another office."

"Thank you, sweet," she murmured. She moved close and reached up to kiss him. "You're a prince!"

He went out the door with a handkerchief to his mouth, wiping off the taste of her on his way to his partner's office.

Chapter 9

Harrison just glared at King when he went into the office and closed the door behind him.

"I don't care what you say, she's history," Harrison told the younger man. "She's meddled in my daughter's affairs for the last time!"

King scowled. He didn't like the look of his partner. "I haven't said a word," he said softly. "Calm down. If you want her to go, she goes. But let her work out her notice."

Harrison relaxed a little. His eyes were still flashing. He looked deathly pale and his breathing was unusually strained. He loosened his tie. "All right. But that's all. That silly woman," he said in a raspy voice. "She's caused…Tiffany…no end of heartache already, and now I've got…to cause her…more…" He paused with a hand to his throat and laughed in surprise. "That's funny. My throat hurts, right up to my jaw. I can't…" He grimaced and suddenly slumped to the floor. He looked gray and sweat covered his face.

King buzzed Harrison's secretary, told her to phone the emergency services number immediately and get some help into Harrison's office.

It was terribly apparent that Harrison was having a heart attack. His skin was cold and clammy and his lips were turning blue. King began CPR at once, and in no time, he had two other executives of the company standing by to relieve him, because he had no idea how long he'd have to keep it up before the ambulance came.

As it happened, less than five minutes elapsed between the call and the advent of two EMTs with a gurney. They got Harrison's heartbeat stabilized, hooked him up to oxygen and rushed him down to the ambulance with King right beside them.

"Any history of heart trouble in him or his family?" the EMT asked abruptly as he called the medical facility for orders.

"I don't know," King said irritably. For the second time in less than a week, he couldn't answer a simple question about the medical backgrounds of the two people he cared for most in the world. He felt impotent. "How's he doing?" he asked.

"He's stabilized, but these things are tricky," the EMT said. "Who's his personal physician?"

Finally, a question he could answer. He gave the information, which was passed on to the doctor answering the call at the medical center.

"Any family to notify?" the man relayed.

"I'm his son-in-law," King said grimly. "My wife is in Jamaica. I'll have to get her back here." He dreaded that. He'd have to tell her on the phone, and it was going to devastate her. But they couldn't afford the loss of time for him to fly down there after her. Harrison might not live that long.

The ambulance pulled up at the hospital, and Harrison, still unconscious, was taken inside to the emergency room. King went with him, pausing just long enough to speak with the physician before he found a pay phone and called the hotel in Jamaica. But more complications lay in store. Mrs. Marshall, he was told, had checked out that very morning. No, he didn't know where she'd gone, he was sorry.

King hung up, running an angry hand through his hair. Playing a grim hunch, he telephoned Harrison's house instead of his own. A maid answered the call.

"This is Kingman Marshall. Is my wife there?" he asked.

"Why, yes, sir. She got in about two hours ago. Shall I get her for you?"

He hesitated. "No. Thank you."

This was one thing he couldn't do on the phone. He told the doctor where he was going, hailed a taxi and had it drive him to Harrison's home.

Tiffany was upstairs, unpacking. She paled when she saw King come in the door. She hadn't expected her father to be at home, since it was a working day. She hadn't expected to see King, either.

"Looking for me?" she asked coolly. "I've decided that I'm going to live here until the divorce."

Divorce! Everything he was going to say went right out of his mind. He'd left her after the most exquisite loving of his life. Hadn't he explained the emergency that had taken him from her side? It wasn't as if he hadn't planned to fly right back. He'd had no idea at all that Carla had manufactured the emergency.

"Tiffany," he began, "I flew back because there was an emergency..."

"Yes, and I know what it was," she replied, having phoned the office just awhile ago. "My father fired your secretary, and you had to rush back to save her job. I've just heard all about it from the receptionist, thanks."

"The receptionist?"

"I wanted to know if you were in. She talked to someone and said I should call back, you were in the middle of some sort of argument with my father..."

He let out a short breath. "We'll talk about that later. There's no time. Your father's had a heart attack. He's in the emergency room at city general. Get your purse and let's go."

She grasped her bedpost. "Is he alive? Will he be all right?"

"He was seeing the doctor when I left to fetch you," he replied. "Come on."

She went out with him, numb and shocked and frightened to death. Her life was falling apart. How would she go on if she lost her father? He was the only human being on earth who loved her, who needed her, who cared about her.

Through waves of fear and apprehension, she sat motionless as he drove her Jaguar to the hospital. When he pulled up at the emergency entrance and stopped, she leapt out and ran for the doors, not even pausing to wait for him.

She went straight to the clerk, rudely pushing in front of the person sitting there.

"Please." She choked, "my father, Harrison Blair, they just brought him in with a heart attack…?"

The clerk looked very worried. "You need to speak with the doctor, Miss Blair. Just one minute…"

King joined her in time to hear the clerk use her maiden name. Under different circumstances, he'd have been furious about that. But this wasn't the time.

The clerk motioned Tiffany toward another door. King took her arm firmly and went with her, sensing calamity.

A white-coated young doctor gestured to them, but he didn't take them into the cubicle where King had left her father. Instead, he motioned them farther down the hall to a small cluster of unoccupied seats.

"I'm sorry. I haven't done much of this yet, and I'm going to be clumsy about it," the young man said solemnly. "I'm afraid we lost him. I'm very sorry. It was a massive heart attack. We did everything we possibly could. It wasn't enough."

He patted her awkwardly on the upper arm, his face contorted with compassion.

"Thank you," King said quietly, and shook his hand. "I'm sure it's hard for you to lose a patient."

The doctor looked surprised, but he recovered quickly. "We'll beat these things one day," he said gently. "It's just that we don't have the technology yet. The worst thing is that his family physician told us he had no history of heart problems." He shook his head. "This was unexpected, I'm sure. But it was quick, and painless, if that's any comfort." He looked at Tiffany's stiff, shocked face and then back at King. "Bring her along with you, please. I'll give you something for her. She's going to need it. Any allergies to medicines?" he asked at once.

"Aspirin," King said. He glanced down at Tiffany, subduing his own sorrow at Harrison's loss. "Are you allergic to anything else, sweetheart?" he added tenderly.

She shook her head. She didn't see, didn't hear, didn't think. Her father was dead. King had argued with him over Carla. Her father was dead because of King.

She pushed his hand away. Her eyes, filled with hatred, seared into his mind as she looked up at him. "This is your fault." She choked. "My father is dead! Was keeping Carla worth his life?"

He sucked in a sharp breath. "Tiffany, that wasn't what happened…"

She moved away from him, toward the cubicle where the doctor was waiting. She was certain that she never wanted to speak to her husband again for as long as she lived.

The next few days were a total black void. There were the arrangements to be made, a service to arrange, minor details that somehow fell into place with King's help. The Blair home became like a great empty tomb. Lettie came to stay, of course, and King did, too, in spite of her protests. He slept in a bedroom down the hall from Tiffany's, watching her go through life in a trance while he dealt with friends and lawyers and the funeral home. She spoke to him only when it became necessary. He couldn't really blame her for the way she felt. She was too upset to reason. There would be plenty of time to explain things to her when she'd had time to recover. Meanwhile, Carla was on her way out of the office despite her plea to work out her notice. On that one point, King had been firm. She had her severance pay and a terse letter of recommendation. If only he could have foreseen, years ago, the trouble it was going to cause him when he put her out of his life, all this anguish with Tiffany might have been avoided. But at that time, Carla had been an exciting companion and he'd never considered marrying anyone. Now he was paying the price for his arrogance.

Undaunted by her firing, Carla showed up at the funeral home, only to be escorted right back out again by King. She made some veiled threat about going to the tabloids with her story, and he invited her to do her worst. She was out of his life. Nothing she did would ever matter to him again, and he said so. She left, but with a dangerous glint in her cold eyes.

She didn't come to the funeral service, Tiffany noted, or to the graveside service. Apparently she'd been told that it wasn't appropriate. Some people, Lettie had said huffily, had no breeding and no sensitivity. She said it deliberately, and within King's hearing. He didn't react at all. Whatever he felt, he was keeping it to himself.

The only chip in his stony front came the night of the funeral, when he sat in Harrison's study with only a lamp burning and downed a third of a bottle of Harrison's fine Scotch whiskey.

Lettie intruded long enough to ask if he wanted anything else from the kitchen before the housekeeper closed it up.

He lifted the glass toward her. "I'm drinking my supper, thanks," he drawled.

Lettie closed the door behind her and paused in front of the big antique oak desk, where his booted feet were propped on its aged, pitted surface.

"What are you going to do about the house?" she asked abruptly. Her eyes were red. She'd cried for Harrison almost as much as Tiffany had. Now her only concern was the girl's future.

"What do you mean, what am I going to do?" he asked. "It belongs to Tiffany."

"No, it doesn't," Lettie said worriedly. "Harrison was certain right up until the wedding ceremony that you weren't going to go through with the marriage. He wanted Tiffany provided for if something happened to him, and he didn't want her to have to be dependent on you. So he went to see his personal accountant about having everything he owned put in trust for her, including the house and his half of the business." She folded her hands at her waist, frowning worriedly. "But the accountant couldn't be located. Then Harrison found out that the man had been steadily embezzling from him for the past three years." She lifted her hands and spread them. "Just this week, he learned that a new mortgage had been taken out on the house and grounds and the money transferred to an account in a Bahamian bank." She grimaced as King lowered his feet to the floor and sat up. "He'd hired a private detective and was to see his attorney this afternoon after filing a lawsuit against the man before he skips the country with what's left of Harrison's fortune. If you can't stop him, Tiffany will be bankrupt."

"Good God!" King got to his feet, weaving a little. "No wonder he was so upset! Lettie, why the hell didn't you say something before this?''

''Because I wasn't sure that I had the right to involve you, except where the business is concerned,'' she said flatly. ''You must know that Tiffany doesn't want to continue your marriage.''

His face was drawn taut like a rope. ''I know it.''

She shrugged. ''But there's no one else who can deal with this. I certainly can't. I can't even balance my checkbook. I wouldn't know how to proceed against the man.''

King leaned forward with his head in his hands. ''Get me a pot of strong coffee,'' he said through heavy breaths. ''Then I want every scrap of information you have on the man and what Harrison planned.''

Lettie brightened just a little. ''We'll all miss him,'' she said gently as she turned toward the door. ''But Tiffany most of all. He was both parents to her, for most of her life.'' She hesitated. ''She needs you.''

He didn't reply. She didn't seem to expect him to. She went out and closed the door behind her.

Tiffany was sitting on the bottom step of the staircase, looking pale and worn. Her eyes were red and she had a crumpled handkerchief in her hand. The long white gown and robe she was wearing seemed to emphasize her thinness.

''Child, you should be in bed,'' Lettie chided softly.

''I can't sleep.'' She stared at the study door. ''Is he in there?''

Lettie nodded.

''What's he doing?''

''Getting drunk.''

That was vaguely surprising. ''Oh.''

''I want to know why my father had a heart attack,'' she said grimly. ''The receptionist wouldn't let me speak with King the day Daddy died because he and my father were arguing. Then at the funeral, one of his co-workers said it was a pity about the blow-up, because it was only seconds later when he collapsed. I know he fired Carla. Was that why King argued with him?''

''I don't know. Tiffany,'' she said, approaching the girl, ''this is a vulnerable time for all of us. Don't say anything, do anything, that you'll have cause to regret later. King's hurt, too. He respected Harrison. Even if they did argue, they were friends as well as business partners for a long time."

"They were friends until I married King." Tiffany corrected her. "My father thought it was a mistake. He was right."

"Was he? It's early days yet, and some marriages can have a rocky beginning. It's no easy thing to make a life with another person. Fairy tales notwithstanding, even the most loving couples have to adjust to a shared coexistence."

"It helps if both partners work at it," Tiffany said.

"I agree. Get in there and do your part," her godmother prodded, jerking her red head toward the closed study door. "If you want answers, he's the only person who's got them."

Tiffany stared at the carpet for a minute and then got slowly to her feet.

"That's the idea," Lettie said. "I'm going to make him a pot of coffee. We have a few complications. Get him to tell you about them. Shared problems are another part of building a marriage."

Tiffany laughed, but without mirth. She went to the door after Lettie vanished down the hall and opened it.

King glanced at her from behind the desk as she came into the room. "I didn't plan to strand you in Montego Bay," he said pointedly. "I would have been on my way back that night."

"Would you?" She went to the chair in front of the desk, a comfortable burgundy leather armchair that she'd occupied so many times when she and her father had talked. She sighed. "The whole world has changed since then."

"Yes. I know."

She leaned back, sliding her hands over the cold leather arms, over the brass studs that secured it to the frame. "Tell me how he died, King."

He hesitated, but only for a second. His chiseled mouth tugged into a mocking smile. "So they couldn't wait to tell you, hmm? I'm not surprised. Gossip loves a willing ear."

"Nobody told me anything. It was inferred."

"Same difference." He spread his hands on the desk and stood up. "Okay, honey, you want the truth, here it is. He fired Carla and they had a royal row over it. I walked in and he started on me. I followed him to his office and got there just in time to watch him collapse.''

She let out the breath she'd been holding. Her nails bit into the leather arms of the chair. ''Why did you follow him? Were you going to talk him out of it?''

''No. But there's more to this than an argument over Carla,'' he added, searching for the right way to explain to her the tangled and devastating fact of her father's loss of wealth.

''Yes, there is. We've already agreed that I maneuvered you into a marriage you didn't want,'' she said curtly. ''We can agree that what happened in Montego Bay was a form of exorcism for both of us and let it go at that,'' she added when he started to speak. ''Charge me with desertion, mental cruelty, anything you like. Let me know when the papers are ready and I'll sign them.''

His eyes flashed like black fires. ''There won't be a divorce,'' he said shortly.

She was surprised by the vehemence in his tone, until she remembered belatedly just what her status was. As her father's heir, by a quirk of fate she was now his business partner. He couldn't afford to divorce her. What an irony.

She cocked her head and looked at him with cold curiosity. ''Oh, yes, I forgot, didn't I? We're business partners now. How nice to have it all in the family. You won't even have to buy me out. What's mine is yours.''

The look on his face was a revelation. Amazing how he could pretend that the thought had never occurred to him.

''That's a nice touch, that look of surprise,'' she said admirably. ''I expect you practiced in front of a mirror.''

''Why are you downstairs at this hour of the night?'' he asked.

''I couldn't sleep,'' she replied, and was suddenly vulnerable. She hated having it show. ''My father was buried today,'' she drawled, ''in case you forgot.''

''We can do without the sarcasm,'' he said. ''Wait a minute.'' He reached into her father's top desk drawer and extracted a bottle. ''Come here.''

She stopped with the width of the desk between them and held her hand out. He shook two capsules into her hand and recapped the bottle.

"Don't trust me with the whole bottle?" she taunted.

That was exactly how he felt, although he wasn't going to admit it. She'd had one too many upsets in the past few weeks. Normally as sound as a rock, even Tiffany could be pushed over the edge by grief and worry. He couldn't add the fear of bankruptcy to her store of problems. That one he could spare her. Let her think him a philanderer, if it helped. When she was strong enough, he'd tell her the truth.

"Take those and try to sleep," he said. "Things will look brighter in the morning."

She stared at the capsules with wounded wet eyes. "He was my rudder," she said in a husky whisper. "No matter how bad things got, he was always here to run to."

His face hardened. Once, he'd been there to run to, before they married and became enemies. "You'll never know how sorry I am," he said tightly. "If you believe nothing else, believe that I didn't cause him to have that heart attack. I didn't argue with him over Carla."

She glanced at him and saw the pain in his eyes for the first time. It took most of the fight out of her. She seemed to slump. "I know you cared about my father, King," she said heavily.

"And in case you're wondering," he added with a mocking smile, "she's gone. She has her severance pay and some sort of reference. You won't see her again."

She studied him silently. "Why?"

"Why, what?"

"Why did my father fire her?"

It was like walking on eggshells, but he had to tell her the truth. "Because she dragged me home from Jamaica with a nonexistent emergency, just to interfere with our honeymoon, and he knew it. He said he'd had enough of her meddling."

"So had I," she returned.

"Not half as much as I had," he said curtly. "Harrison beat me to the punch by five minutes."

"He did?"

"Come here."

He looked faintly violent, and he'd been drinking. She hesitated.

He got up and came around the desk, watching her back away. "Oh, hell, no, you don't," he said in a voice like silk. His arms slid under her and he lifted her clear of the floor. "I've listened to you until I'm deaf. Now you can listen to me."

He went back to his chair and sat down with Tiffany cradled stiffly in his arms.

"No need to do your imitation of a plank," he chided, making himself comfortable. "Drunk men make bad lovers. I'm not in the mood, anyway. Now, you listen!"

She squirmed, but he held her still.

"Carla wasn't supposed to have anything to do with the flowers for our wedding," he said shortly. "I gave that task to Edna, who heads the personnel department, because she grew up in a florist's shop. But I was out of the office and Carla went to her with a forged letter that said I wanted Carla to do it instead."

Tiffany actually gasped.

He nodded curtly. "And she didn't get those arrangements from a florist, she did them herself with wilted flowers that she either got from a florist, or from a florist's trash can! She never had any intention of bringing you a bouquet, either. The whole thing was deliberate."

"How did you find out?"

"I went to see Edna when I flew back from Jamaica and found there was no emergency. I gave her hell about the flowers," he said. "She gave it back, with interest. Then she told me what had really happened. I was livid. I'd gone straight to my office to have it out with Carla when I found your father there."

"Oh."

He searched her stunned eyes. "You don't think much of me, do you?" he asked quietly. "Regardless of how I felt about the wedding, I wouldn't have deliberately hurt you like that."

She grimaced. "I should have known."

"You wore a suit to be married in," he added. "That was a blow to my pride. I thought you were telling me in a nonverbal way that you were just going through the motions."

"And I thought that you wouldn't mind what I wore, because you didn't want to marry me in the first place."

The arm behind her shoulders contracted, and the big, warm hand at the end of it smoothed over her upper arm in an absent, comforting motion. "I drew away from you at a time when we should have been talking about our insecurities," he said after a minute. "We had too many secrets. In fact, we still have them." He took a quick breath. "Tiffany, your father's personal accountant just did a flit with the majority of your inheritance. I'll bet that's what really set your father off, not Carla, although she helped. He was upset because he knew he'd have to tell you what had happened when you came home."

Tiffany's eyes widened. "You mean, Daddy was robbed?"

"In a nutshell," he agreed. He smiled faintly. "So, along with all your other woes, my wife, you may have bankruptcy looming unless I can find that accountant and prosecute him."

"I'm broke?" she said.

He nodded.

She sighed. "There goes my yacht."

"What do you want with one of those?"

She kept her eyes lowered demurely. Her heart was racing, because they were talking as they'd never talked before. "I thought I'd dangle it on the waterfront for bait and see if I could catch a nice man to marry."

That sounded like the girl he used to know. His eyes began to twinkle just faintly and he smiled. "What are you going to do with the husband you've already got?"

She studied his lean face with pursed lips. "I thought you were going to divorce me."

One eyebrow levered up. His eyes dropped to her slender body and traced it with arrogant possession. "Think again."

Chapter 10

The look in his eyes was electric and Tiffany watched him watching her for long, exquisite seconds before his head began to bend.

She lay in his arms, waiting, barely breathing as he drew her closer. It seemed like forever since he'd kissed her, and she wanted him. She reached up, barely breathing, waiting...

The sudden intrusion of Lettie with a tray of coffee and cookies was as explosive as a bomb going off. They both jerked.

She hesitated just inside the door and stared at them. "Shall I go away?" she asked, chuckling.

King recovered with apparent ease. "Not if those are lemon cookies," he said.

Tiffany gasped, but he got up and helped her to her feet with a rakish grin. "Sorry, honey, but lemon cookies are my greatest weakness."

"Do tell," she murmured with her hands on her hips.

He gave her a thorough going-over with acquisitive eyes. "My *second* greatest weakness," he said, correcting her.

"Too late now," she told him and moved a little self-consciously toward Lettie as King swept forward and took the heavy tray from her.

He put it on the coffee table and they gathered around it while Lettie poured coffee into thin china cups and distributed saucers and cookies.

"I'm going to be poor, Lettie," Tiffany told Lettie.

"Not yet, you're not," King murmured as he savored a cookie. "I'll get in touch with the private detective your father hired to trail your elusive accountant, not to mention Interpol. He'll be caught."

"Poor Daddy," Tiffany sighed, tearing a little as she thought of her loss. "He must have only found out."

"About two days before the heart attack, I think," Lettie said heavily. She leaned over to pick up her coffee. "I tried to get him to see a doctor even then. His color wasn't good. That was unusual, too, because Harrison was always so robust—" She broke off, fighting tears.

Tiffany put an arm around her. "There, there," she said softly. "He wouldn't want us to carry on like this."

"No, he wouldn't," King added. "But we'll all grieve, just the same. He was a good man."

Tiffany struggled to get in a deep breath. She bit halfheartedly into a cookie and smiled. "These are good."

"There's a bakery downtown, where they make them fresh every day," Lettie confided.

"I know where it is," King mused. "I stop by there some afternoons to buy a couple to go with my coffee."

Tiffany glanced at him a little shyly and smiled. "I didn't know you liked cookies."

He looked back at her, but he didn't smile. "I didn't know you were allergic to aspirin."

He sounded as if not knowing that fact about her really bothered him, too.

"It's the only thing," she replied. She searched his drawn features. "King, you couldn't have known about Daddy's heart. I didn't even know. You heard what the doctor said. There was no history of heart trouble, either."

He stared at his half-eaten cookie. "It didn't help to have him upset..."

She touched his hand. "It would have happened anyway," she said, and she was sure of it now. "You can only control so much in life. There are always going to be things that you can't change."

He wouldn't meet her eyes. His jaw was drawn tight.

"Yes, I know, you don't like being out of control, in any way," she said gently, surprising him. "But neither of us could have prevented what happened. I remember reading about a politician who had a heart attack right in his doctor's office, and nobody could save him. Do you see what I mean?"

He reached out his free hand and linked it with hers. "I suppose so."

Lettie sipped coffee, lost in her own thoughts. She missed Harrison, too. The house was empty without him. She looked up suddenly. "Good Lord, you only had a one-day honeymoon," she exclaimed.

"It was a good day," King murmured.

"Yes, it was," Tiffany said huskily, and his fingers contracted around hers.

"We'll finish it when we solve our problems here," King replied. "We have all the time in the world."

Tiffany nodded.

"It will be a shame if you can't catch that crook," Lettie said, looking around her at the beauty of the study. "This house is the beginning of a legacy. Harrison had hoped to leave it to his grandchildren."

Tiffany felt King stiffen beside her. Slowly, she unlinked her hand with his and put both hands around her coffee cup.

"We have years to talk about children," she told Lettie deliberately. "Some couples don't ever have them."

"Oh, but you will, dear," Lettie murmured dreamily. "I remember how we used to go shopping, and the nursery department was always the first place you'd stop. You'd touch little gowns and booties and smile and talk about babies..."

Tiffany got to her feet, hoping her sudden paleness wouldn't upset Lettie. She had no way of knowing that King didn't want a child.

"I'm so tired, Lettie," she said, and looked it. She smiled apologetically. "I'd like to try to go back to sleep, if you don't mind."

"Of course not, dear. Can you sleep now, do you think?"

Tiffany reached into the pocket of her robe and produced the two capsules King had given her. She picked up her half-full cup of coffee and swallowed them. "I will now," she said as she replaced the cup in the saucer. "Thank you, King," she added without looking directly at him.

"Will you be all right?" he asked.

She felt that he was trying to make her look at him. She couldn't bear to, not yet. She was thinking about the long, lonely years ahead with no babies. She didn't dare hope that their only night together would produce fruit. That one lapse wasn't enough to build a dream on. Nobody got pregnant the first time. Well, some people did, but she didn't have that sort of luck. She wondered if King remembered how careless he'd been.

"I hope you both sleep well," she said as she went from the room.

"You, too, dear," Lettie called after her. She finished her coffee. "I'll take the tray back to the kitchen."

"I'll do it," King murmured. He got up and picked it up, less rocky on his feet now that he'd filled himself full of caffeine.

"Are you going to try to sleep?"

He shook his head. "I've got too much work to do. It may be the middle of the night here, but I can still do business with half the world. I have to wrap up some loose ends. Tomorrow, I'm going to have my hands full tracing that accountant."

Lettie went with him to the kitchen and sorted out the things that needed washing.

King paused at the door, his face solemn and thoughtful. "Stay close to Tiffany tomorrow, will you?" he asked. "I don't want her alone."

"Of course, I will." She glanced at him. "Are you worried about Carla?"

He nodded. "She's always been high-strung, but just lately she seems off balance to me. I don't think she'd try to do anything to Tiffany. But there's no harm in taking precautions."

"I wish…" she began and stopped.

"Yes. I wish I'd never gotten involved with her, either," he replied, finishing the thought for her. "Hindsight is a grand thing."

"Indeed it is." She searched his bloodshot eyes. "You aren't sorry you married Tiffany?"

"I'm sorry I waited so long," he countered.

"But there are still problems?" she probed gently.

He drew in a long breath. "She wants babies and I don't."

"Oh, King!"

He winced. "I've been a bachelor all my life," he said shortly. "Marriage was hard enough. I haven't started adjusting to it yet. Fatherhood…" His broad shoulders rose and fell jerkily. "I can't cope with that. Not for a long time, if ever. It's something Tiffany will have to learn to live with."

Lettie bit down on harsh words. She sighed worriedly. "Tiffany's still very young, of course," she said pointedly.

"Young and full of dreams," King agreed. He stared at the sink. "Impossible dreams."

Outside the door, the object of their conversation turned and made her way slowly back upstairs, no longer thirsty for the glass of milk she'd come to take to bed with her. So there it was. King would never want a child. If she wanted him, it seemed that she'd have to give up any hopes of becoming a mother. Some women didn't want children. It was a pity that Tiffany did.

She didn't have to avoid King in the days that followed. He simply wasn't home. Business had become overwhelming in the wake of Harrison Blair's death. There were all sorts of legalities to deal with, and King had a new secretary who had to learn her job the hard way. He was very seldom home, and when he was, he seemed to stay on the telephone.

Lettie was still in residence, because Tiffany had begged her to stay. The house was big and empty without Harrison, but Lettie made it bearable. And on the rare occasions when King was home, their meals weren't silent ones. Lettie carried on conversations with herself if no one else participated, which amused Tiffany no end.

She hadn't paid much attention to the date. She'd grieved for two long weeks, crying every time she saw familiar things of her father's, adjusting to life without him. But just as she was getting used to the lonely house, another unexpected complication presented itself.

Tiffany suddenly started losing her breakfast. She'd never had any such problems before, and even if it was too soon for tests, deep inside she knew that she was pregnant. She went from boundless joy to stifling fear in a matter of seconds as she realized how this news was going to affect her husband. Her hands went protectively to her flat stomach and she groaned out loud.

She couldn't tell him. He wouldn't want the baby, and he might even suggest...alternatives. There wasn't an option she was willing to discuss. She was going to have her baby, even if she had to leave him and hide it away. That meant that she had to keep her condition secret.

At first it was easy. He was never home. But as the demands of business slowed a couple of weeks later, he began to come home earlier. And he was attentive, gentle with Tiffany, as if he were trying to undo their rocky beginning and start over.

It wounded her to the quick to have to withdraw from those sweet overtures, because she needed him now more than at any time in their shared past. But it was too great a risk to let him come close. Her body was changing. He wasn't stupid. If he saw her unclothed, there were little signs that even a bachelor might notice.

Her behavior surprised him, though, because they'd become much closer after Harrison's death. He'd had business demands that had kept him away from home, and he'd deliberately made very few demands on Tiffany just after her father's death, to give her time to adjust. But now, suddenly, she was talking about going back to modeling in New York, with Lettie to keep her company.

King worried about her attitude. He'd been kept busy with the transfer of authority and stocks and the implementation of Harrison's will, not to mention tracking down the elusive accountant. Perhaps she'd thought he wasn't interested in her feelings. That wasn't true. But when he tried to talk to her, she found dozens of excuses to get out of his vicinity.

Even Lettie was puzzled and remarked about Tiffany's coldness to the man, when he'd done so much for them. But Tiffany only smiled and ignored every word she said. Even from Lettie, the bouts of nausea were carefully concealed. No one was going to threaten her baby, Tiffany told herself. Not even Lettie, who might unwittingly let the cat out of the bag.

She talked about going to New York, but all the while, she was checking into possible escape routes. She could fly anywhere in the world that she wanted to go. Even without her father's fortune, she had a legacy from her mother, which guaranteed her a tidy fixed sum every month paid into her personal checking account. She could live quite well and take care of her child. All she needed was a place to go.

King found her one afternoon poring over travel brochures, which she gathered with untidy haste and stuffed back into a folder as if she'd been caught stealing.

"Planning a trip?" he asked, scowling as he stood over her.

She sat forward on the sofa. "Who, me? No!" She cleared her throat. "Well, not immediately, at least. I thought..." She hesitated while she tried to formulate an answer that would throw him off the track.

"Heard from your friend Mark?" he asked abruptly.

"Mark?" She'd all but forgotten her modeling friend, although she saw Lisa occasionally, and Lisa certainly heard from him. They were becoming an item. "I believe he's in Greece," she added. "Doing a commercial for some swimwear company."

"Yes, he is," King replied thoughtfully. "I saw Lisa's father at a civic-club meeting this week. He said that the two of them are quite serious."

"I'm glad," Tiffany said. "Mark's had a hard life. So has Lisa, in some ways. She's always had money, but her father is a very domineering sort. I hope he isn't planning to throw a stick into their spokes."

"Apparently Lisa's threatened to run away if he does," he mused, and smiled. "Love does make a woman brave, I suppose."

She could have made a nasty remark about Carla, but she let it go and made some careless remark.

"Don't you eat breakfast anymore?" he asked abruptly.

She jumped. "I... Well, no, I don't, really," she stammered. "I've gotten into bad habits since Daddy died," she added with a nervous laugh. "Breakfast reminds me too much of him."

"Which is still no reason to starve yourself, is it?"

She shifted, tracing a flower in the pattern on her skirt. "I'm not starving myself. I just don't like eating breakfast at the table. I have it in my room."

He stood there without speaking, frowning, jingling the loose change in his pocket.

She glanced at the clock and then at him. "Aren't you home early?" she asked.

"Yes." He moved to the armchair beside the sofa and dropped into it. "I thought you might like to know that we've found the runaway accountant."

"Have you really!"

He chuckled at her radiance. "Vengeful girl. Yes, he thought he'd gotten clean away. He was passing the time in luxurious splendor on a private island in the Bahamas when some rogue popped a bag over his head, trussed him up like a duck, and carted him off to a sailboat. He was hauled onto the beach in Miami and summarily arrested."

"Do we know rogues who would do such a thing?" she asked.

He chuckled. "Of course we do!"

"Does he still have any money?"

"All but a few thousand," he replied. "He confessed wholeheartedly when faced with a long prison term for his pains. He offered to give the money back without any prompting. To do him credit, he was sorry about Harrison."

"My father might still be here, if it hadn't been for that skunk. I won't shed any tears for him," she muttered. "I hope he isn't going to get off with a slap on the wrist."

"Not a chance," he replied. "He'll serve time. And he'll never get another job of trust."

"I suppose that's something. But it won't bring Daddy back."

"Nothing will do that."

She crossed her legs and glanced at King. He was restless and irritable. "What's wrong?" she asked.

"I wish I didn't have to tell you."

She sat up, bracing herself for anything. After what she'd just come through, she felt that she could take it on the chin, though, whatever it was. She was stronger than she'd ever been.

"Go ahead," she said. "Whatever it is, I can take it."

He looked at her, saw the new lines in her face, the new maturity. "How you've changed, Tiffany," he murmured absently.

"Stop stalling," she said.

He let out a hollow laugh. "Am I? Perhaps so." He leaned forward, resting his forearms across his knees. "I want you to see a doctor."

Her eyebrows arched. "Me? What for?"

"Because we're married," he replied evenly. "And I've gone without you for as long as I can. That being the case, you have to make some sort of preparation about birth control. We can't have any more lapses."

Steady, girl, she told herself. You can't give the show away now. She swallowed. "You said that you'd take care of it," she hedged.

"Yes, I did, didn't I?" he reflected with a laugh. "And you remember how efficiently I did it, don't you?" he asked pointedly.

She flushed. "It was…unexpected."

"And exquisite," he said quietly. "I dream about how it was. I've tried to wait, to give you time to get over the trauma of losing Harrison. But, to put it bluntly, I'm hurting. I want you."

She felt her cheeks go hot. She still wasn't sophisticated enough for this sort of blunt discussion. "All right," she said. "I'll see the doctor."

"Good girl." He got up and moved toward the sofa, reaching down to pull her up into his arms with a long sigh. "I miss you in my bed, Tiffany," he murmured as he bent to her mouth. "I want you so badly…!"

His mouth opened on hers and she moaned harshly at the pleasure of his embrace. She reached up and held him around the neck, pressing her body to his, moving provocatively, involuntarily.

He groaned harshly and his hands went to her waist to pull her closer. Then, suddenly, he stilled. Holding her rigidly, he lifted his head. His breath seemed to catch in his throat. His eyes looked straight into hers. And while she was trying to decide what had made him stop, his hands smoothed with deliberation over her thick waist and, slowly, down over the faint swell of her stomach.

His face changed. She knew the instant he began to suspect. It was all there, the tautness, the shock, the horror.

She jerked away from him, her face stiff with pain. The breath she drew was painful.

He let his arms fall to his sides. The look he sent to her belly would have won a photo contest.

"No, I won't." She choked out the words before he could speak. She backed toward the door. "I won't do anything about it, I don't care what you say, what you do! It's mine, and I'm going to have it! Do you hear me, I'm going to have it!"

She whirled and ran toward the staircase, desperate to reach the sanctuary of her room. She could lock the door and he couldn't get in, she could outrun him! But out of the corner of her eye, she saw him racing toward her. She'd never make the staircase, not at the speed he was running.

She turned at the last second and went toward the front door, panic in her movements, nausea in her throat. She jerked open the front door and forgot the rain that had made the brick porch as slick as glass. Her feet went out from under her and she fell with a horrible, sickening thud, right on her back.

"Tiffany!"

King's exclamation barely registered. She knew every bone in her body was broken. She couldn't even breathe, much less talk. She had the breath knocked completely out of her. She stared at his white face and didn't really see it at all.

"My...baby," she moaned with the only bit of breath she could muster.

King knelt beside her, his hands running over her gently, feeling for breaks while he strangled on every breath he took. There was a faint tremor in his long fingers.

"Don't try to move," he said uneasily. "Dear God...!" He got up and went back to the doorway. "Lettie! Lettie, get an ambulance, she's fallen!"

"Is she all right?" Lettie's wail came out the door.

"I don't know. Call an ambulance!"

"Yes, dear, right now...!"

King knelt beside Tiffany and took her cold, nerveless hand in his. The rain was coming down steadily beyond the porch, like a curtain between the two of them and the world.

Tiffany sucked in shallow breaths. Tears ran down her cheek. One hand lifted to her stomach. She began to sob. "My baby," she wept. "My baby!"

"Oh, God, don't!" he groaned. He touched her wet cheeks with the backs of his fingers, trying to dry the tears. "You're all right, sweetheart, you're going to be fine. You're going to be fine...Lettie! For God's sake!"

Lettie came at a run, pausing at the slick porch. "I've phoned, and they're on the way right now." She moved onto the wet surface and looked down at Tiffany. "Oh, my dear," she groaned, "I'm so sorry!"

Tiffany was beyond words. She couldn't seem to stop crying. The tears upset King more than she'd ever seen anything upset him. He found his handkerchief and dried her wet eyes, murmuring to her, trying to comfort her.

She closed her eyes. She hurt all over, and she'd probably lost the baby. She'd never get another one. He'd make sure that she took precautions from now on, she'd grow old without the comfort of a child, without the joy of holding her baby in her arms...

The sobs shook her.

King eased down beside her, regardless of the wet floor, and his big hand flattened gently over her flat stomach, pressing tenderly.

"Try not to worry," he whispered at her lips. He kissed her softly, and his hand moved protectively. "The baby's all right. I know he is."

Chapter 11

Tiffany couldn't believe what she'd just heard. Her eyes opened and looked straight into his.

"You don't want it," she whispered.

He drew in a rough breath and his hand spread even more. "Yes, I do," he said quietly. "I want both of you."

She could barely get enough breath to speak, and before she could find the words, the ambulance drowned out even her thoughts as it roared up at the front steps and two EMTs disembarked.

She was examined and then put into the ambulance. King went with her, promising Lettie that he'd phone the minute he knew anything.

Tiffany felt him grasp her hand as the ambulance started up again. "You're forever taking me away in ambulances," she whispered breathlessly.

He brought her hand to his mouth and kissed the palm hungrily. "Wherever you go, I go, Tiffany," he said. But his eyes were saying other things, impossible things. They took the rest of her breath away.

She was taken to the local emergency room and checked thoroughly, by the family physician who was doing rounds.

Dr. Briggs chuckled at her when he'd finished his tests and had the results, over an hour later. "I heard about your wild ride in Montego Bay. Now, here you are in a fall. Maybe marriage doesn't agree with you," he teased, having known her from childhood.

"It agrees with her," King murmured contentedly, watching her with open fascination. "So will having a baby to nurse." He glanced at Briggs. "Is she?"

He nodded, smiling complacently at Tiffany's gasp and radiant smile. "I don't imagine we'll have much trouble computing a delivery date," he added wickedly.

Tiffany flushed and King chuckled.

"One time," he murmured dryly. "And look what you did," he accused.

"What I did!" she exclaimed.

"I only plant. I don't cultivate."

She burst out laughing. She couldn't believe what she was hearing. All that talk about not wanting babies, and here he sat grinning like a Cheshire cat.

"He'll strut for a while," the doctor told her. "Then he'll start worrying, and he won't do any more strutting until after the delivery. You'll have to reassure him at frequent intervals. Expectant fathers," he said on a sigh, "are very fragile people."

"She'll have to have an obstetrician," King was murmuring aloud. He glanced at Briggs. "No offense."

"None taken," the doctor mused.

"A good obstetrician."

"I don't refer pregnant women to any other kind," he was assured.

"We'll need to find a good college, too…"

Tiffany started to protest, but King was at the window, talking to himself and Dr. Briggs held up a hand.

"Don't interrupt him," he told Tiffany. "He's considering all the other appropriate families in town who have baby daughters. He'll have to have the right wife…"

"It could be a girl," she interjected.

"Heresy!" the doctor said in mock alarm.

"Shouldn't we point that out?" she continued, glancing at King.

Dr. Briggs shook his head. "A man has to have dynastic dreams from time to time." He smiled. "You're fine, Tiffany. A few bruises, but nothing broken and that baby is firmly implanted. Just don't overdo during the first trimester. Call me Monday and I'll refer you to an obstetrician. I do not," he added, "deliver babies. I like sleeping at night."

"Are babies born at night?"

"From what I hear, almost all of them," he said with a chuckle.

King took her home, still reeling with his discoveries. He carried her inside, cradling her like a treasure.

Lettie met them at the door, wringing her hands. "You didn't phone," she said accusingly.

"He was too busy arranging the wedding," Tiffany replied.

Lettie looked blank. "Wedding?"

"Our son's."

"Son." Lettie still looked blank. Then her face flushed with glorious surprise. "You're pregnant!"

"Yes," she said.

Lettie gnawed her lip and shot a worried glance at King.

"I know," he said wearily. "I'll have to eat boiled crow for the next month, and I deserve to." He shrugged, holding Tiffany closer. "I didn't know how it was going to feel," he said in his own defense, and he smiled with such tenderness that electricity seemed to run through her relaxed body. "What an incredible sensation."

Tiffany smiled and laid her cheek against his shoulder. "I'm sleepy," she said, yawning.

King glanced at Lettie. "I'm going to put her to bed."

"That's the best place for her," Lettie said with a warm smile. "Let me know if you need anything, dear," she told Tiffany, and bent to kiss the flushed cheek.

"I'll be fine. Thank you, Lettie."

King was grinning from ear to ear all the way up the staircase, and he never seemed to feel her weight at all, because he wasn't even breathing hard by the time they reached the top.

"You don't want children," she murmured drowsily. "You said so."

"We're all entitled to one stupid mistake." He carried her to his room, not hers, and laid her gently on the coverlet. His eyes were solemn as he looked down at her. "For what it's worth, I do want this child. I want it very much. Almost as much as I want you."

She flushed. "King, Dr. Briggs said..." she began cautiously.

He put a finger over her lips. "He said that the first trimester is tricky," he replied. He nodded. "We won't make love again until the baby is at home." He bent and kissed her with aching tenderness. "But we'll sleep in each other's arms, as we should have been doing from the first night, when you were a virgin bride—a beautiful princess bride. If you're cold, I'll warm you. If you're afraid, I'll cuddle you." He pushed back her soft hair. His eyes looked deeply, hungrily into hers. "And if you want to be loved, I'll love you. Like this." His lips drew softly against her mouth, cherishing, tasting. His cheek rested on hers and he sighed. "I'll love you with all my heart," he whispered a little roughly. "For all my life."

Her caught breath was audible. "You...love me?"

"As much as you love me," he agreed. He lifted his head and searched her eyes. "Didn't you think I knew?"

She sighed. "No. Not really."

"That's the only thing I was ever sure of, with you. And sometimes, I wondered why you loved me. I've been a lot of trouble. Still want to keep me, in spite of everything?"

She smiled slowly. "More than ever. Somebody has to teach the baby how to take over corporations when he or she is old enough."

He chuckled. "Well, you're stuck with me, whether you want me or not." He touched her cheek and looked at her with pale eyes that mirrored his awe and delight. "I never dreamed that it would feel like this to belong to someone, to have someone who belonged to me." He sighed. "I didn't think I could."

"I know why," she replied, tracing his mouth with her fingertip. "But we're not like your parents, King. We won't have their problems. We'll have each other and our child."

He began to smile. "So we will."

She drew him down to her lips and kissed him with pure possession. "Now, try to get away," she challenged under her breath.

He chuckled as he met her lips with his. "That works both ways."

She thought what a wonderful godmother Lettie would be to the new arrival, and how proud her father would have been. It made her a little sad to think of him.

But then her husband's warm, strong arms tightened gently around her and reminded her that in life, for each pain, there is a pleasure. She closed her eyes and her thoughts turned to lullabies as the rain beat softly on the roof.

CALLAGHAN'S BRIDE

Chapter 1

The kitchen cat twirled around Tess's legs and almost tripped her on her way to the oven. She smiled at it ruefully and made time to pour it a bowl of cat food. The cat was always hungry, it seemed. Probably it was still afraid of starving, because it had been a stray when Tess took it in.

It was the bane of Tess Brady's existence that she couldn't resist stray or hurt animals. Most of her young life had been spent around rodeos with her father, twice the world champion calf roper. She hadn't had a lot to do with animals, which might have explained why she loved them. Now that her father was gone, and she was truly on her own, she enjoyed having little things to take care of. Her charges ranged from birds with broken wings to sick calves. There was an unbroken procession.

This cat was her latest acquisition. It had come to the back door as a kitten just after Thanksgiving, squalling in the dark, rainy night. Tess had taken it in, despite the grumbling from two of her three bosses. The big boss, the one who didn't like her, had been her only ally in letting the cat stay.

That surprised her. Callaghan Hart was one tough hombre. He'd been a captain in the Green Berets and had seen action in Operation Desert Storm. He was the next-to-eldest of the five Hart brothers who owned the sweeping Hart Ranch Properties, a conglomerate of ranches and feedlots located in several western states. The headquarter ranch was in Jacobsville, Texas. Simon, the eldest brother, was an attorney in San Antonio. Corrigan, who was four years younger than Simon, had married over a year and a half ago. He and his wife Dorie had a new baby son. There were three other Hart bachelors left in Jacobsville: Reynard, the youngest, Leopold, the second youngest, and Callaghan who was just two years younger than Simon. They all lived on the Jacobsville property.

Tess's father had worked for the Hart brothers for a little over six months when he dropped dead in the corral of a heart attack. It had been devastating for Tess, whose mother had run out on them when she was little. Cray Brady, her father, was an only child. There wasn't any other family that she knew of. The Harts had also known that. When their housekeeper had expressed a desire to retire, Tess had seemed the perfect replacement because she could cook and keep house. She could also ride like a cowboy and shoot like an expert and curse in fluent Spanish, but the Hart boys didn't know about those skills because she'd never had occasion to display them. Her talents these days were confined to making the fluffy biscuits the brothers couldn't live without and producing basic but hearty meals. Everything except sweets because none of the brothers seemed to like them.

It would have been the perfect job, even with Leopold's endless pranks, except that she was afraid of Callaghan. It showed, which made things even worse.

He watched her all the time, from her curly red-gold hair and pale blue eyes to her small feet, as if he was just waiting for her to make a mistake so that he could fire her. Over breakfast, those black Spanish eyes would cut into her averted face like a diamond. They were set in a lean, dark face with a broad forehead and a heavy, jutting brow. He had a big nose and big ears and big feet, but his long, chiseled mouth was perfect and he had thick, straight hair as black as a raven. He wasn't handsome, but he was commanding and arrogant and frightening even to other men. Leopold had once told her that the brothers tried to step in if Cag ever lost his temper enough to get physical. He had an extensive background in combat, but even his size alone made him dangerous. It was fortunate that he rarely let his temper get the best of him.

Tess had never been able to understand why Cag disliked her so much. He hadn't said a word of protest when the others decided to offer her the job of housekeeper and cook after her father's sudden death. And he was the one who made Leopold apologize after a particularly unpleasant prank at a party. But he never stopped cutting at Tess or finding ways to get at her.

Like this morning. She'd always put strawberry preserves on the table for breakfast, because the brothers preferred them. But this morning Cag had wanted apple butter and she couldn't find any. He'd been scathing about her lack of organization and stomped off without a second biscuit or another cup of coffee.

"His birthday is a week from Saturday," Leopold had explained ruefully. "He hates getting older."

Reynard agreed. "Last year, he went away for a week around this time of the year. Nobody knew where he was, either." He shook his head. "Poor old Cag."

"Why do you call him that?" Tess asked curiously.

"I don't know," Rey said, smiling thoughtfully. "I guess because, of all of us, he's the most alone."

She hadn't thought of it that way, but Rey was right. Cag was alone. He didn't date, and he didn't go out "with the boys," as many other men did. He kept to himself. When he wasn't working—which was rarely—he was reading history books. It had surprised Tess during her first weeks as housekeeper to find that he read Spanish colonial history, in Spanish. She hadn't known that he was bilingual, although she found it out later when two of the Hispanic cowboys got into a no-holds-barred fight with a Texas cowboy who'd been deliberately baiting them. The Texas cowboy had been fired and the two Latinos had been quietly and efficiently cursed within an inch of their lives in the coldest, most bitingly perfect Spanish Tess had ever heard. She herself was bilingual, having spent most of her youth in the Southwest.

Cag didn't know she spoke Spanish. It was one of many accomplishments she was too shy to share with him. She kept to herself most of the time, except when Dorie came with Corrigan to the ranch to visit. They lived in a house of their own several miles away—although it was still on the Hart ranch. Dorie was sweet and kind, and Tess adored her. Now that the baby was here, Tess looked forward to the visits even more. She adored children.

What she didn't adore was Herman. Although she was truly an animal lover, her affection didn't extend to snakes. The great albino python with his yellow-patterned white skin and red eyes terrified her. He lived in an enormous aquarium against one wall of Cag's room, and he had a nasty habit of escaping. Tess had found him in a variety of unlikely spots, including the washing machine. He wasn't dangerous because Cag kept him well-fed, and he was always closely watched for a day or so after he ate—which wasn't very often. Eventually she learned not to scream. Like measles and colds, Herman was a force of nature that simply had to be accepted. Cag loved the vile reptile. It seemed to be the only thing that he really cared about.

Well, maybe he liked the cat, too. She'd seen him playing with it once, with a long piece of string. He didn't know that. When he wasn't aware anyone was watching, he seemed to be a different person. And nobody had forgotten about what happened after he saw what was subsequently referred to as the "pig" movie. Rey had sworn that his older brother was all but in tears during one of the scenes in the touching, funny motion picture. Cag saw it three times in the theater and later bought a copy of his own.

Since the movie, Cag didn't eat pork anymore, not ham nor sausage nor bacon. And he made everyone who did feel uncomfortable. It was one of many paradoxes about this complicated man. He wasn't afraid of anything on this earth, but apparently he had a soft heart hidden deep inside. Tess had never been privileged to see it, because Cag didn't like her. She wished that she wasn't so uneasy around him. But then, most people were.

Christmas Eve came later in the week, and Tess served an evening meal fit for royalty, complete with all the trimmings. The married Harts were starting their own tradition for Christmas Day, so the family celebration was on Christmas Eve.

Tess ate with them, because all four brothers had looked outraged when she started to set a place for herself in the kitchen with widowed Mrs. Lewis, who came almost every day to do the mopping and waxing and general cleaning that Tess didn't have time for. It was very democratic of them, she supposed, and it did feel nice to at least appear to be part of a family—even if it wasn't her own. Mrs. Lewis went home to her visiting children, anyway, so Tess would have been in the kitchen alone.

She was wearing the best dress she had—a nice red plaid one, but it was cheap and it looked it when compared to the dress that Dorie Hart was wearing. They went out of their way to make her feel secure, though, and by the time they started on the pumpkin and pecan pies and the huge dark fruitcake, she wasn't worried about her dress anymore. Everyone included her in the conversation. Except for Cag's silence, it would have been perfect. But he didn't even look at her. She tried not to care.

She got presents, another unexpected treat, in return for her home-made gifts. She'd crocheted elegant trim for two pillowcases that she'd embroidered for the Harts, matching them to the color schemes in their individual bedrooms—something she'd asked Dorie to conspire with her about. She did elegant crochet work. She was making things for Dorie's baby boy in her spare time, a labor of love.

The gifts she received weren't handmade, but she loved them just the same. The brothers chipped in to buy her a winter coat. It was a black leather one with big cuffs and a sash. She'd never seen anything so beautiful in all her life, and she cried over it. The women gave her presents, too. She had a delicious floral perfume from Dorie and a designer scarf in just the right shades of blue from Mrs. Lewis. She felt on top of the world as she cleared away the dinner dishes and got to work in the kitchen.

Leo paused by the counter and tugged at her apron strings with a mischievous grin.

"Don't you dare," she warned him. She smiled, though, before she turned her attention back to the dishes.

"Cag didn't say a word," he remarked. "He's gone off to ride the fence line near the river with Mack before it gets dark." Mack was the cattle foreman, a man even more silent than Cag. The ranch was so big that there were foremen over every aspect of it: the cattle, the horses, the mechanical crew, the office crew, the salesmen—there was even a veterinarian on retainer. Tess's father had been the livestock foreman for the brief time he spent at the Hart ranch before his untimely death. Tess's mother had left them when Tess was still a little girl, sick of the nomadic life that her husband loved. In recent years Tess hadn't heard a word from her. She was glad. She hoped she never had to see her mother again.

"Oh." She put a plate in the dishwasher. "Because of me?" she added quietly.

He hesitated. "I don't know." He toyed with a knife on the counter. "He hasn't been himself lately. Well," he amended with a wry smile, "he has, but he's been worse than usual."

"I haven't done anything, have I?" she asked, and turned worried eyes up to his.

She was so young, he mused, watching all the uncertainties rush across her smooth, lightly freckled face. She wasn't pretty, but she wasn't plain, either. She had an inner light that seemed to radiate from her when she was happy. He liked hearing her sing when she mopped and swept, when she went out to feed the few chickens they kept for egg production. Despite the fairly recent tragedy in her life, she was a happy person.

"No," he said belatedly. "You haven't done a thing. You'll get used to Cag's moods. He doesn't have them too often. Just at Christmas, his birthday and sometimes in the summer."

"Why?" she asked.

He hesitated, then shrugged. "He went overseas in Operation Desert Storm," he said. "He never talks about it. Whatever he did was classified. But he was in some tight corners and he came home wounded. While he was recuperating in West Germany, his fiancée married somebody else. Christmas and July remind him, and he gets broody."

She grimaced. "He doesn't seem the sort of man who would ask a woman to marry him unless he was serious."

"He isn't. It hurt him, really bad. He hasn't had much time for women since." He smiled gently. "It gets sort of funny when we go to conventions. There's Cag in black tie, standing out like a beacon, and women just follow him around like pet calves. He never seems to notice."

"I guess he's still healing," she said, and relaxed a little. At least it wasn't just her that set him off.

"I don't know that he ever will," he replied. He pursed his lips, watching her work. "You're very domestic, aren't you?"

She poured detergent into the dishwasher with a smile and turned it on. "I've always had to be. My mother left us when I was little, although she came back to visit just once, when I was sixteen. We never saw her again." She shivered inwardly at the memory. "Anyway, I learned to cook and clean for Daddy at an early age."

"No brothers or sisters?"

She shook her head. "Just us. I wanted to get a job or go on to college after high school, to help out. But he needed me, and I just kept putting it off. I'm glad I did, now." Her eyes clouded a little. "I loved him to death. I kept thinking though, what if we'd known about his heart in time, could anything have been done?"

"You can't do that to yourself," he stated. "Things happen. Bad things, sometimes. You have to realize that you can't control life."

"That's a hard lesson."

He nodded. "But it's one we all have to learn." He frowned slightly. "Just how old are you—twenty or so?"

She looked taken aback. "I'm twenty-one. I'll be twenty-two in March."

Now he looked taken aback. "You don't seem that old."

She chuckled. "Is that a compliment or an insult?"

He cocked an amused eyebrow. "I suppose you'll see it as the latter."

She wiped an imaginary spot on the counter with a cloth. "Callaghan's the oldest, isn't he?"

"Simon," he corrected. "Cag's going to be thirty-eight on Saturday."

She averted her eyes, as if she didn't want him to see whatever was in them. "He took a long time to get engaged."

"Herman doesn't exactly make for lasting relationships," he told her with a grin.

She understood that. Tess always had Cag put a cover over the albino python's tank before she cleaned his room. That had been the first of many strikes against her. She had a mortal terror of snakes from childhood, having been almost bitten by rattlesnakes several times before her father realized she couldn't see three feet in front of her. Glasses had followed, but the minute she was old enough to protest, she insisted on getting contact lenses.

"Love me, love my enormous terrifying snake, hmm?" she commented. "Well, at least he found someone who was willing to, at first."

"She didn't like Herman, either," he replied. "She told Cag that she wasn't sharing him with a snake. When they got married, he was going to give him to a man who breeds albinos."

"I see." It was telling that Cag would give in to a woman. She'd never seen him give in to anyone in the months she and her father had been at the ranch.

"He gives with both hands," he said quietly. "If he didn't come across as a holy terror, he wouldn't have a shirt left. Nobody sees him as the soft touch he really is."

"He's the last man in the world I'd think of as a giver."

"You don't know him," Leo said.

"No, of course I don't," she returned.

"He's another generation from you," he mused, watching her color. "Now, I'm young and handsome and rich and I know how to show a girl a good time without making an issue of it."

Her eyebrows rose. "You're modest, too!"

He grinned. "You bet I am! It's my middle name." He leaned against the counter, looking rakish. He was really the handsomest of the brothers, tall and big with blond-streaked brown hair and dark eyes. He didn't date a lot, but there were always hopeful women hanging around. Tess thought privately that he was probably something of a rake. But she was out of the running. Or so she thought. It came as a shock when he added, "So how about dinner and a movie Friday night?"

She didn't accept at once. She looked worried. "Look, I'm the hired help," she said. "I wouldn't feel comfortable."

Both eyebrows went up in an arch. "Are we despots?"

She smiled. "Of course not. I just don't think it's a good idea, that's all."

"You have your own quarters over the garage," he said pointedly. "You aren't living under the roof with us in sin, and nobody's going to talk if you go out with one of us."

"I know."

"But you still don't want to go."

She smiled worriedly. "You're very nice."

He looked perplexed. "I am?"

"Yes."

He took a slow breath and smiled wistfully. "Well, I'm glad you think so." Accepting defeat, he moved away from the counter. "Dinner was excellent, by the way. You're a terrific cook."

"Thanks. I enjoy it."

"How about making another pot of coffee? I've got to help Cag with the books and I hate it. I'll need a jolt of caffeine to get me through the night."

"He's going to come home and work through Christmas Eve, too?" she exclaimed.

"Cag always works, as you'll find out. In a way it substitutes for all that he hasn't got. He doesn't think of it as work, though. He likes business."

"To each his own," she murmured.

"Amen." He tweaked her curly red-gold hair. "Don't spend the night in the kitchen. You can watch one of the new movies on pay-per-view in the living room, if you like. Rey's going to visit one of his friends who's in town for the holidays, and Cag and I won't hear the television from the study."

"Have the others gone?"

"Leo wouldn't say where he was going, but Corrigan's taken Dorie home for their own celebration." He smiled. "I never thought I'd see my big brother happily married. It's nice."

"So are they."

He hesitated at the door and glanced back at her. "Is Cag nice?"

She shifted. "I don't know."

A light flickered in his eyes and went out. She wasn't all that young, but she was innocent. She didn't realize that she'd classed him with the married brother. No woman who found him attractive was going to refer to him as "nice." It killed his hopes, but it started him thinking in other directions. Cag was openly hostile to Tess, and she backed away whenever she saw him coming. It was unusual for

Cag to be that antagonistic, especially to someone like Tess, who was sensitive and sweet.

Cag was locked tight inside himself. The defection of his fiancée had left Cag wounded and twice shy of women, even of little Tess who didn't have a sophisticated repertoire to try on him. His bad humor had started just about the time she'd come into the house to work, and it hadn't stopped. He had moods during the months that reminded him of when he went off to war and when his engagement had been broken. But they didn't usually last more than a day. This one was lasting all too long. For Tess's sake, he hoped it didn't go on indefinitely.

Christmas Day was quiet. Not surprisingly, Cag worked through it, too, and the rest of the week that followed. Simon and Tira married, a delightful event.

Callaghan's birthday was the one they didn't celebrate. The brothers said that he hated parties, cakes and surprises, in that order. But Tess couldn't believe that the big man wanted people to forget such a special occasion. So Saturday morning after breakfast, she baked a birthday cake, a chocolate one because she'd noticed him having a slice of one that Dorie had baked a few weeks ago. None of the Hart boys were keen on sweets, which they rarely ate. She'd heard from the former cook, Mrs. Culbertson, that it was probably because their own mother never baked. She'd left the boys with their father. It gave Tess something in common with them, because her mother had deserted her, too.

She iced the cake and put Happy Birthday on the top. She put on just one candle instead of thirty-eight. She left it on the table and went out to the mailbox, with the cat trailing behind her, to put a few letters that the brothers' male secretary had left on the hall table in the morning mail.

She hadn't thought any of the brothers would be in until the evening meal, because a sudden arctic wave had come south to promote an unseasonal freeze. All the hands were out checking on pregnant cows and examining water heaters in the cattle troughs to make sure they were working. Rey had said they probably wouldn't stop for lunch.

But when she got back to the kitchen, her new leather coat tight around her body, she found Callaghan in the kitchen and the remains of her cake, her beautiful cake, on the floor below a huge chocolate spot on the kitchen wall.

He turned, outraged beyond all proportion, looking broader than usual in his shepherd's coat. His black eyes glittered at her from under his wide-brimmed Stetson. "I don't need reminding that I'm thirty-eight," he said in a soft, dangerous tone. "And I don't want a cake, or a party, or presents. I want nothing from you! Do you understand?"

The very softness of his voice was frightening. She noticed that, of all the brothers, he was the one who never yelled or shouted. But his eyes were even more intimidating than his cold tone.

"Sorry," she said in a choked whisper.

"You can't find a damned jar of apple butter for the biscuits, but you've got time to waste on things like…that!" he snapped, jerking his head toward the ruin of her cake lying shattered on the pale yellow linoleum.

She bit her lower lip and stood just looking at him, her blue eyes huge in her white face, where freckles stood out like flecks of butter in churned milk.

"What the hell possessed you? Didn't they tell you I hate birthdays, damn it?"

His voice cut her like a whip. His eyes alone were enough to make her knees wobble, burning into her like black flames. She swallowed. Her mouth was so dry she wondered why her tongue didn't stick to the roof of it. "Sorry," she said again.

Her lack of response made him wild. He glared at her as if he hated her.

He took a step toward her, a violent, quick movement, and she backed up at once, getting behind the chopping block near the wall.

Her whole posture was one of fear. He stopped in his tracks and stared at her, scowling.

Her hands gripped the edge of the block and she looked young and hunted. She bit her lower lip, waiting for the rest of the explosion that she knew was coming. She'd only wanted to do something nice for him. Maybe she'd also wanted to make friends. It had been a horrible mistake. It was blatantly obvious that he didn't want her for a friend.

"Hey, Cag, could you—" Rey stopped dead in his tracks as he opened the kitchen door and took in the scene with a glance. Tess, white-faced, all but shivering and not from the cold. Cag, with his big hands curled into fists at his side, his black eyes blazing. The cake, shattered against a wall.

Cag seemed to jerk as if his brother's appearance had jolted him out of the frozen rage that had held him captive.

"Here, now," Rey said, talking quietly, because he knew his brother in these flash-fire tempers. "Don't do this. Cag, look at her. Come on, look at her, Cag."

He seemed to come to his senses when he caught the bright glimmer of unshed tears in those blue, blue eyes. She was shaking, visibly frightened.

He let out a breath and his fists unclenched. Tess was swallowing, as if to keep her fear hidden, and her hands were pushed deep into the pockets of her coat. She was shaking and she could barely get a breath of air.

"We have to get those culls ready to ship." Rey was still speaking softly. "Cag, are you coming? We can't find the manifest and the trucks are here for the cattle."

"The manifest." Cag took a long breath. "It's in the second drawer of the desk, in the folder. I forgot to put it back in the file. Go ahead. I'll be right with you."

Rey didn't budge. Couldn't Cag see that the girl was terrified of him?

He eased around his brother and went to the chopping block, getting between the two of them.

"You need to get out of that coat. It's hot in here!" Rey said, forcing a laugh that he didn't feel. "Come on, pilgrim, shed the coat."

He untied it and she let him remove it, her eyes going to his chest and resting there, as if she'd found refuge.

Cag hesitated, but only for an instant. He said something filthy in elegant Spanish, turned on his heel and went out, slamming the door behind him.

Tess slumped, a convulsive shudder leaving her sick. She wiped unobtrusively at her eyes.

"Thanks for saving me," she said huskily.

"He's funny about birthdays," he said quietly. "I don't guess we made it clear enough for you, but at least he didn't throw the cake *at* you," he added with a grin. "Old Charlie Greer used to bake for us before we found Mrs. Culbertson, whom you replaced. Charlie made a cake for Cag's birthday and ended up wearing it."

"Why?" she asked curiously.

"Nobody knows. Except maybe Simon," he amended. "They were older than the rest of us. I guess it goes back a long way. We don't talk about it, but I'm sure you've heard some of the gossip about our mother."

She nodded jerkily.

"Simon and Corrigan got past the bad memories and made good marriages. Cag..." He shook his head. "He was like this even when he got engaged. And we all thought that it was more a physical infatuation than a need to marry. She was, if you'll pardon the expression, the world's best tease. A totally warped woman. Thank God she had enough rope to hang herself before he ended up with her around his neck like an albatross."

She was still getting her breath back. She took the coat that Rey was holding. "I'll put it up. Thanks."

"He'll apologize eventually," he said slowly.

"It won't help." She smoothed over the surface of the leather coat. She looked up, anger beginning to replace fear and hurt. "I'm leaving. I'm sorry, but I can't stay here and worry about any other little quirks like that. He's scary."

He looked shocked. "He wouldn't have hit you," he said softly, grimacing when he saw quick tears film her eyes. "Tess, he'd never! He has rages. None of us really understand them, because he won't talk about what's happened to him, ever. But he's not a maniac."

"No, of course not. He just doesn't like me."

Rey wished he could dispute that. It was true, Cag was overtly antagonistic toward her, for reasons that none of the brothers understood.

"I hope you can find someone to replace me," she said with shaky pride. "Because I'm going as soon as I get packed."

"Tess, not like this. Give it a few days."

"No." She went to hang up her coat. She'd had enough of Callaghan Hart. She wouldn't ever get over what he'd said, the way he'd looked at her. He'd frightened her badly and she wasn't going to work for with a man who could go berserk over a cake.

Chapter 2

Rey went out to the corral where the culls—the nonproducing second-year heifers and cows—were being held, along with the young steers fattened and ready for market. Both groups were ready to be loaded into trucks and taken away to their various buyers. A few more steers than usual had been sold because drought had limited the size of the summer corn and hay crop. Buying feed for the winter was not cost-productive. Not even an operation the size of the Harts's could afford deadweight in these hard economic times.

Cag was staring at the milling cattle absently, his heavy brows drawn down in thought, his whole posture stiff and unapproachable.

Rey came up beside him, half a head shorter, lither and more rawboned than the bigger man.

"Well, she's packing," he said bluntly.

Cag's eyes glanced off his brother's and went back to the corral. His jaw clenched. "I hate birthdays! I know she was told."

"Sure she was, but she didn't realize that breaking the rule was going to be life-threatening."

"Hell!" Cag exploded, turning with black-eyed fury. "I never raised a hand to her! I wouldn't, no matter how mad I got."

"Would you need to?" his brother asked solemnly. "Damn it, Cag, she was shaking like a leaf. She's just a kid, and it's been a rough few months for her. She hasn't even got over losing her dad yet."

"Lay it on," Cag said under his breath, moving restlessly.

"Where's she going to go?" he persisted. "She hasn't seen her mother since she was sixteen years old. She has no family, no friends. Even cooking jobs aren't that thick on the ground this time of year, not in Jacobsville."

Cag took off his hat and wiped his forehead on his sleeve before he replaced it. He'd been helping run the steers down the chute into the loading corral and he was sweating, despite the cold. He didn't say a word.

Leo came up with a rope in his hand, watching his brothers curiously.

"What's going on?" he asked.

"Oh, nothing," Rey muttered, thoroughly disgusted. "Tess made him a birthday cake and he destroyed it. She's packing."

Leo let out a rough sigh and turned his eyes toward the house. "I can't say I blame her. I got her into trouble at the Christmas party by spiking the holiday punch, and now this. I guess she thinks we're all lunatics and she's better off without us."

"No doubt." Rey shrugged. "Well, let's get the cattle loaded."

"You aren't going to try to stop her?" Leo asked.

"What would be the point?" Rey asked solemnly. His face hardened. "If you'd seen her, you wouldn't want to stop her." He glared at Cag. "Nice work, pal. I hope she can pack with her hands shaking that badly!"

Rey stormed off toward the truck. Leo gave his older brother a speaking glance and followed.

Cag, feeling two inches high and sick with himself, turned reluctantly and went back toward the house.

Tess had her suitcases neatly loaded. She closed the big one, making one last sweep around the bedroom that had been hers for the past few weeks. It was a wrench to leave, but she couldn't handle scenes like that. She'd settle for harder work in more peaceful surroundings. At least, Cag wouldn't be around to make her life hell.

She picked up her father's world champion gold belt buckle and smoothed her fingers over it. She took it everywhere with her, like a lucky talisman to ward off evil. It hadn't worked today, but it usually did. She put it gently into the small suitcase and carefully closed the lid, snapping the latches shut.

A sound behind her caught her attention and she turned around, going white in the face when she saw who had opened the door.

She moved around the bed and behind the wing chair that stood near the window, her eyes wide and unblinking.

He was bareheaded. He didn't speak. His black eyes slid over her pale features and he took a long, deep breath.

"You don't have anywhere to go," he began.

It wasn't the best of opening gambits. Her chin went up. "I'll sleep at a Salvation Army shelter," she said coldly. "Dad and I spent a lot of nights there when we were on the road and he didn't win any events."

He scowled. "What?"

She hated having admitted that, to him of all people. Her face closed up. "Will you let one of the hands drive me to town? I can catch a bus up to Victoria."

He shoved his hands into the pockets of his close-fitting jeans, straining the fabric against his powerful thighs. He stared at her broodingly.

"Never mind," she said heavily. "I'll walk or hitch a ride."

She picked up her old coat, the threadbare tweed one she'd had for years, and slipped it on.

"Where's your new coat?" he asked shortly.

"In the hall closet. Don't worry, I'm not taking anything that doesn't belong to me."

She said it so matter-of-factly that he was wounded right through. "We gave it to you," he said.

Her eyes met his squarely. "I don't want it, or a job, or anything else you gave me out of pity."

He was shocked. He'd never realized she thought of it like that. "You needed a job and we needed a cook," he said flatly. "It wasn't pity."

She shrugged and seemed to slouch. "All right, have it any way you like. It doesn't matter."

She slipped her shoulder bag over her arm and picked up her worn suitcases, one big one and an overnight bag, part of a matched set of vinyl luggage that she and her father had won in a raffle.

But when she reached the door, Cag didn't move out of the way. She couldn't get around him, either. She stopped an arm's length away and stared at him.

He was trying to think of a way to keep her without sacrificing his pride. Rey was right; she was just a kid and he'd been unreasonable. He shocked himself lately. He was a sucker for helpless things, for little things, but he'd been brutal to this child and he didn't know why.

"Can I get by, please?" she asked through stiff lips.

He scowled. A muscle jumped beside his mouth. He moved closer, smiling coldly with self-contempt when she backed up. He pushed the door shut.

She backed up again, her eyes widening at the unexpected action, but he didn't come any closer.

"When I was six," he said with cold black eyes, "I wanted a birthday cake like the other kids had. A cake and a party. Simon had gone to town with Dad and Corrigan. It was before Rey was born. Leo was asleep and my mother and I were in the kitchen alone. She made some pert remark about spoiled brats thinking they deserved treats when they were nothing but nuisances. She had a cake on the counter, one that a neighbor had sent home with Dad. She smashed the cake into my face," he recalled, his eyes darker than ever, "and started hitting me. I don't think she would have stopped, except that Leo woke up and started squalling. She sent me to my room and locked me in. I don't know what she told my father, but I got a hell of a spanking from him." He searched her shocked eyes. "I never asked for another cake."

She put the suitcases down slowly and shocked him by walking right up to him and touching him lightly on the chest with a shy, nervous little hand. It didn't occur to him that he'd never confessed that particular incident to anyone, not even his brothers. She seemed to know it, just the same.

"My father couldn't cook. He opened cans," she said quietly. "I learned to cook when I was eleven, in self-defense. My mother wouldn't have baked me a cake, either, even if she'd stayed with us.

She didn't want me, but Dad did, and he put her into a position where she had to marry him. She never forgave either of us for it. She left before I started school.''

''Where is she now?''

She didn't meet his eyes. ''I don't know. I don't care.''

His chest rose and fell roughly. She made him uncomfortable. He moved back, so that her disturbing hand fell away from his chest.

She didn't question why he didn't like her to touch him. It had been an impulse and now she knew not to do it again. She lifted her face and searched his dark eyes. ''I know you don't like me,'' she said. ''It's better if I get a job somewhere else. I'm almost twenty-two. I can take care of myself.''

His eyes averted to the window. ''Wait until spring,'' he said stiffly. ''You'll have an easier time finding work then.''

She hesitated. She didn't really want to go, but she couldn't stay here with such unbridled resentment as he felt for her.

He glanced down at her with something odd glittering in his black eyes. ''My brothers will drown me if I let you walk out that door,'' he said curtly. ''Neither of them is speaking to me.''

They both knew that he didn't care in the least what his brothers thought of him. It was a peace initiative.

She moved restlessly. ''Dorie's had the baby. She can make biscuits again.''

''She won't,'' he said curtly. ''She's too busy worshiping the baby.''

Her gaze dropped to the floor. ''It's a sweet baby.''

A wave of heat ran through his body. He turned and started back toward the door. ''Do what you please,'' he said.

She still hesitated.

He opened the door and turned before he went through it, looking dark as thunder and almost as intimidating. ''Too afraid of me to stay?'' he drawled, hitting her right in her pride with deadly accuracy.

She drew herself up with smoldering fury. ''I am *not* afraid of you!''

His eyebrows arched. ''Sure you are. That's why you're running away like a scared kid.''

''I wasn't running! I'm not a scared kid, either!''

That was more like it. He could manage if she fought back. He couldn't live with the image of her white and shaking and backing away from him. It had hurt like the very devil.

He pulled his Stetson low over his eyes. "Suit yourself. But if you stay, you'd damned sure better not lose the apple butter again," he said with biting sarcasm.

"Next time, you'll get it right between the eyes," she muttered to herself.

"I heard that."

She glared at him. "And if you ever, ever, throw another cake at me…!"

"I didn't throw it at you," he said pointedly. "I threw it at the wall."

Her face was growing redder by the second. "I spent two hours making the damned thing!"

"Lost apple butter, cursed cake, damned women…" He was still muttering as he stomped off down the hall with the faint, musical jingle of spurs following him.

Tess stood unsteadily by the bed for several seconds before she snapped out of her trance and put her suitcases back on the bed to unpack them. She needed her head read for agreeing to stay, but she didn't really have anywhere else to go. And what he'd told her reached that part of her that was unbearably touched by small, wounded things.

She could see a little Cag with his face covered in cake, being brutally hit by an uncaring woman, trying not to cry. Amazingly it excused every harsh word, every violent action. She wondered how many other childhood scars were hiding behind that hard, expressionless face.

Cag was coldly formal with her after that, as if he regretted having shared one of his deeper secrets with her. But there weren't any more violent outbursts. He kept out of her way and she kept out of his. The winter months passed into a routine sameness. Without the rush and excitement of the holidays, Tess found herself with plenty of time on her hands when she was finished with her chores. The brothers worked all hours, even when they weren't bothered with birthing cattle and roundup, as they were in the warmer months of spring.

But there were fences to mend, outbuildings to repair, upkeep on the machinery that was used to process feed. There were sick animals to treat and corrals to build and vehicles to overhaul. It never seemed to end. And in between all that, there were conferences and conventions and business trips.

It was rare, Tess found, to have all three bachelor brothers at the table at the same time. More often than not, she set places only for Rey and Leo, because Cag spent more and more time away. They assured her that she wasn't to blame, that it was just pressing business, but she wondered just the same. She knew that Cag only tolerated her for the sake of her domestic skills, that he hated the very sight of her. But the other brothers were so kind that it almost made up for Cag. And the ever-present Mrs. Lewis, doing the rough chores, was a fountain of information about the history of the Hart ranch and the surrounding area. Tess, a history buff, learned a lot about the wild old days and stored the information away almost greedily. The lazy, pleasant days indoors seemed to drag and she was grateful for any interesting tidbits that Mrs. Lewis sent her way.

Then spring arrived and the ranch became a madhouse. Tess had to learn to answer the extension phone in the living room while the two secretaries in the separate office complex started processing calving information into the brothers' huge mainframe computer. The sheer volume of it was shocking to Tess, who'd spent her whole life on ranches.

The only modern idea, besides the computers, that the brothers had adapted to their operation was the implantation of computer chips under the skin of the individual cattle. This was not only to identify them with a handheld computer, but also to tag them in case of rustling—a sad practice that had continued unabashed into the computer age.

On the Hart ranch, there were no hormone implants, no artificial insemination, no unnecessary antibiotics or pesticides. The brothers didn't even use pesticides on their crops, having found ways to encourage the development of superior strains of forage and the survival of good insects that kept away the bad ones. It was all very ecological and fascinating, and it was even profitable. One of the local ranchers, J. D. Langley, worked hand in glove with them on these renegade methods. They shared ideas and investment strategies and went together as a solid front to cattlemen's meetings. Tess found J. D. "Donavan" Langley intimidating, but his wife and nephew had softened him, or so people said. She shuddered to think how he'd been before he mellowed.

The volume of business the brothers did was overwhelming. The telephone rang constantly. So did the fax machine. Tess was pressganged into learning how to operate that, and the computer, so that she could help send and receive urgent e-mail messages to various beef producers and feedlots and buyers.

"But I'm not trained!" she wailed to Leo and Rey.

They only grinned. "There, there, you're doing a fine job," Leo told her encouragingly.

"But I won't have time to cook proper meals," she continued.

"As long as we have enough biscuits and strawberry preserves and apple butter, that's no problem at all," Rey assured her. "And if things get too hectic, we'll order out."

They did, frequently, in the coming weeks. One night two pizza delivery trucks drove up and unloaded enough pizzas for the entire secretarial and sales staff and the cowboys, not to mention the brothers. They worked long hours and they were demanding bosses, but they never forgot the loyalty and sacrifice of the people who worked for them. They paid good wages, too.

"Why don't you ever spend any money on yourself?" Leo asked Tess one night when, bleary-eyed from the computer, she was ready to go to bed.

"What?"

"You're wearing the same clothes you had last year," he said pointedly. "Don't you want some new jeans, at least, and some new tops?"

"I hadn't thought about it," she confessed. "I've just been putting my wages into the bank and forgetting about them. I suppose I should go shopping."

"Yes, you should." He leaned down toward her. "The very minute we get caught up!"

She groaned. "We'll never get caught up! I heard old Fred saying that he'd had to learn how to use a handheld computer so he could scan the cattle in the low pasture, and he was almost in tears."

"We hired more help," he stated.

"Yes, but there was more work after that! It's never going to end," she wailed. "If those stupid cows don't stop having calves...!"

"Bite your tongue, woman, that's profit you're scoffing at!"

"I know, but—"

"We're all tired," he assured her. "And any day now, it's going to slack off. We're doing compilation figures for five ranches, you know," he added. "It isn't just this one. We have to record each new calf along with its history, we have to revise lists for cattle that have died or been culled, cattle that we traded, new cattle that we've bought. Besides that, we have to have birth weights, weight gain ratios, average daily weight gain and feeding data. All that information has to be kept current or it's no use to us."

"I know. But we'll all get sick of pizzas and I'll forget how to make biscuits!"

"God forbid," he said, taking off his hat and holding it to his heart.

She was too tired to laugh, but she did smile. She worked her way down the long hall toward her room over the garage, feeling as drained as she looked.

She met Cag coming from the general direction of the garage, dressed in a neat gray suit with a subdued burgundy tie and a cream-colored Stetson. He was just back from a trustee meeting in Dallas, and he looked expensive and sophisticated and unapproachable.

She nodded in a cool greeting, and averted her eyes as she passed him.

He stepped in front of her, blocking her path. One big, lean hand tilted her chin up. He looked at her without smiling, his dark eyes glittering with disapproval.

"What have they been doing to you?" he asked curtly.

The comment shocked her, but she didn't read anything into it. Cag would never be concerned about her and she knew it. "We're all putting herd records into the computer, even old Fred," she said wearily. "We're tired."

"Yes, I know. It's a nightmare every year about this time. Are you getting enough sleep?"

She nodded. "I don't know much about computers and it's hard, that's all. I don't mind the work."

His hand hesitated for just an instant before he dropped it. He looked tougher than ever. "You'll be back to your old duties in no time. God forbid that we should drag you kicking and screaming out of the kitchen and into the twentieth century."

That was sarcastic, and she wished she had enough energy to hit him. He was always mocking her, picking at her.

"You haven't complained about the biscuits yet," she reminded him curtly.

His black eyes swept over her disparagingly. "You look about ten," he chided. "All big eyes. And you wear that damned rig or those black jeans and that pink shirt all the time. Don't you have any clothes?"

She couldn't believe her ears. First the brothers had talked about her lack of new clothes, and now he was going to harp on it! "Now, look here, you can't tell me what to wear!"

"If you want to get married, you'll never manage it like that," he scoffed. "No man is going to look twice at a woman who can't be bothered to even brush her hair!"

She actually gasped. She hadn't expected a frontal attack when he'd just walked in the door. "Well, excuse me!" she snapped, well aware that her curly head was untidy. She put a hand to it defensively. "I haven't had time to brush my hair. I've been too busy listing what bull sired what calf!"

He searched over her wan face and he relented, just a little. "Go to bed," he said stiffly. "You look like the walking dead."

"What a nice compliment," she muttered. "Thanks awfully."

She started to walk away, but he caught her arm and pulled her back around. He reached into his pocket, took something out, and handed it to her.

It was a jewelry box, square and velvet-covered. She looked at him and he nodded toward the box, indicating that he wanted her to open it.

She began to, with shaking hands. It was unexpected that he should buy her anything. She lifted the lid to find that there, nestled on a bed of gray satin, was a beautiful faceted sapphire pendant surrounded by tiny diamonds on a thin gold chain. She'd never seen anything so beautiful in her life. It was like a piece of summer sky caught in stone. It sparkled even in the dim shine of the security lights around the house and garage.

"Oh!" she exclaimed, shocked and touched by the unexpected gift. Then she looked up, warily, wondering if she'd been presumtuous and it wasn't a gift at all. She held it out to him. "Oh, I see. You just wanted to show it to me..."

He closed her fingers around the box. His big hands were warm and strong. They felt nice.

"I bought it for you," he said, and looked briefly uncomfortable.

She was totally at sea, and looked it. She glanced down at the pretty thing in her hand and back up at him with a perplexed expression.

"Belated birthday present," he said gruffly, not meeting her eyes.

"But...my birthday was the first of March," she said, her voice terse, "and I never mentioned it."

"Never mentioned it," he agreed, searching her tired face intently. "Never had a cake, a present, even a card."

She averted her eyes.

"Hell!"

The curse, and the look on his face, surprised her.

He couldn't tell her that he felt guilty about her birthday. He hadn't even known that it had gone by until Leo told him two weeks ago. She could have had a cake and little presents, and cards. But she'd kept it to herself because of the way he'd acted about the cake she'd made for him. He knew without a word being spoken that he'd spoiled birthdays for her just as his mother had spoiled them for him. His conscience beat him to death over it. It was why he'd spent so much time away, that guilt, and it was why he'd gone into a jewelers, impulsively, when he never did anything on impulse, and bought the little necklace for her.

"Thanks," she murmured, curling her fingers around the box. But she wouldn't look at him.

There was something else, he thought, watching her posture stiffen. Something…

"What is it?" he asked abruptly.

She took a slow breath. "When do you want me to leave?" she asked bravely.

He scowled. "When do I what?"

"You said, that day I baked the cake, that I could go in the spring," she reminded him, because she'd never been able to forget. "It's spring."

He scowled more and stuck one hand into his pocket, thinking fast. "How could we do without you during roundup?" he asked reasonably. "Stay until summer."

She felt the box against her palms, warm from his body where it had lain in his pocket. It was sort of like a link between them, even if he hadn't meant it that way. She'd never had a present from a man before, except the coat the brothers had given her. But that hadn't been personal like this. She wasn't sure how it was intended, as a sort of conscience-reliever or a genuinely warm gesture.

"We'll talk about it another time," he said after a minute. "I'm tired and I've still got things to do."

He turned and walked past her without looking back. She found herself watching him helplessly with the jewelery box held like a priceless treasure in her two hands.

As if he felt her eyes he stopped suddenly, at the back door, and only his head pivoted. His black eyes met hers in the distance between them, and it was suddenly as if lightning had struck. She felt her knees quivering under her, her heart racing. He was only looking, but she couldn't get her breath at all.

He didn't glance away, and neither did she. In that instant, she lost her heart. She felt him fight to break the contact of their eyes, and win. He moved away quickly, into the house, and she ground her teeth together at this unexpected complication.

Of all the men in the world to become infatuated with, Cag Hart was the very last she should have picked. But knowing it didn't stop the way she felt. With a weary sigh, she turned and went back toward her room. She knew she wouldn't sleep, no matter how tired she was. She linked the necklace around her neck and admired it in the mirror, worrying briefly about the expense, because she'd seen on the clasp that it was 14K gold—not a trifle at all. But it would have been equally precious to her if it had been gold-tone metal, and she was sure Cag knew it. She went to sleep, wearing it.

Chapter 3

Everything would have been absolutely fine, except that she forgot to take the necklace off the next morning and the brothers gave her a hard time over breakfast. That, in turn, embarrassed Cag, who stomped out without his second cup of coffee, glaring at Tess as if she'd been responsible for the whole thing.

They apologized when they realized that they'd just made a bad situation worse. But as the day wore on, she wondered if she shouldn't have left the necklace in its box in her chest of drawers. It had seemed to irritate Cag that she wanted to wear it. The beautiful thing was so special that she could hardly get past mirrors. She loved just looking at it.

Her mind was so preoccupied with her present that she didn't pay close attention to the big aquarium in Cag's room when she went to make the bed. And that was a mistake. She was bending over to pull up the multicolored Navajo patterned comforter on the big four-postered bed when she heard a faint noise. The next thing she knew, she was wearing Herman the python around her neck.

The weight of the huge reptile buckled her knees. Herman weighed more than she did by about ten pounds. She screamed and wrestled, and the harder she struggled the harder an equally frightened Herman held on, certain that he was going to hit the floor bouncing if he relaxed his clinch one bit!

Leo came running, but he stopped at the doorway. No snake-lover, he hadn't the faintest idea how to extricate their housekeeper from the scaly embrace she was being subjected to.

"Get Cag!" she squeaked, pulling at Herman's coils. "Hurry, before he eats me!"

"He won't eat you," Leo promised from a pale face. "He only eats freeze-dried dead things with fur, honest! Cag's at the corral. We were just going to ride out to the line camp. Back in a jiffy!"

Stomping feet ran down the hall. Torturous minutes later, heavier stomping feet ran back again.

Tess was kneeling with the huge reptile wrapped around her, his head arched over hers so that she looked as if she might be wearing a snaky headdress.

"Herman, for Pete's sake!" Cag raged. "How did you get out *this* time?"

"Could you possibly question him later, *after* you've got him off me?" she urged. "He weighs a ton!"

"There, there," he said gently, because he knew how frightened she was of Herman. He approached them slowly, careful not to spook his pet. He smoothed his big hand under the snake's chin and stroked him gently, soothing him as he spoke softly, all the time gently unwinding him from Tess's stooped shoulders.

When he had him completely free, he walked back to the aquarium and scowled as he peered at the lid, which was ajar.

"Maybe he's got a crowbar in there," he murmured, shifting Herman's formidable weight until he could release the other catches enough to lift the lid from the tank. "I don't know why he keeps climbing out."

"How would you like to live in a room three times your size with no playmates?" she muttered, rubbing her aching shoulders. "He's sprained both my shoulders and probably cracked part of my spine. He fell on me!"

He put Herman in the tank and locked the lid before he turned. "Fell?" He scowled. "From where?"

"There!"

She gestured toward one of the wide, tall sculptured posts that graced his king-size bed.

He whistled. "He hasn't gone climbing in a while." He moved a little closer to her and his black eyes narrowed. "You okay?"

"I told you," she mumbled, "I've got fractured bones every-where!"

He smiled gently. "Sore muscles, more likely." His eyes were quizzical, soft. "You weren't really scared, were you?"

She hesitated. Then she smiled back, just faintly. "Well, no, not really. I've sort of got used to him." She shrugged. "He feels nice. Like a thick silk scarf."

Cag didn't say a word. He just stood there, looking at her, with a sort of funny smile.

"I thought they were slimy."

The smile widened. "Most people do, until they touch one. Snakes are clean. They aren't generally violent unless they're provoked, or unless they're shedding or they've just eaten. Half the work is know-ing when not to pick them up." He took off his hat and ran a hand through his thick hair. "I've had Herman for twelve years," he added. "He's like family, although most people don't understand that you can have affection for a snake."

She studied his hard face, remembering that his former fiancée had insisted that he get rid of Herman. Even if he loved a woman, it would be hard for him to give up a much-loved pet.

"I used to have an iguana," she said, "when I was about twelve. One of the guys at the rodeo had it with him, and he was going off to college. He asked would I like him." She smiled reminiscently. "He was green and huge, like some prehistoric creature, like a real live dragon. He liked shredded squash and bananas and he'd let you hold him. When you petted him on the head he'd close his eyes and raise his chin. I had him for three years."

"What happened?"

"He just died," she said. "I never knew why. The vet said that he couldn't see a thing wrong with him, and that I'd done everything right by the book to keep him healthy. We could have had him au-topsied, but Dad didn't have the money to pay for it. He was pretty old when I got him. I like to think it was just his time, and not anything I did wrong."

"Sometimes pets do just die." He was looking at Herman, coiled up happily in his tank and looking angelic, in his snaky fashion. "Look at him," he muttered. "Doesn't look like he's ever thought of escaping, does he?"

"I still remember when I opened up the washing machine to do clothes and found him coiled inside. I almost quit on the spot."

"You've come a long way since then," he had to admit. His eyes went to the blue and white sparkle of the necklace and he stared at it.

"I'm sorry," she mumbled, wrapping her hand around it guiltily. "I never should have worn it around your brothers. But it's so lovely. It's like wearing a piece of the sky around my neck."

"I'm glad you like it," he said gruffly. "Wear it all you like. They'll find something else to harp on in a day or so."

"I didn't think they'd notice."

He cocked an eyebrow. "I haven't bought a present for a woman in almost seven years," he said shortly. "It's noteworthy around here, despite my intentions."

Her face colored. "Oh, I know it was just for my birthday," she said quickly.

"You work hard enough to deserve a treat now and again," he returned impatiently. "You're sure you're okay?"

She nodded. "A little thing like a broken back won't slow me down."

He glowered at her. "He only weighs a hundred and ten pounds."

"Yeah? Well, I only weigh a hundred!"

His eyes went over her suddenly. "You've lost weight."

"You said that before, but I haven't. I've always been thin."

"Eat more."

Her eyebrows arched. "I'll eat what I like, thank you."

He made a rough sound in his throat. "And where are those new clothes we've been trying to get you to buy?"

"I don't want any more clothes. I have plenty of clothes."

"Plenty, the devil," he muttered angrily, "You'll go into town tomorrow and get some new jeans and shirts. Got that?"

She lifted her chin stubbornly. "I will not! Listen here, I may work for you, but you don't tell me what I can wear!"

He stared at her for a minute with narrowed eyes. "On second thought,'' he muttered, moving toward her, ''why wait until tomorrow? And like hell I can't tell you what to wear!''

''Callaghan!'' she shrieked, protesting.

By the time she got his name out of her shocked mouth, he had her over his shoulder in a fireman's lift. He walked right down the hall with her, passing Leo, who was just on his way back in to see what had happened.

''Oh, my gosh, did Herman bite her?'' he gasped. ''Is she killed?''

''No, of course he didn't bite her!'' Cag huffed and kept walking.

''Then where are you taking her?''

''To the nearest department store.''

''To the...you are? Good man!''

''Turncoat!'' Tess called back to him.

''Get her a dress!'' Leo added.

''I hate dresses!''

''In that case, get her two dresses!''

''You shut up, Leo!'' she groaned.

Rey was standing at the back door when Cag approached it with his burden.

''Going out?'' Rey asked pleasantly, and opened the door with a flourish. ''Have fun, now.''

''Rescue me!'' Tess called to him.

''Say, wasn't there a song about that?'' Rey asked Leo, who joined him on the porch.

''There sure was. It went like this... 'Rescue me!''' he sang.

The two of them were still singing it, arm in arm, off-key, at the top of their lungs, when Cag drove away in the ranch truck with a furious Tess at his side.

''I don't want new clothes!'' she raged.

He glanced toward her red face and grinned. ''Too late. We're already halfway to town.''

This strangely jubilant mood of his surprised her. Cag, of all the brothers, never seemed to play. Of course, neither did Simon, but he was rarely around. Leo and Rey, she'd been told, had once been just as taciturn as the older Harts. But since Dorie came back into Corrigan's life, they were always up to their necks in something. All

Cag did was work. It was completely unlike him to take any personal interest in her welfare.

"Leo could have taken me," she muttered, folding her arms over her chest.

"He's too polite to carry you out the door," he replied. "And Rey's too much a gentleman. Most of the time, anyway."

"These jeans just got broke in good."

"They've got holes in them," he said pointedly.

"It's fashionable."

"Most fashionable jeans have holes in them when you buy them. Those—" he gestured toward the worn knees "—got like that from hard work. I've seen you on your knees scrubbing the kitchen floor. Which reminds me, we bought you one of those little floor cleaners that's specially made for linoleum. They're sending it out with the butane and lumber we ordered at the same time."

"A floor cleaner?" she asked, stunned.

"It will make things a little easier for you."

She was delighted that he was concerned about her chores. She didn't say another word, but she couldn't quite stop smiling.

Minutes later, he pulled up in front of the downtown department store and led her inside to the women's section. He stopped in front of Mrs. Bellamy, the saleslady who'd practically come with the store.

He tilted his hat respectfully. "Mrs. Bellamy, can you fit her out with jeans and shirts and new boots and a dress or two?" he asked, nodding toward Tess, who was feeling more and more like a mannequin. "We can't have our housekeeper looking like *that!*" He gestured toward her faded shirt and holey jeans.

"My goodness, no, Mr. Hart," Mrs. Bellamy agreed at once. She frowned thoughtfully. "And we just received such a nice shipment of summer things, too! You come right along with me, Miss Tess, and we'll fix you up!" She took Tess's arm and waved her hand at Cag. "Shoo, now, Mr. Hart," she murmured absently, and Tess had to stifle a giggle at his expression. "She'll be ready to pick up in about an hour."

I'm a parcel, Tess thought, and Cag's a fly. She put a hand over her wobbly mouth as she went meekly along with the older woman. Hysterical laughter would not save her now.

Cag watched her go with an amused smile. So she didn't want new clothes, huh? They'd see about that! Mrs. Bellamy wasn't going to let a potential commission walk away from her!

An hour later, Cag went back for Tess and found her trying on a royal blue and white full-skirted dress with spaghetti straps and a shirred bodice. Against her white skin the sapphire-and-diamond necklace was brilliant. With her freckled white shoulders bare and the creamy tops of her breasts showing, she took his breath away.

"Isn't that dress just the thing, Tess?" Mrs. Bellamy was murmuring. "You wait right here. I want to show you one more! Oh, hello, Mr. Hart!" she called as she passed him. She waved a hand toward Tess. "What do you think? Isn't it cute? Now where did I see that pretty black lacy thing…"

Tess turned as Cag joined her. His face gave nothing away, but his black eyes glittered over the soft skin left bare by the dress. It certainly made her eyes bluer.

"Is it…too revealing?" Tess asked nervously, because of the way he was watching her.

He shook his head. "It suits you. It even matches the necklace." His voice sounded deep and husky. He moved closer and one big, lean hand lifted involuntarily to her throat where the small sapphire lay in its bed of diamonds and gold. His hand rested there for an instant before it moved restlessly over the thin strap of the dress. His fingertips absently traced over her soft skin as he studied her, noticing its silky warmth.

Her breath caught in her throat. She felt her heartbeat shaking the dress even as she noticed his black eyes lowering to the flesh left bare by the shirred bodice.

His fingers contracted on her shoulder and her intake of breath was suddenly audible.

He met her eyes relentlessly, looking for hidden signs that she couldn't keep from him.

"This is the sort of dress," he said gruffly, "that makes a man want to pull the bodice down."

"Mr….Hart!" she exclaimed.

He scowled faintly as he searched her shocked eyes. "Don't you know anything about dresses and the effect they have on men?'' he wanted to know.

Her trembling hands went to tug the bodice up even more. ''I do not! But I know that I won't have it if it makes you...makes a man think...such things!''

His hand jerked suddenly, as if her skin had burned it. ''I was teasing!'' he lied sharply, moving away. ''It's fine. You look fine. And yes,'' he added firmly, ''you'll have it, all right!''

She didn't know what to think. He was acting very strangely, and now he wouldn't look at her at all. Teasing? Then why was he so stiff and uncomfortable looking if he was teasing? And why keep his back to her and Mrs. Bellamy, who'd just rejoined them.

''Here, Tess, try on this one. I'll box that one while you're dressing.'' She rushed the girl off before she could say anything to Cag.

That was just as well. He was fighting a raging arousal that had shocked him senseless. Tess was beginning to have a very noticeable effect on him, and he was quite sorry that he'd insisted on bringing her here. If she wore that dress around him, it was going to cause some major problems.

He stood breathing deliberately until his rebellious body was back under control. He noticed that Tess didn't show him the black dress she'd tried on. But she shook her head when Mrs. Bellamy asked her about it. She was trying to refuse the blue one, too. He wasn't having that. She looked so beautiful in it. That was one she had to have.

''You're not turning that blue one back in,'' he said firmly. ''You'll need something to wear if you're asked out anywhere.'' He hated thinking about her in that dress with another man. But she didn't date. It shouldn't worry him. ''Did you get some jeans and blouses, and how about those boots?''

After Mrs. Bellamy rattled off an inventory, he produced a credit card and watched her ring up a total. He wouldn't let Tess see it. She looked worried enough already.

He took the two large bags and the dress bag from Mrs. Bellamy with thanks and hustled Tess back out to the double-cabbed truck. He put the purchases on the back seat and loaded Tess into the passenger seat.

She sat without fastening her belt until he got in beside her.

"You spent too much," she said nervously, her big blue eyes echoing her mood. "I won't be able to pay you back for months, even if you take so much a week out of my salary."

"Think of the clothes as a uniform," he said gently. "You can't walk around in what you've been wearing. What will people think of us?"

"Nobody ever comes to see you."

"Visiting cattlemen do. Politicians do. We even have the occasional cookout. People notice these things. And you'll look neater in new stuff."

She shrugged and sighed with defeat. "Okay, then. Thanks."

He didn't crank the truck. He threw a long arm over the back of the seat and looked at her openly. Her barely contained excitement over the clothes began to make sense to him. "You've never had new things," he said suddenly.

She flushed. "On the rodeo circuit, when you lose, you don't make much. Dad and I bought most of our stuff from yard sales, or were given hand-me-downs by other rodeo people." She glanced at him nervously. "I used to compete in barrel racing, and I won third place a few times, but I didn't have a good enough horse to go higher. We had to sell him just before Dad gave up and came here to work."

"Why, Tess," he said softly. "I never knew you could ride at all!"

"I haven't had much chance to."

"I'll take you out with me one morning. Can you ride a quarter horse?"

She smiled. "If he's well trained, sure I can!"

He chuckled. "We'll see, after the biggest part of the roundup's over. We'd never get much done with all the cowboys showing off for you."

She flushed. "Nobody looks at me. I'm too skinny."

"But you're not," he protested. His eyes narrowed. "You're slender, but nobody could mistake you for a boy."

"Thanks."

He reached out unexpectedly and tugged a short reddish-gold curl, bringing her face around so that he could search it. He wasn't smiling.

His eyes narrowed as his gaze slid lazily over her eyes, cheekbones and down to her mouth.

"The blue dress suited you," he said. "How did the black one look?"

She shifted restlessly. "It was too low."

"Low what?"

She swallowed. "It was cut almost to the waist. I could never wear something like that in public!"

His gaze fell lower, to the quick rise and fall of her small breasts. "A lot of women couldn't get away with it," he murmured. "But you could. You're small enough that you wouldn't need to wear a bra with it."

"Mr. Hart!" she exclaimed, jerking back.

His eyebrows arched. "I've been Callaghan for months and today I've already been Mr. Hart twice. What did I say?"

Her face was a flaming red. "You...you know what you said!"

He did, all at once, and he chuckled helplessly. He shook his head as he reached for the ignition and switched it on. "And I thought Mrs. Lewis was old-fashioned. You make her look like a hippie!"

She wrapped her arms over her chest, still shaken by the remark. "You mustn't go around saying things like that. It's indecent!"

He had to force himself not to laugh again. She was serious. He shouldn't tease her, but it was irresistible. She made him feel warm inside, when he'd been empty for years. He should have realized that he was walking slowly toward an abyss, but he didn't notice. He enjoyed having her around, spoiling her a little. He glanced sideways at her. "Put your belt on, honey."

Honey! She fumbled it into the lock at her side, glancing at him uncertainly. He never used endearments and she didn't like them. But that deep, rough voice made her toes curl. She could almost imagine him whispering that word under his breath as he kissed a woman.

She went scarlet. Why had she thought of that? And if the thought wasn't bad enough, her eyes went suddenly to his hard mouth and lingered there in spite of her resolve. She wondered if that mouth could wreak the devastation she thought it could. She'd only been kissed a time or two, and never by anybody who knew how. Callaghan would know how, she was sure of it.

He caught her looking at him and one eyebrow went up. "And what sort of scandalous thoughts are going through that prudish mind now?" he taunted.

She caught her breath. "I don't know what you mean!"

"No?"

"No! And I do not have a prudish mind!"

"You could have fooled me," he said under his breath, and actually grinned.

"Hold your breath until you get any more apple butter with your biscuits," she muttered back. "And wait until you get another biscuit, too!"

"You can't starve me," he said smugly. "Rey and Leo will protect me."

"Oh, right, like they protected me! How could you do that? Carrying me out like a package, and them standing there singing like fools. I don't know why I ever agreed to work for such a loopy family!"

"Loopy? Us?"

"You! You're all crazy."

"What does that make you?" he murmured dryly. "You work for us."

"I need my head read!"

"I'll get somebody on it first thing."

She glanced at him sourly. "I thought you wanted me to quit."

"I already told you, not during roundup!" he reminded her. "Maybe when summer comes, if you're determined."

"I'm not determined. You're determined. You don't like me."

He pursed his lips, staring straight ahead. "I don't, do I?" he said absently. "But you're a fine housekeeper and a terrific cook. If I fired you, the others would stick me in a horse trough and hold me under."

"You destroyed the cake I baked for you," she recalled uneasily. "And you let your snake fall on me."

"That was Herman's own idea," he assured her. His face hardened. "The cake—you know why."

"I know now." She relented. "I'm sorry. I don't know what nice mothers are like, either, because I never had one. But if I had little kids, I'd make their birthdays so special," she said almost to herself, smiling. "I'd bake cakes and give them parties, and make ice cream. And they'd have lots and lots of presents." Her hand went involuntarily to the necklace he'd given her.

He saw that, and something warm kindled in his chest. "You like kids?" he asked without wanting to.

"Very much. Do you?"

"I haven't had much to do with them. I like Mack's toddler, though," he added. The foreman had a little boy two years old who always ran to Cag to be picked up. He always took something over for the child when he went to see Mack and his wife. Tess knew, although he never mentioned it.

She looked out the window. "I don't suppose I'll ever have kids of my own."

He scowled. "Why do you say that?"

She wrapped her arms around her chest. "I don't like…the sort of thing that you have to do to get them."

He stepped on the brakes so hard that the seat belt jerked tight and stared at her intently.

She flushed. "Well, some women are cold!"

"How do you know that you are?" he snapped, hating himself for even asking.

She averted her gaze out the window. "I can't stand to have a man touch me."

"Really?" he drawled. "Then why did you gasp and stand there with your heartbeat shaking you when I slid my hand over your shoulder in the dress shop?"

Her body jerked. "I never!"

"You most certainly did," he retorted, and felt a wave of delight wash over him at the memory of her soft skin under his hands. It had flattered him, touched him, that she was vulnerable with him.

"It was…I mean, I was surprised. That's all!" she added belligerently.

His fingers tapped on the steering wheel as he contemplated her with narrowed eyes. "Something happened to you. What?"

She stared at him, stunned.

"Come on. You know I don't gossip."

She did. She moved restlessly against the seat. "One of my

mother's lovers made a heavy pass at me," she muttered. "I was sixteen and grass green, and he scared me to death."

"And now you're twenty-two," he added. He stared at her even harder. "There aren't any twenty-two-year-old virgins left in America."

"Says who?" she shot at him, and then flushed as she felt herself fall right into the trap.

His lips pursed, and he smiled so faintly that she almost missed it.

"That being the case," he said in a soft, mocking tone, "how do you know that you're frigid?"

She was going to choke to death trying to answer that. She drew in an exasperated breath. "Can't we go home?"

She made the word sound soft, mysterious, enticing. He'd lived in houses all his life. She made him want a home. But it wasn't a thing he was going to admit just yet, even to himself.

"Sure," he said after a minute. "We can go home." He took his foot off the brake, put the truck in gear and sent it flying down the road.

It never occurred to him that taking her shopping had been the last thing on his mind this morning, or that his pleasure in her company was unusual. He was reclusive these days, stoic and unapproachable; except when Tess came close. She was vulnerable in so many ways, like the kitten they'd both adopted. Surely it was just her youth that appealed to him. It was like giving treats to a deprived child and enjoying its reactions.

Except that she trembled under his hands and he'd been years on his own. He liked touching her and she liked letting him. It was something he was going to have to watch. The whole situation was explosive. But he was sure he could handle it. She was a sweet kid. It wouldn't hurt if he spoiled her just a little. Of course it wouldn't.

Chapter 4

The brothers, like Tess and the rest of the staff, were worn to a frazzle by the time roundup was almost over.

Tess hadn't thought Cag meant it when he'd invited her to ride with him while he gathered strays, but early one morning after breakfast, he sent her to change into jeans and boots. He was waiting for her at the stable when she joined him there.

"Listen, I'm a little rusty," Tess began as she stared dubiously toward two saddled horses, one of whom was a sleek black gelding who pranced in place.

"Don't worry. I wouldn't put you on Black Diamond even if you asked. He's mine. This is Whirlwind," he said, nodding toward a pretty little red mare. "She's a registered quarter horse and smart as a whip. She'll take care of you." He summed her up with a glance, smiling at the blue windbreaker that matched her eyes and the Atlanta Braves baseball cap perched atop her red-gold curls.

"You look about ten," he mused, determined to put an invisible Off Limits sign on her mentally.

"And you look about—" she began.

He cut her off in midsentence. "Hop aboard and let's get started."

She vaulted easily into the saddle and gathered the reins loosely in her hands, smiling at the pleasure of being on a horse again. She hadn't ridden since her father's death.

He tilted his tan Stetson over his eyes and turned his mount expertly. "We'll go out this way," he directed, taking the lead toward the grassy path that wound toward the line camp in the distance. "Catch up."

She patted the horse's neck gently and whispered to her. She trotted up next to Cag's mount and kept the pace.

"We do most of this with light aircraft, but there are always a few mavericks who aren't intimidated by flying machines. They get into the brush and hide. So we have to go after those on horseback." He glanced at her jean-clad legs and frowned. "I should have dug you out some chaps," he murmured, and she noticed that he was wearing his own—bat-wing chaps with stains and scratches from this sort of work. "Don't ride into the brush like that," he added firmly. "You'll rip your legs open on the thorns."

"Okay," she said easily.

He set the pace and she followed, feeling oddly happy and at peace. It was nice riding with him like this across the wide, flat plain. She felt as if they were the only two people on earth. There was a delicious silence out here, broken only by the wind and the soft snorting of the horses and occasionally a distant sound of a car or airplane.

They worked through several acres of scrubland, flushing cows and calves and steers from their hiding places and herding them toward the distant holding pens. The men had erected several stockades in which to place the separated cattle, and they'd brought in a tilt-tray, so that the calves could be branded and ear-tagged.

The cows, identified with the handheld computer by the computer chips embedded in their tough hides, were either culled and placed in a second corral to be shipped out, or driven toward another pasture. The calves would be shipped to auction. The steers, already under contract, would go to their buyers. Even so far away from the ranch, there was tremendous organization in the operation.

Tess took off her Braves cap and wiped her sweating forehead on her sleeve.

Hardy, one of the older hands, grinned as he fetched up beside her on his own horse. "Still betting on them Braves, are you? They lost the pennant again last fall…that's two years in a row."

"Oh, yeah? Well, they won it once already," she reminded him with a smug grin. "Who needs two?"

He chuckled, shook his head and rode off.

"Baseball fanatic," Cag murmured dryly as he joined her.

"I'll bet you watched the playoffs last fall, too," she accused.

He didn't reply. "Hungry?" he asked. "We can get coffee and some stew over at the chuck wagon."

"I thought only those big outfits up in the Rockies still packed out a chuck wagon."

"If we didn't, we'd all go hungry here," he told her. "This ranch is a lot bigger than it looks."

"I saw it on the map in your office," she replied. "It sure covers a lot of land."

"You should see our spread in Montana," he mused. "It's the biggest of the lot. And the one that kept us all so busy a few weeks ago, trying to get the records on the computer."

She glanced back to where two of the men were working handheld computers. "Do all your cowboys know how to use those things?" she asked.

"Most of them. You'd be amazed how many college boys we get here between exams and new classes. We had an aeronautical engineer last summer and a professor of archaeology the year before that."

"Archaeology!"

He grinned. "He spent more time digging than he spent working cattle, but he taught us how to date projectile points and pottery."

"How interesting." She stretched her aching back. "I guess you've been to college."

"I got my degree in business from Harvard."

She glanced at him warily. "And I barely finished high school."

"You've got years left to go to college, if you want to."

"Slim chance of that," she said carelessly. "I can't work and go to school at the same time."

"You can do what our cowboys do—work a quarter and go to school a quarter." He fingered the reins gently. "In fact, we could arrange it so that you could do that, if you like. Jacobsville has a community college. You could commute."

The breath left her in a rush. "You'd let me?" she asked.

"Sure, if you want to."

"Oh, my goodness." She thought about it with growing delight. She could study botany. She loved to grow things. She might even learn how to cultivate roses and do grafting. Her eyes sparkled.

"Well?"

"I could study botany," she said absently. "I could learn to grow roses."

He frowned. "Horticulture?"

"Yes." She glanced at him. "Isn't that what college teaches you?"

"It does, certainly. But if you want horticulture, the vocational school offers a diploma in it."

Her face became radiant at the thought. "Oh, how wonderful!"

"What an expression," he mused, surprised at the pleasure it gave him. "Is that what you want to do, learn to grow plants?"

"Not just plants," she said. *"Roses!"*

"We've got dozens of them out back."

"No, not just old-fashioned roses. Tea roses. I want to do grafts. I want to...to create new hybrids."

He shook his head. "That's over my head."

"It's over mine, too. That's why I want to learn it."

"No ambition to be a professional of some sort?" he persisted. "A teacher, a lawyer, a doctor, a journalist?"

She hesitated, frowning as she studied his hard face. "I like flowers," she said slowly. "Is there something wrong with that? I mean, should I want to study something else?"

He didn't know how to answer that. "Most women do, these days."

"Sure, but most women don't want jobs working in a kitchen and keeping house and growing flowers, do they?" She bit her lip. "I don't know that I'd be smart enough to do horticulture..."

"Of course you would, if you want to do it," he said impatiently. His good humor seemed to evaporate as he stared at her. "Do you want to spend your life working in somebody else's kitchen?"

She shifted. "I guess I will," she said. "I don't want to get married, and I don't really see myself teaching kids or practicing medicine. I enjoy cooking and keeping house. And I love growing things.'' She glanced at him belligerently. ''What's wrong with that?''

''Nothing. Not a damned thing.''

''Now I've made you mad.''

His hand wrapped around the reins. He didn't look at her as he urged his mount ahead, toward the chuck wagon where several cowboys were holding full plates.

He couldn't tell her that it wasn't her lack of ambition that disturbed him. It was the picture he had of her, surrounded by little redheaded kids digging in the rose garden. It upset him, unsettled him. He couldn't start thinking like that. Tess was just a kid, despite her age, and he'd better keep that in mind. She hadn't even started to live yet. She'd never known intimacy with a man. She was likely to fall headlong in love with the first man who touched her. He thought about that, about being the first, and it rocked him to the soles of his feet. He had to get his mind on something else!

They had a brief lunch with several of the cowboys. Tess let Cag do most of the talking. She ate her stew with a biscuit, drank a cup of coffee and tried not to notice the speculative glances she was getting. She didn't know that it was unusual for Cag to be seen in the company of a woman, even the ranch housekeeper. Certainly he'd never brought anyone female out to a roundup before. It aroused the men's curiosity.

Cag ignored the looks. He knew that having Tess along was innocent, so what did it matter what anyone else thought? It wasn't as if he was planning to drag her off into the brush and make love to her. Even as he thought it, he pictured it. His whole body went hot.

''We'd better get going,'' he said abruptly, rising to his feet.

Tess thanked the cook for her lunch, and followed Cag back to the horses.

They rode off toward the far pastures without a word being spoken. She wondered what she'd done to make Cag mad, but she didn't want to say anything. It might only make matters worse. She wondered if he was mad because she wanted to go back to school.

They left the camp behind and rode in a tense silence. Her eyes kept going to his tall, powerful body. He seemed part of the horse he rode, so comfortable and careless that he might have been born in the saddle. He had powerful broad shoulders and lean hips, with long legs that were sensuously outlined by the tight-fitting jeans he wore under the chaps. She'd seen plenty of rodeo cowboys in her young life, but none of them would have held a candle to Cag. He looked elegant even in old clothes.

He turned his head and caught her staring, then frowned when she blushed.

"Did you ever go rodeoing?" she asked to cover her confusion.

He shook his head. "Never had much use for it," he said honestly. "I didn't need the money, and I always had enough to do here, or on one of the other ranches in the combine."

"Dad couldn't seem to stay in one place for very long," she murmured thoughtfully. "He loved the rodeo circuit, but he didn't win very often."

"It wasn't much of a life for you, was it?" he asked. "It must have been hard to go to school at all."

She smiled. "My education was hit-and-miss, if that's what you mean. But there were these correspondence courses I took so I could get my high school diploma." She flushed deeper and glanced at him. "I know I'm not very educated."

He reined in at a small stream that crossed the wooded path, in the shade of a big oak tree, and let his horse drink, motioning her to follow suit. "It wasn't a criticism," he said. "Maybe I'm too blunt sometimes, but people always know where they stand with me."

"I noticed."

A corner of his mouth quirked. "You aren't shy about expressing your own opinions," he recalled. "It's refreshing."

"Oh, I learned to fight back early," she murmured. "Rodeo's a tough game, and some of the other kids I met were pretty physical when they got mad. I may not be big, but I can kick like a mule."

"I don't doubt it." He drew one long leg up and hooked it over the pommel while he studied her. "But despite all that male company, you don't know much about men."

This was disturbing territory. She averted her gaze to the bubbling stream at their feet. "So you said, when we went to the store." She

remembered suddenly the feel of his hard fingers on her soft skin
and her heart began to race.

His black eyes narrowed. "Didn't you ever go out on dates?"

Her lithe body shifted in the saddle. "These days, most girls don't
care what they do and they're clued up about how to take care of
themselves." She glanced at him and away. "It makes it rough for
the few of us who don't think it's decent to behave that way. Men
seem to expect a girl to give out on the first date and they get mad
when she won't."

He traced a cut on his chaps. "So you stopped going out."

She nodded. "It seemed the best way. Besides," she murmured
uncomfortably, "I told you. I don't like...that."

"That?"

He was going to worry the subject to death. "That," she emphasized. "You know, being grabbed and forcibly fondled and having a
man try to stick his tongue down your throat!"

He chuckled helplessly.

"Oh, you don't understand!"

"In fact, I do," he replied, and the smile on his lips was full of
worldly knowledge and indulgent amusement. "You were lucky that
your would-be suitors didn't know any more than you did."

She frowned because she didn't understand.

His black eyes searched her face. "Tess, an experienced man
doesn't grab. Ever. He doesn't have to. And French kisses need to
be worked up to, very slowly."

Her heart was really going now. It shook the cotton blouse she
was wearing. She stared at the chaps where Cag's long fingers were
resting, and remembered the feel of his lean, strong hands.

"Embarrassed?" he asked softly.

She hesitated. Then she nodded.

His heart jumped wildly as he stared at her, unblinking. "And
curious?" he added in a deep, slow drawl.

After a few seconds, she nodded again, but she couldn't make
herself meet his eyes.

His hand clenched on the pommel of his saddle as he fought the
hunger he felt to teach her those things, to satisfy her curiosity. His
gaze fell to her soft mouth and he wanted it. It was crazy, what he

was thinking. He couldn't afford a lapse like that. She was just a kid and she worked for him...

She heard the creak of leather as he swung down out of the saddle. After a minute, she felt his lean hands hard on her waist. He lifted her down from the horse abruptly and left the horses to drink their fill.

The sun filtered down to the ground in patterns through the oak leaves there, in the middle of nowhere, in the shelter of the trees where thick grass grew on the shallow banks of the stream and open pasture beyond the spot. The wind whipped around, but Tess couldn't hear it or the gurgle of the stream above the sound of her own heart.

His hands felt rough against her skin. They felt as if he wasn't quite in control, and when she looked up at him, she realized that he wasn't. His face was like steel. The only thing alive in it was those black Spanish eyes, the legacy of a noble Madrid ancestry.

She felt her knees wobble because of the way he was looking at her, his eyes bold on her body, as if he knew exactly what was under her clothing.

The thought of Callaghan Hart's mouth on her lips made her breath catch in her throat. She'd always been a little afraid of him, not because she thought he might hurt her, but because late at night she lay wondering how it would feel if he kissed her. She'd thought about it a lot lately, to her shame. He was mature, experienced, confident, all the things she wasn't. She knew she couldn't handle an affair with him. She was equally sure that he wouldn't have any amorous interest in a novice like her. She'd *been* sure, she amended. Because he was looking at her now in a way he'd never looked at her before.

Her cold hands pressed nervously into the soft cotton of his shirt, feeling the warmth and strength of his chest under it.

"Callaghan," she whispered uncertainly.

His hard lips parted. "Nobody else calls me that," he said tersely, dropping his gaze to her mouth. He liked the way she made his name sound, as if it had a sort of magic.

Her fingers spread. She liked the feel of warm muscle under the shirt, and the soft, spongy feel of thick hair behind the buttons. He was hairy there, she suspected.

He wasn't breathing normally. She could feel his heartbeat against her skin. Her hands pressed gingerly against him, to explore, hesitantly, the hardness of his chest.

He stiffened. His hands on her waist contracted. His breathing changed.

Her hands stilled immediately. She looked up into glittery black eyes. She didn't understand his reactions, never having experienced them before.

"You don't know anything at all, do you?" he asked tersely, and it sounded as if he was talking to himself. He looked down at her short-nailed, capable little hands resting so nervously on top of his shirt. "Why did you stop?"

"You got stiff," she said.

He lifted an eyebrow. "Stiff?"

He looked as if he was trying not to smile, despite the tautness of his face and body.

"You know," she murmured. "Tense. Like you didn't want me to touch you."

He let out a slow breath. His hands moved from her waist to cover her cold fingers and press them closer. They felt warm and cozy, almost comforting. They flattened her hands so that she could feel his body in every cell.

She moved her fingers experimentally where the buttons ran down toward his belt.

"Don't get ambitious," he said, stilling her hands. "I'm not taking off my shirt for you."

"As if I would *ever...!*" she burst out, embarrassed.

He smiled indulgently, studying her flushed face, her wide, bright eyes. "I don't care whether you would, ever, you're not going to. Lift your face."

"Why?" she expelled on a choked breath.

"You know why."

She bit her lip, hard, studying his face with worried eyes. "You don't like me."

"Liking doesn't have anything to do with this." He let go of her hands and gripped her elbows, lifting her easily within reach of his mouth. His gaze fell to it and his chest rose and fell roughly. "You said you were curious," he murmured at her lips. "I'm going to do something about it."

Her hands gripped his shirt, wrinkling it, as his mouth came closer. She could taste the coffee on his warm breath and she felt as if the whole world had stopped spinning, as if the wind had stopped blowing, while she hung there, waiting.

His hard lips just barely touched hers, brushing lightly over the sensitive flesh to savor it. Her eyes closed and she held herself perfectly still, so that he wouldn't stop.

He lifted his head fractionally. She looked as if she couldn't bear to have him draw back. Whatever she felt, it wasn't fear.

He bent again. His top lip nudged under hers, and then down to toy with her lower lip. He felt her gasp. Apparently the kisses she'd had from other men hadn't been arousing. He felt her hands tighten on his shirt with a sense of pure arrogant pleasure.

He brought both lips down slowly over her bottom one, letting his tongue slide softly against the silky, moist inner tissue. She gasped and her mouth opened.

"Yes," he whispered as his own mouth opened to meet it, press into it, parting her lips wide so that he could cover them completely.

She made a tiny sound and her body stiffened, but he ignored the faint involuntary protest. His arms reached down, enclosing, lifting, so that she was completely off the ground in a hungry, warm embrace that seemed to swallow her whole.

The kiss was hard, slow, insistent and delicious. She clasped her hands at the back of Cal's neck and clung to it, her mouth accepting his, loving the hard crush of it. When she felt his tongue slipping past her lips, she didn't protest. She opened her mouth for him, met the slow, velvety thrust with a husky little moan, and closed her eyes even tighter as the intimacy of the kiss made her whole body clench with pleasure.

It seemed a long time before he lifted his head and watched her dazed, misty eyes open.

He searched them in the heady silence of the glade. Nearby a horse whinnied, but he didn't hear it. His heart was beating in time with Tess's, in a feverish rush. He was feeling sensations he'd almost forgotten how to feel. His body was swelling, aching, against hers.

He watched her face color and knew that she felt it and understood it.

He eased her back down onto her feet and let her move away a few inches. His eyes never left hers and he didn't let her go completely.

She looked as stunned as he felt. He searched her eyes as his big hand lifted and his fingers traced a blatant path down her breast to the hard tip.

She gasped, but she didn't try to stop him. She couldn't, and he knew it.

His hand returned to her waist.

She leaned her forehead against him while she got her breath back. She wondered if she should be embarrassed. She felt hot all over and oddly swollen. Her mouth was sore, but she wished his hard lips were still covering it. The sensations curling through her body were new and exciting and a little frightening.

"Was it just...a lesson?" she whispered, because she wanted to know.

His hands smoothed gently over her curly head. He stared past it, toward the stream where the horses were still drinking. "No."

"Then, why?"

His fingers slid into her curls. He sighed heavily. "I don't know."

Her eyes closed. She stood against him with the wind blowing all around them and thought that she'd never been so happy, or felt so complete.

He was feeling something comparable, but it disturbed him and made him angry. He hadn't wanted it to come to this. He'd always known, at some level, that it would be devastating to kiss her. This little redhead with her pert manner and fiery temper. She could bring him to his knees. Did she know that?

He lifted his head and looked down at her. She wasn't smiling, flirting, teasing, or pert. She looked as shattered as he felt.

He put her away from him, still holding her a little too tightly by the arms.

"Don't read anything into it," he said shortly.

Her breath was jerky. "I won't."

"It was just proximity," he explained. "And abstinence."

"Sure."

She wasn't humoring him. She really believed him. He was amazed that she didn't know how completely he'd lost control, how violently his body reacted to her. He frowned.

She shifted uneasily and moved back. His hands fell away. Her eyes met his and her thin brows wrinkled. "You won't...you won't tell the brothers?" she asked. She moved a shoulder. "I wouldn't want them to think I was, well, trying to... I mean, that I was flirting or chasing you or...anything."

"I don't think you're even real," he murmured half-absently as he studied her. "I don't gossip. I told you that. As if I'd start telling tales about you, to my own damned brothers, just because a kiss got a little out of hand!"

She went scarlet. She whirled away from him and stumbled down the bank to catch the mare's reins. She mounted after the second try, irritated that he was already comfortably in the saddle by then, watching her.

"As for the rest of it," he continued, as if there hadn't been any pause between words, "you weren't chasing me. I invited you out here."

She nodded, but she couldn't meet his eyes. What she was feeling was far too explosive, and she was afraid it might show in her eyes.

Her embarrassment was almost tangible. He sighed and rode closer, putting out a hand to tilt up her chin.

"Don't make such heavy weather of a kiss, Tess," he said quietly. "It's no big deal. Okay?"

"Okay." She almost choked on the word. The most earthshaking event of her life, and it was no big deal. Probably to him it hadn't been. The way he kissed, he'd probably worked for years perfecting his technique. But she'd never been kissed like that, and she was shattered. Still, he wasn't going to know it. He didn't even like her, he'd said as much. It had been an impulse, and obviously it was one he already regretted.

"Where do we go next?" she asked with a forced smile.

He scowled. She was upset. He should never have touched her, but it had been irresistible. It had been pure delight to kiss her. Now he had to forget that he ever had.

"The next pasture," he said curtly. "We'll roust out whatever cattle wildlife we find and then call it a day. You're drooping."

"I guess I am, a little," she confessed. "It's hot."

In more ways than one, he thought, but he didn't dare say it aloud. "Let's go, then."

He rode off, leaving her to follow. Neither of them mentioned what had happened. By the end of the day, they only spoke when they had to. And by the next morning, Cag was glaring at her as if she was the reason for global warming. Everything was back to normal.

Chapter 5

Spring turned to summer. Cag didn't invite Tess to go riding again, but he did have Leo speak to her about starting horticulture classes in the fall.

"I'd really like to," she told Leo. "But will I still be here then?" she added on a nervous laugh. "Cag's worse than ever lately. Any day now, he's going to fire me."

"That isn't likely," Leo assured her, secretly positive that Cag would never let her leave despite his antagonism, because the older man cared too much about her. Oddly Tess was the only person who didn't seem to realize that.

"If I'm still here," she said. "I'd love to go to school."

"We'll take care of it. Cheer up, will you?" he added gently. "You look depressed lately."

"Oh, I'm not," she assured him, lying through her teeth. "I feel just fine, really!"

She didn't tell him that she wasn't sleeping well, because she laid awake nights remembering the way Cag had kissed her. But if she'd hoped for a repeat of that afternoon, it had never come. Cag was all but hostile to her since, complaining about everything from the way she dusted to the way she fastened his socks together in the drawers. Nothing she did pleased him.

Mrs. Lewis remarked dryly that he acted lovesick, and Tess began to agonize about some shadowy woman that he might be seeing on those long evenings when he left the ranch and didn't come home until midnight. He never talked about a woman, but then, he didn't gossip. And even his brothers knew very little about his private life. It worried Tess so badly that even her appetite suffered. How would she survive if Cag married? She didn't like thinking about him with another woman. In fact, she hated it. When she realized why, she felt even worse. How in the world was it that she'd managed to fall in love with a man who couldn't stand to be around her, a man who thought of her only as a cook and housekeeper?

What was she going to do about it? She was terrified that it might show, although she saw no signs of it in her mirror. Cag paid her no more attention than he paid the housecleaning. He seemed to find her presence irritating, though, most especially at mealtimes. She began to find reasons to eat early or late, so that she didn't have to sit at the table with him glaring at her.

Oddly that made things worse. He started picking at her, and not in any teasing way. It got so bad that Leo and Rey took him aside and called him on it. He thought Tess had put them up to it, and blamed her. She withdrew into herself and sat alone in her room at night crocheting an afghan while she watched old black-and-white movies on the little television set her father had given her for Christmas four years ago. She spent less time with the brothers than ever, out of self-defense. But Cag's attitude hurt. She wondered if he was trying to make her quit, even though it was his idea to get her into school in the fall quarter. Perhaps, she thought miserably, he meant her to live in at the school dormitory and quit her job. The thought brought tears to her eyes and made her misery complete.

It was a beautiful summer day when haying got underway on the ranch to provide winter forage for the cattle. It hadn't rained for over a week and a half, and while the danger of drought was ever present, this was a necessary dry spell. The hay would rot in the field if it rained. Besides, it was a comfortable heat, unseasonably cool. Even so, it was hot enough for shorts.

Tess had on a pair of denim cutoffs that she'd made from a torn pair of jeans, and she was wearing socks and sneakers and a gray tank top. She looked young and fresh and full of energy, bouncing across the hayfield with the small red cooler in her hands. She hadn't wanted to go near Cag, but Leo had persuaded her that his older brother would be dying of thirst out there in the blazing sun with nothing to drink. He sent a reluctant Tess out to him with a cooler full of supplies.

Cag, driving the tractor that was scooping the hay into huge round bales, stopped and let the engine idle when he saw her coming toward him. He was alone in the field, having sent two other men into adjacent fields to bale hay in the same fashion. It was blazing hot in the sun, despite his wide-brimmed straw hat. He was bare-chested and still pouring sweat. He'd forgotten to bring anything along to drink, and he hadn't really expected anyone to think about sending him something. He smiled ruefully to himself, certain that Tess wouldn't have thought of it on her own. She was still too nervous of him to come this close willingly, especially considering the way he'd treated her since that unfortunate kiss in the pasture.

It wasn't that he disliked her. It was that he liked her far too much. He ached every time he looked at her, especially since he'd kissed her. He found himself thinking about it all the time. She was years younger, another generation. Some nice boy would come along and she'd go head over heels. He had to remember that and not let a few minutes of remembered pleasure blind him to reality. Tess was too young for him. Period.

He cut off the tractor and jumped down as she approached him. Her eyes seemed to flicker as they brushed his sweaty chest, thick with black hair that ran down into his close-fitting jeans.

He wiped his hand on a work cloth. "Brought survival gear, did you?" he asked.

"Just a couple of cans of beer and two sandwiches," she said tautly. "Leo asked me to."

"Naturally," he drawled sarcastically. "I'd hardly expect you to volunteer."

She bit her lower lip to keep from arguing with him. She was keenly aware of his dislike. She offered the cooler.

He took it from her, noticing how she avoided touching him as it changed hands.

"Go back along the path," he said, irritated by his own concern for her. "I've seen two big rattlesnakes since I started. They won't like the sun, so they'll be in a cool place. And that—" he indicated her shorts and sneakers "—is stupid gear to wear in a pasture. You should have on thick jeans and boots. Good God, you weren't even looking where your feet were!"

"I was watching the ravens," she said defensively, indicating two of them lighting and flying away in the field.

"They're after field mice." His narrowed black eyes cut into her flushed, averted face. "You're all but shaking. What the hell's wrong with you today?" he demanded.

Her eyes shot back up to his and she stepped back. "Nothing. I should go."

He realized belatedly that the sight of him without his shirt was affecting her. He didn't have to ask why. He already knew. Her hands had been shyly exploring his chest, even through the shirt, the day he'd kissed her, and she'd wanted to unfasten it. But she'd acted as if she couldn't bear to be near him ever since. She avoided him and it made him furious.

"Why don't you run along home?" he asked curtly. "You've done your duty, after all."

"I didn't mind."

"Hell!" He put the cooler down. "You can't be bothered to come within five feet of me unless somebody orders you to." He bit off the words, glaring at her. He was being unreasonable, but he couldn't help himself. "You won't bring me coffee in the office when I'm working unless the door's open and one of my brothers is within shouting distance. What do you expect, you scrawny little redhead, that the sight of you maddens me with such passion that I'm likely to ravish you on the floor? You don't even have a woman's body yet!" he muttered, his eyes on her small, pert breasts under the tank top.

She saw where he was looking and it wounded her. The whiplash of his voice hit her like a brick. She stared at him uncomprehendingly, her eyes wounded. "I never...never said..." she stammered.

"As if you could make me lose my head," he continued coldly, his voice like a sharp blade as his eyes went over her disparagingly.

Her face flamed and the eyes that met his were suddenly clouded not with anger, but with pain. Tears flooded them and she whirled with a sob, running in the direction from which she'd come.

She hated him! *Hated* him! He was the enemy. He'd never wanted her here and now he was telling her that she didn't even attract him. How obvious it was now that he'd only been playing with her when he kissed her. He didn't want her, or need her, or even like her, and she was dying of love for him! She felt sick inside. She couldn't control her tears or the sobs that broke from her lips as she ran blindly into the small sweep of thick hay that he hadn't yet cut.

She heard his voice, yelling something, but she was too upset to hear him. Suddenly her foot hit something that gave and she stopped dead, whirling at a sound like frying bacon that came from the ground beside her.

The ugly flat, venomous head reared as the tail that shot up from the coil rattled its deadly warning. A rattler—five feet long at least—and she'd stepped on it! Its head drew back ominously and she was frozen with fear, too confused to act. If she moved it would strike. If she didn't move it would strike. She could already feel the pain in her leg where the fangs would penetrate....

She was vaguely aware of a drumming sound like running, heavy footsteps. Through her tears she saw the sudden flash of something metallic go past her. The snake and its head abruptly parted company, and then long, powerful arms were around her, under her, lifting her to a sweat-glistening hard chest that was under her cheek.

"God!"

Cag's arms contracted. He was hurting her and she didn't care. Her arms tightened around his neck and she sobbed convulsively. He curled her against him in an ardent fever of need, feeling her soft breasts press hard into his bare, sweaty, hair-roughened chest as his face burrowed into her throat. She thought he trembled, but surely she imagined it. The terror came full force now that the threat was over, and she gave way to her misery.

They clung to each other in the hot sunlight with the sultry breeze wafting around them, oblivious to the man running toward them. Tess felt the warm, hard muscles in his back strain as she touched them, felt Cag's breath in her ear, against her hair. His cheek drew across hers and her nails dug into him. His indrawn breath was audible. His arms contracted again, and this time it wasn't comfort, it was a deep, dragging hunger that found an immediate response in her.

His face moved against hers jerkily, dragging down from her cheek, so that his lower lip slowly, achingly, began to draw itself right across her soft, parted mouth. Her breath drew in sharply at the exquisite feel of it. She wanted his lips on hers, the way they had been that spring day by the stream. She wanted to kiss him until her young body stopped aching.

He hesitated. His hand was resting at the edge of her breast and even as the embrace became hungry, she stopped breathing altogether as she felt his hard lips suddenly part and search for hers, felt the caressing pressure of those lean fingers begin to move up....

On the edge of the abyss, a barely glimpsed movement in the distance brought Cag's dark head up and he saw Leo running toward them. He was almost trembling with the need to take Tess's soft mouth, but he forced himself to breathe normally. All the hot emotion slowly drained out of his face, and he stared at his young brother as if he didn't recognize him for the first few seconds.

"What was it, a rattler?" Leo asked, panting for breath as he came up beside them.

Cag nodded his head toward the snake. It lay in two pieces, one writhing like mad in the hot sun. Between the two pieces was the big hunting knife that Cag always carried when he was working alone in the fields.

"Whew!" Leo whistled, shaking his head. "Pretty accurate, for a man who was running when he threw it. I saw you from the south field," he added.

"I've killed a few snakes in my time," Cag replied, and averted his eyes before Leo could ask if any of them had had two legs. "Here," he murmured to Tess, his voice unconsciously tender. "Are you all right?"

She sniffed and wiped her red eyes and nodded. She was embarrassed, because at the last, it hadn't been comfort that had brought them so close together. It was staggering after the things he said, the harshness of his manner before she'd stepped on the snake.

Cag put her down gingerly and moved back, but his turbulent eyes never left her.

"It didn't strike you?" he asked belatedly, and went on one knee to search over her legs.

"No," she faltered. The feel of those hard fingers on her skin made her weak. "No, I'm fine." She was looking down at him with eyes full of emotion. He was beautiful, she thought dazedly, and when he started to stand up again, her eyes lingered helplessly on that broad, sexy chest with its fine covering of hair. Her hand had touched it just as he put her down, and her fingers still tingled.

"Heavens, Tess!" Leo breathed, taking off his hat to wipe the sweat from his brow. "You don't run across a hayfield like that, without looking where you're going! When we cut hay, we always find half a dozen of the damned things!"

"It's not her fault," Cag said in a surprisingly calm voice. "I upset her."

She didn't look at Cag. She couldn't. She turned to Leo with a wan smile. "Could you walk me back, just to the track that leads up to the house?" she asked. "I'm a little shaky."

"Sure," he said gently. "I'll carry you, if you like."

"No, I can walk." She turned away. With her back to Cag she added carefully, "Thanks for what you did. I've never seen anybody use a knife like that. It would have had me just a second later."

Cag didn't say anything. He turned away and retrieved his knife, wiping it on his jeans before he stuck it back into the sheath on his belt. He stalked back toward the tractor. He never looked back.

"What did he do to upset you?" Leo asked when they were out of earshot.

"The usual things," she said with resignation in her voice. "I can't imagine why he doesn't fire me," she added. "First he said I could go in the spring, but we got too busy, then he said I could go in the summer. But here it is, and I'm still here."

He didn't mention that he had his own suspicions about that. Cag was in deep, and quite obviously fighting a defensive battle where Tess was concerned. But he'd seen the look on Cag's face when he was holding her, and dislike was not what it looked like to him.

"Did you see him throw the knife?" she asked, still awed by the skill of it. "Dad used to have a throwing knife and he could never quite get the hang of hitting the target. Neither could I. It's a lot harder than it looks. He did it running.''

"He's a combat veteran," he said. "He's still in the reserves. Nothing about Cag surprises us anymore.''

She glanced at him with twinkling eyes. "Did you really hit Turkey Sanders to keep Cag from doing it?''

"Dorie told you!" He chuckled.

"Yes. She said you don't let Cag get into fights.''

"We don't dare. He doesn't lose his temper much, but when he does, it's best to get out of the line of fire.''

"Yes, I know," she said uneasily, still remembering the birthday cake.

He glanced at her. "You've had a hard time.''

"With him?" She shrugged. "He's not so bad. Not as bad as he was around Christmas," she added. "I guess I'm getting used to sarcasm and insults. They bounce off these days.''

He made a rough sound under his breath. "Maybe he'll calm down eventually.''

"It doesn't matter. I like my job. It pays well.''

He laughed, sliding a friendly arm around her shoulders as they walked. "At least there are compensations.''

Neither of them saw a pair of black eyes across the field glaring after them hotly. Cag didn't like that arm around Tess, not one bit. He was going to have something to say to Leo about it later.

Blissfully unaware, Leo stopped at the trail that led back to the house. "Okay now?" he asked Tess.

"Yes, thanks.''

He studied her quietly. "It may get worse before it gets better, especially now," he said with some concern.

"What do you mean?''

"Never you mind," he replied, and his eyes held a secret amusement.

That evening, after the brothers cleaned up and had supper, Cag motioned Leo into the study and closed the door.

"Something wrong?" Leo asked, puzzled by his brother's taciturn silence since the afternoon.

Cag perched himself on the edge of his desk and stared, unblinking, at the younger man.

"Something," he agreed. Now that he was facing the subject, he didn't want to talk about it. He looked as disturbed as he felt.

"It's Tess, isn't it?" Leo asked quietly.

"She's twenty-two," Cag said evenly, staring hard at his brother. "And green as spring hay. Don't hit on her."

It was the last thing Leo expected the older man to say. "Don't *what?*" he asked, just to make sure he wasn't hearing things.

Cag looked mildly uncomfortable. "You had your arm around her on the way out of the field."

Leo's dark eyes twinkled. "Yes, I did, didn't I?" He pursed his lips and glanced at his brother with pure calculation. "She's a soft little thing, like a kitten."

Cag's face hardened and his eyes became dangerous. "She's off limits. Got that?"

Leo lifted both eyebrows. "Why?"

"Because she's a virgin," Cag said through his teeth. "And she works for us."

"I'm glad you remembered those things this afternoon," Leo returned. "But it's a shame you'd forgotten all about them until you saw me coming toward you. Or are you going to try and convince me that you weren't about to kiss the breath out of her?"

Cag's teeth ground together. "I was comforting her!"

"Is *that* what you call it?" came the wry response. "Son of a gun. I'm glad I have you to tell me these things."

"I wasn't hitting on her!"

Leo held up both hands. "Of course not!"

"If she's too young for you, she's damned sure too young for me."

"Was I arguing?"

Cag unruffled a little. "Anyway, she wants to go to school and study horticulture in the fall. She may not want to stay on here, once she gets a taste of younger men."

Why, he really believed that, Leo thought, his attention diverted. Didn't he see the way Tess looked at him, the way she acted around him lately? Or was he trying not to see it?

"She won't have to wait for that to happen," Leo murmured. "We hired a new assistant sales manager last week, remember? Sandy Gaines?"

Cag scowled. "The skinny blond fellow?"

"Skinny, sure, but he seems to have plenty of charm when it comes to our Tess. He brought her a teddy bear from his last trip to St. Louis, and he keeps asking her out. So far she won't go."

Cag didn't want to think about Tess with another man, especially the new salesman. "She could do worse, I guess," he said despite his misgivings.

"You might ask her out yourself," Leo suggested carelessly.

Cag's dark eyes held a world of cynicism. "I'm thirty-eight and she works for me."

Leo only smiled.

Cag turned away to the fireplace and stared down at the gas logs with resignation. "Does it show?" he asked after a minute.

That he cared for her, he meant. Leo smiled affectionately. "Only to someone who knows you pretty well. She doesn't. You won't let her close enough," Leo added.

Broad shoulders rose and fell. His eyes lifted to the huge painting of a running herd of horses tearing across a stormy plain. A great-uncle had painted it. Its wildness appealed to the brothers.

"She's grass green," Cag said quietly. "Anybody could turn her head right now. But it wouldn't last. She's too immature for any-thing...serious." He turned and met his brother's curious eyes. "The thing is," he said curtly, "that I can't keep my head if I touch her."

"So you keep her carefully at a distance to avoid complications."

Cag hesitated. Then he nodded. He stuffed his hands into the pockets of his jeans and paced. "I don't know what else to do. Maybe if we get her into school this fall, it will help. I was thinking we might even get her a job somewhere else."

"I noticed," Leo said dryly. "And then you tell her to wait one more season. She's waited two already."

Cag's black eyes cut into him. "I haven't been serious about a woman since I was sent to the Middle East," he said through his teeth. "I've been pretty bitter. I haven't wanted my heart twisted out of my chest again. Then, she came along." He nodded in the general direction of the kitchen. "With her curly red hair and big blue eyes and that pert little boyish figure." He shook his head as if to clear the image from it. "Damn it, I ache just looking at her!" He whirled. "I've got to get her out of here before I do something about it!"

Leo studied his hand. "Are you sure you don't want to do something about it?" he asked softly. "Because she wants you to. She was shaking when you put her down."

Cag glared at him. "The snake scared her."

"*You* scared her," came the wry response. "Have you forgotten how to tell when a woman's aroused?"

"No, I haven't forgotten," he replied grimly. "And that's why she's got to go. Right now."

"Just hold on. There's no need to go rushing into anything," Leo counseled.

"Oh, for God's sake, it's just a matter of time, don't you see?" Cag groaned. "You can't hold back an avalanche!"

"Like that, is it?"

"Worse." Cag lowered his head with a hard sigh. "Never like this. Never."

Leo, who'd never felt what passed for love in the world, stared at his brother with compassion but no real understanding of what he was going through.

"She fits in around here," Leo murmured.

"Sure she does. But I'm not going to marry her!"

Leo's eyebrows lifted. "Why not? Don't you want kids?"

"Corrigan's got one."

"Kids of your own," Leo persisted with a grin. "Little boys with big feet and curly red hair."

Cag lifted a paperweight from the desk and tossed it deliberately in one hand.

Leo held up both hands in a defensive gesture. "Don't throw it. I'm reformed. I won't say another word."

The paperweight was replaced on the desk. "Like I said before, I'm too old for her. After all the other considerations have been taken into account, that one remains. Sixteen years is too much."

"Do you know Ted Regan?"

Cag scowled. "Sure. Why?"

"Do you know how much older he is than Coreen?"

Cag swallowed. "Theirs is a different relationship."

"Calhoun Ballenger and Abby?"

Cag glared at him.

"Evan and Anna Tremayne?"

The glare became a black scowl.

Leo shrugged. "Dig your own grave, then. You should hear Ted groan about the wasted years he spent keeping Coreen at bay. They've got a child of their own now and they're talking about another one in the near future. Silver hair and all, Ted's the happiest fellow I know. Coreen keeps him young."

"I'll bet people talked."

"Of course people talked. But they didn't care."

That grin was irritating. Cag turned away from him. He didn't dare think about kids with curly red hair. He was already in over his head and having enough trouble trying to breathe.

"One day, a young man will come along and sweep her off her feet."

"You've already done that, several times," Leo said pointedly. "Carrying her off to the store to buy new clothes, and just today, out of the path of a rattler."

"She doesn't weigh as much as a good sack of potatoes."

"She needs feeding up. She's all nerves lately. Especially when you're around."

Cag's big hands clenched in his pockets. "I want to move the heifers into the west pasture tomorrow. What do you think?"

"I think it's a week too soon."

The broad shoulders shrugged. "Then we'll wait one more week. How about the pastures on the bottoms?"

"We haven't had rain, but we will. If they flood, we'll have every cowboy on the place out pulling cows out of mud." His eyes narrowed. "You know all that better than I do."

"I'm changing the subject."

Leo threw up his hands. "All right. Don't listen to me. But Sandy Gaines means business. He's flirting with her, hard. He's young and personable and educated, and he wears nice suits and drives a red Corvette."

Cag glared at him. "She can see through clothes and a car, even a nice car."

"She's had digs and sarcasm and insults from you," Leo said and he was serious. "A man who tells her she's pretty and treats her gently might walk up on her blind side. She's warming to him a little. I don't like it. I've heard things about him."

"What sort of things?" Cag asked without wanting to.

"That he's fine until he gets his hands on a bottle of liquor, and then he's every woman's worst nightmare. You and I both know the type. We don't want our Tess getting into a situation she can't handle."

"She wouldn't tolerate that sort of behavior from a man," he said stiffly.

"Of course not, but she barely weighs a hundred pounds sopping wet! Or have you forgotten that she couldn't even get away from Herman, and he only outweighs her by ten pounds? Gaines is almost your size!"

Cag's teeth clenched. "She won't go out with him," he said doggedly. "She's got better sense."

That impression only lasted two more days. Sandy Gaines, a dark-haired, blue-eyed charmer, came by to discuss a new advertising campaign with the brothers and waylaid Tess in the hall. He asked her to a dance at the Jacobsville dance hall that Friday night and she, frustrated and hurt by Cag's sarcasm and coldness, accepted without hesitation.

Chapter 6

Sandy picked her up early for the dance in his low-slung used red Corvette. Cag was nearby and he watched them with cold eyes, so eaten up with jealousy that he could hardly bear it. She was wearing their dress, to top it all, the blue dress he'd helped her pick out when he'd taken her shopping. How could she wear it for that city dude?

"Get her home by midnight," he told Sandy, and he didn't smile.

"Sure thing, Mr. Hart!"

Sandy put Tess into the car quickly and drove off. Tess didn't even look at Cag. She was uncomfortably aware of the dress she had on, and why Cag glared at her. But he didn't want to take her anywhere, after all, so why should he object to her going out on a date? He didn't even like her!

"What's he, your dad?" Sandy drawled, driving far too fast.

"They all look out for me," she said stiffly.

Sandy laughed cynically. "Yeah? Well, he acts like you're his private stock." He glanced at her. "Are you?"

"Not at all," she replied with deliberate carelessness.

"Good." He reached for her hand and pressed it. "We're going to have a nice time. I've looked forward to this all week. You're a pretty little thing."

She smiled. "Thanks."

"Now you just enjoy yourself and don't worry about heavy-handed surrogate parents, okay?"

"Okay."

But it didn't work out that way. The first two dances were fun, and she enjoyed the music. But very quickly, Sandy found his way to the bar. After his second whiskey sour, he became another man. He held her too closely and his hands wandered. When he tried to kiss her, she struggled.

"Oh, no, you don't," he muttered when she tried to sidestep him. He caught her hand and pulled her out of the big structure by a side door. Seconds later, he pushed her roughly up against the wall in the dim light.

Before she could get a hand up, he was kissing her—horrible wet, invasive kisses that made her gag. She tasted the whiskey on his breath and it sickened her even further. His hands grasped her small breasts roughly, hurting, twisting. She cried out and fought him, trying to get away, but his hips levered down over hers with an obscene motion as he laughed, enjoying her struggles as she tried valiantly to kick him.

It was like that other time, when she was sixteen and she'd been at the mercy of another lecherous man. The memories further weakened her, made her sick. She tried to get her knee up, but she only gave him an opening that brought them even more intimately together and frightened her further. She was beating at his chest, raging at him, and his hand was in the neckline of her dress, popping buttons off in his drunken haste, when she felt the pressure against her body suddenly lessen.

There were muffled curses that stopped when Sandy was suddenly pushed up against the wall himself with one arm behind him and a mercilessly efficient hand at his neck, the thumb hard under his ear. Cag looked violent as Tess had rarely seen him. The hold was more than dangerous, it was professional. She didn't have the slightest doubt that he could drop the other man instantly if it became necessary.

"Move, and I'll break your neck," Cag said in a voice like hot steel. His black eyes cut to Tess and took in her disheveled clothing, her torn bodice. He jerked his head toward the ranch pickup that was parked just at the edge of the grass. "It's unlocked. Go and get inside."

She hesitated, sick and wobbly and afraid.

"Go on," Cag said softly.

She turned. She might have pleaded for Sandy, except that she didn't think he deserved having her plead for him. He might have...God only knew what he might have done if Cag hadn't shown up! She resisted the urge to kick him while Cag had him powerless, and she wobbled off toward the truck.

She was aware of dull thuds behind her, but she didn't turn. She went to the truck, climbed in and sat shivering until a cold, taciturn Cag joined her.

Before he got into the cab, he pulled off the denim shirt he was wearing over a black T-shirt and put it over her shoulders the wrong way. He didn't attempt to touch her, probably aware that she was sick enough of being touched at the moment.

"Get into that," he said as he fastened his seat belt, "and fasten your belt."

He reached for the ignition and she noticed that his knuckles were bleeding. As she struggled into the shoulder harness she glanced toward the barn and saw Sandy leaning against the wall, looking very weak.

"I couldn't make him stop," she said in a thin voice. "I didn't expect him to...to get drunk. He seemed so nice. I never go out with big men usually—" Her voice broke. "Damn him! Oh, damn him! I never dreamed he'd be like *that!* He seemed like such a nice man!"

He glanced toward her with a face like black thunder, but he didn't speak. He put the truck in gear and drove her home.

The others were out for the evening. They were alone in the house. She started to go down the hall toward her room, but he turned her into the study and closed the door.

He seated her on the big black antique leather divan that graced the corner near the picture window and went to pour brandy into a snifter.

He came back and sat beside her, easing her cold, trembling hands around the bowl and offering it at her swollen lips. It stung and she hesitated, but he tilted it up again.

She let out a single sob and quickly controlled herself. "Sorry," she said.

"Why did you go out with him?"

"He flattered me," she said with pure self-disgust. "He was sweet to me and he seemed sort of boyish. I thought…I thought he'd be a perfect gentleman, the sort of man I'd never have to fight off. But he was different when we were alone. And then he started drinking."

"You're grass green," he muttered. "You can't size up men even now, can you?"

"I haven't dated much."

"I noticed."

She glanced up at his set features and then down into the brandy.

"Why haven't you?" he persisted.

She tried not to notice how sexy he looked in that black T-shirt that clung to every muscle he had. He was big, lean, all powerful muscle and bristling vitality. It made her weak to look at him, and she averted her eyes.

"My mother came to see us one day, when I was sixteen," she said uneasily. "She wanted to see how much I'd grown up, she said." She shifted. "She brought her latest lover. He was a playboy with lots of money and apparently he saw that it irritated her when he paid me some attention, so he put on the charm and kept it up all day. After supper, she was miffed enough to take my dad off into another room. Dad was crazy about her, even then." She swallowed. "It made her lover furious and vengeful. He closed the door and before I knew what was happening, he locked it and threw me down onto the sofa. He tore my clothes and touched me…." She closed her eyes at the horrible memory. "It was like tonight, only worse. He was a big man and strong. I couldn't get away, no matter how hard I fought, and in the end I just screamed. My father broke in the door to get to him. I'll never forget what he said to that man, and my mother, before he threw them off the place. I never saw her again. Or wanted to."

Cag let out the breath he'd been holding. So many things made sense now. He searched her wan little face with feelings of possession. She'd had so much pain and fear from men. She probably had no idea that tenderness even existed.

"You're tied up in bad memories, aren't you, little one?" he asked quietly. "Maybe they need to be replaced with better ones."

"Do they?" Her voice was sad, resigned. She finished the brandy and Cag put the snifter on the table.

She started to get up, only to find him blocking her way. He eased her back down onto the wide divan and slid down alongside her.

She gasped, wondering if she'd gotten out of the frying pan only to fall into the fire. She frantically put her hands against his broad chest and opened her mouth to protest, but his fingers touched it lightly as he laid beside her and arched over her prone body resting his formidable weight on his forearm.

"There's nothing to be afraid of, Tess," he said quietly. "Whatever disagreements we've had, you know that I'd never hurt you physically. Especially after the ordeal you've just been through."

She knew, but she was still nervous of him. He was even more powerfully built than Sandy, and in this way, in an intimate way, he was also an unknown quantity.

While she was thinking, worrying, he bent and she felt the warm threat of his big body as his mouth drew softly over her eyes, closing the lids. It moved to her temples, her eyebrows. He kissed her closed eyes, his tongue lightly skimming the lashes. She jerked, and his lean hand eased under her nape, soothing her, calming her.

She had little experience, but she wasn't so naive that she couldn't recognize his. Every touch, every caress, was expert. He eased down so slowly that she only realized how close he really was when she moved and felt his warm, hard chest move with her. By then, she was a prisoner of her own sensual curiosity, sedated by the exquisite pleasure his mouth was giving her as it explored her face.

By the time he reached her lips, the feel and smell of him were already familiar. When his hard mouth eased her lips apart and moved into them, she felt the increased pressure of his chest against her breasts, and she stiffened with real fear.

He lifted away immediately, but only a breath. His black eyes searched her blue ones slowly.

"You still don't know me like this," he murmured, as if he were talking to himself as he studied her flushed face, understanding the fear he read in it. "You're afraid, aren't you?"

She swallowed. Her mouth felt dry as she looked at him. "I think I am," she whispered.

He smiled lazily and traced her lips with a lean forefinger. "Will you relax if I promise to go so far and stop?" he whispered.

"So...far?" she asked in a hushed tone, searching his black eyes curiously.

He nodded. He teased her lips apart and touched the inside of her lower lip with the tip of his finger. "We'll make a little love," he whispered as he bent. "And then you'll go to bed. Your own, not mine," he added with dry mischief.

Her fingers clenched and unclenched on the soft fabric of his undershirt, like a kitten kneading a new place to lay. She could hear her own breath sighing out against his mouth as it came closer.

"You don't like me," she breathed.

His thumb rubbed quite roughly over her mouth. "Are you sure? You must know that I want you!" he said, and it came out almost as a growl. "Taunting you was the only way I knew to keep you at arm's length, to protect you. I was a fool! I'm too old for you, but at least I'm not like that damned idiot who took you out tonight!"

Nothing got into her sluggish brain except those first three feverish words. "You want me?" she whispered as if it was some dark secret. She looked up at him with wonder and saw the muted ferocity in his eyes.

His hand was on her waist now and it contracted until it all but bruised. "Yes, Tess. Is it shocking to hear me say it?" His gaze fell to her mouth and lower, to the two little peaks that formed suddenly against the torn bodice of her dress and were revealed even under the thick fabric of his concealing shirt. "You want me, too," he whispered, bending. "I can see it...."

She wanted to ask how he knew, but the taste of his breath against her lips weakened her. She wanted him to kiss her. She wanted nothing more in the world. Her nails curled into his powerful chest and she felt him shiver again just as his mouth slowly, tenderly, eased down on her parted lips.

He drew back almost at once, only to ease down again as his lips toyed with hers, brushing lightly from the upper lip to the lower one, teasing and lifting away in a silence that smoldered. She felt the warm pressure increase from second to second, and the leisure of his movements reassured her. She began to relax. Her body lost its rigor and softened against him. After a few seconds of the lazy, tender pressure, her lips opened eagerly for him. She heard a soft intake of breath as he accepted the unspoken invitation with increasingly intimate movements of his hard mouth.

The spicy fragrance of his cologne surrounded her. She knew that as long as she lived, every time she smelled it, it would invoke these images of Cag lying against her on the leather divan in the muted light of the study. She would hear the soft creak of the leather as his body moved closer to her own; she would hear the faint ticking of the old-fashioned grandfather clock near the desk. Most of all, she would feel the hard warmth of Cag's mouth and the slow caress of his lean hands up and down her rib cage, making her body ache with new pleasures.

His head lifted and he looked at her again, this time reading with pinpoint accuracy the sultry look of her eyes, the faint pulse in her throat, the hard tips of her breasts rising against the slip that her half-open bodice revealed. Somewhere along the way, he'd unbuttoned his shirt that she was wearing and it was lying back away from her torn dress.

He traced the ragged edge of the fabric with returning anger. "Did it have to be this dress?" he groaned.

She winced. "You never seemed to look at me," she defended herself. "He wanted to take me out, and it was the nicest thing I had in my closet."

He sighed heavily. "Yes, I know." He smiled wryly. "I didn't think I could risk taking you out. But look what happened because I didn't."

"He was so drunk," she whispered hoarsely. "He would have forced me..."

"Not while there was a breath in my body," he returned intently.

"How did you know?" she asked suddenly.

He pushed a stray curl away from her cheek. "I don't know," he said, frowning as if it disturbed him. "Something I'd heard about Gaines bothered me. One of the men said that he was fine as long as there wasn't a bottle anywhere nearby, and another one mentioned a threatened lawsuit over a disastrous date. I remembered that you'd gone to the dance at the bar.'' He shrugged. ''Maybe it was a premonition. Thank God I paid attention to it.''

''Yes.'' A thick strand of jet black hair had fallen onto his broad forehead. Hesitantly she reached up and pushed it back, her fingers lingering on its coolness.

He smiled because it was the first time that she'd voluntarily touched him.

She sought his eyes, sought permission. As if he understood the new feelings that were flaring up inside her, he drew her hand down to his chest and opened her fingers, pressing them there, firmly.

Her hand moved experimentally, pressing down and then curling into the thick hair she could feel under the soft fabric of his shirt.

Impatiently he lifted himself and peeled off the T-shirt, tossing it to the floor. He lay back down again beside her, curling his leg into hers as he guided her hand back to his chest.

She hesitated again. This was another step, an even bigger one.

''Even teenagers do this,'' he mused, smiling gently at her inhibitions. ''It's perfectly permissible.''

''Is it?'' Her fingers touched him as if she expected them to be burned. But then they pressed into the thick pelt of hair and explored, fascinated by the size and breadth of his chest, the warmth and strength of it.

He arched with pure pleasure and laughed delightedly at the sensations she aroused. It had been a long time since a woman had touched him like that.

She smiled shyly, fascinated by his reaction. He seemed so stoic, so reserved, that this lack of inhibition was surprising.

''Men are like cats,'' he murmured. ''We love to be stroked.''

''Oh.'' She studied him as if he were an exhibit in a museum, curious about every single cell of his body.

''Feeling more secure now?'' he asked softly. ''More adventurous?''

''I'm not sure.'' She looked up at him, quizzically.

''Nothing heavy,'' he promised. His black eyes were softer than she'd ever seen them. ''It's no news to me that you're a rank beginner.''

''What are you...going to do?'' she stammered, wide-eyed.

"Kiss you," he breathed, letting his gaze fall to her bare breasts.

"Th...there?" she gasped.

He touched her lightly, smiling at the expression on her taut face. "There," he whispered. He bent and drew his cheek softly over the bruised flesh, careful not to hurt her with the light pressure.

While she was trying to cope with so many new and shocking sensations, his mouth smoothed back over the soft, silky flesh and she felt it open. He tasted her flushed skin in a heated fever of need. Her hands curled up into his thick hair and she held him to her, whimpering softly with pleasure as she found herself drawing his face hungrily to where the flesh was very taut and sensitive.

"Here?" he whispered, hesitating.

"Oh...yes!" she choked.

His mouth opened obediently and he drew the hard nipple into it with a faint, soft suction that brought a sharp cry from her dry lips.

She thought she felt him tremble, and then he was moving onto his back, breathing roughly as he carried her with him. He held her at his side, their legs intimately entangled, while he fought to get his breath back.

His skin was cool against her hot breasts where they were pressed together above the waist. Her cheek was against the hard muscle of his upper arm and she caught again that elusive spicy scent that clung to him.

Her hand eased onto the thick hair at his chest, but he caught it and held it a little roughly at her side.

"No," he whispered.

She didn't understand what she'd done wrong. A minute later, he got to his feet and bent to retrieve his undershirt. While he shrugged into it, she tugged up her bodice and tried to fasten it.

But when she would have gotten to her feet, he pressed her back down.

"Stay put," he said quietly. He turned and left the room.

She'd barely gotten her breathing calm when he was back, sitting down beside her with a cold can of beer in his hand.

He popped it open and took a sip before he pulled her up beside him and held it to her lips.

"I don't like beer," she murmured dazedly.

"I'm going to taste of it," he replied matter-of-factly. "If you swallow some, you won't find the taste so unpleasant when I kiss you."

Her heart jumped wildly.

He met her surprised expression with a smile. "Did you think we were finished?" he asked softly.

She blushed.

"I was getting too aroused," he murmured dryly. "And so were you. I'm not going to let it go that far."

She searched his hard face with open curiosity. "What does it feel like to you, when you kiss me like that?" she asked quickly, before she lost her nerve.

"How does it feel when I do it?"

"I don't know. Shivery. Hot. I never felt anything like that before."

He took a sip of the beer and looked down at her hungrily. "Neither did I," he said tersely. His eyes seemed to possess her as they ran like caressing hands all over her. "Your breasts are freckled," he said with an intimate smile and chuckled when she blushed. He held her face up to his and kissed her nose. "I'm not going to rush out to the nearest bar and gossip about it," he whispered when he saw the faint apprehension in her wide eyes. "It's a lover's secret; a thing we don't share with other people. Like the scar on my belly."

She frowned slightly. He tugged down the waistband of his jeans and drew her hand against him where a long, thick scar was just visible above his belt.

"It runs down to my groin," he said solemnly. "Fortunately, it missed the more...vital areas. But it was touch and go for a few days and the scar is never going to go away."

Her fingers lingered there. "I'm sorry you were hurt."

He held her hand to him and smiled. "This is something I haven't shown to anyone else," he told her. "Except my brothers."

It made sense then. She looked up into his eyes. "A...lover's secret," she whispered, amazed that she could think of him like that, so easily.

He nodded. He wasn't smiling. "Like the freckles on your breasts, just around the nipples."

She felt her breath gathering speed, like an old-time steam engine. Her breasts felt tight, and not because of Sandy's rough handling. She frowned a little because it was uncomfortable and she still didn't quite understand it.

"We swell, both of us, when we're aroused," he said quietly, glancing at the small hand that had come up to rest a little gingerly against one taut nipple. "It's uncomfortable, isn't it?"

"Just...just a little." She felt like a child in a candy store, breathless with delight as she looked at him. "I liked...what you did," she whispered.

"So did I. Have a few sips of this and I'll do it again."

Her breath caught. She sipped and wrinkled her nose. He took two more huge swallows before he put the can on the table and came back to her.

He stretched out beside her and this time when he slid his leg in between both of hers, it wasn't shocking or frightening. It felt natural, right. His hands slid under her as he bent again to her mouth. Now the kisses weren't tentative and seeking. They were slow and insistent and arousing. They were passionate kisses, meant to drag a response from the most unwilling partner.

Tess found herself clinging to him as if she might drown, her nails biting into his nape, and every kiss was more intimate than the last, more demanding, more arousing, more complete.

When his powerful body eased completely down over hers, she didn't protest at all. Her arms slid around his waist, her legs parted immediately, and she melted into the leather under them, welcoming the hard crush of him, the sudden heat and swelling that betrayed his hunger.

"You can feel it, can't you?" he whispered intimately at her ear and moved a little, just to make sure she could.

"Cag...!"

"I want you so badly, Tess!" he whispered, and his mouth slid over her cheek and onto her lips. He bit at them with a new and staggering intimacy that set her body on fire. When his tongue eased into her mouth, she opened her lips to accept it. When he pressed her legs further apart so that he could settle intimately between them, she arched into him. When he groaned and his hands found her breasts, she gave everything that she was into his keeping. He never thought he could draw back in time. He shook convulsively with the effort. He dragged his hips away and turned, lying on his back with Tess settled close against his side while he fought his own need, and hers.

"Don't...move!" he stated when she turned closer to him.

She stilled at once, half-heard bits of advice from a parade of motherly women coming back to her and making sudden sense.

She could feel Cag's powerful body vibrating with the hunger the kisses had built in it. He was like corded wood, breathing harshly. It fascinated her that he'd wanted her that much, when she was a rank beginner. He certainly wasn't!

When she felt him begin to relax, she let out a sigh of relief. She hadn't known what to do or say. Men in that condition were a mystery to her.

She felt his hand in her curly hair, holding her cheek to his chest. Under it, she heard the heavy, hard beat of his heart, like a fast drum.

"I haven't touched a woman since my fiancée threw me over," he said in a harsh tone.

Years ago. He didn't say it, but Tess knew that was what he was implying. She lifted her head and raised up, resting her hand on his shoulder to steady her as she searched his face. There was a hard flush along his high cheekbones, but his eyes were quiet, soft, full of mystery as they met hers.

"You want to know why I drew back."

She nodded.

He let go of her hair and touched her soft, swollen mouth with his. "You're a virgin."

He sounded so certain of it that she didn't bother to argue. It would have been pretty pointless at the moment, anyway.

"Oh. I see." She didn't, but it sounded mature.

He chuckled gently. "You don't know beans," he corrected. He moved suddenly, turning her over so that his body half covered hers and his eyes were inches from her own. His big hand caught her hip and curved it up into his intimately. The reaction of his body was fierce and immediate; and very stark. She flushed.

"I don't date anymore," he said, watching her mouth. "I don't have anything to do with women. This—'' he moved her subtly against that part of him that was most obvious ''—is delicious and heady and even a little shocking. I haven't felt it in a very long time.''

Curiosity warred with embarrassment. ''But I'm not experienced,'' she said.

He nodded. ''And you think it should take an experienced woman to arouse me this much.''

''Well, yes.''

He bent and drew his lips over her open mouth in a shivery little caress that made her breath catch. ''It happens every time I touch you,'' he whispered into her lips. ''An experienced woman would have realized immediately why I was so hostile and antagonistic toward you. It's taken you months.''

He covered her mouth with his, kissing her almost violently as his hand slid back inside her dress and played havoc with her self-control. But it only lasted seconds. He got up abruptly and pulled her up with him, holding her a few inches away from him with steely hands at her waist.

''You have to go to bed. Alone. Right now,'' he said emphatically.

Her breath came in soft spurts as she looked up at him with her heart in her eyes.

He actually groaned and pulled her close, into a bearish embrace. He stood holding her, shivering as they pressed together.

''Dear God,'' he whispered poignantly, and it sounded reverent, almost a plea for divine assistance. ''Tess, do you know how old I am?'' he groaned at her ear. ''We're almost a generation apart!''

Her eyes were closed. She was dreaming. It had all been a dream, a sweet, sensuous dream that she never wanted to end.

''I can still feel your mouth on my breasts when I close my eyes,'' she whispered.

He made another rough sound and his arms tightened almost to pain. He didn't know how he was going to let her go.

''Baby,'' he whispered, ''this is getting dangerous.''

''You never called me 'baby' before,'' she murmured.

''I was never this close to being your lover before,'' he whispered gruffly. His head lifted and his black eyes glittered down into her pale blue ones. "Not like this, Tess," he said roughly. "Not in a fever, because you've had a bad experience."

"You made love to me," she said, still dazed by the realization of how much their turbulent relationship had changed in the space of a few minutes.

"You wanted me to," he returned.

"Oh, yes," she confessed softly. Her lips parted and she watched, fascinated at the expression on his face when he looked down at them.

She reached up to him on tiptoe, amazed that it took such a tiny little tug to bring his hard mouth crashing passionately down onto her parted lips. He actually lifted her off the floor in his ardor, groaning as the kiss went on endlessly.

She felt swollen all over when he eased her back down onto her feet.

"This won't do," he said unsteadily. He held her by the shoulders, firmly. "Are you listening?"

"I'm trying to," she agreed, searching his eyes as if they held the key to paradise. His hands contracted. "I want you, honey," he said curtly. "Want you badly enough to seduce you, do you understand?" His gaze fell to her waist and lingered there with the beginnings of shock. All at once, he was thinking with real hunger of little boys with curly red hair...

Chapter 7

"Why are you looking at me like that?" Tess asked softly.

His hands contracted on her waist for an instant before he suddenly came to his senses and realized what he was thinking and how impossible it was. He closed his eyes and breathed slowly, until he got back the control he'd almost lost.

He put her away from him with an odd tenderness. "You're very young," he said. "I only meant to comfort you. Things just...got out of hand. I'm sorry."

She searched his eyes and knew that what they'd shared hadn't made a whit of difference to their turbulent relationship. He wanted her, all right, but there was guilt in his face. He thought she was too young for anything permanent. Or perhaps that was the excuse he had to use to conceal the real one—that he was afraid to get involved with a woman again because he'd been so badly hurt by one.

She dropped her gaze to his broad chest, watching its jerky rise and fall curiously. He wasn't unaffected by her. That was oddly comforting.

"Thanks for getting rid of the bad memory, anyway," she said in a subdued tone.

He hesitated before he spoke, choosing his words. "Tess, it wasn't only that," he said softly. "But you have to realize how things are. I've been alone for a long time. I let you go to my head." He took a long, harsh breath. "I'm not a marrying man. Not anymore. But you're a marrying woman."

She ground her teeth together. Well, that was plain enough. She looked up at him, red-cheeked. "I didn't propose! And don't get your hopes up, because I won't. Ever. So there."

He cocked his head, and for an instant something twinkled deep in his eyes. "Never? I'm devastated."

The humor was unexpected and it eased the pain of the awkward situation a little. She peeked up at him. "You're very attractive," she continued, "but it takes more than looks to make a marriage. You can't cook and you don't know which end of a broom to use. Besides that, you throw cakes at people."

He couldn't deny that. His firm mouth, still swollen from the hot kisses they'd shared, tugged up at the corners. "I missed you by a mile. In fact," he reminded her, "you weren't even in the room when I threw it."

She held up a hand. "I'm sorry. It's too late for excuses. You're right off my list of marriage prospects. I hope you can stand the shock."

He chuckled softly. "So do I." She was still flushed, but she looked less tormented than she had. "Are you all right now?" he asked gently.

She nodded and then said, "Yes. Thank you," she added, her voice softer then she intended it to be.

He only smiled. "He won't be back, in case you're worried about that," he added. "I fired him on the spot."

She drew in a breath. "I can't say I'm sorry about that. He wasn't what he seemed."

"Most men aren't. And the next time you accept a date, I want to know first."

She stared at him. "I beg your pardon?"

"You heard me. You may not consider me good husband material," he murmured, "but I'm going to look out for your interests just the same." He studied her seriously for a moment. "If I can't seduce you, nobody else can, either."

"Well, talk about sour grapes!" she accused.

"Count on it," he agreed.

"And what if I want to be seduced?" she continued.

"Not this week," he returned dryly. "I'll have to look at my calendar."

"I didn't mean you!"

His black eyes slid up and down her body in the torn dress that she'd covered with his shirt. "You did earlier," he murmured with a tender smile. "And I wanted to."

She sighed. "So did I. But I won't propose, even if you beg."

He shrugged powerful shoulders. "My heart's broken."

She chuckled in spite of herself. "Sure it is."

She turned and reached for the doorknob.

"Tess."

She glanced back at him. "Yes?"

His face was solemn, no longer teasing. "They told you about her, didn't they?"

He meant his brothers had told her about his doomed engagement. She didn't pretend ignorance. "Yes, they did," she replied.

"It was a long time ago, but it took me years to get over it. She was young, too, and she thought I was just what she wanted. But the minute I was out of sight, she found somebody else."

"And you think I would, too, because I'm not mature enough to be serious," she guessed.

His broad chest rose and fell. "That's about the size of it. You're pretty green, honey. It might be nothing more concrete than a good case of repressed lust."

"If that's my excuse, what's yours?" she asked with pursed lips. "Abstinence?"

"That's my story and I'm sticking to it like glue."

She laughed softly. "Coward."

He lifted one eyebrow. "You can write a check on that. I've been burned and I've got the scars to prove it."

"And I'm too young to be in love with you."

His heart jerked in his chest. The thought of Tess being in love with him made his head spin, but he had to hold on to his common sense. "That's right." His gaze went homing to her soft mouth and he could taste it all over again. He folded his arms over his broad chest and looked at her openly, without amusement or mockery. "Years too young."

"Okay. Just checking." She opened the door. A crash of thunder rumbled into the silence that followed. Seconds later, the bushes outside his window scratched against the glass as the wind raged.

"Are you afraid of storms?" he asked.

She shook her head. "Are you?"

"I'll tell you tomorrow."

She looked puzzled.

"You've spent enough time around livestock to know that thunderstorms play hell with cattle from time to time. We'll have to go out and check on ours if this keeps up. You can lie in your nice, soft dry bed and think about all of us getting soaked to the skin."

She thought about how bad summer colds could be. "Wear a raincoat," she told him.

He smiled at that affectionate concern, and it was in his eyes this time, too. "Okay, boss."

She grinned. "That'll be the day."

He lifted an eyebrow. "You're big on songs these days," he murmured. "That was one of Buddy Holly's. Want me to sing it to you?"

She realized belatedly which song he was talking about, and she shook her head. "No, thanks. It would upset the neighbors' dogs."

He glowered at her. "I have a good voice."

"Sure you do, as long as you don't use it for singing," she agreed. "Good night, Callaghan. Thanks again for rescuing me."

"I can't let anything happen to the family biscuit chef," he said casually. "We'd all starve."

She let him get away with that. He might not believe in marriage, but he was different after their ardent interlude. He'd never picked at her, teased her, before. Come to think of it, she'd never teased him. She'd been too afraid. That was ancient history now. She gave him one last shy, smiling glance and went out the door.

He stood where she left him, his eyes narrowed, his body still singing with the pleasure she'd given him. She was too young. His mind knew it. If he could only convince the rest of him...

Surprisingly Tess slept that night, despite the storms that rippled by, one after another. The memory of Cag's tender passion had all but blotted out the bad memories Gaines had given her. If only Cag wanted her on a permanent basis. At least they'd gotten past the awkwardness that followed that physical explosion of pleasure. It would make things easier for both of them.

She made breakfast the following morning and there was nobody to eat it. One of the men, wet and bedraggled looking, came to the back door to explain why breakfast went untouched.

It seemed that the high winds combined with drenching rain had brought down some huge old oak trees, right through several fences. While she slept soundly, in the outer pastures, cattle had gotten loose and had to be rounded up again, and the broken fences had to be mended. Half the outfit was soaked and all but frozen from the effort. The brothers had dragged in about daylight and fallen asleep, too tired even for their beloved biscuits.

It was almost noon before they came wandering into the kitchen. Breakfast had gone to the ranch dogs and the chickens, but she had beef and potatoes in a thick stew—with biscuits—waiting.

Rey and Leo smiled at her. To her astonishment, Cag gave her an openly affectionate glance as he sat down at the head of the table and reached for the coffeepot.

"It amazes me how you always keep food hot," Leo remarked. "Thanks, Tess. We were dead on our feet when we finally got back this morning."

"It was a rough night, I gather," she murmured as she ferried butter and jam to the table.

Leo watched her curiously. "We heard that you had one of your own," he said, regretting the careless remark when he saw her flush. "I'm sorry we didn't get our hands on Gaines before he ran for the border," he added, and the familiar, funny man she'd come to know suddenly became someone else.

"That goes double for me," Rey added grimly.

"Well, he had plenty of attention without counting on either of you," Cag remarked pleasantly. "I understand that he left tire marks on his way out in the early hours of the morning. The sniveling little weasel," he added.

"Amazing, isn't it, that Gaines actually walked away under his own steam," Leo told Rey.

Rey nodded. "And here we've been wasting our time saving people from him—" he indicated Cag "—for years."

"People don't need saving from me," Cag offered. "I'm not a homicidal maniac. I can control my temper," he added.

Leo pursed his lips. "Say, Tess, did the chocolate icing stain ever come completely off the wall...?"

She was fumbling with a lid that wouldn't come off, flustered from the whole conversation and wishing she could sink through the floor.

"Here, give me that," Cag said softly.

She gave it to him. Their hands touched and they looked at each other for just a second too long, something the brothers picked up on immediately.

Cag opened the jar and put it on the table while she went to get spoons.

"At least he's stopped throwing cakes at people," Rey remarked.

Cag lifted the jar of apple butter and looked at his brother intently.

Rey held up a hand and grinned sheepishly as he fell to eating his stew.

"If it's all right, I thought I'd go ahead and apply to the local technical school," Tess said quickly, before she lost her nerve. "For fall classes in horticulture, you know."

"Sure," Leo said. "Go ahead."

Cag lifted his gaze to her slender body and remembered how sweet it had been to hold in the silence of the study. He let his gaze fall back to his plate. He couldn't deter her. She didn't belong to him. She did need an occupation, something that would support her. He didn't like the idea of her keeping house for anyone else. She was safe here; she might not be in some other household. And if she went as a commuter, she could still work for the brothers.

"I could...live in the dormitory, if you want," she continued doggedly.

That brought Cag's head up. "Live in the dormitory? What the hell for?" he exclaimed.

His surprise took some of the gloom out of her heart. She clasped her hands tight in front of her, against her new jeans. "Well, you only said I could stay until summer,'' she said reasonably. "It's summer now. You didn't say anything about staying until fall.''

Cag looked hunted. "You won't find another job easily in the fall, with all the high school seniors out grabbing them,'' he said curtly. He glanced back at his plate. "Stay until winter.''

She wondered why Rey and Leo were strangling on their coffee.

"Is it too strong?'' she asked worriedly, nodding toward the cups.

"Just…right.'' Leo chocked, coughing. "I think I caught cold last night. Sorry. I need a tissue…''

"Me, too!'' Rey exploded.

They almost knocked over their chairs in their rush to get out of the room. Muffled laughter floated back even after the door had been closed.

"Idiots,'' Cag muttered. He looked up at Tess, and something brushed against his heart, as softly as a butterfly. He could hardly breathe.

She looked at him with eyes that loved him, and hated the very feeling. He wanted her to go, she knew he did, but he kept putting it off because he was sorry for her. She was so tired of being pitied by him.

"I don't mind living in the dormitory at school, if you want me to leave here,'' she repeated softly.

He got up from his chair and moved toward her. His big, lean hands rested on her shoulders and he looked down from his great height with quiet, wondering eyes. She was already like part of him. She made him bubble inside, as if he'd had champagne. The touch of her, the taste of her, were suddenly all too familiar.

"How would you manage to support yourself, with no job?'' he asked realistically.

"I could get something part-time, at the school.''

"And who'll bake biscuits for us?'' he asked softly. "And worry about us when we're tired? Who'll remember to set the alarm clocks and remind me to clean Herman's cage? Who'll fuss if I don't wear my raincoat?'' he added affectionately.

She shrugged. His hands felt nice. She loved their warmth and strength, their tenderness.

He tilted her chin up and searched her quiet eyes. Fires kindled deep in his body and made him hungry. He couldn't afford to indulge what he was feeling. Especially not here, in the kitchen, where his brothers could walk in any minute.

But while he was thinking it, his rebellious hands slid up to frame her face and he bent, brushing his mouth tenderly over her soft lips.

"You shouldn't let me do this," he whispered.

"Oh, I'm not," she assured him softly. "I'm resisting you like crazy." She reached up to link her arms around his neck.

"Are you?" He smiled as he coaxed her lips under his and kissed her slowly.

She smiled against his mouth, lifting toward him. "Yes. I'm fighting like mad. Can't you tell?"

"I love the way you fight me...!"

The kiss became possessive, insistent, feverish, all in the space of seconds. He lifted her against him and groaned at the fierce passion she kindled in him so effortlessly.

Only the sound of booted feet heading their way broke them apart. He set her down gently and struggled to get back in his chair and breathe normally. He managed it, just.

Tess kept her back to the brothers until she could regain her own composure. But she didn't realize that her mouth was swollen and the softness in her eyes was an equally vivid giveaway.

Cag was cursing himself and circumstances under his breath for all he was worth. Having her here was going to be an unbearable temptation. Why hadn't he agreed to letting her live in at the school?

Because he ached for her, that was why. He was alive as he hadn't been in seven long years and the thought of going back into his shell was painful.

His black eyes settled on Tess and he wondered how he could ever have lived from day to day without looking at her at least once. He was getting a fixation on red curly hair and pale freckled skin. She was too young for him. He knew that, but he couldn't seem to keep his hands off her. He didn't know what he was going to do. If he didn't find something to occupy him, and quickly, he was going to end up seducing her. That would be the end of the world. The absolute end.

* * *

Tess borrowed one of the ranch trucks the next morning after breakfast and drove herself to the campus of the Jacobsville Vocational-Technical School. The admissions office was easy to find. She was given forms to fill out, a course schedule for the fall quarter, and advice on financial assistance. From there, she went to the financial office and filled out more forms. It took until lunch to finally finish, but she had a sense of accomplishment by the time she left the campus.

On her way back to the ranch, she stopped in at the local café and had coffee and a sandwich while she did some thinking about her situation.

Cag said he didn't want her to move out, but did he really mean it, or was he just sorry for her? He liked kissing her, but he didn't want to keep doing it. He seemed not to be able to stop. Maybe, she thought, that was the whole problem. She made him forget all the reasons why he shouldn't get involved with her, every time he came close.

If she was gone, of course, he wouldn't get close enough to have his scruples damaged. But he'd said that he didn't want her to leave. It was a puzzle she couldn't seem to solve.

The sandwich tasted flat, although it was roast beef, one of her favorites. She put it down and stared at it without seeing.

"Thinking of giving it its freedom, huh?" Leo asked with a grin, and sat down across from her. He took off his hat, laid it on the chair beside him and gestured toward the sandwich. "I hate to tell you this, but there's absolutely no way known to science that a roast beef sandwich can be rejuvenated." He leaned forward conspiratorially. "Take it from a beef expert."

She chuckled despite her sadness. "Oh, Leo, you're just impossible," she choked.

"It runs in the family." He held up a hand and when the waitress came to see what he wanted, he ordered coffee.

"No lunch?" Tess asked.

He shook his head. "No time. I'm due at the Brewsters's in forty-five minutes for a business meeting over lunch. Rubber chicken and overdone potatoes, like last time," he muttered. He glanced at her. "I wish you were cooking for it instead of Brewster's daughter. She's pretty as a picture and I hear tell she had operatic aspirations, but she couldn't make canned soup taste good.''

He sounded so disgusted that Tess smiled in spite of herself. ''Are you going by yourself, or are the brothers going, too?''

''Just Cag and me. Rey escaped on a morning flight to Tulsa to close a land deal up there.''

She lowered her eyes to the half-finished sandwich. ''Does Cag like her...Miss Brewster?''

He hesitated. ''Cag doesn't like women, period. I thought you knew.''

''You said she was pretty.''

''Like half a dozen other women who have fathers in the cattle business,'' he agreed. ''Some of them can even cook. But as you know Cag gave up on women when he was thrown over for a younger man. Hell, the guy was only three years younger than him, at that. She used his age as an excuse. It wasn't, really. She just didn't want him. The other guy had money, too, and she did want him.''

''I see.''

He sipped coffee and pursed his lips thoughtfully. ''I've told you before how Cag reacts to women most of the time,'' he reminded her. ''He runs.'' He smiled. ''Of course, he's been doing his best to run from you since last Christmas.''

She looked at him with her heart in her eyes. ''He has?'' she asked.

''Sure! He wants you to go off to school so you'll remove temptation from his path. But he also wants you to stay at the ranch while you go to school, in case you run into any handsome eligible bachelors there. I think he plans to save you from them, if you do.''

She was confused and it showed.

''He said,'' he related, ''that you shouldn't be exposed to potential seducers without us to protect you.''

She didn't know whether to laugh or cry.

He held up a hand when she started to speak. ''He thinks you should commute.''

''But he doesn't want me at the ranch, don't you see?'' she asked miserably, running a hand through her short, curly hair. ''He keeps leaving to get away from me!''

"Why would he leave if you weren't getting to him?" he asked reasonably.

"It's still a rotten way to live," she said pointedly. "Maybe if I go to school I'll meet somebody who'll think I'm old enough for them."

"Oh, that's just sour grapes," he murmured dryly.

"You have no idea *how* sour," she replied. "I give up. I can't spend the rest of my life hoping that he'll change his mind about me. He's had almost a year, and he hasn't changed a thing."

"He stopped throwing cakes," he said.

"Because I stopped baking them!"

He checked his watch and grimaced. "I'd love to stay here and talk recipes with you, but I'm late." He got up and smiled at her. "Don't brood, okay? I have a feeling that things are going to work out just fine."

That wasn't what she thought, but he was gone before she could put the thought into words.

Chapter 8

It was inevitable that Leo would bring up the matter of the Brewster girl's cooking the next day. Breakfast was too much of a rush, and they didn't get to come home for lunch. But when two of the three brothers and Tess sat down to supper, Leo let it fly with both barrels.

"That Janie Brewster isn't too bad-looking, is she?" Leo murmured between bites of perfectly cooked barbecued chicken. "Of course, she can ruin a chicken."

Cag glanced at him quickly, as if the remark puzzled him. Then he glanced at Tess's studiously downbent head and understood immediately what Leo was trying to do.

He took a forkful of chicken and ate it before he replied, "She'll never make a cook. Or even much of a wife," he added deliberately. "She knows everything."

"She does have a university degree."

"In psychology," Cag reminded him. "I got psychoanalyzed over every bite of food." He glanced at Tess. "It seems that I have repressed feelings of inadequacy because I keep a giant reptile," he related with a twinkle in his black eyes.

Tess's own eyes widened. "You do?"

He nodded. "And I won't eat carrots because I have some deep-seated need to defy my mother."

She put a napkin to her mouth, trying to ward off laughter.

"You forgot the remark she made about the asparagus," Leo prompted.

Cag looked uncomfortable. "We can forget that one."

"But it's the best one!" Leo turned to Tess. "She said that he won't eat asparagus because of associations with impo—"

"Shut up!" Cag roared.

Leo, who never meant to repeat the blatant sexual remark, only grinned. "Okay."

Tess guessed, quite correctly, that the word Cag had cut off was "impotence." And she was in a perfect position to tell Leo that it certainly didn't apply to his older brother, but she wouldn't have dared.

As it was, her eyes met Cag's across the table, and she flushed at the absolutely wicked glitter in those black eyes, and almost upset her coffee.

Leo, watching the byplay, was affectionately amused at the two of them trying so hard not to react. There was a sort of intimate merriment between them, despite Cag's attempts to ward off intimacy. Apparently he hadn't been wholly successful.

"I've got a week's worth of paperwork to get through," Cag said after a minute, getting up.

"But I made dessert," Tess said.

He turned, surprised. "I don't eat sweets. You know that."

She smiled secretively. "You'll like this one. It isn't really a conventional dessert."

He pushed in his chair. "Okay," he said. "But you'll have to bring it to me in the office. How about some coffee, too?"

"Sure."

Leo put down his napkin. "Well, you do the hard stuff. I'm going down to Shea's Bar to see if I can find Billy Telford. He promised me faithfully that he was going to give me a price on that Salers bull we're after. He's holding us up hoping that he can get more from the Tremaynes."

"The Tremaynes don't run Salers cattle," Cag said, frowning.

"Yes, but that's because Billy's only just been deluging them with facts on the advantages of diversification." He shrugged. "I don't think they'll buy it, but Billy does. I'm going to see if I can't get him dru...I mean," he amended immediately, "get him to give me a price."

"Don't you dare," Cag warned. "I'm not bailing you out again. I mean it."

"You drink from time to time," Leo said indignantly.

"With good reason, and I'm quiet about it. You aren't. None of us have forgotten the last time you cut loose in Jacobsville."

"I'd just gotten my degree," Leo said curtly. "It was a great reason to celebrate."

"To celebrate, yes. Not to wreck the bar. And several customers."

"As I recall, Corrigan and Rey helped."

"You bad boys," Tess murmured under her breath.

Cag glanced at her. "I never drink to excess anymore."

"Neither do I. And I didn't say that I was going to get drunk," Leo persisted. "I said I was going to get *Billy* drunk. He's much more malleable when he's not sober."

Cag shook a finger at him. "Nothing he signs inebriated will be legal. You remember that."

Leo threw up both hands. "For heaven's sake!"

"We can do without that bull."

"We can't! He's a grand champion," Leo said with pure, naked hunger in his tone. "I never saw such a beautiful animal. He's lean and healthy and glossy, like silk. He's a sire worthy of a foundation herd. I want him!"

Cag exchanged an amused glance with Tess. "It's love, I reckon," he drawled.

"With all due respect to women," Leo sighed, "there is nothing in the world more beautiful than a pedigree bull in his prime."

"No wonder you aren't married, you pervert," Cag said.

Leo glared at him. "I don't want to marry the bull, I just want to own him! Listen, your breeding program is standing still. I have ideas. Good ideas. But I need that bull." He slammed his hat down on his head. "And one way or another, Billy's going to sell him to me!"

He turned and strode out the door, looking formidable and determined.

"Is it really that good a bull?" Tess asked.

Cag chuckled. "I suppose it is." He shook his head. "But I think Leo has ulterior motives."

"Such as?"

"Never you mind." He studied her warmly for a minute, approving of her chambray shirt and jeans. She always looked neat and feminine, even if she didn't go in for seductive dresses and tight-fitting clothes. "Bring your mysterious dessert on into the office when you get it ready. Don't forget the coffee."

"Not me, boss," she replied with a pert smile.

She put the finishing touches on the elegant dessert and placed it on a tray with the cup of coffee Cag liked after supper. She carried the whole caboodle into the study, where he was hunched over his desk with a pencil in one hand and his head in the other, going over what looked like reams of figure-studded pages of paper.

He got up when she entered and took the tray from her, placing it on the very edge of the desk. He scowled.

"What is it?" he asked, nodding toward a saucer of what looked like white foam rubber with whipped cream on top.

"It's a miniature Pavlova," she explained. "It's a hard meringue with a soft center, filled with fresh fruit and whipped cream. It takes a long time to make, but it's pretty good. At least, I think it is."

He picked up the dessert fork she'd provided and drew it down through the dessert. It made a faint crunching sound. Intrigued, he lifted a forkful of the frothy-looking substance to his mouth and tasted it. It melted on his tongue.

His face softened. "Why, this is good," he said, surprised.

"I thought you might like it," she said, beaming. "It isn't really a sweet dessert. It's like eating a cloud."

He chuckled. "That's a pretty good description." He sat down in the big leather swivel chair behind his desk with the saucer in his hand. But he didn't start eating again.

He lifted his chin. "Come here."

"Who, me?" she asked.

"Yes, you."

She edged closer. "You said that I mustn't let you do things to me."

"Did I say that?" he asked in mock surprise.

"Yes, you did."

He held out the arm that wasn't holding the saucer. "Well, ignore me. I'm sure I was out of my mind at the time."

She chuckled softly, moving to the chair. He pulled her down onto his lap so that she rested against his broad chest, with his shoulder supporting her back. He dipped out a forkful of her dessert and held it to her lips.

"It's not bad, is it?" she asked, smiling.

He took a bite of his own. "It's unique. I'll bet the others would love it, too." He glanced down at her expression and lifted an eyebrow. "Mm-hmm," he murmured thoughtfully. "So you made it just for me, did you?"

She shifted closer. "You work harder than everybody else. I thought you deserved something special."

He smiled warmly at her. "I'm not the only hard worker around here. Who scrubbed the kitchen floor on her hands and knees after I bought her a machine that does it?"

She flushed. "It's a very nice machine. I really appreciate it. But it's better if you do it with a toothbrush. I mean, the dirt in the linoleum pattern just doesn't come up any other way. And I do like a nice kitchen."

He grimaced. "What am I going to do with you? A modern woman isn't supposed to scrub floors on her hands and knees. She's supposed to get a degree and take a corporate presidency away from some good old boy in Houston."

She snuggled close to him and closed her eyes, loving his warm strength against her. Her hand smoothed over his shirt just at the pocket, feeling its softness.

"I don't want a degree. I'd like to grow roses."

"So you said." He fed her another bite of the dessert, which left one for himself. Then he sat up to put the saucer on the desk and reach for the coffee.

"I'll get it." She slid off his lap and fixed the coffee the way he liked it.

He took it from her and coaxed her back onto his lap. It felt good to hold her like that, in the pleasant silence of the office. He shared the coffee with her, too.

Her hand rested on his while she sipped the hot liquid, staring up into eyes that seemed fascinated by her. She wondered at their sudden closeness, when they'd been at odds for such a long time.

He was feeling something similar. He liked holding her, touching her. She filled an empty place in him with joy and delight. He wasn't lonely when she was close to him.

"Why roses?" he asked when they finished the coffee and he put the cup back on the desk.

"They're old," she said, settling back down against his chest. "They have a nobility, a history. For instance, did you know that Napoleon's Empress Josephine was famous for her rose garden, and that despite the war with England, she managed to get her roses shipped through enemy lines?"

He chuckled. "Now how did you know about that?"

"It was in one of my gardening magazines. Roses are prehistoric," she continued. "They're one of the oldest living plants. I like the hybrids, too, though. Dad bought me a beautiful tea rose the last year we lived in Victoria. I guess it's still where I planted it. But the house was rented, and we weren't likely to have a permanent home after that, so I didn't want to uproot my rosebush."

He smoothed his fingers over her small, soft hand where it pressed over his pocket. His fingers explored her neat, short nails while his breath sighed out at her forehead, ruffling her hair.

"I never had much use for flowers. Our mother wasn't much of a gardener, either."

She leaned back against his shoulder so that she could see his face. He looked bitter.

Her fingers went up to his mouth and traced his hard, firm lips. "You mustn't try to live in the past," she said. "There's a whole world out there waiting to be seen and touched and lived in."

"How can you be so optimistic, after the life you've had?" he wanted to know.

"I'm an incurable optimist, I guess," she said. "I've seen so much of the ugly side of life that I never take any nice thing for granted.

It's been great, living here, being part of a family, even though I just work for you."

His lips pursed against her exploring fingers. He caught them and nibbled absently at their tips while he looked down into her eyes. "I like the way you cook."

"I'm not pretty, though," she mused, "and I can't psychoanalyze you over the vegetables."

"Thank God."

She chuckled.

He tugged at a lock of her hair and searched her eyes. "Cute of Leo to bring up the asparagus." His eyes narrowed and his smile faded as he looked down at her with kindling desire. "You knew what he was going to say, didn't you?"

She nodded. Her heart was racing too fast to allow for speech.

"Well, it was interesting, having asparagus signify impotence," he murmured dryly, smiling at her blush. "But we could have told Miss Brewster that the asparagus lied, couldn't we, Tess?" he drawled.

She hid her hot face against him, feeling his laughter as his chest rippled with it.

"Sorry," he said at her ear, bending to gather her even closer against him. "I shouldn't tease you. It's irresistible. I love the way you blush." His arms tightened and his face nuzzled against hers, coaxing it around so that his lips could find her soft mouth. "I love...so much about you, Tess," he growled against her lips.

She reached up to hold him while the kiss grew and grew, like a spark being fanned into a bonfire.

He lifted away from her for an instant, to search her eyes and look down at her soft, yielding body.

Without the slightest hesitation, his hand smoothed over the chambray shirt she was wearing and went right to her small breast, covering it boldly, teasing the nipple to immediate hardness with his thumb.

Her lips parted with the excitement he aroused, and he bent and took her soft sigh right into his mouth.

She didn't have the experience to know how rare this mutual delight was, but he did. It was pleasurable with some women, but with Tess, it was like walking through fireworks. He enjoyed every single thing about her, from the way she curled into him when he touched her to the way her mouth opened eagerly for his. It made him feel vaguely invincible.

He made a rough sound in his throat as his hand edged between them, feeling blindly for her shirt buttons. She wasn't coy about that, either. She lay submissively in his arms, letting him open the shirt, letting him unclip her bra and push it away.

She didn't have to tell him that she liked his gazing on her body. It was even in the way her breath caught and fluttered.

He touched her delicately, lifting his gaze to her face to watch the way she reacted to it.

It occurred to him that she might love him, must love him, to let him be so familiar with her body, which he knew instinctively was innocent.

His heart jumped up into his throat as he traced around one tight little pink nipple.

"What did you do for experience before I came along?" he murmured half-teasingly.

"I watched movies on cable," she said, her own voice breathless. She shivered and her short nails dug into his shoulder. "Callaghan, is it supposed to...do that?" she whispered.

"What?"

She bit her lip and couldn't quite look at him.

He bent to her mouth and liberated her lower lip with a soft, searching kiss. "It's supposed to make your body swell," he whispered into her lips. "Does it?"

She swallowed hard. "All over?"

"All over."

She nuzzled her face into his hot throat while his hands worked magic on her. "It makes me ache."

"It's supposed to do that, too."

He had the weight of her in one big palm and he bent his head to put his mouth, open, on the nipple.

She shivered again and he heard a tight sob pass her lips. He knew he was going to get in over his head, and it didn't seem to matter anymore.

With a rough curse, he suddenly got to his feet and stripped her out of the shirt and bra before he lifted her and, with his mouth hard on hers, carried her to the divan.

He stretched her out on it, yielding and openly hungry, and came down beside her, one long leg inserted boldly between both of hers.

"Do you have any idea how dangerous this is?" he ground out against her breasts.

Her hands were fumbling for buttons. "It isn't, because we aren't...doing anything," she whispered with deathbed humor as she forced the stubborn shirt buttons apart and pushed the fabric away from hard, warm, hair-covered muscles. "You are...so beautiful," she added in a hushed, rapt whisper as she touched him and felt him go tense.

His teeth clenched. "Tess..." He made her name sound like a plea for mercy.

"Oh, come here. Please!" She drew him down on her, so that her bare breasts merged with his hard chest. She held him close while they kissed hungrily, feeling his long legs suddenly shift so that he was between them, pressing against her in a new and urgent way.

He lifted his head and looked into her eyes. His own were coal black, glittering with desire, his face drawn and taut.

She watched him openly, all too aware of his capability, and that he could lose his head right here and she wouldn't care.

He shifted against her deliberately, and his head spun with pleasure. He laughed, but without humor.

"If I'd ever imagined that a virgin—" he stressed the word in a harsh, choked tone "—could make an utter fool of me!"

Her hands had been sliding up and down the hard muscles of his back with pure wonder. Now they stilled, uncertain. "A...fool?" she whispered.

"Tess, have you gone numb from the waist down?" he asked through his teeth. "Can't you feel what's happened to me?"

"Well...yes," she said hesitantly. "Isn't it normal?"

He laughed in spite of the stabbing ache she'd given him. "Baby, you haven't got a clue, have you?"

"Did I do something wrong?"

"No!" He eased down again, giving in to his need, and hers, but careful not to give her too much of his formidable weight. His mouth moved lazily over her forehead, down to close her wide, wounded eyes. "You haven't done anything wrong. I want you," he whispered tenderly.

"I want you, too," she whispered back shyly.

He sighed as if he had the weight of the world on him. One big, lean hand slid under her hips and lifted them slowly, sensually into the hard thrust of him, and held her there.

She stiffened suddenly and a tiny little cry crawled out of her tight throat as she registered the heat and power of him in such stark intimacy.

"When it gets this bad," he whispered at her ear, "a man will lie, cheat, steal, kill to get rid of it! If I had just a little less honor, I'd tell you anything that would get those jeans off you in the least possible time."

"Get my jeans off...!"

The shock in her voice broke the tension. He lifted his head and burst out laughing despite the urgency in his body when he saw her face.

"You don't imagine that we could make love *through* them?" he asked.

She was scarlet. And he was laughing, the animal! She hit his shoulder angrily. "You stop that!"

He chuckled helplessly, shifting suddenly to lie beside her on the wide leather divan. He pulled her against him and lay there fighting for breath and control, deliciously aware of her bare breasts pressing warmly against his rib cage.

"Just when I think I'll go mad, you act your age."

"I'm not a kid!" she protested.

He smoothed her ruffled hair lazily and his chest rose and fell in a long sigh while the urgency slowly passed out of his body. "Yes, you are," he contradicted, his voice soft and affectionate. "And if we keep doing this, eventually, blushes or not, you're coming out of those jeans."

"As if I'd let you!"

"You'd help me," he returned. "Tess, I haven't really tried to seduce you," he added quietly. "You're as hungry for me as I am for you, and I know tricks I haven't used yet."

She drank in the male smell of his body with pleasure. "Such as?"

"You really want to know?" He drew her close and whispered in her ear.

"Callaghan!"

He kissed her shocked face, closing her open mouth with warm, tender kisses. "You've got a lot to learn, and I ache to teach it to you," he said after a minute. "But you aren't geared for an affair, and I have far too many principles to seduce a woman who works for me." He sighed wearily and drew her closer, wrapping her up against him. "Good God, Tess, how did we ever get into this situation?"

"You insisted that I sit on your lap while you ate dessert," she replied reasonably.

"It happened long before that. Months ago. I fought you like mad to keep you at arm's length."

"It didn't work," she informed him.

"So I noticed."

He didn't speak again and neither did she for a long time. They lay in each others' arms in the silence of the study, listening to the muted sounds of the night outside the window.

"Do you want me to go?" she asked finally.

His arms contracted. "Sure," he replied facetiously. "Like I want to give up breathing."

That was reassuring. She felt the same way. But he still wasn't mentioning anything permanent. Even through the euphoria of lying half nude against him, she did realize that.

Finally he let go of her and got up from the divan, careful not to look at her as he fetched her shirt and bra and put them beside her.

"You'd better..." He gestured, not putting it into words.

She dressed quickly, watching his long back as he stood beside the desk, idly touching the papers on it.

She got to her feet at last and after a minute she went around him to get the tray.

"I'll take this back to the kitchen."

He nodded without speaking. He was too choked with conflicting emotions to put a single one of them into words.

But when she went to pick up the tray, his hand covered the back of hers, briefly.

"I've put off a conference that I meant to attend in Kansas City," he said quietly. "I'm going to go. Rey will be back in the morning before I leave, and Leo will be here."

She looked up at him with wide, soft eyes in a face that made his heart ache.

He cursed softly. "Tess, it wouldn't work," he said through his teeth. "You know it wouldn't!"

She made a motion with her shoulders and lowered her revealing eyes so that he couldn't read what was in them. "Okay."

"You'll like school," he forced himself to say. "There will be boys your own age, nice boys, not like some of the toughs you meet on the rodeo circuit."

"Sure."

"You can commute," he added after a minute. "None of us want you to give up your job while you're going to school. And I'll make sure we aren't alone again, like this."

She swallowed the lump in her throat and even forced a smile. "Okay."

He watched her pick up the tray and go out of the room. When he finally closed the door behind her, it was like putting the finishing touches on a high wall. He actually winced.

Chapter 9

Cag was dressed in a lightweight gray vested suit the next morning when he came in to breakfast. His suitcase was packed and waiting by the front door, along with his silver belly Stetson. He looked elegant when he dressed up. Tess had to force herself not to stare at him too closely while she served the meal.

Rey had walked in, still dressed in a suit himself, just as Tess started to put breakfast down on the table. He, like Callaghan, would never win any beauty contests, but he paid for dressing. He looked elegant and faintly dangerous, in a sexy sort of way. Tess was glad she was immune to him, and wondered vaguely if there had ever been a special woman in his life.

"I feel like Cinderella before the ball," Leo muttered, glancing from one of his brothers to the other. He was in jeans and a blue-checked shirt and boots, his blond-streaked brown hair shining like gold in the ceiling light.

Cag didn't react, but Rey took him up on it, peering deliberately under the table to see if Leo was wearing a dress.

"Cute, cute," Leo drawled. He picked up his fork and stabbed the air toward his brother. "I meant figuratively speaking. I don't wear dresses."

"Good thing, with your hairy legs," Rey retorted. He glanced toward Cag. "You leaving?"

Cag nodded as he finished a mouthful of eggs and washed it down with coffee. "I'm going to that legislative cattlemen's conference in Kansas City. I decided that I'd better go. The journals don't keep us completely up-to-date on pending legislation, and I've heard some rumors I don't like about new regulations."

"I've heard those same rumors," Leo remarked.

"We have to start policing our own industry better," Cag said. "All the rules and regulations and laws in the world won't work without better enforcement." He looked up. "You should have kept your seat on the legislative committee at the state cattlemen's association."

"Hindsight is a fine thing," Leo agreed. "I had too much to do at the time."

"If they ask you again, take it."

"You bet I will." He glanced at Cag. "Why don't you do it?"

Cag smiled. "I've got more than I can do already, as you'll discover when you look at the paperwork in the study. I only got half the figures keyed into the computer. You'll need to take the rest down to Margie in the office and get her to finish."

"Sure."

Neither Leo nor Rey noticed that Tess had turned away to the sink deliberately, because she knew why Cag hadn't finished that paperwork. She didn't want the other two brothers to see her flush.

Cag noticed. He didn't look at her, though, because he'd become more readable lately where she was concerned. He finished his coffee and got up.

"Well, I'm off. I'll try to be back by next weekend. You can reach me at the Airport Hilton in Kansas City if you need me."

"We won't," Leo said with a grin. "Have a good time."

Cag glanced involuntarily at Tess, thinking how empty life without her was going to be, even for a few days. He'd grown all too fond of that red curly head of hair and those heavenly blue eyes.

"Take care of Tess while I'm gone," he said, trying to make a joke of it and failing miserably.

"I'll take care of myself, thanks very much," she shot right back and forced a smile, so that he'd think it wasn't killing her to watch him walk out the door.

"You never told us how your application went," Leo said suddenly.

"Oh, I was accepted on the spot," Tess said. "They've scheduled me for three classes when fall quarter begins. I went to the financial aid office and applied for tuition, which they say I can get, and it will pay for my books."

Cag frowned. "You've already applied?"

"Yes," she said with determined brightness. "I start in three weeks. I can hardly wait."

"So I see." Cag finished his goodbyes, added a few things for his brothers to take care of while he was away and left without another word.

Tess wondered why he was irritated that she'd applied for admission to the vocational school, when he'd already said he wanted her to do it. She knew he hadn't changed his mind. His behavior was puzzling.

Cag was thinking the same thing as he slammed his hat on his head, picked up his suitcase, and went out the front door. He'd known she was applying, but now it was definite. He thought of her in his arms the night before, hungry for his kisses, and then he thought of all the young men she'd meet when she started classes. She might meet a young man who liked roses, too. He had visions of her youthful crush on him melting quickly away in the heat of a new romance, and it made him vaguely sick.

He'd tried not to get in over his head, but it looked as if he was only fooling himself. Tess had wormed her way under his skin, right where his heart was. He wondered how he'd ever imagined that he could make a little love to her and walk away. He'd never been quite so confused or worried in his life. He wanted Tess as he'd never wanted anything. But he was afraid that she was in love with love, not him, because he was the first man who'd ever been intimate with her even in a slight way. He couldn't forget the fiancée who'd dropped him for someone younger. He couldn't bear to go through that a second time.

He got into the ranch truck and drove toward the airport, but his heart wasn't in it. Tess was going to go away to school, and he was going to lose her. But not right away, he comforted himself. She'd still be living at the ranch. He'd have time to get himself sorted out. And it wasn't as if she was going to meet someone else at once. He had plenty of time. The thought comforted him, and he put that worry aside.

Cag wouldn't have been quite so comforted if he'd seen the big black limousine that drew up in front of the Hart ranch house barely two hours after he'd left.

Rey and Leo had already gone out with the men to look over a new batch of bulls when someone rang the doorbell.

Tess wiped her hands on a kitchen towel and left the pots she'd been scrubbing in the sink when she went to answer it.

A tall, taciturn man in a suit, carrying a briefcase, was standing there.

"Miss Theresa Brady?" the man asked politely.

It was a shock to hear her given name. She'd been called Tess for so long that she'd all but forgotten that it was a contraction of Theresa.

"Yes," she said hesitantly.

He held out a hand. "I'm Clint Matherson," he said, shaking hands. "Your late mother's attorney."

Her hand went limp in his. "My... *late*... mother?"

"I'm sorry to tell you that your mother passed away almost a month ago in Singapore. It wasn't possible to get word to you until now. I found you through a detective agency, but I've been out of town and the message only reached me a week ago. I'm very sorry," he said belatedly.

She hadn't thought of her mother in years, and only then with regret. It might have been sad to lose her if she'd ever shown the slightest affection for her only child, but she hadn't.

"I didn't know where she was," Tess said honestly. "We hadn't communicated since I was sixteen."

"Yes, she, uh, made me aware of that. She left you a portfolio of stocks in a trading company out of Singapore," he added. "If we could sit down and discuss her will?"

"I'm sorry. Of course. Come into the living room, please."

He sat down in an armchair and laid out the documents on the spotless oak coffee table, moving her flower arrangement aside to make room for them.

"I can't tell you much about this company. Frankly the stocks are as much a surprise to you as they are to me. She didn't ask my advice before she sank her money into them. You did know that she married a wealthy Singapore importer six years ago?"

"No," Tess said stiffly. "As I said, we haven't corresponded."

"A pity," he replied. "She gave up drinking and led a fairly admirable life in her last years. She was widowed about the time she contracted cancer. Her illness perhaps changed her outlook somewhat. I understand that she had plans to ask you to come out and visit with her, but she never carried them out." He smiled thinly. "She told me she was ashamed of the way she'd treated you, Miss Brady, and not too hopeful of making amends."

Tess clasped her hands together on the knees of her jeans. "I would have listened, if she'd wanted to talk to me."

He shrugged. "Perhaps it's just as well. But time is a great healer." He indicated the documents. "I'll have these stocks checked out by the end of the week. I should be able to give you some idea of their current worth on the Asian market then. You can decide whether you'd rather keep them or sell them. There are a few odds and ends, like her jewelry, which will be sent on to me and I'll forward them to you."

The thought of having something, anything, of her mother's made her uneasy. "Wasn't there any other relative?"

"A stepdaughter who still lives in Singapore. But she was already provided for by her father's will."

"Wouldn't she like the jewelry?"

He was surprised. "Well, she was fond of your mother, I understand. They were good friends. Yes, I imagine she would like it. But it's yours, Miss Brady. You were a blood relative."

"I never felt like one," she replied stiffly. "I'd like the daughter to have the jewelry and the other…personal things." She glanced at him and away. "It's hard to put into words, but I don't really want anything of hers. Not even the stock."

"Ah, but you have no choice about that," he said, surprising her. "There's no provision if you don't accept it. There must be some goal you've set in life that it would help you achieve. I understand that you work as a housekeeper here since your father's untimely death. Wouldn't you like to be financially independent?''

That remark changed her life. If she had a little money of her own, Callaghan wouldn't have to keep her on here because he was sorry for her. It would give her some measure of independence, even if leaving Callaghan broke her heart.

"Yes, I would," she answered the lawyer. "And I'll accept the stock. Thank you."

He indicated the places her signature was required, closed the documents up in his briefcase, shook hands and promised to be in touch soon about the stock.

"How much do you think it could be worth?" she asked hesitantly when he was on the verge of leaving.

"Hard to tell. It was bought for eighty dollars a share, but that was last year."

"And how much was bought?"

He smiled musingly. "About a million dollars worth."

She was pale. Her hand found the door and held on for support. "Oh."

"So you see, you won't be dependent on other people for your livelihood. Your mother may have neglected you in life, but she didn't forget you at the end. That must be some comfort."

It wasn't, but she smiled and pretended that it was. She closed the door and leaned back against it. Everything had changed in the course of a few minutes. She was a woman of means. She could do what she pleased. But it would be without Callaghan Hart, and that was the hardest pill of all to swallow.

She told the brothers about her visitor at the supper table.

They were silent after she related the size of the inheritance, glancing at each other as if communicating in some mysterious fashion.

"I can still go to school, but I'll be able to support myself now," she told them. "And I guess," she added reluctantly, "I won't need to work. I'm sorry to leave, but we've known for a long time that Callaghan really would prefer to have another cook."

"Why don't you ever call him Cag, like we do?" Leo asked gently.

She stared at her coffee cup. "It never seemed comfortable, I guess."

They exchanged another mysterious glance.

"Well, we'll advertise as soon as Cag comes home and we have time to discuss what we want to do," Rey said. "We'll miss you, Tess. Especially your biscuits."

"Amen to that. A good biscuit chef is really hard to find in these liberated times. I guess we'll be eating them out of tins from now on."

"Now, now," Tess chided, "Dorie can bake biscuits and even real bread. I'll bet she won't mind keeping you supplied. But you'll find a cook. I know you will."

They looked at her silently. "She won't be you," Leo said, and he smiled wistfully.

Tess got used to the idea of leaving in the days that followed. She was almost reconciled to it when Cag showed up late the next Friday afternoon. He looked tired and worn and unhappy until he saw Tess. His black eyes began to light up at once, and her heart ached, because it could have been so different if he'd loved her. She stood quietly in the kitchen when she wanted to fling herself into his arms and kiss him to death.

"Missed me?" he drawled.

She nodded, but she wouldn't look at him. "I've got to gather eggs. I forgot this morning. Welcome home," she said belatedly as she carried a small wicker basket out the back door.

"There you are!" Leo called, joining his brother in the kitchen. He clapped a hand on the taller man's shoulder. "How'd it go?"

"Fine. What's wrong with Tess?"

"What do you mean?"

Cag's eyes darkened. "She wouldn't look at me."

"Oh. Well, she's been unsettled since the lawyer came," Leo replied, carefully choosing his words. "Sudden wealth would do that to most people."

Cag's face lost a few shades of color. "Wealth?"

"Her mother died and left her a small fortune in stocks," he told the older man, watching with compassion the effect it had on him.

"She says she'll be leaving as soon as we can hire a replacement. No need for her to work with a million dollars worth of stock, is there?"

Cag went to the sink and poured himself a glass of water that he didn't want, just to keep from groaning aloud. Tess had money. She was quitting. He'd thought he had time to work out his own feelings, and suddenly it was all up. She was leaving and he'd never see her again. She'd find somebody younger and get married and have babies. Tess would love having children of her own....

He put the glass down with a thud. "I've got things to do. How about those new bulls?"

"They came in, and I got Billy to sell me that Salers bull," he added smugly. "I've put him in a pasture all to himself with his own salt lick and a nice clean stall to keep him out of bad weather when it comes."

Cag didn't rise to the occasion which he would have only days before. He looked thoughtful and worried. Very worried.

"It won't be the same without Tess, will it?" Leo prompted gently.

Cag's face closed up completely. "I'll change and get back to the paperwork."

"Aren't you going to tell me how the conference went?"

"Later," Cag said absently. He walked out of the room without a backward glance.

He acted oddly for the rest of the day. And he wasn't at the supper table.

"Said he had to go into town, God knows what for," Rey murmured as he buttered a flaky biscuit. "They pull in the sidewalks at six. He knows that."

"Maybe he's got something on his mind," Leo mused, watching Tess fuss over the chicken dish she was putting into a serving bowl.

Rey sighed. "Something big. He wasn't going toward Jacobsville," he added. "He was headed toward Shea's."

That brought Leo's head up. "He was?"

Tess finished putting food on the table, so preoccupied by Cag's reappearance that she couldn't put two thoughts together in any sort of order. It was much harder to leave than she'd even anticipated.

She missed the comment about Shea's Bar entirely, and she barely touched her own food. She cleaned up the kitchen, blind to the brothers' troubled glances, and went to bed early. She felt like it was the end of the world.

So did Cag, who sat quietly at a corner table at Shea's Bar, drinking one whiskey highball after another until he was pleasantly numb and barely coherent.

No fool, he left the truck locked at the bar and took a cab back to the ranch. If the driver wondered at the identity of his overly-quiet passenger, he didn't ask. He took the bills that were fumbled out of the cowhide wallet and drove away.

Cag managed to get through the living room without falling over anything, amazing considering the amount of whiskey he'd imbibed. He made it to his own room and even into the shower, an undertaking of mammoth proportions.

With his hair still damp and only a short robe covering his nudity, it occurred to him that he should ask Tess why the rush to get away from the ranch. That it was three in the morning didn't seem to matter. If she was asleep, why, she could just wake up and answer him.

He knocked at her door, but there was no answer. He opened it and walked in, bumping into a chair and the side table before he ever reached the bed.

He sat down on the side of it and noticed how hot the room was. She hadn't turned on the air conditioner, and then he remembered that his brothers had told him they'd shut the unit off temporarily while it was being worked on. No wonder it was so hot.

He reached out and pushed gently at Tess's shoulder under the cover. She moaned and kicked the cover away and he caught his breath. She was lying there just in her briefs, without any other covering, her beautiful little breasts bare and firm in the muted light of the security lamp outside her window.

He couldn't help himself. He reached out and traced those pretty breasts with the tips of his fingers, smiling when she arched and they went hard-tipped at once.

It seemed the most natural thing in the world to slide out of his robe and into bed beside her.

He turned her against his nude body, feeling her quiver softly and then ease closer to him. She felt like heaven in his arms. The feel of her soft, warm skin so intimately kindled a raging arousal in him.

He moved her onto her back and slid over her, his mouth gently smoothing across her lips until they parted and responded despite the sharp tang of whiskey on his breath.

Half-asleep, and sure that she was dreaming, her arms went under his and around him, her legs moved to admit him into an intimacy that made his head spin. He moved against her blindly, hungrily, urgently, his mouth insistent on her mouth as he felt surges of pleasure breaking like waves inside him.

"Ca...Callaghan? Callaghan?" she whimpered.

"Yes, Tess...!" He caught her mouth again and his hand went to her thigh, pulling her even closer, straining against the thin nylon barrier that was all that separated them.

She didn't fight his seduction. If this was what he wanted, it was what she wanted, too. She relaxed and gave in to the sweet, fierce sensations that came from the intimate contact with his powerful body.

But even as his fingers sought her hips in a fierce urgency, the liquor finally caught up with him. He gave a soft, explosive sigh and a curse and suddenly went limp on her, the full weight of his body pressing her hard into the sheets.

She lay dazed, wondering exactly what had happened. Cag had no clothes on. She was wearing briefs, but nothing more. Not being totally stupid, she realized that sex involved a little more contact than this, but it was blatant intimacy, all the same. She shifted experimentally, but nothing happened. He'd been very aroused, but now he was relaxed all over.

She eased away a little and pushed. He went over onto his back in a liquid sprawl and with a long sigh.

Curious, she sat up in bed and looked at him, surprised at how much she enjoyed the sight of him like that. He might have been a warm statue for all the movement in him, but he was a delight even to her innocent eyes. She smiled secretively as she studied him unashamedly, thinking that for tonight he belonged to her, even if he didn't want to. After all, she hadn't coaxed him in here. He'd come of his own free will. He had to feel something for her, if he'd had to go out and get himself drunk to express what he really wanted.

While she looked at him she weighed her options. She could leave him here and shoo him out first thing in the morning—unless, of course, he awoke in the same condition he'd just been in except sober. In which case, her innocence was really going to be gone. Or she could try to get him back to his room. That would be impossible. He was deadweight. She could call the brothers to help her—but that would create a scandal.

In the end, she curled up beside him, pulled the sheet over both of them and went to sleep in his arms. Let tomorrow take care of itself, she mused while she enjoyed the feel of all that latent strength so close against her nudity. She loved him. If this was all she could ever have, she was going to have this one night. Even if he never knew about it.

Cag felt little hammers at either side of his head. He couldn't seem to open his eyes to discover what was the sound that had disturbed him. He remembered drinking a glass of bourbon whiskey. Several glasses. He remembered taking a shower and falling into bed. He remembered....

His eyes flew open and he sat straight up. But instead of looking at the bare back beside him, covered just decently by a sheet, he scanned his own nudity to the door, where Rey and Leo were standing frozen in place.

He jerked the sheet over his hips, held his throbbing head and said, predictably, "How did I get in here?"

"You bounder," Leo murmured, so delighted by his brother's predicament that he had to bite his tongue to keep from smiling. Finally he'd got Cag just where he wanted him!

"That goes double for me," Rey said, acting disgusted as he glanced toward Tess's prone figure barely covered by the sheet. "And she works for us!"

"Not anymore," Leo said with pure confidence as he folded his arms over his chest. "Guess who's getting married?" He raised his voice, despite Cag's outraged look. "Tess? Tess! Wake up!"

She forced her eyes open, glanced at Cag and froze. As she pulled up the sheet to her chin, she turned and saw the brothers standing poker-faced in the doorway.

Then she did what any sane woman might do under the circumstances. She screamed.

Chapter 10

An awkward few minutes later, a cold sober and poleaxed Cag jerked into his robe and Tess retreated under the sheet until he left. He never looked at her, or spoke. She huddled into the sheet and wished she could disappear.

She felt terrible. Even though it wasn't her fault, any of it. She hadn't gone and climbed into bed with him, after all, and she certainly hadn't invited him into bed with her! When she'd dozed off, she'd been almost convinced that the whole episode had been a dream. Now it was more like a nightmare.

Tess went into the kitchen to make the breakfast that the brothers had found missing at its usual time. That was why they'd come looking for her, and how they knew Cag was in bed with her. She groaned as she realized what she was going to have to endure around the table. She decided beforehand that she'd eat her breakfast after they finished and keep busy in another part of the house until they were gone.

The meal was on the table when three subdued men walked into the kitchen and sat down. Tess couldn't look at any of them. She mumbled something about dusting the living room and escaped.

Not ten minutes later, Leo came looking for her.

She was cleaning a window that she'd done twice already. She couldn't meet his eyes.

"Was everything okay? I'm sorry if the bacon was a little over-done...."

"Nobody's blaming you for anything," he said, interrupting her quietly. "And Cag's going to do the right thing."

She turned, red-faced. "But he didn't do anything, Leo," she said huskily. "He was drunk and he got into the wrong bed, that's all. Nothing, absolutely nothing, went on!"

He held up a hand. "Cag doesn't know that nothing went on," he said, lowering his voice. "And you aren't going to tell him. Listen to me," he emphasized when she tried to interrupt, "you're the only thing that's going to save him from drying into dust and blowing away, Tess. He's alone and he's going to stay that way. He'll never get married voluntarily. This is the only way it will ever happen, and you know it."

She lifted her head proudly. "I won't trick him into marriage," she said curtly.

"I'm not asking you to. *We'll* trick him into it. You just go along."

"I won't," she said stubbornly. "He shouldn't have to marry me for something he didn't do!"

"Well, he remembers some of it. And he's afraid of what he can't remember, so he's willing to get married."

She was still staring at him with her eyes unblinking. "I love him!" she said miserably. "How can I ever expect him to forgive me if I let him marry me when he doesn't want to!"

"He does want to. At least, he wants to right now. Rey's gone for the license, you both go to the doctor in thirty minutes for a blood test and you get married Friday in the probate judge's office." He put a gentle hand on her shoulder. "Tess, if you love him, you have to save him from himself. He cares about you. It's so obvious to us that it's blatant. But he won't do anything about it. This is the only way he has a chance at happiness, and we're not letting him throw it away on half-baked fears of failure. So I'm sorry, but you're sort of the fall guy here. It's a gamble. But I'd bet on it."

"What about when he remembers, if he does, and we're already married?" she asked plaintively.

"That's a bridge you can cross when you have to." He gave her a wicked grin. "Besides, you need an insurance policy against anything that might...happen."

"Nothing's going to happen!" she growled, her fists clenched at her side.

"That's what you think," he murmured under his breath, smiling—but only after he'd closed the door between them. He rubbed his hands together with gleeful satisfaction and went to find his sibling.

It was like lightning striking. Everything happened too fast for Tess's protests to make any differences. She wanted to tell Cag the truth, because she hadn't been drunk and she remembered what had gone on. But somehow she couldn't get him to herself for five minutes in the three days that followed. Before she knew what was happening, she and Cag were in the probate judge's office with Corrigan and Dorie, Simon and Tira, Leo and Rey behind them, cheering them on.

Tess was wearing a white off-the-shoulder cotton dress with a sprig of lily of the valley in her hair in lieu of a veil, and carrying a small nosegay of flowers. They were pronounced man and wife and Cag leaned down to kiss her—on the cheek, perfunctorily, even reluctantly. He looked more like a man facing an incurable illness than a happy bridegroom, and Tess felt more guilty by the minute.

They all went to a restaurant to have lunch, which Tess didn't taste. Afterward, Leo and Rey went on a hastily arranged business trip to California while Corrigan and Simon and their respective wives went to their own homes.

Cag put Tess into the Mercedes, which he drove for special occasions, and took her back to the ranch.

She wanted to tell him the truth, but the look on his face didn't invite confidences, and she was certain that it would only make things worse and get his brothers into big trouble if she confessed now.

She knew that nothing had happened that night, but if she slept with Cag, he was going to know it, too. Besides, sleeping with him would eliminate any ideas of an annulment. She'd been thinking about that all day, that she could give him his freedom before any more damage was done. She had to talk to him before tonight, before their wedding night.

It was almost time to put on dinner and she'd just started changing out of her wedding dress when the door opened and Cag came in, closing the door deliberately behind him.

In nothing but a bra and half-slip, she turned, brush in hand, to stare at him as if he were an apparition. He was wearing his jeans and nothing else. His broad chest was bare and there was a look in his black eyes that she didn't like.

"Cag, I have to tell you...."

Before she could get the rest of the sentence out, he had her up in his arms and he was kissing her. It wasn't like other kisses they'd shared, which had an affectionate, teasing quality to them even in passion. These were rough, insistent, arousing kisses that were a prelude to out-and-out seduction.

Tess didn't have the experience to save herself. A few feverish minutes later, she was twisting under him on the cover of the bed trying to help him get rid of the last little bit of fabric that concealed her from his eyes.

He was out of his jeans by then, and his mouth was all over her yielding body. He touched and tasted her in ways she'd never experienced, until she was writhing with hunger.

By the time he slid between her legs and began to possess her, she was so eager that the tiny flash of pain went almost unnoticed.

But not by Cag. He stopped at once when he felt the barrier give and lifted his head. His arms trembled slightly with the effort as he arched over her and put a rein on his desire long enough to search her wide, dazed eyes.

"I tried...to tell you," she stammered shakily when she realized why he was hesitating.

"If I could stop, I swear to God...I would!" he said in a hoarse, harsh whisper. He shuddered and bent to her mouth. "But it's too late! I'd rather die than stop!"

He kissed her hungrily as his body eased down and found a slow, sweet rhythm that brought gasps from the mouth he was invading. He felt her nails biting into his hips, pulling him, pleading, her whole body one long aching plea for satisfaction. She sobbed into his mouth as he gave her what she wanted in waves of sweet, hot ecstasy that built into a frightening crescendo just at the last.

She cried out and felt him shiver above her with the same exquisite delight she was feeling. Seconds later, he collapsed in her arms and she took the weight of him with joy, clinging as he fought to get his breath. His heartbeat shook both of them in the damp, lazy aftermath.

She felt his breath at her ear, jerky and hot. "Did I hurt you?" he asked.

"No. Oh, no," she breathed, burrowing closer.

Her body moved just slightly and his own clenched. It had been years. He'd ached for Tess, for the fulfillment she'd just given him. It was too soon, and he wasn't going to get over this subterfuge that had made him her husband, but just now his mind wasn't the part of his body that was in control.

He moved experimentally and heard her breath catch even as sharp pleasure rippled up his spine. No, he thought as he pulled her under him again, it wasn't too soon. It wasn't too soon at all!

It was dark when he got out of bed and pulled his jeans back on. Tess was lying in a damp, limp, spent sprawl on the cover where he'd left her. She looked up at him with dazed blue eyes, her face rosy in the aftermath of passion, her body faintly marked where his hands and his mouth had explored her. She was his. She belonged to him. His head lifted with unconscious, arrogant pride of possession.

"How was it?" he asked.

She couldn't believe he'd said anything so blatant to her after the lovemaking that had been nothing short of a revelation. She hadn't dreamed that her body was capable of such sensations as she'd been feeling. And he asked her that question with the same interest he'd have shown about a weather report.

She stared at him, confused.

"Was it worth a sham wedding?" he continued, wounded by her silence that had made him feel obliged to go through with a wedding he didn't want. She'd trapped him and he felt like a fool, no matter how sweet the bait had been.

She drew the cover back over her nudity, ashamed because of the way he was looking at her. He made her feel as if she'd done something terrible.

"You knew nothing happened that night," he continued quietly. "I didn't. I was too drunk to care what I did, but I remembered all too well that I lost my head the minute I touched you. For all I knew, I might have gone through with it. But you knew better, and you let me marry you in spite of it, knowing it wasn't necessary."

She clutched the coverlet. "I tried to tell you, but I couldn't seem to get you alone for five minutes," she murmured defeatedly.

"Of course you couldn't," he returned. His voice was as cold as his eyes. "I wasn't going to make matters worse by seducing you a second time."

"I thought it was your brothers...."

She didn't finish, but her face gave the game away. His eyes positively glittered. "My brothers? Of course. My brothers!" He glared down at her. "They were in on it, too, weren't they? No wonder they did their best to make me feel like a heel! Did you convince them to go along with the lie?"

She wanted to tell him that it had been Leo's idea in the first place, but what good would it do now? He was making it clear that he'd married her against his will and blamed her for making it necessary. Nothing she could say would be much of a defense.

Her silence only made him madder. He turned toward the door.

"Where...are you going? Do you want supper?"

He looked at her over one broad, bare shoulder. "I've had all I want. Of everything."

He went through the doorway and slammed the door behind him.

Tess dissolved into tears of misery. Well, she was married, but at what cost? If Cag had ever been close to loving her, he wasn't anymore. He hated her; she'd seen it in his eyes. She'd trapped him and he hated her.

She got up, feeling unusually stiff and sore in odd places, and went to take a shower. The sooner she could get back to normal, or nearly normal, the better.

She bathed and dressed in a neat flowered shirtwaist dress, combed her freshly washed and dried curly hair and went to the kitchen to make supper. But even as she went into the room, she heard one of the ranch trucks crank up and roar away in a fury.

Curious, she searched the house for Cag, even braving his own bedroom. His closet was still open and she caught a whiff of after-shave. She leaned against the doorjamb with a long sigh. So he'd run out, on their wedding night. Well, what did she expect, that he'd stay home and play the part of the loving husband? Fat chance, after the things he'd said.

She fixed herself a sandwich with some cold roast beef and drank a glass of milk. Then she waited for Cag to come home.

When he hadn't come back by midnight, she went to her room and crawled into bed. She was certain that she laid awake for an hour, but she never heard him come in. She slept alone and miserable, still tingling with the memories of the past few hours. If only he'd loved her, just a little, she might have had hope. She had none, now.

By morning, she knew what she had to do. She went looking for Cag, to tell him she was leaving. She had the promise of her mother's legacy and a small savings account, plus last week's salary that she hadn't spent. She could afford a bus ticket and a cheap apartment somewhere, anywhere, out of Jacobsville.

It might have been just as well that Cag still hadn't come home. His room was empty, his bed hadn't been slept in. The brothers were still out of town and Mrs. Lewis wasn't coming again until the next week. Nobody would be here to say goodbye to her. But what did it matter? Cag had made his disgust and contempt very clear indeed. He wouldn't care if she left. She could get the divorce herself and have the papers sent to him. He didn't love her, so what reason was there to stay here and eat her heart out over a man who didn't want her?

She blushed a little as her mind provided vivid proof that it wasn't a case of his not wanting her physically. He'd been insatiable, in-exhaustible. Perhaps that was why he left. Perhaps he was ashamed of how hungry he'd been for her, of letting her see that hunger. Her own inexperience had been her worst drawback, because she had no real knowledge of how men behaved after they'd soothed an ache. She didn't think a man in love would insult his new bride and leave her alone all night. Apparently he was still furious with her and in no mood to forgive what he saw as a betrayal of the worst kind.

Well, he needn't expect her to be sitting at home mourning his loss! She'd had enough of being alternately scorned, rejected and passionately kissed. He could find another object for his desires, like the noncooking Miss Brewster! And she wished the woman joy of him. Such a narrow-minded, hard-nosed man deserved a woman who'd lead him around by the ear!

Tess packed, took a long last look around the first real home she'd ever known and called a cab. She thought about leaving a note. But, after all, Cag hadn't left her one when he'd stayed out all night. He must have known that she'd be worried, but he hadn't cared about her feelings. Why should she care about his? Now it was her turn. But she was staying out much longer than a night.

She took the cab to the airport and walked into the terminal, staying only until the cab pulled away. She hailed another cab, climbed in and went to the bus station, just in case Cag tried to trace her. She wasn't going to make it easy for him! She bought a ticket for St. Louis and sat down to wait for the bus.

A plane ticket would have been nice, but she couldn't afford the luxury. She had to conserve her small store of cash. It would be enough to keep her for at least a week or two. After that, she could worry about getting enough to eat. But if she ran out of luck, there was always the shelter. Every city had one, full of compassionate people willing to help the down and out. If I ever get rich, she thought, I'll donate like crazy to keep those shelters open!

She *was* rich, she remembered suddenly, and bit her lip as she realized that she hadn't left the lawyer a forwarding address. She went to the nearest phone and, taking his card from her wallet, phoned and told his secretary that she was going out of town and would be in touch in a week or so. That business accomplished, she sat back down on one of the long benches and waited for the bus to arrive.

St. Louis was huge. Tess noticed barges going down the wide Mississippi and thought how much fun it would be to live in a river town. She'd lived inland all her life, it seemed.

She found a small efficiency apartment and paid a week's rent in advance. Then she bought a newspaper and got a sandwich from a nearby deli and went back to her room to read and eat.

There weren't a lot of jobs available. She could wait, of course, and hope for something she could do that paid a nice salary. But her skills were limited, and cooking was her best one. It seemed like kindly providence that there was a cooking job available at a local restaurant; and it was nearby!

She went the very next morning just after daylight to apply. The woman who interviewed her was dubious when Tess told her how old she was, but Tess promised she could do the job, which turned out to be that of a pastry chef.

The woman, still skeptical but desperate to fill the position, gave Tess a probationary job. Delighted, she got into the apron and cap and got started.

By the end of the day, her employer was quite impressed and Tess was hired unconditionally.

She went back to her apartment tired but satisfied that things had worked out for her so quickly. She spared a thought for Cag. If he'd come home, he probably wondered where she was. She didn't dare expand on that theme or she'd be in tears.

Running away had seemed the answer to all her problems yesterday, but it wasn't so cut-and-dried today. She was in a strange city where she had no family or friends, in a lonely apartment, and all she had to show for it was a job. She thought of the brothers waiting patiently for their breakfast and nobody there to fix it. She thought of Cag and how happy she'd felt that night she'd taken him the special dessert in his study. Things had been magical and for those few minutes, they'd belonged together. But how soon it had all fallen apart, through no real fault of her own.

"I should have stayed," she said, thinking aloud. "I should have made him listen."

But she hadn't. Now she had to live with the consequences. She hoped they wouldn't be too bad.

Callaghan dragged back into the house a day and a half after he'd left it with his misery so visible that it shocked his brothers, who'd come back from their business trip to an ominously empty house.

They surged forward when he walked through the door.

"Well?" Leo prompted impatiently, looking past Cag to the door. "Where is she?"

Cag's tired mind took a minute to work that question out. "Where is she? What do you mean, where is she? She isn't here?" he exploded.

Rey and Leo exchanged worried glances as Cag pushed past them and rushed down the hall to Tess's room. It was empty. Her suitcase was gone, her clothes were gone, her shoes were gone. He looked over her dresser and on the bed, but there was no note. She hadn't left a trace. Cag's heart turned over twice as he realized what she'd done. She'd run away. She'd left him.

His big fists clenched by his sides. His first thought was that he was glad she'd gone; his life could get back to normal. But his second thought was that he felt as if half his body was missing. He was empty inside. Cold. Alone, as he'd never been.

He heard his brothers come up behind him.

"Her things are gone," he said without any expression in his voice.

"No note?" Leo asked.

Cag shook his head.

"Surely she left a note," Rey murmured. "I'll check the office."

He went back down the hall. Leo leaned against the wall and stared unblinking at his big brother.

"Gave her hell, did you?" he asked pointedly.

Cag didn't look at him. His eyes were on the open closet door. "She lied. She tricked me into marriage." He turned his black eyes on Leo. "You helped her do it."

"Helped her? It was my idea," he said quietly. "You'd never have married her if it was left up to you. You'd have gone through life getting older and more alone, and Tess would have suffered for it. She loved you enough to risk it. I'd hoped you loved her enough to forgive it. Apparently I was wrong right down the line. I'm sorry. I never meant to cause this."

Cag was staring at him. "It was your idea, not hers?"

Leo shrugged. "She didn't want any part of it. She said if you didn't want to marry her, she wasn't going to do anything that would force you to. I talked her into keeping quiet and then Rey and I made sure you didn't have much time to talk to each other before the wedding." His eyes narrowed. "All of us care about you, God knows why, you're the blooming idiot of the family. A girl like that, a sweet, kind girl with no guile about her, wants to love you and you kick her out the door.'' He shook his head sadly. ''I guess you and Herman belong together, like a pair of reptiles. I hope you'll be very happy.''

He turned and went back down the hall to find Rey.

Cag wiped his forehead with his sleeve and stared blindly into space. Tess was self-sufficient, but she was young. And on top of all his other mistakes, he'd made one that caused the others to look like minor fumbles. He hadn't used anything during that long, sweet loving. Tess could be pregnant, and he didn't know where she was.

Chapter 11

Tess was enjoying her job. The owner gave her carte blanche to be creative, and she used it. Despite the aching hurt that Cag had dealt her, she took pride in her craft. She did a good job, didn't watch the clock and performed beautifully under pressure. By the end of the second week, they were already discussing giving her a raise.

She liked her success, but she wondered if Cag had worried about her. He was protective toward her, whatever his other feelings, and she was sorry she'd made things difficult for him. She really should call that lawyer and find out about her stock, so that she wouldn't have to depend on her job for all her necessities. And she could ask him to phone the brothers and tell them that she was okay. He'd never know where she was because she wasn't going to tell him.

She did telephone Clint Matherson, the lawyer, who was relieved to hear from her because he had, indeed, checked out those stocks her mother had left her.

"I don't know quite how to tell you this," he said heavily. "Your mother invested in a very dubious new company, which had poor management and little operating capital from the very start. The owner was apparently a friend of hers. To get to the point, the stock is worthless. Absolutely worthless. The company has just recently gone into receivership."

Tess let out a long breath and smiled wistfully. "Well, it was nice

while it lasted, to think that she did remember me, that I was inde-
pendently wealthy,'' she told the lawyer. ''But I didn't count on it,
if you see what I mean. I have a job as a pastry chef in a restaurant,
and I'm doing very well. If you, uh, speak to the Hart brothers....''

''*Speak* to them!'' he exclaimed. ''How I'd love to have the
chance! Callaghan Hart had me on the carpet for thirty minutes in
my own office, and I never got one word out. He left his phone
number, reminded me that his brother was acting attorney general of
our state and left here certain that I'd call him if I had any news of
you.''

Her heart leaped into her throat. Callaghan was looking for her?
She'd wondered if he cared enough. It could be hurt pride, that she'd
walked out on him. It could be a lot of things, none of which concerned missing her because he loved her.

''Did you tell him about the stock?'' she asked.

''As I said, Miss Brady, I never got the opportunity to speak.''

''I see.'' She saw a lot, including the fact that the attorney didn't
know she was married. Her spirits fell. If Callaghan hadn't even
mentioned it, it must not matter to him. ''Well, you can tell them
that I'm okay. But I'm not telling you where I am, Mr. Matherson.
So Callaghan can make a good guess.''

''There are still papers to be signed...'' he began.

''Then I'll find a way to let you send them to me, through someone
else,'' she said, thinking up ways and means of concealing her where-
abouts. ''Thanks, Mr. Matherson. I'll get back to you.''

She hung up, secure in her anonymity. It was a big country. He'd
never find her.

Even as she was thinking those comforting thoughts, Clint Matherson was reading her telephone number, which he'd received auto-
matically on his Caller ID box and copied down while they were
speaking. He thought what a good thing it was that Miss Brady didn't
know how to disable that function, if she even suspected that he had
it. He didn't smirk, because intelligent, successful attorneys didn't do
that. But he smiled.

Callaghan hadn't smiled for weeks. Leo and Rey walked wide
around him, too, because he looked ready to deck anybody who set

him off. The brothers had asked, just once, if Cag knew why Tess had left so abruptly and without leaving a note. They didn't dare ask again.

Even Mrs. Lewis was nervous. She was standing in for Tess as part-time cook as well as doing the heavy housework, but she was in awe of Callaghan in his black mood. She wasn't sure which scared her more, Cag or his scaly pet, she told Leo when Cag was out working on the ranch.

Always a hard worker, Cag had set new records for it since Tess's disappearance. He'd hired one private detective agency after another, with no results to date. A cabdriver with one of Jacobsville's two cab companies had been found who remembered taking her to the airport. But if she'd flown out of town, she'd done it under an assumed name and paid cash. It was impossible to find a clerk who remembered selling her a ticket.

Jacobsville had been thoroughly searched, too, but she wasn't here, or in nearby Victoria.

Callaghan could hardly tell his brothers the real reason that Tess had gone. His pride wouldn't let him. But he was bitterly sorry for the things he'd said to her, for the callous way he'd treated her. It had been a last-ditch stand to keep from giving in to the love and need that ate at him night and day. He wanted her more than he wanted his own life. He was willing to do anything to make amends. But Tess was gone and he couldn't find her. Some nights he thought he might go mad from the memories alone. She loved him, and he could treat her in such a way. It didn't bear thinking about. So he'd been maneuvered into marriage, so what? He loved her! Did it matter why they were married, if they could make it work?

But weeks passed with no word of her, and he had nightmares about the possibilities. She could have been kidnapped, murdered, raped, starving. Then he remembered her mother's legacy. She'd have that because surely she'd been in touch with…the lawyer! He could have kicked himself for not thinking of it sooner, but he'd been too upset to think straight.

Cag went to Matherson's office and made threats that would have taken the skin off a lesser man. She'd have to contact Matherson to get her inheritance. And when she did, he'd have her!

Sure enough, a few days after his visit there, the attorney phoned him.

He'd just come in from the stock pens, dirty and tired and worn to a nub.

"Hart," he said curtly as he answered the phone in his office.

"Matherson," came the reply. "I thought you might like to know that Miss Brady phoned me today."

Cag stood up, breathless, stiff with relief. "Yes? Where is she?"

"Well, I have Caller ID, so I got her number from the unit on my desk. But when I had the number checked out, it was a pay phone."

"Where?"

"In St. Louis, Missouri," came the reply. "And there's one other bit of helpful news. She's working as a pastry chef in a restaurant."

"I'll never forget you for this," Cag said with genuine gratitude. "And if you're ever in need of work, come see me. Good day, Mr. Matherson."

Cag picked up the phone and called the last detective agency he'd hired. By the end of the day, they had the name of the restaurant and the address of Tess's apartment.

Unwilling to wait for a flight out, Cag had a company Learjet pick him up at the Jacobsville airport and fly him straight to St. Louis.

It was the dinner hour by the time Cag checked into a hotel and changed into a nice suit. He had dinner at the restaurant where Tess worked and ordered biscuits.

The waiter gave him an odd look, but Cag refused to be swayed by offers of delicate pastries. The waiter gave in, shrugged and took the order.

"With apple butter," Cag added politely. He had experience enough of good restaurants to know that money could buy breakfast at odd hours if a wealthy customer wanted it and was willing to pay for the extra trouble.

The waiter relayed the order to Tess, who went pale and had to hold on to the counter for support.

"Describe the customer to me," she asked curtly.

The waiter, surprised, obliged her and saw the pale face go quite red with temper.

"He found me, did he? And now he thinks I'll cook him biscuits at this hour of the night!"

The assistant manager, hearing Tess's raised voice, came quickly over to hush her.

"The customer at table six wants biscuits and apple butter," the waiter said with resignation. "Miss Brady is unsettled."

"Table six?" The assistant manager frowned. "Yes, I saw him. He's dressed very expensively. If the man wants biscuits, bake him biscuits," he told Tess. "If he's influential, he could bring in more business."

Tess took off her chef's hat and put it on the counter. "Thank you for giving me the opportunity to work here, but I have to leave now. I make biscuits for breakfast. I don't make them for supper."

She turned and walked out the back door, to the astonishment of the staff.

The waiter was forced to relay the information to Cag, whose eyes twinkled.

"Well, in that case, I'll have to go and find her," he said, rising. "Nobody makes biscuits like Tess."

He left the man there, gaping, and went back to his hired car. With luck, he could beat Tess to her apartment.

And he did, with only seconds to spare as she got off the downtown bus and walked up the steps to her second-floor apartment.

Cag was standing there, leaning against the door. He looked worn and very tired, but his eyes weren't hostile at all. They were... strange.

He studied her closely, not missing the new lines in her face and the thinner contours of her body.

"You aren't cut out for restaurant work," he said quietly.

"Well, I'm not doing it anymore, thanks to you. I just quit!" she said belligerently, but her heart was racing madly at the sight of him. She'd missed him so badly that her eyes ached to look at him. But he'd hurt her. The wound was still fresh, and the sight of him rubbed salt in it. "Why are you here?" she continued curtly. "You said you'd had enough of me, didn't you?" she added, referring to what he'd said that hurt most.

He actually winced. "I said a lot of stupid things," he replied slowly. "I won't expect you to overlook them, and I'll apologize for every one, if you'll give me a chance to."

She seemed to droop. "Oh, what's the point, Callaghan?" she asked wearily. "I left. You've got what you wanted all along, a house without me in it. Why don't you go home?"

He sighed. He'd known it wouldn't be easy. He leaned his forearm against the wall and momentarily rested his head there while he tried to think of a single reason that would get Tess back on the ranch.

"Mrs. Lewis can't make biscuits," he said. He glanced at her. "We're all starving to death on what passes for her cooking. The roses are dying," he added, playing every card he had.

"It's been so dry," she murmured. Blue eyes met his. "Haven't you watered them?"

He made a rough sound. "I don't know anything about roses."

"But they'll die," she said, sounding plaintive. "Two of them are old roses. Antiques. They're precious, and not because of the cost."

"Wellll," he drawled, "if you want to save them, you better come home."

"Not with you there!" she said haughtily.

He smiled with pure self-condemnation. "I was afraid you'd feel that way."

"I don't want to come back."

"Too rich to bother with work that's beneath your new station?" he asked sarcastically, because he was losing and he couldn't bear to.

She grimaced. "Well, there isn't going to be any money, actually," she said. "The stocks are worthless. My mother made a bad investment and lost a million dollars." She laughed but it sounded hollow. "I'll always have to work for my living. But, then, I always expected to. I never really thought she'd leave anything to me. She hated me."

"Maybe she hated herself for having deserted you, did you think of that?" he asked gently. "She couldn't love you without having to face what she'd done, and live with it. Some people would rather be alone, than admit fault."

"Maybe," she said. "But what difference does it make now? She's dead. I'll never know what she felt."

"Would you like to know what I feel?" he asked in a different tone.

She searched his eyes coolly. "I already know. I'm much too young for you. Besides, I'm a weakness that you can't tolerate. And I lie," she added shortly. "You said so."

He stuck his hands deep into his pockets and stared at her with regret. "Leo told me the wedding was all his idea."

"Of course you'd believe your brother. You just wouldn't believe me."

His chest rose and fell. "Yes, that's how it was," he admitted, not bothering to lie about it. "I made you run away. Then I couldn't find you." His black eyes glittered. "You'll never know how that felt."

"Sure I know," she returned grimly. "It felt just the same as when you walked out the door and didn't come back all night!"

He leaned against the wall wearily. He'd avoided the subject, walked around it, worried it to death. Now here it was. He lifted his gaze to her face. "I wanted you too badly to come home," he said. "I couldn't have kept my hands off you. So I spent the night in the bunkhouse."

"Gee, thanks for saving me," she muttered.

He stood erect with one of those lightning moves that once had intimidated her. "I should have come home and ravished you!" he said shortly. "At least you'd still be there now. You'd have been too weak to walk when I got through with you!"

She caught her breath. "Well!"

He moved forward and took her by the shoulders. He shook her gently. "Listen, redhead, I love you!" he said through his teeth, and never had a man looked less loverlike. "I want you, I need you and you're going home with me or I'll..."

Her breath was suspended somewhere south of her collarbone. "Or you'll what?" she asked.

He eased her back against the door and bent to her mouth. "Or you'll get what you escaped when I left you that night."

She lifted her mouth to his, relaxing under his weight as he pinned her there and kissed her so hungrily that she moaned. She clung to him. The past weeks had been so empty, so lonely. Cag was here, in her arms, saying that he loved her, and it wasn't a dream!

After a few feverish seconds, he forced himself to lift away from her.

"Let's go inside," he said in a tortured voice.

She only nodded. She fumbled her key into the lock and apparently he closed and locked it behind them. He didn't even turn on a light. He picked her up, purse and all, and carried her straight into the bedroom.

"Amazing how you found this room so easily when you've never been in here before," she whispered shakily as he laid her on the bed and began to remove everything that was in the way of his hands.

"Nesting instinct," he whispered, his hands urgent.

"Is that what it is?" She reached up, pushing at his jacket.

"First things first," he murmured, resisting her hands. When he had her out of her clothes, he started on his own.

Minutes later, he was beside her in the bed, but he did nothing about it, except to pull her completely against him and wrap her up under the covers.

"Oh, dear God," he groaned reverently as he held her close. "Tess, I was so afraid that I'd lost you! I couldn't have borne it."

She melted into him, aware of the stark arousal of his body. But he wasn't doing anything about it.

"I don't like being alone," she replied, nuzzling her face against his warm, bare chest.

"You won't be, ever again." His hands smoothed over her back. One eased between them to lie gently against her stomach. "How are you feeling?" he asked suddenly.

She knew what he was asking. "I don't think I'm pregnant," she answered the question he hadn't put into words. "I'm tired a lot, but that could be work stress."

"But you could be."

She smiled against him. If this was a dream, she hoped she didn't wake up too soon. "I guess so." She sighed. "Why? Nesting instinct?"

He chuckled. "Yes. I'm thirty-eight. I'd love kids. So would you. You could grow them along with your precious roses."

She stiffened. "My roses! Oh, Cag...!"

His intake of breath was audible. "That's the first time you've ever shortened my name."

"You didn't belong to me before," she said shyly.

His arms tightened. "And now I do?"

She hesitated. "I hope so."

"I know so. And you belong to me." He moved so that she was on her back. "I've been rough with you. Even the first time. Tonight, it's going to be so slow and silky sweet that you won't know your name by the time I've satisfied you." He bent and touched his mouth with exquisite tenderness to her parted lips.

"How conceited," she teased daringly.

He chuckled with a worldliness she couldn't match. "And we'll see about that...."

It was unexpectedly tender this time, a feast of exquisite touches and rhythms that progressed far too slowly for the heat he roused in her slim young body. She arched toward him and he retreated. He touched her and just as she trembled on the brink of ecstasy, he stopped touching her and calmed her. Then he started again.

On and on it went, so that time seemed to hang, suspended, around them. He taught her how to touch him, how to build the need and then deny it. She moaned with frustration, and he chuckled with pure joy.

When he heard her sob under the insistent pressure of his mouth, he gave in to the hunger. But even then, he resisted her clinging hands, her whispered pleadings.

"Make it last," he whispered at her open mouth, lazily moving against her. "Make it last as long as you can. When it happens, you'll understand why I won't let you be impatient."

She was shuddering already, throbbing. She met the downward motion of his hips with upward movements of her own, her body one long plea for satisfaction.

"It's so...good," she whispered, her words pulsing with the rhythm of his body, the same throb in her voice that was in her limbs. "So good...!"

"It gets better," he breathed. He moved sinuously against her, a new movement that was so arousing that she cried out and clung to him with bruising fingers. ''There?'' he whispered. ''Yes. There. And here....''

She was sobbing audibly. Her whole body ached. It was expanding, tense, fearsome, frightening. She was never going to live through it. She was blind, deaf, dumb, so much a part of him that she breathed only through him.

He felt her frantic motions, heard the shuddering desire in her voice as she begged him not to stop. He obliged her with smooth, quick, deep motions that were like stabs of pure pleasure. She closed her eyes and her teeth ground together as the tension suddenly built to unbearable heights and she arched up to him with her last ounce of strength.

''Yes. Now. Now, finally, now!'' he said tightly.

There was no time. She went over some intangible edge and fell, throbbing with pleasure, burning with it, so oblivious to her surroundings that she had no idea where she was. She felt the urge deep in her body, growing, swelling, exploding. At some level she was aware of a harsh groan from the man above her, of the fierce convulsion of his body that mirrored what was happening to hers.

She lost consciousness for a few precious seconds of unbearable pleasure, and then sobbed fiercely as she lost it even as it began.

He held her, comforted her. His mouth touched her eyes, her cheeks, her open mouth. Her body was still locked closely into his, and when she was able to open her eyes, she saw his pupils dilated, glittering with the remnants of passion.

''Do you know that I love you, after that,'' he whispered unsteadily, ''or would you like to hear it a few dozen more times?''

She managed to shake her head. ''I...felt it,'' she whispered back, and blushed as she realized just how close they were. ''I love you, too. But you knew that already.''

''Yes,'' he replied tenderly, brushing back her damp, curly hair. ''I knew it the first time you let me touch you.'' He smiled softly at her surprise. ''You were so very innocent, Tess. Not at all the sort of girl who'd permit liberties like that to just any man. It had to be love for you.''

''It wasn't for you,'' she said quietly. ''Not at first.''

''Oh, yes, it was,'' he denied. His fingers lingered near her ear. ''I started fighting you the day you walked into the kitchen. I wanted you so badly that I ached every time I looked at you.'' He smiled ruefully. "I was so afraid that you'd realize it.''

"Why didn't you say so?'' she asked.

His fingers contracted. "Because of the bad experience I had with a younger woman who threw me over because she thought I was too old for her.'' His shoulders moved. "You were even younger than she was at the time.'' His eyes were dark, concerned. "I was in over my head almost at once, and I thought I'd never be enough for you...''

"Are you nuts?'' she gasped. "Enough for me? You're too *much* for me, most of the time! I can't match you. Especially like this. I don't know anything!''

"You're learning fast,'' he mused, looking down their joined bodies in the light from the night-light. "And you love like a poem,'' he whispered. "I love the way you feel in my arms like this. You make me feel like the best lover in the world.''

"You are,'' she said shyly.

"Oh, no,'' he argued. "It's only because you don't have anyone to compare me with.''

"It wouldn't matter,'' she said.

He touched her cheek gently. "I don't guess it would,'' he said then. "Because it's like the first time, every time I'm with you. I can't remember other women.''

She hit him. "You'd better not!''

He grinned. "Love me?''

She pressed close. "Desperately.''

"Try to get away again,'' he invited. "You're my wife. You'll never get past the first fence.''

She traced a path on his shoulder and frowned. "I just thought of something. Where are your brothers?''

"Leo and Rey are in Denver.''

"What are they doing in Denver?'' she asked.

He sighed. "Getting away from me. I've been sort of hard to get along with.''

"You don't say! And that's unusual?''

He pinched her lightly, making her squeal. "I'll be a model of courtesy starting the minute we get home. I promise."

Her arms curled around his neck. "When are we going home?"

He chuckled and moved closer, sensuous movements that began to have noticeable results. "Not right now...."

It was two days later when they got back to the Hart ranch. And they still hadn't stopped smiling.

Tess had decided not to pursue her horticulture education just yet, because she couldn't leave Cag when she'd only just really found him. That could wait. So she had only one last tiny worry, about sleeping in the same room with an escaping Herman, although she loved Cag more than enough to tolerate his pet—in another bedroom.

But when she opened the door to Cag's room, which she would now share, the big aquarium was gone. She turned to Cag with a worried expression.

He put his arms around her and drew her close, glad that his brothers and Mrs. Lewis hadn't arrived just yet.

"Listen," he said softly, "remember that nesting instinct I told you I had?"

She nodded.

"Well, even the nicest birds don't keep a snake in the nest, where the babies are," he said, and his whole face smiled tenderly as he said it.

She caught her breath. "But you love him!"

"I love you more," he said simply. "I gave him to a friend of mine, who, coincidentally, has a female albino python. Speaking from experience, I can tell you that deep down any bachelor is far happier with a female of his own species than with any pet, no matter how cherished it is."

She touched his cheek lovingly. "Thank you."

He shrugged and smiled down at her. "I built the nest," he reminded her. "Now it's your turn."

"Want me to fill it, huh?"

He grinned.

She hugged him close and smiled against his broad chest. "I'll do my very best." Her heart felt full unto bursting. "Cag, I'm so happy."

"So am I, sweetheart." He bent and kissed her gently. "And now, there's just one more thing I need to make me the most contented man on earth."

She looked up at him expectantly, with a wicked gleam in her blue eyes. "Is there? What is it?" she asked suggestively.

"A pan of biscuits!" he burst out. "A great, big pan of biscuits! With apple butter!"

"You fraud! You charlatan! Luring me back here because of your stomach instead of your...Cag!"

He was laughing like a devil as he picked her up and tossed her gently onto the bed.

"I never said I wouldn't sing for my supper," he murmured dryly, and his hands went to his shirt buttons as he stood over her.

She felt breathless, joyful, absolutely gloriously loved. "In that case," she whispered, "you can have *two* pansful!"

By the time the brothers arrived that evening, Cag had already gone through half a panful. However, he seemed more interested in Tess than the food, anyway, so the brothers finally got their fill of biscuits after a long, dry spell.

"What are you two going to do when I build Tess a house like Dorie's got?" Cag asked them.

They looked horrified. Just horrified.

Rey put down his half-eaten biscuit and stared at Leo. "Doesn't that just beat all? Every time we find a good biscuit-maker, somebody goes and marries her and takes her away! First Corrigan, now him!"

"Well, they had good taste, you have to admit," Leo continued. "Besides, Tira can't bake at all, and Simon married her!"

"Simon isn't all that crazy about biscuits."

"Well, you do have a point there," Leo conceded.

Rey stared at Tess, who was sitting blatantly on her husband's lap feeding him a biscuit. He sighed. He'd been alone a long time, too.

"I'm not marrying anybody to get a biscuit," he said doggedly.

"Me, neither," Leo agreed, stuffing another one into his mouth.

"Tell you what—" he pointed his apple butter spoon at Rey "—he can put up his house in the daytime and we'll take it down at night."

"You can try," Cag said good-naturedly.

"With our luck, we'll never find wives. Or if we do," Leo added dolefully, "they won't be able to cook at all."

"This is a great time to find a veteran housekeeper who can make bread," Cag stated. "Somebody who can take care of both of you when we move out."

"I can take care of myself," Rey muttered.

"So can I," Leo agreed.

"Be stubborn," Cag said. "But you'll change your tune one day."

"In a pig's eye!" they both said at once.

Later, lying in Tess's soft arms, Cag remembered when he'd said the same things his brothers just had.

"They'll fall like kingpins one day," he told Tess as he smoothed her hair.

"If they're lucky," she agreed.

He looked down into her gentle eyes and he wasn't smiling. "If they're very lucky," he whispered. "Was I worth all the trouble, Tess?"

She nodded. "Was I?"

"You were never any trouble." He kissed her tenderly. "I'm sorry I gave you such a hard time."

"You're making up for it," she returned, pulling him down to her. "I'd rather have you than that million dollars, Cag," she breathed into his lips. "I'd rather have you than the whole world!"

If Cag hadn't been so busy following his newly acquired nesting instinct, he could have told her the same thing. But he was certain that she knew it already.

*   *   *   *   *

USA *Today* Bestselling Author

SHARON SALA

has won readers' hearts with thrilling tales
of romantic suspense. Now Silhouette Books
is proud to present five passionate stories from
this beloved author.

Available in August 2000:
ALWAYS A LADY
A beauty queen whose dreams have been dashed in a
tragic twist of fate seeks shelter for her wounded spirit
in the arms of a rough-edged cowboy....

Available in September 2000:
GENTLE PERSUASION
A brooding detective risks everything to protect the
woman he once let walk away from him....

Available in October 2000:
SARA'S ANGEL
A woman on the run searches desperately for a reclusive
Native American secret agent—the only man who can
save her from the danger that stalks her!

Available in November 2000:
HONOR'S PROMISE
A struggling waitress discovers she is really a rich heiress—
and must enter a powerful new world of wealth and
privilege on the arm of a handsome stranger....

Available in December 2000:
KING'S RANSOM
A lone woman returns home to the ranch where she was
raised, and discovers danger—as well as the man she once
loved with all her heart....

**Don't miss
an exciting opportunity
to save on the purchase of
Harlequin and Silhouette books!**

Buy any two Harlequin or
Silhouette books and save
$10.00 off future Harlequin
and Silhouette purchases

OR

buy any three
Harlequin or Silhouette books
and save **$20.00 off** future
Harlequin and Silhouette purchases.

**Watch for details
coming in October 2000!**

PHQ400TR

HARLEQUIN®
*M*akes any time special ™

Silhouette®
Where love comes alive ™